John Stuart Ogilvie

The Life and Death of James A. Garfield from the Tow Path to the White House

Vol. 1

John Stuart Ogilvie

The Life and Death of James A. Garfield from the Tow Path to the White House
Vol. 1

ISBN/EAN: 9783337408930

Printed in Europe, USA, Canada, Australia, Japan

Cover: Foto ©Raphael Reischuk / pixelio.de

More available books at **www.hansebooks.com**

THE

LIFE AND DEATH

OF

JAMES A. GARFIELD

FROM THE

TOW PATH TO THE WHITE HOUSE

TOGETHER WITH A

*Complete Account of his Assassination ; History of Charles J. Guiteau,
the assassin: The Comments of the Press on the Assassination:
The Feeling throughout the Country ; Words of Sympathy
from all parts of the World; Voices from the Pulpit,
including Sermons by Rev. Henry Ward Beecher,
Rev. Dr. Storrs, Rev. Robert S. McArthur,
Rev. Dr. J. P. Newman, and other
Prominent Clergymen*

CINCINNATI
CINCINNATI PUBLISHING CO.
174 WEST FOURTH STREET

CONTENTS.

ILLUSTRATIONS.

ASSASSINATION OF PRESIDENT GARFIELD.

THE PRESIDENT'S PROGRAMME FOR A BRIEF VACATION—WHO WAS TO ACCOMPANY THE PARTY—PREPARATIONS FOR A JOYOUS TIME COMPLETED.

JAMES A. GARFIELD, the President of the United States and the subject of this history, had determined to take two weeks' relaxation from his important duties, and had invited the members of the Cabinet and their ladies with several other friends to accompany him.

The party was to leave Washington Saturday, July 2, 1881, at 9.30 A.M., on the limited express train from the Baltimore and Potomac Depot, in the city of Washington, for an extended journey through New England. The party was to comprise the President and Mrs. Garfield, who was to meet him in New York, their two elder sons, Harry and James, Miss Mollie Garfield, their daughter, who is now with her mother; Colonel and Mrs. Rockwell, with Don Rockwell, their son, and Miss Lulu Rockwell, their daughter; Dr. W. H. Hawkes, the classical tutor of the three young gentlemen above named; the Secretary of the Treasury and Mrs. Windom; Postmaster-General James and Mrs. James, the Secretary of the Navy and Mrs. Hunt, the Secretary of War, Judge Advocate General Swaim and Colonel Jamison, of the Post Office Department. From New York they were to go directly to Irvington, on the Hudson, where they were to spend Sunday. On Monday morning they were to go to Williamstown, Mass., to attend the commencement exercises of Williams College, of which the President is a graduate. They were to remain there until Thursday noon, and then take the cars for St. Albans, Vt., spending Friday at that place. From there they were to go to the White Mountains, staying at

Maplewood or Bethlehem, and remaining over Sunday. On Monday they were to go to the top of Mount Washington, and on Tuesday to Portland, Me.; from thence to Augusta, where they were to be the guests of Secretary Blaine. The Secretary had secured a revenue cutter, and the party were to take a trip along the Maine coast, visiting Mount Desert and other places of interest. They were then to return to Bangor, Me., and from there to Boston. The Legislature of New Hampshire, having by resolution invited the President to make them a visit, the party was to go to Concord. From there they were to go to New Concord, Mass., then begin the homeward trip, going to New York by way of Hartford and New Haven, expecting to get back to this city about the 17th or 18th of July.

THE PRESIDENT SHOT DOWN.

This was the programme marked out for a pleasant vacation, and the last of the party to complete it had not arrived when the twenty minutes past nine A.M. train, preceding the limited express, departed from the depot. A few moments later the President's carriage drove in front of the depot, and the President and his only companion, Secretary Blaine, alighted and both entered the depot by the main entrance on B Sstreet. There was a slight pause on the steps, and a moment later the President and Secretary of State, side by side, were walking across the ladies' reception room, in which there was not at the time half a dozen persons. One of these was a man of short stature, a wicked expression in his face, who moved about nervously until the two statesmen had half crossed the reception room, a distance of not more than ten feet from the door. A report as of a big fire-cracker challenged the attention of the policemen at the main door, who thought some boy had fired it in honor of the President's departure. Instantly another report was heard, and President Garfield lay prostrate upon the floor of the reception room, wounded in the right arm and in the side just above the hip. The first ball from the assassin's revolver struck the President near the left shoulder and passed out by the shoulder blade; the second struck him in the back over the left kidney. The President turned at the first shot and fell forward on his knees at receiving the second bullet. Post-master-General James and others of his party who had preceded him rushed to his assistance. The assassin was instantly over-powered and arrested.

The mysterious nervous individual was Charles J. Guiteau, about forty years of age, who had been imploring the President to give him a consulate in France. His excited condition had changed in the presence of his intended victim, and he stood as firm and as calm as a statue, the "English bull-dog" pistol still drawn and in his right hand. Secretary Blaine had, in turning the corner of the seat near the main entrance to the hall of the depot, gone just a little ahead of the President. The first shot not being noticed by the President or his companion, the second and the fatal one found Mr. Blaine on the sill of the door, who instantly called for help. It is believed that the second shot was intended for Secretary Blaine. Guiteau wanted to be Consul at Paris. Last fall he bored Blaine with simple-minded letters proposing to take the stump in Maine, and was not regarded as a useful man in the campaign. He has been stopping at the Riggs House, and has shown no peculiarities during his stay to lead to the belief that he is of unsound mind. Secretary Blaine's private secretary says, from what he knows of the persistent appeals of Guiteau, that he must have intended to shoot Blaine. The second shot gave him a very narrow escape.

GREAT EXCITEMENT AT THE DEPOT.

Colonel Jamison, who was to have had charge of the President's party, was the first to communicate the sad news to the Cabinet officers. From the scene to the rear of the train was a distance of perhaps two hundred feet. As though drawn by an invisible power, the Presidential party in a second was surging towards the room where the prostrate form of the President lay. Five members of the Cabinet were then present, Messrs. Blaine, Windom, Lincoln, Hunt, and James. In a few minutes Attorney-General McVeagh, who was at his office when the deed was done, had arrived. The President's son Harry, scarcely realizing what had happened, for but little blood fell from the wounds, stood ready to fight or die in his father's defence. The scene beggars description. A beautiful summer morn, warm and tranquil as the face of nature in early spring, encouraged the brightest thoughts and happiest feelings in the hearts of the company that was to journey with the President. Now their countenances were black with sorrow. "President Garfield assassinated!" exclaimed Secretary Hunt. "Impossible!" No, if a meteoric stone had singled him out as its victim it could not be more improbable. Secretary Lincoln realized in an instant his position. The son of an assassinated President and the Secretary of War of another victim by the assassin's hand, he quickly gave the order for the troops stationed at the arsenal to hold themselves for immediate orders. The same was done by the Secretary of the Navy, who directed that the marines should be held for similar orders. Meanwhile word was sent to Surgeon-General Barnes, Drs. Norris, Lincoln, and Woodward, requiring their immediate presence at the depot. With the messengers trooping over the pavements it was not long before every part of Washington was informed of what had happened, and the fact became generally known. Then a crowd soon assembled, and in less than ten minutes Sixth Street and B Street were packed with people, and the news of the horrible affair flew from mouth to mouth and spread over the city like wildfire. An attempt was made to rush into the building, and cries were raised to lynch the assassin; but a strong force of policemen, summoned by telephone, had arrived promptly on the scene and preserved order. In the mean time the President had been carried to a room up-stairs and the physicians summoned.

POLICEMAN KEARNEY'S STORY.

Policeman Kearney, of the Island precinct, who first tried to arrest the assassin, makes the following statement of the shooting:

Guiteau arrived at the depot about half an hour ahead of the Presidential party, and moved about and acted quite restlessly. The officer's attention was attracted by his movements, but he did not watch the assassin particularly until he heard him ask a hackman at the Sixth Street depot if he could drive him off in a hurry if required. "I thought," said Kearney, "that that was a peculiar thing, but before I could follow it up closer I saw the President's party driving down Sixth Street to the depot, and I had to go and look after them. They drove to the B Street entrance. Secretary Blaine was with the President, and the two entered the depot together. The President walked up to me, and asked how much time he had before the train left. It was twenty minutes after nine o'clock I saw by looking at my watch, and I told the President that he had ten minutes. Just as he thanked me I heard a pistol shot, and turning, I saw the man that I had been watching previously standing about ten feet away, in the shadow of the main entrance to the waiting-room, levelling his pistol across his arm. He fired a second shot before I could speak to him, and darted between myself and the President and Secretary Blaine into the street. The President reeled and fell just in front of me. As he fell he said something I could not exactly understand, and Secretary Blaine, with a terrified look, pushed towards him, exclaiming, 'My God, he has been murdered! What is the meaning of this?'

" 'In God's name, man,' I shouted, 'what did you shoot the President for?' "

JAMES R. YOUNG'S STATEMENT.

Mr. James R. Young, of the Philadelphia *Star*, says of the occurrence: "I reached the depot of the Baltimore and Potomac Railroad at about nine o'clock, intending to take the limited express train for New York. It leaves at half-past nine. I found the depot full of people, some going south, some west, and others on the train I was to take north. I passed through the ladies' reception room, where the shooting took place, to the main or general reception room, where the ticket office is located. After purchasing my ticket I proceeded immediately to the train, which was standing on the track south of the main building of the depot, say about a hundred yards from the ladies' reception room. After locating my seat in the car I descended to the depot platform. There I met Mr. Barclay, the old journal clerk of the House, and Messrs. Kilburn and Adams of the newspaper press of the city, who were about to leave with their families for the north. We stood just opposite the special train which was waiting for the President. In it were some dozen people, more than half of whom were ladies, the wives, sons, and daughters of Secretaries Windom and Hunt, Postmaster-General James, Colonel Rockwell, and others of the Presidential party. They were a merry party, laughing and joking with the numerous friends who had come down to see them off for a fortnight's holiday and frolic. Soon Secretaries Windom and Hunt came out of the car and began promenading up and down the platform, quietly smoking their cigars. Later Postmaster-General James alighted from the car and joined our party.

"NEWS THAT HORRIFIED.

"We began congratulating him and ourselves that we were to escape the fearfully hot weather, and were trying to joke him about the administration leaving business for pleasure, when a young man stepped up to Mr. James and said to him, excitedly, that the President had been shot.

"Mr. James turned and said, 'What! There is no joke in a thing like that.'

"His informant, almost scared to death, replied, 'I assure you it is true.'

"Without another word Mr. James turned and ran to the depot building, and we all naturally followed him. When I reached the ladies' reception rooms the doors were being closed. There were at least two hundred people in and around the building, and I began to inquire if the news I had heard was true. It took only a moment to find out that it was. I could not gain admission at the inside door of the room where the President was, so I ran out into the street, hoping to be more successful at the street entrance. There I found a big crowd already gathered, and a policeman and some others hurriedly hustling a man outside. This was the assassin. I did not follow, as my desire was to learn the extent of the President's wound. Not being able to gain admittance at the door, I saw an open window, say about ten feet from the ground. A colored newsboy was climbing in, and I concluded to follow suit. It was not more than a half minute's work before I got inside. The first person I saw was Secretary Windom. He was standing alone, as pale as death, and the tears were trickling down his cheeks. Knowing him well I said:

"'Mr. Secretary, where is the President, and what does this mean?'

"He replied, 'There he lies in yonder corner in that group. It is as much of a mystery to me as it is to you.'

"I moved over about two yards, and there I saw the President lying on a mattress which had been hastily brought from the sleeping apartments of one of the depot employees. There were probably thirty people around him, many of whom were women, who had been waiting for the southern trains.

"Secretary Blaine had hold of one of the President's hands, and Postmaster-General James was assisting to get him into a sitting posture. His face showed a deathly paleness, and he had a look of surprise, as if caused by pain and despair. He was vomiting and seemed to have no control of himself. His coat and vest had been ripped from him and his trousers loosened. The matter he had vomited had fallen on his shirt below the bosom, which made it seem as if the ball of the assassin had penetrated the intestines. Near him was his son, a lad of sixteen. Poor boy, he was almost beside himself. He wrung his hands and cried in a piteous manner. With him were the son of Colonel Rockwell, and Secretary Hunt, who, in every way natural to human beings, were trying to comfort him. In less than ten minutes Secretary Blaine gave orders to have the President removed to the upper floor of the depot, to the officers' room, where there would be plenty of air and a freedom from the mob which was rapidly gathering. Colonel Rockwell and Adjutant-General Corbin soon made a passage-way, and the President was borne by a number of the colored porters of the depot to the upper floor. I waited down-stairs, and in about half an hour he was carried down, placed in an ambulance, and under a strong guard of mounted police was driven to the White House. I immediately left the depot and hurriedly went up Pennsylvania Avenue. Although it was not an hour since the shooting took place, I found the avenue crowded with people, some standing in groups, regardless of the broiling hot sun, discussing the event, others hurrying towards the depot, and others pushing and rushing and wending their way no one knows where."

WHAT A PASSENGER SAW.

Mr. Everett Foss, of Dover, N. H., who was in the gentlemen's room at the depot at the time of the shooting, says: "At twenty-two minutes past nine A.M., two shots in rapid succession rang through the depot, startling people who were gathered there waiting the movement of the train, and to witness the departure of the Presidential party. Almost at the same instant Secretary Blaine rushed from the ladies' room and called for an officer. The cry of murder came through an open door at the same time. In a moment Officer Kearney, of the Metropolitan police force, appeared with the assassin, who waved in his hand a letter, which he vociferated he wanted delivered to General Sherman. On entering the room I found General Garfield with his head resting upon the lap of the lady in charge of the room, with Secretary Blaine bending over him, exclaiming, 'O my poor President!'"

STATEMENT OF THE LADIES' ATTENDANT.

Mrs. White, the woman in charge of the ladies' waiting room, was an eye-witness to all that transpired, and the first to reach the President. She is a modest little woman, petite in form, has a narrow face, but very intelligent countenance, light brown hair, and blue eyes. She was attired in a becomingly trimmed black alpaca dress with white apron, and large lace bow at the neck. She gives her account of the affair as follows :

" I was standing in the ladies' room, and saw the President as he entered in company with Secretary Blaine. The latter had stepped a little in advance as they entered the door, as if to give the President more room. I had noticed this man Guiteau lounging around the ladies' room for a half hour before the arrival of the President. I did not like his appearance from the first time I saw him. It is my business to see that such characters do not loaf around the ladies' room, and I thought seriously of having him pointed out to our watchman, Mr. Scott, so that he should be made stay in the gentlemen's room. When the President and Secretary Blaine entered he was standing near the entrance door. He wheeled to the left and fired, evidently aiming for the heart. It was a quick shot and struck the President in the left arm. The President did not at first seem to realize that he had been struck, although Secretary Blaine instantly stepped to one side as though dazed at this unexpected movement. The President then partly turned around and the assassin advancing two steps fired the second time—the whole thing being the work of a few moments. The President advanced one step, then fell to the floor. I ran to him at once and raised his head and held it in that position until some gentlemen came, and we remained until his son came from the car where he was seated, with the rest of the Presidential party, awaiting the arrival of his father. The entire party followed him to the scene, and a large crowd gathered about the prostrate form very quickly. When I had a chance to look about me I saw Guiteau trying to wrench his arm from those who held him. When the President fell it was about twenty-five minutes past nine A.M. There was no blood visible. A mattress was brought in, and the President was removed to the upper floor of the depot. The President had on a light drab travelling suit and a silk hat, which latter was badly battered in the fall. When I ran to him he was deathly pale, but perfectly conscious. In about two or three minutes he vomited. His son was kneeling beside him at this time. He asked me if I saw who shot his father, and I replied, ' Yes, and he is caught.' He said somebody would have to pay for this. The young man and I thought the President was dying, so pale was he. He tried to raise his head and get his hand on the wound near the thigh, but he was too weak to do so. I noticed Guiteau at the depot either early this week or the latter part of last."

ANOTHER WHO SAW THE ASSASSINATION.

Mr. Parks, the ticket agent at the depot, was the first person to lay hands upon the assassin. Mr. Parks, when questioned in regard to the sad occurrence, said : " I had been watching for the arrival of the President through the small window between my office and the ladies' waiting room, and saw this man Guiteau, who was a small man, slight in physique, with short pointed beard on his chin. His movements were those of an uneasy, nervous man. At that time there were but few persons present, and nearly all ladies. I was attracted by the report of a pistol. I immediately peered into the ladies' room and saw the assassin, pistol in hand, standing about two feet inside of the entrance door. I saw him advance two paces and fire the second shot. The President had then advanced more than half way across the room on his way to the train, Secretary Blaine slightly in advance. The President turned around, after receiving the first wound in the shoulder, and received the second shot in the region of the thigh, towards the back. There was an interval of about four seconds between the first and second shots. Just as soon as the second shot was fired I took in the situation, and ran out of the office for the purpose of securing the assassin. In the mean time Guiteau tried to make his escape by the main door on Sixth Street, but being headed off he turned to make away by the exit of the ladies' room on C Street, when I grappled him by the left hand and the left shoulder, and held him until Officer Kearney and Depot Watchman Scott came to my assistance in a few moments, the former holding him by the right shoulder and the latter securing him by his clothing in the back. He said that this letter which he held in his hand and flourished frantically about his head was going to General Sherman and explained all. When I first laid my hand on him he made desperate efforts to release himself, but upon finding that it was useless he subsided."

THE PATIENT AT THE WHITE HOUSE.

It was evident that whatever was to be done must be done quickly, and as it would be impossible to proceed with medical and surgical treatment at the depot, it was decided to remove the wounded President to the mansion. Carefully the mattress on which he lay was taken up and borne down the long flight of stairs to the police ambulance now awaiting his coming. It was a pitiable sight to see the somewhat shabby looking ambulance which contained the prostrate form of the President driving rapidly along Pennsylvania Avenue to the White House, surrounded by mounted police, when one remembered in what excellent spirits General Garfield had ridden over the same pavement scarcely an hour before, or how joyously he had ridden along it to and from his inauguration four months ago. And by the same route, in the rear of the Treasury Building, as the President drove on the 4th of March, surrounded by the Cleveland Horse Troops, to-day drove the ambulance surrounded by the mounted police. Arrived at the mansion, the President was carried up-stairs to the large chamber in the south side, and the bedside was soon surrounded by physicians and agonized friends. The regular troops shortly after arrived, and all the gateways leading to the President's grounds were closed. Armed sentries took their places at the main gateway, and only those having passes were permitted to enter.

It was now half-past ten. A feverish excitement added to the intense heat of the day. "Will he die?" "Is he badly wounded?" "What do the doctors say?" and a hundred similar inquiries were addressed to anybody supposed to have superior facilities in getting news from the White House. The sidewalks fronting the White House grounds, and the square opposite were packed with people peering through the iron railing at the house a hundred yards distant, as though something could be discovered in the atmosphere that would tell them just the condition of the President's wounds. At eleven o'clock Dr. Barnes, the Surgeon-General, sent over the wires from the White House a statement that the wound in the loin would probably prove fatal, though nothing could be decided until consultation. It was not five minutes that this sad news was on the wing, and the eager crowd whispered it and sent it to every part of the city. The possibility of the President's dying was realized now for the first time. There had been hope that Providence which prepends the aims of assassins had turned the bullet in a harmless direction ; but too soon was it suspected that the lower wound was of a nature from which the President could scarcely recover, and that death was only a question of a few hours.

DIAGNOSIS BY THE DOCTORS.

Dr. Smith Townshend, the District Health Officer, who was the first physician to reach the President, gives the following statement: "I arrived at the depot four minutes after he was shot, and found him lying upon the floor of the depot, surrounded by an immense gathering. He was then in a fainting condition. From his appearance and the pulsations at the wrist I thought he was dying. I took some of the pillows from under his head that he might rest easier. I prescribed aromatic spirits of ammonia and brandy, which revived him. I ordered the police to get the crowd back, and had the President removed to an upper room. He rallied considerably, and I proceeded to examine his wounds. I found that the last bullet had entered his back about two and a half inches to the right of the vertebræ. When I placed my finger in the wound some hemorrhage followed. I then administered another dose of the stimulant, which' again revived him. In the mean time Drs. Purvis and Bliss arrived. I had, however, previously asked him how he felt and where the most pain was felt, and he answered in his right leg and feet. I asked him the character of his pain, and he said that it was a pricking sensation. Dr. Woodward, of the army, also came in afterwards, and after a consultation we concluded to remove him to the White House. It was then about ten o'clock, and all the members of the Cabinet were present. I forgot to tell you that after I made the examination of the wounds the President looked up and asked me what I thought of it. I answered that I did not consider it serious. He continued, ' I thank you, doctor, but I am a dead man.' When we arrived at the White House, and just before he was removed from the ambulance, he asked me to call to Major Brock to clear the hall, as there might be another assassin around. Quite a number of the doctors and others went along with the ambulance. When taken from the ambulance he was in a fainting condition, and we revived him with stimulants, and upon consultation we concluded to give a hypodermic injection of morphia and allow him to rest until three o'clock. Afterwards we gave him an injection of atropia and morphia, which brought his pulse up to eighty. At three o'clock, when we had another consultation, we found his pulse 102 and temperature 96, or two and a half below normal. While we were in consultation he became very much nauseated and vomited considerably. Upon examining the wound we found much dulness and tension of the right hypogastric region, restlessness and pain, which indicated internal hemorrhage. We immediately gave him one hypodermic injection of a quarter of a grain of morphia, which relieved him of the pain and quieted him. At half-past four o'clock this afternoon, when I left him, he was in a partially comatose state and unconscious. He was not talking much, but answered some of our questions."

Said Dr. Ford, one of the attending physicians: "He is bearing his sufferings with remarkable patience, and when I took hold of his leg the President requested me to squeeze it a little harder, as it greatly relieved him." Dr. Ford stated further that the President desired to know his exact condition, and made his wish known to Dr. Bliss. The latter told him that he was seriously injured; that some slight symptoms of internal hemorrhage were visible, and that if such was really the case it was a very serious matter. But if the ball had simply penetrated the muscles, it would put a different face upon matters, and he would very probably recover. The President replied, " I am very glad to know my condition; I can bear it." "These words," said Dr. Ford, "were spoken as calmly and peaceably as anything I had ever heard in my life." Dr. Ford further stated that at the consultation at three o'clock it was resolved to hold another at seven o'clock this P.M., and it was unanimously agreed that the condition of the President would not admit of probing for the ball.

HOW THE NEWS WAS BROKEN TO MRS. GARFIELD AT LONG BRANCH.

ELBERON, LONG BRANCH, July 2.—The sea air has done wonders for Mrs. Garfield, who came here two weeks ago to-day, enfeebled by malaria contracted in the White House. Her first week ended last Saturday happily. She was a loved wife and mother, surrounded by her husband and children, and rapidly regaining health and strength. Her second week ends in the deepest sorrow. " Who would have thought," said one of the most prominent lady friends of Mrs. Garfield, in this house this morning, "that that strong man who went away from here on Monday morning, waving adieus to those he left behind him for only a few days, would be lying at the point of death to-night?" Never was more profound sympathy expressed than that which I hear from all sides to-night. The corridor of the hotel is filled with prominent men from every quarter of the country, and they have apparently but one sentiment: deep sorrow for the dying President, and pity for his bereaved household. Many ladies came in with their escorts to look at the latest bulletins. General Grant also came a moment ago, but his impassive face showed no emotion. He declined to express himself further than he had done in a telegram that he had sent to Secretary Lincoln. That telegram was as follows:

To Robert T. Lincoln, Secretary of War, Washington, D. C.:
Please despatch the condition of the President. News received is conflicting. I hope the favorable may be confirmed. Express to the President my deep sympathy and hope that he may speedily recover.　　　　　　　　　　　U. S. GRANT.

The reply came only a short time ago, after the General had bought some cigars and gone away puffing impassively. It is as follows:

　　　　　　　　　　　WASHINGTON, D. C., July 2.
General U. S. Grant, Elberon, N. J.:
The President's condition is very serious, and excites our greatest apprehensions. There is internal hemorrhage. The surgeons are evidently very anxious and guarded in their expressions. He is perfectly clear in mind, and desires me to thank you for your telegram, which I just gave to him in substance.　　　　　　　　ROBERT T. LINCOLN,
　　　　　　　　　　　　　　　Secretary of War.

Mrs. Garfield, Miss Mollie Garfield, and General and Mrs. Swaim came from their rooms this morning. Mrs. Garfield admired the beauty of the morning, and spoke with evident pleasure of the reunion with President Garfield in New York later in the day. It had been arranged that the party was to set out for New York in a train of the Long Branch Division from this station at 12.22. From New York it was the purpose to proceed to the residence of Mr. Cyrus W. Field, in Irvington, in Mr. Field's steam yacht. The cool, bright morning gave abundant promise of a delightful journey. From the drawing-room the party went to the dining-room and sat down to break-fast together. The breakfast lasted until 10 o'clock. Then Mrs. Garfield and her friends returned to the drawing-room, whose windows command a view of the ocean. Soon after 10 a bell-boy summoned General Swaim to the office, where Mr. C. T. Jones, the proprietor, handed him a telegram. General Swaim tore the telegram open indifferently, supposing that it was from some friend on business. But he read the following:

WASHINGTON, D. C., July 2, 1881.
To General J. Swaim, Elberon:
The President has been shot and, I am afraid, is seriously wounded. Keep it from Mrs. Garfield till you hear further.
Later—Doctors say not dangerous.   ROCKWELL.

General Swaim was evidently deeply moved. He reflected for a moment, and then returned the telegram to its envelope and put it in his breast pocket. He returned to the drawing-room and conversed with the ladies as though nothing was upon his mind. Several minutes later the bell-boy again summoned him to the office, where this telegram awaited him:

EXECUTIVE MANSION,
WASHINGTON, D. C., July 2.
To General Swaim:
We have the President safely and comfortably settled in his room at the Executive Mansion, and his pulse is strong and nearly normal. So far as I can determine, and from what the surgeons say, and from his general condition, we feel very hope-ful. Come on as soon as you can get a special train. Advise us of the movements of your train, and when you can be ex-pected. As the President said on a similar occasion sixteen years ago, "God reigns, and the Government in Washington still lives."   A. F. ROCKWELL.

General Swaim went into the drawing-room again, and, with as much calmness as he could assume, said, "Mrs. Garfield, it may be necessary for us to go direct to Washington. An acci-dent has happened to General Garfield." Mrs. Garfield and Miss Mollie turned pale, and looked anxiously at General Swaim.

"So far as I am informed," he went on, hoping to avoid close questioning, "the accident is not so serious as was at first supposed." Mrs. Garfield begged General Swaim to tell her the whole truth, and as gently and sympathetically as possible he told her. She and Miss Mollie and Mrs. Swaim retired at once to their rooms. Mrs. Garfield was too much affected to do anything towards hurrying the preparations for departure, but Mollie and Mrs. Swaim relieved her. Just before 11 o'clock a telegram for Mrs. Garfield was received and sent to her room. It was as follows:

Mrs. Garfield, Elberon, Long Branch:
The President desires me to say to you, from him, that he has been seriously hurt, how seriously he cannot yet say. He is himself, and hopes you will come to him soon. He sends his love to you. A. F. ROCKWELL.

Hardly had it been delivered when another:

EXECUTIVE MANSION,
WASHINGTON, D. C., July 2, 1881.
To Mrs. J. A. Garfield, Elberon, N. J.:
Don't believe sensational despatches about the President. Will keep you constantly advised. J. S. BROWN.

Close upon this telegram was the following:

EXECUTIVE MANSION,
ALBANY, N. Y., July 2, 1881.
To Mrs. Garfield:
Please accept my earnest sympathy and sincere hope for the early and complete restoration of the President. Intense feeling of indignation prevails throughout our State.
ALONZO B. CORNELL.

General Swaim at once made arrangements for a special train. He telegraphed to Jersey City, and the reply came that a special train, with parlor car for Mrs. Garfield, would reach the Elberon station at 12.45. Mr. Jones had had a carriage at the door at a few minutes after 12 o'clock, and Mrs. Garfield and her friends were driven to the station. Mr. Jones sent his own body servant to wait upon Mrs. Garfield on the swift journey to Washington, so as to spare her the intrusion of stranger attendants.

The train got under way on time, and dashed away at express speed. It was calculated that the trip to Philadelphia would be accomplished in a little over two hours, and that Mrs. Garfield would arrive in Washington at 7 P.M.

MRS. GARFIELD WITH HER HUSBAND.

Shortly after seven o'clock this evening a carriage rolled up to the White House entrance, and Mrs. Garfield alighted. With her were her daughter and Mrs. and Miss Rockwell. She hurried to the bedside of the President, who recognized her at once, and she began to converse with him in a low tone. She exhibited great self-control while in the sick-room, and did not betray the slightest evidence of emotion. The President spoke to her in a whisper that was audible at the other end of the room. The physicians, who were then holding consultation in an adjoining room, decided it unwise to allow the interview to last beyond a few minutes, and persuaded Mrs. Garfield to take her leave for the time being at least. She very readily assented, and was escorted out by two of the doctors. When she had left the room she completely broke down and sobbed aloud most piteously.

Mrs. Garfield pleaded for a second interview with her husband, which was acceded to by the physicians. The room was cleared at her request, and she, with some other members of the family, remained thirty minutes with the President. During this period the first favorable symptoms were exhibited, and from that moment up to twelve o'clock everything looked brighter.

SEARCHING THE ASSASSIN.

Lieutenant Eckloff, of the Metropolitan Police force, received the prisoner at police headquarters, and when interviewed said: "When he was brought in we searched him, but he took from his pocket unassisted the pistol that he had used. It was too large for the hip pocket, and he had considerable difficulty in getting it out. He said to us that we need not be excited at all, that if we wanted to know why he did the act we would find it in his papers in the breast pocket of his coat. We took the pistol out of his hand and found it to be a five-shooter, with two barrels empty. It was what is termed an 'English bull-dog,' and carries a ball as large as a navy revolver does."

The assassin was taken to jail by Lieutenants Austin and Eckloff and Detective McElfresh, when the following conversation took place on the way out:

Mr. McElfresh said, "Where are you from?"

"I am a native-born American; born in Chicago."

"Why did you do this?" asked the officer.

He replied, "I did it to save the Republican party."

"What is your politics?"

He said, "I am a stalwart among the stalwarts. With Garfield out of the way we can carry all the Northern States, and with him in the way we can't carry a single one. Who are you?"

"A detective officer of this department."

"You stick to me and have me put in the third story front at the jail. General Sherman is coming down to take charge. Arthur and all these men are my friends, and I'll have you made Chief of Police. When you get back to the police you will find that I left two bundles of papers at the news stand, which will explain all."

"Is there anybody else with you in this matter?"

"Not a living soul; I contemplated this thing for the last few weeks."

On reaching the jail the people there did not seem to know anything about the assassination, and when inside the door Mr. Russ, the deputy warden, said, "This man has been here before." The detective then asked him, "Have you ever been here before?" He replied, "No, sir."

"Well, the deputy warden seems to identify you," said the officer.

"Yes," replied Guiteau. "I was down here last Saturday morning and wanted them to let me look through, and they told me that I could not, but to come on Monday."

"What was your object in looking through?"

"I wanted," he said, "to see what kind of quarters I would have to occupy."

The detective then searched him, and when he pulled off his shoes he said, "Give me my shoes, I will catch cold on the stone pavement." The detective then told him he could not have them.

TRACING THE BULLET.

At half-past eight o'clock, when the physicians saw great retching going on, they determined to make an effort to ascertain the exact location of the ball, and to treat the patient.

accordingly. They began by administering stimulants, but nothing would stay down. However, a hypodermic injection was given and the examination procceded with. It was found that the ball had fractured the eleventh rib and passed into the liver; but it could not be traced further, though it is supposed to have lodged in the locality of the spinal column, the result of which would be hemorrhage of the liver. At a quarter of nine his pulse was 158, as near as could be computed, for it was so faint it was scarcely perceptible at the wrist. At this hour the doctors thought that he could not last beyond twelve o'clock, while some looked for his death momentarily, and he had lost consciousness.

At thirty-five minutes after twelve o'clock the following bulletin was issued:

EXECUTIVE MANSION, 12.35 P.M.

The reaction from the shock of the injury has been very gradual. He is suffering some pain, but it is thought best not to disturb him by making any exploration for the ball until after the consultation at three P.M.   D. W. BLISS, M.D.

At this time the following physicians were in attendance, viz.: Drs. Bliss, Ford, Huntingdon, Woodward, United States Army; Townshend, Lincoln, Reyburn, Norris, Purvis, Patterson, Surgeon-General Barnes, and Surgeon-General Wales. As soon as possible after consultation Mr. Blaine sent a cable message to this effect, announcing the misfortune to General Garfield to our representatives abroad:

DEPARTMENT OF STATE,
WASHINGTON, July 2, 1881.

James Russell Lowell, Minister, etc., London:

The President of the United States was shot this morning by an assassin named Charles Guiteau. The weapon was a large-sized revolver. The President had just reached the Baltimore and Potomac station at about twenty minutes past nine, intending, with a portion of his Cabinet, to leave on the limited express for New York. I rode in the carriage with him from the Executive Mansion, and was walking by his side when he was shot. The assassin was immediately arrested, and the President was conveyed to a private room in the station building and surgical aid at once summoned. He has now, at twenty minutes past ten, been removed to the Executive Mansion. The surgeons on consultation regard his wounds as very serious, though not necessarily fatal. His vigorous health gives strong hopes of his recovery. He has not lost consciousness for a moment. Inform our Ministers in Europe.

JAMES G. BLAINE,
Secretary of State.

GUITEAU IN JAIL.

Guiteau on being arrested was hurried off to the District jail. When the prisoner arrived there he was neatly attired in a suit of blue, and wore a drab hat pulled down over his eyes, giving him the appearance of an ugly character. It may be worthy of note to state that some two or three weeks ago Guiteau went to the jail for the purpose of visiting it, but was refused admittance on the ground that it was not "visitors' day." He at that time mentioned his name as Guiteau, and said that he came from Chicago. When brought to the jail to-day he was admitted by the officer who had previously refused to allow him to enter, and a mutual recognition took place, Guiteau saying, "You are the man who wouldn't let me go through the jail some time ago." The only other remark he made before being placed in his cell was that General Sherman would arrive at the jail soon. The two jailors state that they have seen him around the jail several times recently, and that on one occasion he appeared to be under the influence of liquor. On one of his visits, subsequent to the first one mentioned, these officers say that Guiteau succeeded in reaching the rotunda of the building, where he was noticed examining the scaffold from which the Hirth murderers were hanged.

Pursuant to his orders from the Attorney-General the officer in charge of the jail declined to give any further information, nor would he state in what cell the prisoner was confined. This officer was an attendant at the old city jail at the time of the assassination of President Lincoln.

THE MURDERER'S FORETHOUGHT.

The following letter was taken from the prisoner's pocket at police headquarters:

July 2, 1881.

To the White House:

The President's tragic death was a sad necessity, but it will unite the Republican party and save the Republic. Life is a flimsy dream, and it matters little when one goes; a human life is of small value. During the war thousands of brave boys went down without a tear. I presume the President was a Christian, and that he will be happier in Paradise than here. It will be no worse for Mrs. Garfield, dear soul, to part with her husband this way than by natural death. He is liable to go at any time, any way. I had no ill-will towards the President. His death was a political necessity. I am a lawyer, a theologian, and a politician. I am a Stalwart of the Stalwarts. I was with General Grant and the rest of our men in New York during the canvass. I have some papers for the press, which I shall leave with Byron Andrews and his company, journalists, at No. 1420 New York Avenue, where all the reporters can see them. I am going to the jail.   CHARLES GUITEAU.

On his way to jail the prisoner said that the President's assassination was premeditated, and that he went to Long Branch for the purpose of shooting him there, and was deterred by the enfeebled and saddened condition of Mrs. Garfield, which appealed so strongly to his sense of humanity that he came back without carrying out his intention. Those by whom Guiteau has been examined since the shooting say that he shows no symptoms of insanity, and it is understood that the letter "To the White House" is the only document in the collection which supports the theory of insanity. Byron Andrews, who is the Washington correspondent of the Chicago *Inter-Ocean*, says that while it is true a package of papers are in the hands of the police, accompanied by a note addressed to himself (Andrews), he has no personal acquaintance with Guiteau, and never heard of his existence until this morning. From what he has gathered from the police Andrews believes that Guiteau's home is in Freeport, Ill.

A LETTER TO GENERAL SHERMAN.

This letter was found on the street shortly after the arrest. The envelope was unsealed and addressed: "Please deliver at once to General Sherman (or his first assistant in charge of the War Department)":

To General Sherman:
I have just shot the President. I shot him several times, as I wished him to go as easily as possible. His death was a political necessity. I am a lawyer, theologian, and politician; I am a

Stalwart of the Stalwarts. I was with General Grant and the rest of our men in New York during the canvass. I am going to the jail. Please order out your troops and take possession of the jail at once. Very respectfully,

CHARLES GUITEAU.

On receiving the above General Sherman gave it the following endorsement:

HEADQUARTERS OF THE ARMY,
WASHINGTON, D.C., July 2, 1881, 11.35 A.M.

This letter . . . was handed me this minute by Major William J. Twining, United States Engineers, Commissioner of the District of Columbia, and Major William G. Brock, Chief of Police. I don't know the writer, never heard of or saw him to my knowledge, and hereby return it to the keeping of the above-named parties as testimony in the case.

W. T. SHERMAN, *General.*

THE PRISONER ISOLATED.

The District jail was visited by the press reporter shortly after eleven o'clock for the purpose of obtaining an interview with Guiteau. The officers refused admittance to the building, stating as the reason therefor that they were acting under instructions received from Attorney-General MacVeagh, the purport of which were that no one should be allowed to see the prisoner. At first, indeed, the officers emphatically denied that the man had been conveyed to the jail, fearing, it appears, that should the fact be made known that he was there, the building would be attacked by a mob. Information had reached them that such a movement was contemplated. A large guard, composed of regulars from the barracks, and a Metropolitan Police force are at the jail, to be in readiness to repel an attack.

The following despatch was sent by the Secretary of State to Vice-President Arthur, at New York:

WASHINGTON, D. C., July 2, 1881.

At this hour (1 P.M.) the President's symptoms are not regarded as unfavorable, but no definite assurance can be given until after the probing of the wound at three o'clock. There are strong grounds for hope, and, at the same time, the gravest anxiety as to the final result.

JAMES G. BLAINE,
Secretary of State

There is a theory which has many adherents that the attempted assassination was not the work of a lunatic, but the result of a plot much deeper and darker than has been suspected. It is cited in support of this theory that Guiteau arranged beforehand with a hackman to be in readiness to drive him swiftly in the direction of the Congressional Cemetery as soon as he made his appearance on returning from the depot. In the mean time he had left a bundle of papers in the hands of a boy with a view, it is maintained, to creating a belief in his insanity in the event of his capture. It is also reported that Guiteau had an accomplice whose description is in the hands of the police.

ENGLAND'S OFFICIAL SYMPATHY.

Sir Edward Thornton and Mr. Victor Drummond called upon the Secretary of State, who was in attendance upon the President at the Executive Mansion, between four and five o'clock, and delivered to him a copy of the following despatch, with many expressions of deep sorrow at the great tragedy:

LONDON, July 2, 5 P.M.

Thornton, Washington:
Is it true that President Garfield has been shot at? If so, express at once great concern of Her Majesty's government and our hope that report that he has sustained serious injury is not true.   EARL GRANVILLE, *Foreign Office.*

Also the following:

LONDON, 10.25 P.M.

To Sir Edward Thornton, British Embassy, Washington:
The Queen desires that you will at once express the horror with which she has learned of the attempt upon the President's life, and her earnest hope for his recovery. Her Majesty wishes for full and immediate reports as to his condition.
LORD GRANVILLE.

MESSAGES FROM HANCOCK AND GRANT.

GOVERNOR'S ISLAND, N. Y.

To General W. T. Sherman, Washington:
I trust that the result of the assault upon the life of the President to-day may not have fatal consequences, and that in

the interest of the country the act may be shown to have been that of a madman. Thanks for your despatch and for your promise of further information. W. S. HANCOCK.

ELBERON, N. J., July 2, 1881.

To Secretary Lincoln, Washington :

Please despatch me the condition of the President. News received conflicts. I hope the most favorable may be confirmed. Express to the President my deep sympathy and hope that he may speedily recover. U. S. GRANT.

The *Star* says in an extra that when the assassin was arrested he said :

"I did it, and want to be arrested. I am a stalwart, and Arthur is President now. I have a letter here that I want you to give to General Sherman. It will explain everything. Take me to the police station."

MRS. GARFIELD IN WASHINGTON.

Mrs. Garfield travelled from Elberon in a special car. One engine broke down during the journey, and the Pennsylvania Company immediately supplied another. Mrs. Garfield arrived at fifteen minutes to seven o'clock P.M., and was immediately conducted to the President's apartment. At seven o'clock this telegram was sent by Secretary Blaine to Vice-President Arthur :

Mrs. Garfield has just arrived—a quarter before seven o'clock. The President was able to recognize and converse with her, but in the judgment of his physicians he is rapidly sinking.

JAMES G. BLAINE.

HALF HOURLY BULLETINS.

During the evening half hourly bulletins of the President's condition were sent out, among which were the following :

EXECUTIVE MANSION,
WASHINGTON, D. C., July 2, 7.40 P.M.

The President's condition is not perceptibly changed either for the better or the worse. His voice is strong, his mind unimpaired, and he talks freely with those about him.

EXECUTIVE MANSION, 8.25 P.M.

The President is again sinking, and there is little if any hope.

EXECUTIVE MANSION, 9.20 P.M.

The President has rallied a little within the past three-quarters of an hour, and his symptoms are a little more favorable. He continues brave and cheerful. About the time he began to rally he said to Dr. Bliss, "Doctor, what are the indications?" Dr. Bliss replied, "There is a chance of recovery." "Well, then," replied the President, cheerfully, "we will take that chance." The President is still sleeping.

EXECUTIVE MANSION, 10.20 P.M.

The President's symptoms continue to grow more favorable and to afford more ground for hope. His temperature is now normal, his pulse has fallen four beats since the last official bulletin, and the absence of blood in the discharges from the bladder shows that that organ is not injured as had been feared.

WASHINGTON, 11 P.M.

Mrs. Garfield, although weak from her recent illness and shocked by the suddenness of the grief which has come to her, has behaved since her arrival with a courage and self-control equal to those of her husband. Not only has she not given way to the terror and grief which she necessarily feels, but she has been constantly by the President's side encouraging him with her presence and sympathy, and giving efficient aid, so far as has been in her power, to the attending physicians.

WASHINGTON, July 2, 12 P.M.

The improvement in the President's condition is still maintained. He is resting quietly.

THRILLING STORY OF THE SHOOTING BY AN EYE-WITNESS.

The train by which President Garfield was to have travelled to New York arrived at the Pennsylvania depot in Jersey City at a quarter to four o'clock. It left Washington à little after half-past nine and was due at Jersey City at twenty-four minutes to four. It was composed of three Pullman cars and an engine. There were not many passengers on it, and most of those were ladies. Great crowds of people, anxious to learn some particulars of the shooting, thronged the depot and the streets in the neighborhood. The moment passengers by what at that time had come to be called the President's train alighted they were accosted and challenged for information. Very few of them knew anything more than they had gleaned from the newspapers along the route, and so the multitude had to disperse unsatisfied. The conductor in charge of the train informed a reporter of the *Herald* that there was a gentleman on the train who had witnessed the whole occurrence of the assassination of the President and he seemed to be deeply distressed about it. After a search among the passengers scattered through the depot and ferry-house, the reporter at length found the gentleman. He proved to be Mr. Simon Camacho, the Minister from Venezuela, and though he was somewhat reluctant at first to speak on the subject, being deeply moved when it was spoken of to him, he subsequently consented to describe what he heard and saw. To the reporter's first question Mr. Camacho said: "I went to the Baltimore and Potomac depot early, because I had to meet some friends."

"What time did you get there?"

"About nine o'clock. I had to wait for Mrs. General Blake and daughters, as they were going to New York with me on the half-past nine train. It was the limited express."

"Were you waiting in the depot?"

"No; I was standing at the entrance to the station on B Street."

"Did you see anything of the man who shot the President while you were there?"

"No, not there; that is the ladies' entrance, and there were not many people about. I saw Secretary Lincoln drive up in his carriage. He was alone. Some little time after, the Secretary of the Navy drove up in his carriage, accompanied by a lady."

"How soon after that did the President arrive?"

"Not long after."

"What hour was it when he got to the station?"

"A quarter past nine o'clock exactly. He and Secretary Blaine drove up together in a carriage."

"Did you notice how the President was dressed?"

"Yes; he wore a long duster, and was out of the carriage before I recognized him. Mr. Blaine and he sat and talked a while before leaving the carriage. They seemed to be in capital spirits. Mr. Blaine was tossing his cane up and down as he talked."

"Did you remain at the ladies' entrance?"

"When the bell signalled the approaching departure of the train I turned and went into the depot. I gave up all hope of meeting my friends, and concluded to go on the cars and take my place."

"Where were you when the shooting occurred?"

"On my way to the train yard through the station. I was already very near the door which divides the ladies' room from the large hall, and I heard the noise of quick steps on the floor. The report of a pistol followed immediately. I turned quickly and saw a man firing a second shot into the back of President Garfield. The second shot succeeded the first one very rapidly."

"Would you be kind enough to explain to me how the President was going at that instant?"

"He entered with Mr. Blaine by the door at which I was standing. There is an almost similar door at the opposite end of the building that leads to the train yard, and he was moving across the building in that direction."

"What happened when he was hit the second time?"

"Well, he fell—that is, he dropped or sank as it might be, and fell forward near the wall. His knees seemed to bend, and he leaned a little towards the right as he fell face downwards."

"Did he speak?"

"No; not a word."

"Nor utter a cry?"

"I heard none."

"What did Mr. Blaine do?"

"At the first shot he turned, but in a minute he regained his ground and went to the assistance of the President."

"Were both shots fired into the President's back?"

"No. The first was fired at his side, a sort of three-quarter side, and the second was directly in his back."

"Was the assassin arrested at once?"

"No; he made a dash for the B Street door, and at the same moment I started to intercept and arrest him."

"Had he the pistol?"

"Yes; he held the pistol in his right hand; but I knew that a man bent on killing a man would not readily attack a third; at all events I meant to take the consequences. I could have crossed the space in the building to him but for the heater, which stood in the center. I had to go round that way. When he saw that he must be caught at that door he wheeled and ran to the other, at what I may call the rear end of the building. By that move he escaped me and got into the yard."

" He was arrested there ?"

" Yes; by a number of men, and almost instantly the cry went up, ' Lynch! lynch! lynch!' It was an awful moment— dreadful."

" What did the assassin look like ?"

" He was white, sunburned, short, stout; what I should call powerful. He had auburn hair and looked angry and full of resolution."

" You did not think he was a lunatic ?"

" No, sir; nothing of the kind. He looked like a man who had come there prepared and determined, and he carried out his terrible purpose."

" Mr. Blaine, you say, made a motion as if to escape at the first shot ?"

" At the first moment he jumped towards the door, but he came back immediately to help the President."

" Could he have saved the President ?"

" No, sir; the shooting was too rapid and unexpected. I might have been able to do something if the heater had not been between me and the assassin; but as it was, all present were powerless."

" What had become of Secretaries Lincoln and Hunt ?"

" When a mattress was brought to place the President on I saw them entering from the large hall into the ladies' reception room."

" Were there none of the station authorities about the place ?"

" The B Street door was shut by a tall man, who compelled the people to keep back from the spot where the President was lying."

" The people soon understood what had occurred ?"

" Yes, instantly. The news spread like wildfire, and the excitement was intense. The voice of the gateman started me to go to the train. I found my friends at that moment. They were entering the car, and I followed them."

" Did you tell no one what you had witnessed !"

" Yes; as Secretary Blaine was moving towards the fallen President I said to him, ' Mr. Secretary, I have seen everything.' "

" I suppose you met Mrs. Garfield on the road ?"

" We passed her, poor lady, at Trenton. This murderous attack reminds me of the one by which President Prado per-

ished. He was going with two friends into the senate chamber
of Lima when a soldier shot him in the back. Prado staggered
some few feet and fell just as did President Garfield."

MRS. GARFIELD AND THE CABINET OFFICERS.

Secretary Lincoln, who, with his wife and little girl, remained
in constant attendance at the White House from the time the
President arrived, seemed to feel the blow more deeply, perhaps, than any one except Mr. Blaine. The memories of that
terrible night, sixteen years ago, when his father was assassinated,
were evidently uppermost in his mind, and he referred to that
sad event several times.

"My God!" he exclaimed this afternoon when the news was
brought out from the doctors that the case was well-nigh hopeless. "How many hours of sorrow I have passed in this
town."

Postmaster-General James here interposed and said to Mr.
Lincoln, "Do you remember how often General Garfield has
referred to your father during the past few days?"

"Yes," replied Mr. Lincoln, "and it was only night before
last that I entered into a detailed recital of the events on that
awful night."

Secretary Kirkwood said very little during the day except to
refer to the remarkably good spirits of the President yesterday.
"I never saw him so light-hearted as yesterday afternoon. We
had a long Cabinet session, and the President was the life of
the meeting. He interspersed the proceedings with anecdotes
and jokes. He especially referred to the convalescence of Mrs.
Garfield, and the anticipated pleasures of his visit to his old
Alma Mater, the meeting with his old schoolmates, and his trip
to New England."

About three o'clock this afternoon his son, James, could not
contain his pent-up grief any longer, and broke out into sobs.
His father sadly said, "Jimmy, my son, hope for the best."

The President talked considerably during the day. According to Dr. Bliss he was at times jocular, and the vein of his
conversation was of a light character and calculated to cheer up
his friends and attendants. A short time after he was put to
bed a messenger was despatched to a neighboring establishment
for one bottle of brandy. The man brought two, and the President, perceiving it, joked with Dr. Bliss about a double allowance. The President informed Dr. Bliss that he desired to be

kept accurately informed about his condition. Conceal nothing from me, doctors," said he, " for remember that I am not afraid to die." Towards four o'clock, when the evidence of internal hemorrhage became unmistakable and all the indications pointed to his dissolution, the President asked Dr. Bliss what the prospects were. He said, " Are they bad, doctor? Don't be afraid; tell me frankly. I am ready for the worst."

"Mr. President," replied Dr. Bliss, "your condition is extremely critical. I do not think you can live many hours."

"God's will be done, doctor; I'm ready to go if my time has come," firmly responded the wounded man.

Of all the Cabinet, Secretary Blaine was, to all outward appearances, the most distressed. He was very pale, and evidently was making a strong effort to keep up his strength. When Mrs. Garfield alighted from her carriage, weeping, and followed by her daughter, Mr. Blaine broke completely down and wept for several minutes.

Mrs. Garfield was escorted by her son James up the stairs, the boy, a lad of fifteen, holding her tightly by the waist and constantly whispering words of comfort in her ear. Upon entering the apartment over which the shadow of death was beginning to hover, all present silently retired, and the dying President and his wife were left alone. This was at precisely 6.50. They remained together for fifteen minutes. At the end of that time the doctors were again admitted to the room. They found the President perfectly conscious, but much weaker, his pulse being 146. "There is no hope for him," said Dr. Bliss; "he will not probably live three hours, and may die in half an hour. The bullet has pierced the liver, and it is a fatal wound."

Colonel Corbin, who came up with the President a few moments after he was shot, said he regarded his wound as mortal from the moment he saw him lying on the floor of the depot. "I had seen too many men die on the battle-field not to know death's mark. In my opinion he was virtually a dead man from the moment he was shot."

Telegrams from all parts of the country and Europe kept pouring in at the White House all the afternoon. Great surprise was expressed that neither General Grant, Conkling, Arthur, nor any of the leading Stalwarts had sent despatches of sympathy up to a late hour in the afternoon. Many prominent Democrats, among them Senators Beck, Pugh, and Jones, of Florida, and Representative Randolph Tucker, of Virginia,

spent several hours at the White House, and were deeply concerned in the bulletins from the physicians. Senator Pugh
said he regarded the death of the President as a great calamity,
and one that might tend to check the present prosperity of the
country and of his section.

The room to which General Garfield was taken is on the south-
eastern corner of the mansion. The one occupied by him when
Mrs. Garfield is in the city adjoins this apartment. Besides the
half-dozen attending physicians and three or four attendants, there
was an average of five or six other persons in the room during
the entire day. The library, the Cabinet room, and the private
secretaries' rooms were filled with officers during the afternoon
and evening. The correspondents of the press were given every
facility to observe the progress of events by private secretary
Brown, and were also given access to the doors of the sick-
room.

GUITEAU'S STORY.

The excitement and indignation became so great among the
crowds that were rapidly assembling in all parts of the city that
the authorities grew apprehensive for the safety of the prisoner,
and in order that any attempt at lynching might be frustrated it
was determined to remove him to the District jail, and General
Sherman was applied to for the assistance of the military in
case of an emergency. General Sherman, after consulting Secretary Lincoln, ordered out three companies of United States
artillery from the arsenal, one company being mounted as
cavalry and two serving as infantry. One mounted and one
foot company were stationed about the White House and
grounds, and one was stationed at the jail. The District militia
were also ordered to hold themselves is readiness, and remained
under arms at their armories all day. Guiteau was taken to jail
in a carriage by Lieutenants Austin and Eckloff and Detective
McElfresh, of the District police. The last named officer reports
the following conversation with the prisoner while being conducted to jail: "I asked him, Where are you from?"

"I am a native-born American. Born in Chicago, and am a
lawyer and a theologian."

"Why did you do this?"

"I did it to save the Republican party."

"What are your politics?"

"I am a Stalwart among the Stalwarts. With Garfield out of

the way, we can carry all the Northern States, and with him in the way we can't carry a single one."

Upon learning that McElfresh was a detective, Guiteau said: "You stick to me and have me put in the third story, front, at the jail. General Sherman is coming down to take charge. Arthur and all those men are my friends, and I'll have you made chief of police. When you go back to the depot you will find that I left two bundles of papers at the news-stand which will explain all."

"Is there anybody else with you in this matter?"

"Not a living soul. I have contemplated the thing for the last six weeks, and would have shot him when he went away with Mrs. Garfield, but I looked at her, and she looked so bad that I changed my mind."

On reaching the jail the officers of the institution did not seem to know anything about the assassination, and when taken inside Mr. Russ, the deputy warden, said: "This man has been here before."

The detective then asked Guiteau, "Have you ever been here before?" He replied, "No, sir."

"Well, the deputy warden seems to identify you."

"Yes, I was down here last Saturday morning and wanted them to let me look through, and they told me that I couldn't, but to come Monday."

"What was your object in looking through?"

"I wanted to see what sort of quarters I would have to occupy."

Continuing, the detective said: "I then searched him, and when I pulled off his shoes he said, 'Give me my shoes; I will catch cold on this stone pavement.' I told him he couldn't have them, and then he said, 'Give me a pair of pumps, then.'"

The pistol used by the prisoner is a bulldog, 44 calibre, five-shooter, and there are three loads remaining in it. Guiteau did not throw it away, but had it in his hands when arrested. Guiteau had been noticed lounging about the White House and State Department since the 4th of March last. He was regarded as a harmless lunatic by the officers, and was frequently refused admission. When denied admission to the Executive Mansion he would linger about the grounds, and when told at the State Department that he could not see Secretary Blaine he would linger in the corridors, and earned the reputation of being one of the most determined and persistent of office-seekers in the

field.   His application was filed for appointment as Minister to
Austria, also as Consul to Liverpool and Consul-General to
Paris.   These papers would seem to indicate some aberration
or failing of the mind, as there was no signature to give them
weight.   His papers were written by himself, and were accompanied by a printed speech, which he said he had delivered
during the late campaign in the State of New York.   He is a
man apparently between 35 and 40 years of age, about 5 feet 8
inches in height, of medium weight, with an ordinary countenance, without a single marked feature.   He has a sandy
complexion, light gray eyes, with a very closely-cropped beard
and hair.   He was rather poorly dressed when he made his first
appearance at the State Department.   As time passed by he
grew more shabby, and when last seen he had reached that point
when the worn sleeves were pulled down over his hands and his
coat buttoned close and high to denote the disappearance of
collar, and perhaps other linen.

Guiteau, while waiting at the White House in the hope of
securing an interview, has frequently addressed notes to the
President, of which the following is a specimen:

"I regret the trouble that you are having with Senator Conkling.   You are right and should maintain your position.   You
have my support and that of all patriotic citizens.   I would like
an audience of a few moments."

While thus waiting he would help himself to stationery and
write innumerable letters.   He would also utilize blank cards.
Writing his name upon them, he would place them in his pocket.
One day Colonel Crook, the disbursing clerk, said to him, "You
seem to make yourself at home here, and to be laying in a supply of stationery."   Guiteau replied to him, in an insolent manner, "Do you know who I am?   I am one of the men who
made Garfield President."   Colonel Crook told Mr. Brown, the
President's private secretary, of this, when that gentleman informed Colonel Crook of the true character of Guiteau, and he
has not been allowed to take liberties with the White House stationery since.   He has not been at the White House for about a
week until last evening, when Colonel Crook discovered him,
about seven o'clock, standing on the porch at the main entrance.

Dr. Townshend, Health Officer of the District, in conversation
this afternoon said: "I found the President, when I arrived at
the Baltimore and Potomac depot, about five minutes after the
shooting, in a vomiting and fainting condition.   I had his head

lowered—it had been elevated by the attendant—and administered aromatic spirits of ammonia and brandy to revive him. This had the desired effect, and the President regaining consciousness, was asked where he felt the most pain. He replied in the leg and foot. I then examined the wound, introducing my fingers, which caused a slight hemorrhage. I then decided to have him moved up-stairs from the crowd. Soon after getting him there, Drs. Smith and Purvis arrived, and, upon consultation with them, it was decided to remove him to the White House. Dr. Smith and myself accompanied the President in the ambulance to the White House, where another examination was made, and stimulants again administered. An ineffectual attempt was made to trace the course of the wound, and at 12.20 the President suffering much pain, a hypodermic injection of morphine was administered."

One of the telegraphers who carried a telegram to the President during the afternoon was asked by the wounded man if there had been many despatches received to-day regarding his misfortunes. The operator replied, "Yes, sir, quite a number expressing sympathy for you." The President responded good-humoredly, "Excuse me for correcting you, but 'sympathy with me' would be better. Be careful of your grammar."

GUITEAU IN JAIL.

The Assassin Saved from the Mob and Locked in a Cell.

WASHINGTON, July 2.

The District jail, a large brown-stone structure situated at the eastern extremity of the city, was visited by an Associated Press reporter a few minutes after eleven o'clock this morning for the purpose of obtaining an interview with Charles Guiteau, the assassin of President Garfield. The officers refused admittance to the building, stating that they were acting under instructions from Attorney-General MacVeagh, the purport of which were that no one should be allowed to see the prisoner. At first, indeed, the officers emphatically denied that the man had been conveyed to the jail, fearing, it appears, that should the fact be made known that he was there the building would be attacked by a mob. Information had reached them that such a movement was contemplated. The statement that the assassin's name is Guiteau was verified by the officer in charge of the jail. The prisoner arrived and was placed in a

cell about 10.30 o'clock, just one hour after the shooting occurred. He gave his name as Charles Guiteau, of Chicago. In
appearance he is about thirty years of age, and is supposed to be
of French descent. His height is about 5 feet 5 inches. He
has a sandy complexion, and is slight, weighing not more than
125 pounds. He wears a moustache and light chin whiskers, and
his sunken cheeks and eyes, far apart from each other, give him a
sullen, or, as the officers described it, a "loony" appearance. The
officer in question gave it as his opinion that Guiteau is a Chicago
Communist, and stated that he has noticed it to be a peculiarity
of nearly all murderers that their eyes are far apart, and Guiteau,
he said, proves no exception to the rule. When the prisoner
arrived at the jail he was neatly attired in a suit of blue, and wore
a drab hat, pulled down over his eyes, giving him the appearance
of an ugly character. It may be worthy of note that about two
or three weeks ago Guiteau went to the jail for the purpose of
visiting it, but was refused admittance on the ground that it was
not "visitors' day." He at that time mentioned his name as
Guiteau, and said that he came from Chicago. When brought to
the jail to-day he was admitted by the officer who had previously
refused to allow him to enter, and a mutual recognition took
place, Guiteau saying, "You are the man who wouldn't let me
go through the jail some time ago." The only other remark he
made before being placed in his cell was that Gen. Sherman
would arrive at the jail soon. The two jailors who are guarding
his cell state that they have seen him around the jail several
times recently, and that on one occasion he appeared to be
under the influence of liquor. On one of his visits subsequent
to the one mentioned these officers say that Guiteau succeeded
in reaching the rotunda of the building, where he was noticed
examining the scaffold from which the Hirth murderers were
hanged. Pursuant to his orders from the Attorney-General, the
officer in charge of the jail declined to give any further information, nor would he state in what cell the prisoner was confined.
This officer was an attendant at the old City Jail at the time of
the assassination of President Lincoln.

Charles Guiteau came here in the month of February, with
recommendations from various persons in Illinois, to secure the
United States Consulship at Marseilles, France. He went in
March to the well-known boarding-house of Mrs. Lockwood
(formerly Mrs. Rines) No. 810 Twelfth Street, and tried to secure
board. Mrs. Lockwood did not like his appearance, and gave

him an out-of-the-way room in the house, in the hope of getting rid of him. He pretended to know Gen. Logan and others then boarding there. He appeared to get along very well with himself, but not with the boarders, who avoided him as much as possible. "He appeared to have a cat-like tread," said one of the boarders, "and walked so easily that he was always up alongside persons before they knew it." He was said to be rude at the table, too, so much so that a gentleman and his wife stopping there would not sit beside him at the table. Mrs. Lockwood states that he acted strangely at times, and about the middle of the month, when she presented his bill, he could not pay it. He afterwards left the house, and sent Mrs. Lockwood a note stating that he was expecting a six-thousand-dollar position and would soon pay his bill. Mrs. Lockwood showed this note to Gen. Logan, who said the man was crazy. Three weeks ago he met Mrs. Ricksford, of Mrs. Lockwood's boarding-house, on the street, and requested her not to say anything about the bill he owed as it would injure him in his efforts to secure a position. He expressed great pleasure at the fact that Mrs. Lockwood had treated him kindly while he was at her house. Mrs. Lockwood said that Guiteau was a great bother to Gen. Logan, so persistent was he in his attempts to secure that gentleman's efforts in his behalf. Since leaving Mrs. Lockwood's house he has been boarding at various places, but never for a great length of time, for the reason that he appeared to have no money. He told one of the boarders at Mrs. Lockwood's that he expected to be appointed Minister to France, but did not desire it to be known. Up to the day before yesterday, when he registered at the Riggs House, Guiteau has been stopping for six weeks, with no baggage except a paper box, at No. 920 Fourteenth Street.

There is a theory, which has many adherents, that the attempted assassination was not the work of a lunatic, but the result of a plot much deeper and darker than has been suspected. It is cited, in support of this theory, that Guiteau arranged beforehand with a hackman, to be in readiness to drive him swiftly in the direction of the Congressional Cemetery as soon as he came out of the depot. In the mean time he had left a bundle of papers in the hands of a boy, with a view, it is maintained, to create a belief in his insanity, in the event of his capture.

Guiteau said, on his way to jail, that the President's assassination was premeditated, and that he went to Long Branch for the purpose of shooting him there, and was deterred by the enfeebled and saddened condition of Mrs. Garfield, which appealed so strongly to his sense of humanity that he came back without carrying out his intention. Those by whom Guiteau has been examined since the shooting say that he shows no symptoms of insanity, and it is understood that the letter addressed " To the White House" is the only document in the collection which supports the theory of insanity. It is reported that Guiteau had an accomplice, whose description is in the hands of the police, and further developments are anxiously looked for.

The librarian of the Navy Department says that Guiteau was one of Farwell's supporters in the effort to break the unit rule in the Chicago Convention, and that he was in the habit of calling at the librarian's room and telling how he had been treated by Secretary Blaine.

GEN. ARTHUR'S MOVEMENTS.

The Vice-President's Receipt of the News—Still Remaining in the City.

Gen. Arthur stopped at the Fifth Avenue Hotel in the morning soon after his arrival in this city prior to going to his home in Lexington Avenue. For an hour or more before noon he was in consultation with ex-Senator Conkling in the apartments of the latter. Numerous cards were sent to the general and the ex-senator, but they declined to see the greater number of the visitors. Both said that they had been so much shocked upon receipt of the terrible intelligence that they had no disposition to talk with any one. Ex-Senator Conkling was disinclined to express his feelings to the newspaper representatives who called, and said to one of them that he felt very bad. His countenance plainly showed that he was sorely distressed. Gen. Arthur and the ex-senator eagerly seized the telegraphic despatches which were brought to them. When Gen. Arthur went to his residence he asked his servants to see that he was not disturbed. In the evening he sat in a front parlor reading the newspaper reports from Washington. He said to a reporter, " What can I say? What is there to be said by me? I am overwhelmed with grief over the awful news." He was asked whether he would go to Washington last night, and at first said that he did not know what he should do. A few minutes later he said that in all probability he would not start for Washington until officially notified of the President's death. He received the following despatches during the day and evening from Secretary of State Blaine:

WASHINGTON, July 2, 1881.

The Hon. Chester A. Arthur, Vice-President of the United States, No. 123 *Lexington Avenue:*

The President of the United States was shot this morning by an assassin named Charles Guiteau. The weapon was a large-sized revolver. The President had just reached the Baltimore and Potomac station at about 9.20, intending, with a portion of his Cabinet, to leave on the limited express for New York. I rode in the carriage with him from the Executive Mansion, and was walking by his side when he was shot. The assassin was immediately arrested, and the President was conveyed to a private room in the station building and surgical aid at once summoned. He has now, at 10.20, been removed to the Executive Mansion. The surgeons are in consultation. They regard his wounds as very serious, but not necessarily fatal. I will keep you advised of his condition. His vigorous health gives strong hopes of his recovery. He has not lost consciousness for a moment.

JAMES G. BLAINE,
Secretary of State.

WASHINGTON, July 2, 1881.

Hon. Chester A. Arthur, Vice-President United States, No. 123 *Lexington Avenue:*

At this hour, 1 o'clock P.M., the President's symptoms are not regarded as unfavorable, but no definite assurance can be given until after the probing of the wound at 3 o'clock. There is strong ground for hope, and at the same time the greatest anxiety as to the final results. JAMES G. BLAINE,
Secretary of State.

EXECUTIVE MANSION,
WASHINGTON, July 2, 1881.

The Hon. Chester A. Arthur, Vice-President United States, No. 123 *Lexington Avenue:*

At this hour, 3.30, the symptoms of the President are not favorable. Anxiety deepens. JAMES G. BLAINE,
Secretary of State.

WASHINGTON, July 2, 1881.

The Hon. Chester A. Arthur, Vice-President:

At this hour, 6 o'clock, the condition of the President is very alarming. He is losing his strength, and the worst may be apprehended.   JAMES G. BLAINE,
Secretary of State.

EXECUTIVE MANSION,
WASHINGTON, July 2, 1881.

The Hon. Chester A. Arthur, Vice-President, New York:

Mrs. Garfield has just arrived, at 6.45 o'clock. The President was able to recognize and converse with her, but, in the judgment of his physicians, he is rapidly sinking.
JAMES G. BLAINE,
Secretary of State.

In reply to Secretary Blaine, Gen. Arthur sent the following:

NEW YORK, July 2, 1881.

Hon. James G. Blaine, Secretary of State, Washington, D. C.:

Your telegram, with its deplorable narrative, did not reach me promptly, owing to my absence. I am profoundly shocked at the dreadful news. The hopes you express relieve somewhat the horror of the first announcement. I await further intelligence with the greatest anxiety. Express to the President and those about him my great grief and sympathy, in which the whole American people will join.   C. A. ARTHUR.

NEW YORK, July 2, 1881.

The Hon. James G. Blaine, Secretary of State, Washington, D.C.:

Your 6.45 telegram is very distressing. I still hope for more favorable tidings, and ask you to keep me advised. Please do not fail to express to Mrs. Garfield my deepest sympathy.
.C. A. ARTHUR.

About 7 o'clock last evening, Gen. Arthur entered a coupé at his residence, and was rapidly driven to the Fifth Avenue Hotel, where he met ex-Senator Conkling, Police Commissioner Stephen B. French, John F. Smyth, of Albany, and ex-Senator John P. Jones, of Nevada, and remained until 8.30. Then he ordered a coupé, and, with Commissioner French, went to his residence. Prior to leaving the hotel, Gen. Arthur repeated his remark that he would not go to Washington until officially notified of the death of the President. At 9 o'clock Gen. Arthur was at home, and was talking over the event of the day with Commissioner French.

A short time before 10 o'clock it was rumored in the Fifth Avenue Hotel that Gen. Arthur had decided to start at once for Washington; but the servant who opened the door of his residence in answer to the reporter's ring of the bell, said that though the Vice-President had left the house he had not gone to Washington. The general returned to the Fifth Avenue Hotel, and was with ex-Senator Conkling, John F. Smyth, Senator Jones, and others. A telegraphic despatch sent from Washington at 9.30 o'clock to Gen. Arthur, and signed by the Secretary of the Navy and the Postmaster-General, was as follows:

WASHINGTON, July 2, 1881.

Hon. Chester A. Arthur, New York:

Sincere thanks for your expressions of sympathy. The President is no better, and we fear sinking.

WILLIAM H. HUNT,
THOMAS L. JAMES.

After the receipt of this despatch, Gen. Arthur consulted with his friends again upon the advisability of his going to Washington, and he at length declared his attention of taking the midnight train for Washington.

Gen. Arthur, ex-Senator Conkling, Senator Jones, and Commissioner French entered a coach at the Fifth Avenue Hotel a few minutes after 11 o'clock last night, and took the last boat of the Desbrosses Street Ferry, arriving before the departure of the midnight train for Washington. At the Jersey City depot Commissioner French was the first to alight. Following him was Mr. Conkling, who carried two large satchels. Behind were Gen. Arthur and Senator Jones, and Detective Frank Cosgrove, of the Central Office. A section had been secured in the Pullman sleeper Kensington, which was just forward of the sleeper Chester. Gen. Arthur reiterated his opinion that there was nothing for him to say for publication when accosted by reporters. He hurried to his section with Senator Jones and the detective. Ex-Senator Conkling shook the general's hand warmly, and saying, "God bless you, I'll see you on Thursday," stepped out on the platform. Commissioner French then bade the general good-by and went to the platform. As the train started Commissioner French stepped off, but Mr. Conkling remained on the lower step of the platform until the train had almost emerged from the depot. Then he too left the car and joined Mr. French. Mr. Conkling said that it was decidedly proper for Gen. Arthur to go to Washington without further delay, as in the event of the President's death he would be in Washington, and if the President did not die it was equally proper that the Vice-President should be there. Mr. Conkling and Mr. French returned to New York at 12.30 this morning by way of the Desbrosses Street Ferry.

MRS. GARFIELD'S SORROW.

A Day of Expected Pleasure turned into one of Endless Mourning—Her Departure for Washington — General Grant's Sentiments.

ELBERON, N. J., July 2, 1881.

The wife of the President received the dreadful news this morning as bravely as the bravest woman could. It reached her under no ordinary circumstances, and the worst effects might have been justly apprehended. It came at a time when Mrs. Garfield was barely convalescent from a severe illness, and in an hour when she was looking forward with pleasant anticipations to a meeting with the President. She was waiting for the train which would convey her to Jersey City, the place of meeting, when the information came that her husband had fallen by the bullet of an assassin. The millions of hearts that throbbed for the sick and patient wife all over the land would have ached to see her acute suffering. But she bore it all with pale, firm lips, and in the two long hours she had to pass before starting for Washington her self-control never once deserted her. Perhaps it was fortunate that her daughter, Mollie, was the only one of her children that remained with her. The two little boys, Irving and Abram Garfield, had left Elberon on Friday noon in the care of Mrs. Dr. Boynton. The dangerous illness of her sister-in-law had called Mrs. Boynton to Ohio, and as the two boys would have to return soon for school it was decided that they should go with her. Thus Mrs. Garfield was spared at least the additional burden of their care in such a harrowing time.

PREPARING FOR PLEASURE.

Last evening General D. D. Swaim, United States Army, reached Elberon from Washington to accompany the party to

Jersey City. The programme was that the President would join them there, at the Pennsylvania depot, and all were to embark upon the yacht of Mr. Cyrus W. Field, with whom they were to spend Sunday and Monday at Irvington on the Hudson. The trunks were packed last evening and everything made ready for the trip. The Elberon party consisted of Mrs. Garfield, Miss Mollie Garfield, Mrs. A. F. Rockwell and her daughter, and General Swaim. Mrs. Garfield had been improving so rapidly that her friends declared with pleasure she was her old self once more. Each day of late she had been driving and walking and getting all the benefit which the breath of old ocean could afford her. This morning she was in better spirits than usual, and spoke gayly of the expected meeting with the President. All things augured well for their excursion, and the day itself was one of Elberon's best. The hotel was early filled with people from the neighboring cottages, who were one and all bent upon sharing the excitement of the first day's racing at Monmouth Park. The regular guests of the hotel were sauntering leisurely from their breakfast tables; some had gone for a stroll along the beach; a few energetic ones were playing tennis upon the lawn, and every minute saw fresh arrivals in handsome equipages at the Elberon's doors. The races were uppermost in the anticipation of all. Mrs. Garfield and her companions breakfasted in their rooms, according to their custom, and were whiling away the time until the 12.22 train should arrive to take them to their rendezvous.

THE FIRST DESPATCH.

At about ten minutes after ten o'clock a messenger ran in breathless haste from the Elberon station to the hotel bearing a despatch for Mrs. Garfield. It was signed by A. S. Brown, the Superintendent of the Western Union Telegraph Company at Washington, and urged Mrs. Garfield not to put too much weight upon the many rumors that were flying in every direction about the President's injuries. This was the first intimation received that the President had been injured; but fast upon the heels of the first despatch came another from Colonel Corbin to General Swaim that the President had been shot in the depot of the Baltimore and Potomac Railway, and asking him to break the news gently to Mrs. Garfield. While General Swaim went to perform this duty the alarming news spread among the people in the hotel and around the grounds and filled every mind with consternation. Pleasure faded instantly from the scene and mourning took its place. Deserting their amusements they crowded around the little telegraph stall in the office of the hotel, and a solemn silence ensued as if they were in the presence of death itself. General Swaim came down stairs pale and agitated after his distressing interview with Mrs. Garfield. What she said was only known to the few who stood around her; but General Swaim replied, when dozens of persons asked him how the lady bore it, that she stood the ordeal without a single outcry.

" GOD REIGNS."

Soon followed a despatch from the President's secretary, which read:

EXECUTIVE MANSION,
WASHINGTON, D. C., July 2, 1881.

General Swaim, Elberon, N. J.:

We have the President safely and comfortably settled in his room at the Executive Mansion. His pulse is strong and nearly normal. So far as I can detect, from what the surgeons say and from his general condition, I feel very hopeful. Come on as soon as you can get special. Advise me of movements of your train and when you can be expected. As the President said upon a similar occasion sixteen years ago, "God reigns and the government at Washington still lives."

A. F. ROCKWELL.

This was immediately conveyed to Mrs. Garfield by General Swaim, and a copy of it was read with tear-filled eyes by the spectators. Only a few days before the President, as well as the writer of that despatch, had stood where they stood, at a time when the Chief Magistrate had taken a few days' respite from the cares of his great office, and was enjoying his wife's returning health and the first quiet he himself had experienced since he accepted the Presidential chair in March. The sudden transition was more than those who saw him then could bear, and imprecations upon the head of his assailant mingled with their tremulous words of sorrow. The news had meanwhile spread all over Long Branch, and it was there believed that the President was dead. Several of the hotels had their flags at half-mast, business stands were deserted, amusements were forgotten, and thousands of people gathered around the West End to await further tidings. The knowledge that Mrs. Garfield was at the Elberon took a continuous string of carriages in that direction. General Grant's cottage was not far away, and some of them went there upon the supposition that the General might have received fuller information. They were disappointed and returned to the Elberon. All of General Grant's despatches came by the Elberon line, and they were no more complete than the others.

GENERAL GRANT CALLS.

About eleven o clock General Grant drove up to the Elberon unaccompanied, and obtained an interview with the President's wife. When he came down-stairs again he stopped for a moment to speak with a group of gentlemen, among whom were Messrs. Robert Lennox Kennedy, H. Victor Newcombe, and D. G. Goodwin, U. S. A. The General said that he was astonished at the firmness and courage displayed by Mrs. Garfield. He was very much moved himself, and said that he could not understand how such a thing could happen in America. He surmised that it was the work of either an insane man or a Nihilist; and "if it was a Nihilist," he added with determination, "it is time that this country suppressed Nihilism."

Despatches came pouring in now, and bit by bit the situation of affairs in Washington began to be understood. The operator was overrun by people who wanted to send inquiries to the capital at the very time that they were coming thence as fast as he could possibly receive them. The proprietor of the Elberon, Mr. C. T. Jones, had some of the despatches posted at the hotel office, where all might read them. One came from Dr. Bliss, at Washington, offering Mrs. Garfield such encouragement as was possible under the circumstances. Another from Colonel Corbin to General Swaim informed him that they were trying to arrange for a special train to take the Presidential party from Jersey City to Washington. It was decided, partly to save Mrs. Garfield from further suspense in waiting, and partly to be in readiness for taking the Washington train as soon as it was ready, that she should go to the Long Branch station at once. Mr. Newcombe promptly tendered the use of his coupé, and in that Mrs. Garfield was taken to the railway station, about an eighth of a mile distant. Mr. Jones took the rest of the party to the station in carriages, and provided a man servant to accompany them all the way to the capital. When Mrs. Garfield emerged from the hotel her face was terribly pale, but her features were composed.

OFF FOR WASHINGTON.

The party got in the last car on the 12.22 train of the Central Railroad of New Jersey and alighted five minutes later at the Long Branch station. Despatches were flying up and down the road in the mean time, and it was arranged that instead of going by way of Jersey City a special train should be made up at Long Branch to go by way of Monmouth Junction. Mr. Watts, the train superintendent on the New York division of the Pennsylvania Railroad, telegraphed to Mr. Stearns, superintendent of the New Jersey Central at Long Branch, that an engine and special car at Long Branch were at the immediate service of Mrs. Garfield for the through trip to Washington. This engine (No. 729) and car had run as a special train from Philadelphia in the morning and was waiting orders at Long Branch. Mr. Stearns communicated with General Swaim, and the offer was promptly accepted. Mr. Neiman, the train despatcher at Long Branch, hurriedly arranged for the start, and at half-past twelve o'clock all was ready. Mrs. Garfield left the station, in which she had been waiting, to take a seat in the car, with Mrs. Rockwell beside her. All the baggage belonging to the party was stowed at the rear end of the car, and they started at full speed and with a clear track. There was one stop at Seabright to change conductors, and again the train sped on for the capital. They expected to pass Philadelphia at twenty-two minutes past two by way of Mantua, reach Baltimore at about half-past four, where they would change locomotives, and then run through to Washington.

LATER DESPATCHES.

After Mrs. Garfield left Elberon a multitude of despatches reached the hotel, some of which were forwarded to Mrs. Garfield *en route*. One addressed to General Grant read as follows:

NEW YORK, July 2, 1881.

General U. S. Grant, Elberon, N. J.:

At noon Blaine reports the President's condition to be serious, but the wounds are not necessarily fatal. Other despatches indicate his condition as precarious, but it is hoped that his vigorous constitution may pull him through.   J. R. Y.

Another came to the Elberon and was telegraphed to the special train, which read:

WASHINGTON, D. C., July 2, 1881.

To Mrs. Garfield, Elberon, N. J.:

The President wishes me to say to you for him that he has been seriously hurt. How seriously he cannot say. He is himself and hopes you will come to him soon. He sends his love to you.

(2) Rec'd.   A. F. ROCKWELL.

Despatches were afterwards bulletined from Mr. G. C. Clarke at Washington, and were eagerly scanned by the people who yet clung about the hotel. They were as follows:

WASHINGTON, D. C., July 2, 1881.

To the Elberon:

The best information we can obtain is that the President is lying in a critical condition. One of the balls is supposed to have entered his bowels.   G. C. CLARKE.

WASHINGTON, D. C., July 2, 1881.

To the Elberon:

Garfield hopeful, but one of his wounds may prove fatal. Indications are rather favorable.   CLARKE.

THE WORST EXPECTED.

Just when the people at Elberon and Long Branch were beginning to be hopeful for the recovery of the President these feelings were again depressed by the receipt of the following:

WASHINGTON, D. C., July 2, 1881.

To the Elberon:

Report says that the President is sinking rapidly. Stimulants are being administered.   G. C. CLARKE.

At three o'clock or a little thereafter the following was received amid expressions of the greatest sorrow:

WASHINGTON, D. C., July 2, 2.45 P.M.

To Elberon Hotel:

Physicians say that President Garfield cannot recover.

A. S. BROWN.

4

THE PRESIDENT'S MOTHER.

CLEVELAND, O., July 2.—The President's aged mother is in Solon, forty miles from Cleveland, and the first thought was what effect the shock might have on her great age and feebleness. She is a guest of her daughters, Mrs. Mary G. Larabee and Mrs. Mehetable Trowbridge, upon their farms, one mile east of Solon. A reporter visited Solon to-day, and drove out to the Larabee homestead, where he met Mrs. Larabee, Mrs. Trowbridge, and the daughter of the former. "What have you heard from Washington?" was the anxious inquiry that greeted him, as he appeared at the doorway. Upon being informed that the news at two o'clock was of an encouraging nature, the ladies were partly relieved of their anxiety, and entered into conversation concerning the sad event. "How does Mrs. Garfield bear the news?" "She has not heard a word of what has happened," replied Mrs. Larabee, "and we are afraid to break the news to her. Mother has had so much trouble of late, that we dare not excite her at this time. She was not informed of Mrs. Arnold's death, which occurred on Thursday night, until this morning, and it has prostrated her. The death of Uncle Thomas produced a great shock on her nerves and she was unable to attend his funeral. Mother is so wrapped up in James that this will certainly kill her." "Have you received tidings from any members of the President's family?" was asked. "We received a telegram a short time ago from Harry Garfield, addressed to his grandmother, but further than this we have heard nothing from the family," was the reply of Mrs. Trowbridge. The following is a copy of the message mentioned above:

EXECUTIVE MANSION, WASHINGTON, D. C., July 2.
To Mrs. Eliza Garfield, Solon, Ohio:
Don't be alarmed by sensational rumors; doctor thinks it will not be fatal. Don't think of coming until you hear further.
HARRY A. GARFIELD.

"You had learned of the attempted assassination before the receipt of this message?" suggested the reporter inquiringly. "We knew nothing of what had happened until the arrival of the noon train with copies of an extra," replied Mrs. Trowbridge. "My daughter from Brooklyn Village came down from Cleveland this morning, and brought us a copy containing the terrible news. We could not at first believe it. But as we read the

MRS. ELIZA GARFIELD, MOTHER OF JAMES A. GARFIELD.

bulletins we became satisfied they were only too true. A short time later we received Harry's despatch, from which we drew as much comfort as possible. After that we had no news until you arrived." It was decided that the aged lady should not be told the awful news, at least until morning, when better news might be at hand, and when she might have more strength to bear it.

BREAKING THE NEWS TO HER AS GENTLY AS POSSIBLE.

CLEVELAND, O., July 3.—The news of the shooting of the President was broken to his mother this forenoon at Scion. She had been so much overcome by the fatal accident which resulted in the death of Thomas Garfield and Mrs. Arnold that the family had kept from her the intelligence of the attempted assassination. But this morning she felt better, and spoke of attending Mrs. Arnold's funeral, which took place at Bedford to-day. In announcing her intention she remarked, "Last Saturday, Thomas was buried; to-day, Cornelia. I wonder who it will be next Sunday."

Mrs. Trowbridge, at whose house she then was, sent for Mrs. Larabee, another daughter. When the latter arrived Mrs. Garfield inquired whether she was going to Mrs. Arnold's funeral. Mrs. Larabee replied that she guessed she could not, as something had happened, so the sister thought it best not to go.

"What has happened?" inquired Mrs. Garfield.

"We have heard that James is hurt," replied Mrs. Larabee.

"How? By the cars?" asked the mother.

"No, he was shot by an assassin, but he was not killed," answered the daughter.

"The Lord help me!" exclaimed Mrs. Garfield.

Mrs. Larabee assured her mother that the latest reports were favorable, and showed that the President was resting quietly and in a fair way to recover.

"When did you hear this?" queried Mrs. Garfield.

"Yesterday noon, but we thought it best not to tell you. The news was not as favorable as to-day," was the reply.

"You were very thoughtful. I am glad you did not tell me," said Mrs. Garfield, adding that she thought something had happened, as she had noticed that the manner of her daughter had been peculiar towards her yesterday. She bore up under the intelligence with much fortitude. She was shown despatches received from Major Swaim, Secretary Judd, and Harry Garfield, the one from the last-named reading as follows:

WASHINGTON, D. C., July 3.

Mrs. Eliza Garfield, Solon, Ohio:

Thank God, he lives this morning, and the doctors are very hopeful. He has been perfectly himself all the time.

HARRY A. GARFIELD.

She read the despatches calmly, and said, "How could anybody be so cold-hearted as to want to kill my baby?"

In general conversation she expressed wonder as to what was coming next, and inquired what would probably be done with the assassin. Upon some one saying "Hang him," she replied, "He deserves it."

She does not contemplate going to Washington unless sent for, thinking she will be telegraphed for if necessary to go on. It being remarked to her that the news continued to grow favorable, she said, "I am glad to hear it, but I am afraid we are hoping against fate. It seems terrible."

This afternoon she dictated the following despatch to her grandson:

Harry A. Garfield, Executive Mansion, Washington:

The news was broken to me this morning and shocked me very much. Since receiving your telegram I feel much more hopeful. Tell James that I hear he is cheerful, and that I am glad of it. Tell him to keep in good spirits, and accept the love and sympathy of a mother, sisters, and friends.

ELIZA GARFIELD.

VICE-PRESIDENT ARTHUR AND SENATOR CONKLING APPALLED BY THE TRAGEDY.

No description could do justice to the scenes about the Fifth Avenue and other uptown hotels yesterday. The news of the assassination was received in the forenoon, and as it went from mouth to mouth, people wondered and speculated and hoped that the President would recover. As later despatches were received and the crowd grew greater the interest increased and the Fifth Avenue Hotel corridors became almost one mass of men. They talked with bowed heads of the tragic event, and everybody had a sympathetic word for the stricken President and the members of his family.

Senator Conkling received the news as he left the Albany boat. He was very much affected, and for a time said nothing. Finally he raised his head and said: "My God, can this be true!" He went to the Fifth Avenue Hotel and walked across his room once or twice and then sank into a chair. He was very greatly affected, and remained seated for some time. At about noon he was joined by Vice-President Arthur. The General had read a despatch announcing the assassination while he was leaving the Albany boat, and hastily repaired to Senator Conkling. The two gentlemen remained together for some time. They were both very much grieved, and whatever political differences they may have had with the President it was plain to be seen that they very greatly deplored the assassination. The Senator and the Vice-President remained secluded for some time and refused to see any friends. Shortly after noon General Arthur hurriedly left the hotel and went to his residence. He returned later and remained with Senator Conkling during the evening.

Senator Conkling did not desire to make any statement for publication. His sorrow at the event was plainly to be seen, and nothing he could say would make it the more evident.

General Arthur said he could say nothing about the matter. "What can I say," he remarked, "except that I am like everybody else, overwhelmed with grief? I was thunderstruck at the news when I received it, and have not as yet recovered. I will not go to Washington until I receive official notification of the death of the President."

At about fourteen minutes past twelve P.M. General Arthur received the following despatch:

WASHINGTON, D. C., July 2, 1881.

To the Hon. Chester A. Arthur, Vice-President of the United States, No. 120 *Lexington Avenue, New York City, N. Y.:*

The President of the United States was shot this morning by an assassin named Charles Guiteau. The weapon was a large-sized revolver. The President had just reached the Baltimore and Potomac Station at about twenty minutes past nine, intending, with a portion of his Cabinet, to leave on the limited express for New York. I rode in the carriage with him from the Executive Mansion. Was walking by his side when he was shot. The assassin was immediately arrested and the President was conveyed to a private room in the station building and surgical aid at once summoned. He has now, at twenty past ten, been

removed to the Executive Mansion. The surgeons, on consultation, regard his wounds as very serious, though not necessarily fatal. I will keep you advised of his condition. His vigorous health gives strong hopes of his recovery. He has not lost consciousness for a moment.   JAMES G. BLAINE,
Secretary of State.

At two o'clock General Arthur received the following:

EXECUTIVE MANSION,
WASHINGTON, D. C., July 2, 1881.
To Chester A. Arthur, Vice-President of the United States, No.
120 *Lexington Avenue, New York City:*
At this hour, one o'clock P.M., the President's symptoms are not regarded as unfavorable, but no definite assurance can be given until after the probing of the wound at 3 o'clock. There is strong ground for hope, and at the same time the gravest anxiety as to the final result.
JAMES G. BLAINE,
Secretary of State.

At four P.M. the Vice-President received the following despatch:

EXECUTIVE MANSION,
WASHINGTON, D. C., July 2, 1881.
To Chester A. Arthur, Vice-President of the United States, No.
120 *Lexington Avenue, or Fifth Avenue Hotel, New York City,*
N. Y.:
At this hour—half-past three—the symptoms of the President are not favorable. Anxiety deepens.
JAMES G. BLAINE,
Secretary of State.

This telegram was followed by the following:

EXECUTIVE MANSION,
WASHINGTON, D. C., July 2, 1881.
To Chester A. Arthur, Vice-President of the United States, New
York City, N. Y.:
At this hour—six o'clock—the condition of the President is very alarming. He is losing his strength and the worst may be apprehended.   JAMES G. BLAINE,
Secretary of State.

Later the following was received :

EXECUTIVE MANSION,
WASHINGTON, D. C., July 2, 1881.

*To Hon. Chester A. Arthur, Vice-President, New York City,
N. Y.:*

Mrs. Garfield has just arrived—a quarter before seven o'clock. The President was able to recognize and converse with her, but in the judgment of his physicians he is rapidly sinking.

JAMES G. BLAINE,
Secretary of State.

ARTHUR REPLIES.

General Arthur, in reply to these despatches, sent the following :

NEW YORK, July 2, 1881.

*To the Hon. James G. Blaine, Secretary of State, Washington,
D. C.:*

Your telegram, with its deplorable narrative, did not reach me promptly, owing to my absence. I am profoundly shocked at the dreadful news. The hopes you express relieve somewhat the horror of the first announcement. I await further intelligence with the greatest anxiety. Express to the President and those about him my great grief and sympathy, in which the whole American people will join. C. A. ARTHUR.

NEW YORK, July 2, 1881.

*To the Hon. James G. Blaine, Secretary of State, Washington,
D. C.:*

Your six forty-five telegram is very distressing. I still hope for more favorable tidings, and ask you to keep me advised. Please do not fail to express to Mrs. Garfield my deepest sympathy. C. A. ARTHUR.

THE NIGHT IN THE FIFTH AVENUE.

Senator Conkling remained in his room nearly all the evening. Early in the night he came down in the large corridor of the Fifth Avenue Hotel and conversed with ex-Governor Goodwin, of Arizona. When he returned to his room he was joined by ex-Insurance Superintendent Smyth and Police Commissioner French. General Arthur formed one of the party. The gentlemen remained together until late, and a number of despatches were received from Washington giving information about the President's condition. Senator Conkling spent most of the time in walking up and down his room, and several times gave vent to his feelings in remarks as to the horror he felt for the assassination. General Arthur was laboring under great emotion, and several times remarked that he thought the President would recover. Neither Mr. Smyth nor Mr. French seemed to share the Vice-President's opinion, but they said nothing. Senator Conkling still continued to pace up and down his room, and when General Arthur suggested the possibility of the President's recovery he shook his head sorrowfully and resumed his walk. The group was certainly as sad a one as could be expected. Every one was full of sorrow at the terrible calamity that has befallen the President and his family, and all had a sympathetic word for the Chief Magistrate.

Towards eight o'clock the corridors of the Fifth Avenue Hotel became very crowded. Ingress and egress were extremely difficult, and policemen were stationed at the staircases and entrances to the hotel. There was most intense excitement and everybody conversed in whispers. Sorrow was depicted on every face, and the feeling was universal that the death of the President would be an almost irreparable loss.

A TERRIBLE DEATH-WATCH.

Scenes in the President's Chamber Saturday Night—His Anxiety about Mrs. Garfield and His Joy on Her Arrival— Touching Incidents.

WASHINGTON, July 3.—Never since the 14th of April, 1865, when the citizens of the entire nation were looking for the momentary death of the martyred Lincoln, has the White House been the scene of such a terrible death-watch as it was last night. Whether the President lives or dies, the night of the 2d of July will forever mark an era in the history of the Executive Mansion, and the incidents of that night, when the life of President Garfield hung trembling in the balance, will be read with interest so long as the English language is read or spoken. The full particulars of that night of anxious watching and fearful forebodings will probably never be written. The actors in the scene were too busy and too much excited by their fears to remember half of the little incidents which go to make up the tragic story; but some dim picture of the terrible life drama which was enacted in the President's chamber, while the whole world was awaiting with breathless anxiety its culmination, may be drawn at this time, while the actors of it still hold its prominent features fresh in their memory. The *Times* correspondent has seen and conversed with most of the ladies and gentlemen who passed the night in the White House, hoping and fearing alternately for the safety of the life of the chief Executive of a great nation, and the stories which they relate, while they serve to make a graphic picture of a scene which all Americans will look upon with intense interest, serve still more forcibly to depict the character of President Garfield, and to place him before the world as a husband and father as he never could have been known but for the attempt made upon his life yesterday by the assassin Guiteau

From the time of the shooting in the Baltimore and Potomac depot yesterday morning until very nearly midnight, but little, if any, hopes of saving the President's life were entertained by the physicians who attended him. It is safe to say that but for the remarkably abstemious course of life which he had pursued from boyhood up he never would have rallied from the shock. His one thought, when it became possible for him to think calmly at all after being removed to his chamber in the Executive Mansion, was for his wife and children. He feared the effect of the terrible news upon Mrs. Garfield, and he was anxious to have her and their daughter Mollie with him, that he might reassure them, if possible, and look upon them for the last time if it was decreed that he should die. He was very weak at this time, and to all appearances sinking fast. He was told by Mrs. James, wife of the Postmaster-General, and Mrs. Hunt, who were doing all that sympathetic women could do to make him comfortable, that Mrs. Garfield would be with him by six o'clock. Every moment seemed an age to the fast sinking father and husband. He turned restlessly in his bed and asked the time of day continually. It was evident that his anxiety to meet Mrs. Garfield was aggravating the effect of the wounds which he had received, but nothing could be done. Six o'clock came, and with it, instead of Mrs. Garfield, the news that the engine of her train had broken down seventeen miles outside of Washington. This news was carefully kept from the suffering President, and a fresh engine started off to take the place of the disabled one. It brought Mrs. Garfield, Mollie Garfield, Gen. Swaim, and Mrs. Rockwell to the city, at the rate of sixty miles

4*

an hour, and at 6.50 the party drove up to the private entrance in the rear of the White House.

Here the almost heart-broken wife was met by her son James A. Garfield, Jr., Mrs. James, and Attorney-General MacVeagh. She placed her hands in those of Mrs. James, and directing a piercing inquiry into her eyes, exclaimed interrogatively, "Well?" "Oh, everything is going on beautifully," said Mrs. James, in reply, "only he must not be excited. You must be very calm when you meet him." Mrs. Garfield had nerved herself for the ordeal and she answered simply, but with great firmness, "I can do it." The party then went sadly up the stairs, young James A. Garfield with his arm about his mother's waist. Arrived in the library, everybody but Mrs. Garfield paused, and the doctors withdrew with bowed heads from the President's chamber. Mrs. Garfield passed quickly in, and the door was closed. Of that solemn meeting between husband and wife no record will ever be given. The two were alone together, without witnesses. At the end of about fifteen minutes the door opened, and Mrs. Garfield came slowly out. There were no tears in her eyes, and she walked with a firm step and took her seat in the library. She was very brave and bore up nobly under the great blow which had fallen upon her. As she left the room Mrs. James passed in. The President was smiling and he beckoned with his finger to the lady to approach. She leaned over the President and he said, "Have you met Crete?" Mrs. Garfield's Christian name is Lucretia, and Crete is the pet name by which the President always speaks of her. "Yes, I have met her," said Mrs. James. "And how does she act; how did she bear it?" was the next eager question. "She bore it like the true wife of a true soldier," answered Mrs. James. "Ah, the dear little woman," exclaimed the President. "I would rather die than that this should cause a relapse to her."

Soon after Miss Mollie entered the room. She, too, was very brave, and forced herself to assume a calmness which she could not feel. Advancing steadily towards her father as he lay on what was supposed to be his death-bed, she said, "O papa! I'm so glad to get back to you, but I'm so sorry to see you in this way." Then she kissed him, and the President, putting his arm around her neck, exclaimed, "Mollie, you are a brave, good little girl." "Well, I'm not going to talk with you now," said the stout-hearted little girl, as she tenderly removed his arm from her neck; "wait till you get well," and with these parting words she kissed him again and turned and walked from the room, followed by a beaming smile from the President.

From the moment of Mrs. Garfield's visit to him, the President seemed to gain in strength and spirits, and if he recovers the doctors say that it will be due greatly to the presence of his devoted wife. After Mollie had left him he turned over, and with one hand clasped firmly in one of Mrs. James's, and his head resting upon her other hand, he fell into a gentle sleep. In half an hour, however, he awoke and complained of a pain in his feet. It did not last long, and he dozed off again, still holding the hand of Mrs. James. This time he slept a little over half an hour, and when he awoke he said to Mrs. James, "Do you know where Mrs. Garfield is now?" "Oh, yes," Mrs. James answered, "she is close by, watching and praying for her husband." He looked up to the lady with an anxious face, and said, "I want her to go to bed. Will you tell her that I say if she will undress and go to bed I will turn right over, and I feel sure that when I know she is in bed I can go to sleep and sleep all night. Tell her," he exclaimed with sudden energy, "that I *will* sleep all night if she will only do what I ask." Mrs. James conveyed the message to Mrs. Garfield, who said to her at once, "Go back and tell him that I am undressing." She returned with the answer, and the President turned over on his right side and dropped into a quiet sleep almost instantly.

THE PRESIDENT'S CONDITION ON SUNDAY MORNING.

Joyful News for the Patient Watchers in and about the White House Followed by Discouraging Tidings—His Tender Nurses —A Good Omen—No Visitors Allowed to see the Patient— Incidents of the Day.

WASHINGTON, July 3.—The feeling in this city has changed within the past twenty-four hours from that of the utmost alarm to one of hope and joy. On all sides the news has gone forth that the life of President Garfield is not despaired of by his physicians, and that they now believe, unless some totally unexpected crisis should be precipitated, that the President will live to continue the work which was begun with his administration. In this great crisis of his life, the President's early habits have come to his rescue. But for his robust frame and magnificent physique, the result of his abstinence and youthful training in the struggle for existence, there is not the slightest doubt that the shock of the assault would have terminated fatally within twenty-four hours. The President, however, was prepared by long years of careful obedience to the laws of nature to resist the effects of the shock successfully, and when they had once passed away he had strength and energy enough left to fight for his life, and he is doing it now with the most encouraging prospects of eventual success in the conflict. His recovery, if he should recover, will require a long time, during which he will be forced to remain in his bed and to be kept perfectly quiet. All danger from internal hemorrhage is now passed, and the only thing to be feared is inflammation of the wound. The healthy condition of the patient and the strictly abstemious course of life which he has pursued, together with the favorable weather, render this danger much less than might be anticipated. The wound has been carefully bathed in cold water at frequent intervals during the entire day, and up to this evening no symptoms of inflammation have been observed. The mind of the President is perfectly clear and his nerves have recovered their normal condition. He is cheerful at all times, and manifests a disposition to talk freely to his medical and other attendants. This disposition is discouraged as much as possible by Dr. Bliss, who insists that his patient must be kept perfectly quiet and composed in his mind, and to secure this condition, all visitors, except Mrs. Garfield and the ladies of the Cabinet, have been excluded from the sick-room to-day, and these have been warned not to talk to the President except when it is absolutely necessary.

The care and attention bestowed upon the wounded man have been all that could possibly be given, and no person had ever more tender nurses than President Garfield has had since the assassin marked him in the Baltimore and Potomac depot yesterday morning. The Cabinet ladies are nearly worn out by their long and anxious watching, but they look better to-day than they did yesterday, for the light of hope has taken the place of despair in their weary eyes. Mrs. James, Mrs. Hunt, Mrs. Blaine, Mrs. Windom, Mrs. MacVeagh, and Mrs. Lincoln have had very little sleep during the past forty-eight hours; but the nature of the work in which they are engaged has nerved them to their task, and they show few signs of the weariness which they must feel.

THE EARLY HOURS AT THE WHITE HOUSE.

The sun rose upon the capital of the nation this morning to find a throng of vigilant and anxious watchers at the gates of the Executive Mansion, many of whom had not left the spot during the entire night. The crowd was not so great and the excitement was not so intense as it had been yesterday, the reassuring bulletins issued late last night having sent many to their homes full of hope for the recovery of the President. But a large enough throng remained to make the early morning scene one of grave and intense interest. Sentries paced in front of the gate and kept the carriage-way clear, and within the grounds, on the lawn between the Executive Mansion and the Treasury building, the two military companies, which Secretary Lincoln had stationed at the White House, were bivouacked. Within the mansion, the only person who had slept for any considerable time during the night was the wounded sufferer himself, and his sleep had been fitful and uneasy. Postmaster-General James, who had left the White House at three o'clock to secure a little needful rest, returned at five o'clock and passed up to the library. He remained nearly two hours, and upon his return the crowd pressed eagerly around him for news of the President. He brought good news. The favorable symptoms which had begun at about eleven o'clock last night had increased, and the doctors were really hopeful of saving the life of the chief Executive of the nation, upon which so much depends. The announcement was received with heartfelt joy by those who heard it, and it was soon spread all over the city. Washington people are not, as a rule, early risers, but to-day the streets were alive with men whom anxiety would not allow to sleep after the rising of the sun. The good news met them as a boon from heaven, and there were probably more devout thanksgivings silently rendered on this beautiful Sabbath than have ever gone up from this community before. The excitement expended itself yesterday. Men went to bed late last night or early this morning hoping for the best, but prepared for the worst, and to-day when they received the glad tidings of hope, they accepted them calmly and almost without comment. There were no large gatherings such as were to be seen yesterday. The newspapers were read eagerly, and when the New York journals arrived at noon the supply was exhausted before a fiftieth part of the demand had been met.

THE ATTENDANTS ON THE SUFFERER.

The experience of the crowds at the Executive Mansion yesterday, and the inconvenience which they occasioned, with the possible danger to the President, was not lost upon the doctors, and to-day they insisted that no person except the Cabinet Ministers and members of the diplomatic corps should be allowed to pass beyond the vestibule of the White House. Only a few favored ones were furnished with cards admitting them to the grounds, and the result was that the noise and confusion and excitement of yesterday were avoided. The Executive Mansion was comparatively deserted, only those whose business demanded their presence being allowed to enter. Mrs. Garfield, who, at the request of her husband, had retired at about midnight, made her appearance in the library, which communicates with the sick-chamber, at 5.30 o'clock. The President was awake, and Mrs. Hunt and Mrs. Blaine, with Dr. Bliss, were in attendance upon him. Mrs. Garfield, who has borne up with remarkable courage ever since she was brought face to face with the terrible realities of the position, passed into the President's room and greeted the sufferer with a smile of encouragement, receiving in return a happy smile of welcome. It was evident that the President was in a much more hopeful condition than when she had left him last night, and Dr. Bliss assured her that the prospects for his recovery were now good. The President suffered terribly at times from pain in his feet and limbs, but he was stronger than he had been, and his pulse was slowly but most surely falling towards its normal condition. Mrs. Garfield seated herself by the bed of her husband, and took his hand in her own. She remained with him for the greater part of the entire day, only leaving him at intervals for a few moments at a time.

At about 8 o'clock this morning the President fell into a gentle slumber which lasted, with occasional breaks, until 9.30. Half an hour later the first official bulletin of the day, signed by Dr. Bliss, was posted on the gates of the grounds of the Executive Mansion and in all the prominent hotels of the city. It announced that the President had rested quietly and awakened much refreshed, and that his improved condition gave additional hopes of his gradual recovery. His pulse at this time registered 114, his respiration was recorded at 18, and his temperature was nearly normal. The news was received throughout the city with universal expressions of joy and thanksgiving, and telegraphed all over the country to reassure the waiting and anxious citizens.

A GOOD OMEN.

In the mean time, the members of the Cabinet who had been snatching little seasons of sleep after the exhausting watch of last night, began to appear in the Cabinet room and the library with their ladies. The gentlemen looked far more weary and careworn than the ladies, who had done the actual watching at the bedside of the President. They had waited during the night in the outer rooms with nothing but their sad thoughts and fears to bear them company, while their wives had been occupied in attending to the duties of the sick-room, and this had to a certain extent relieved them from the wear and tear of their anxious forebodings. Secretary Blaine wore the most woebegone look of all the Cabinet. He flitted in and out of the library like a spirit who could find no rest. Postmaster-General James and Mrs. James started from the Arlington for the Executive Mansion at 9.30. As they were stepping to the sidewalk fronting the grounds, a passing horse cast a shoe, and it fell directly in front of Mrs. James. "That is a good omen," she said, as she stooped and picked it up, "and it will please the President." It is well known that Gen. Garfield is inclined to attach some slight importance to omens, and Mrs. James faithfully carried the horseshoe to the Executive Mansion and deposited it in the chamber of the sick man, who smiled pleasantly as she told the story of the incident. Secretary Hunt looked sad and gloomy as he strode silently around the library. Secretary Windom was not inclined to talk, and Attorney-General MacVeagh wore a face of mingled sternness and sorrow as he glided in and out of the Cabinet chamber. Sir Edward Thornton, the British Minister, was early at the White House, with a message from Sir H. Ponsonby stating that the Queen desired to have the latest news of the President's condition sent by cable. Commissioner Raum, the Hon. Marshall Jewell, Prince de Camporeale, the Italian Chargé d'Affaires, and Señor Don Francisco Barca, Envoy Extraordinary and Minister Plenipotentiary of Spain, with cable messages of sympathy and condolence, also called in the early morning hours and at different times throughout the day. Nobody, however, was allowed to penetrate beyond the library, and the greater number of the

callers were not permitted to approach nearer to the President
than the room of his private secretary, Stanley Brown. The
physicians were imperative in their orders that none but the
ladies in attendance upon him should be allowed to enter the
presence of the wounded Chief Magistrate, and their orders were
faithfully obeyed to the letter. Senator John P. Jones, of Nevada, called later in the day and sent in his card, with a message
expressing the deepest regret for the assault, to the President.

MORE JOYFUL NEWS.

At 11 o'clock the second official bulletin appeared, with the
signature of Dr. Bliss attached. The good news of the preceding
hour was confirmed and increased. "The President's condition,"
it read, "is greatly improved. He secures sufficient refreshing
sleep, and during his waking hours is cheerful and inclined to
discuss pleasant topics. His pulse stands at 106, with more
fulness and a soft expression. His temperature and respiration
are now normal." This announcement was hailed with joy by
the waiting crowd in front of the Executive Mansion and throughout the city. Soon after it was made Dr. Bliss was standing by
the bedside of the President. Gen. Garfield extended his hand
and pressed that of the doctor, and a smile lighted up his pale
face. The grasp of his hand was almost as firm and steady as
it had been when in the enjoyment of perfect health. "Doctor,"
he said, "you have changed my programme a little. I had prepared to meet death philosophically, but you have changed all
that." The confidence in his own power of resistance, which is
better than all the medicine to a sinking man, had taken possession of the President. "I believe he has made up his mind
that he won't die, and that he will fight it off," said one of the
attendants in describing this scene. An hour later the confidence of both Dr. Bliss and the President in his ultimate recovery was demonstrated by an order given to Private Secretary
Brown to inform Drs. Smith, Townshend, of the Health Office;
C. M. Ford, P. S. Wales, Surgeon-General of the Navy; C. B.
Purvis, C. C. Patterson, Basil Norris, N. S. Lincoln, and J. B.
Hamilton, Surgeon-General of the Marine Hospital Service, who
have been attending on the President with Dr. Bliss, that the
symptoms of recovery were so favorable that, for the present at
least, their further attendance would not be necessary, and
thanking them for their valuable services. The case was thus

left entirely in the hands of Dr. Bliss, who was the first physician called in after the shooting.

The President, however, was by no means easy on his bed of sickness. The twitching pains in the feet and limbs attacked him at intervals, and he suffered terribly while they lasted. At 1 o'clock he called for the New York papers, and Mrs. Garfield read the editorial columns to him. He then fell into a gentle sleep, from which he awoke, however, in about half an hour, with the pains attacking him again. At 2 o'clock a fresh bulletin was issued for the information of the public. It said: "The President has slept a good deal since the last bulletin, though occasionally suffering from pain in both feet and ankles. His pulse is now 104, respiration 18, and temperature nearly normal. While the President is by no means out of danger, yet his symptoms continue favorable." It was evident from this bulletin that Dr. Bliss still feared a relapse, and the hopeful feelings which had been created by the announcements since 10 o'clock were slightly dampened. At about this time a despatch was received from Mrs. Garfield, the mother of the President, who is at Mentor, asking if she might come to see her son. A reassuring answer was sent to her, and she was advised not to come, for the present at least.

SOME UNFAVORABLE SYMPTOMS.

The President rested well until about 3 o'clock, when Mrs. James left the White House for the Arlington, Mrs. Hunt deciding to remain all night. She took a little rest, however, in the library, and turns at watching the President were taken by Mrs. Blaine, Mrs. Windom, Mrs. Lincoln, and Mrs. MacVeagh. At a little after 3 o'clock the President awoke, and seeing Dr. Bliss standing by his bed asked him what the chance for his recovery was. "The symptoms are very critical," was the answer. "Do you think I shall get well?" asked the President, pressing for a direct answer. "There is a possibility of your recovery," said the doctor, declining to commit himself to the direct answer which the President evidently sought. "Then, doctor," said the sick man, grasping his arm with a firm hand, "we'll accept the possibility, and I'll help you all I can." After this little episode the President again dropped into a sleep, but it was not a continuous one, being composed of short naps from which he was constantly awakening. About 5 o'clock this morning, when the sun was well up in the heavens, he awoke from one of these short naps, and, in answer to a question by Dr. Bliss, said, "I feel much better every way, except that I still have that terrible pain in my feet." Throughout the night, whenever he was attacked by these pains, his sufferings were excruciating, but he bore them all bravely and made no complaints. His one thought seemed to be that his wife and children must not be made to suffer more than was absolutely necessary from the crime which had attacked his life.

While these mournful scenes which are to form a part of the nation's history were being enacted in the President's chamber at the south-west corner of the Executive Mansion, the rooms of his private secretary in the eastern wing were crowded by scores of men who were waiting anxiously for bulletins from the sick-room. A great number of cards of admission had been issued, and many not having cards managed to pass through the gate to the grounds and gain an entrance to the White House. The throng in the secretary's rooms annoyed the doctors, but everybody wanted to stay all night in order to get the latest news of the President's condition. The people who had gained admittance showed no signs of retiring, and finally, at 11 o'clock, Secretary Brown gave the order to put out the lights, and by this action succeeded in clearing the rooms.

At 10 o'clock to-night the condition of the President was reported by the physicians to be less favorable. The pulse had risen to 120, temperature to 100°, and respiration to 20. He was also more restless at that hour, and again complained of pain in his feet. The physicians, however, say that this changed condition of their patient does not necessarily imply that the chances of recovery are decreased. The increased pulse and temperature are partially accounted for by the fact that a few minutes before the 10 o'clock bulletin was issued the President's clothing was changed, which would have the effect to produce some restlessness, and thus increase the pulse and temperature. Besides, the time has about arrived when inflammation may be naturally expected. Thus far there has been less than the usual amount of inflammation considering the character of the wound; but the physicians say inflammation is an inevitable consequence, and that during its continuance the patient will exhibit less favorable conditions. "The President," said one of the physicians, "is approaching the critical period.

We look for him to get worse before he can get better. The result will depend upon the violence of the inflammation." Dr. Bliss gives out that he still has hopes of recovery, but it is understood that all that occurs in the treatment of the wounded man is not made public. It is known that the President at times experiences what he has termed "tiger's claws" in his feet and legs, and that to allay these acute pains hypodermic injections are resorted to.

After 7 o'clock to-night the order for admission to the White House was changed, and no one was permitted to ascend to the second story except members of the Cabinet and their families and foreign Ministers. Representatives of the press and others who held cards of admission to the house were stopped in the vestibule, where the bulletins from the President's chamber were brought and read. This new order was made necessary in order that the sufferer might not be disturbed by the slightest noise. An order was also issued to-day by the physicians that no one be permitted to enter the President's room except members of his family and those necessary for proper attendance, and the President was forbidden to hold any long conversation with any one.

ONLY SLIGHT GROUND FOR HOPE.

The Latest Symptoms Regarded as Very Unfavorable—No Bulletin till Morning.

WASHINGTON, July 4, 2 A.M.—At 12.40 o'clock Surgeon-General Barnes left the White House. In reply to a question as to the President's condition, he said there had been no change for some hours, and that he had had some fever during the evening. At 12.45 Secretary and Mrs. Windom, Secretary and Mrs. Hunt, Attorney-General and Mrs. MacVeagh, and Secretary Blaine and Mr. Walker Blaine left the White House. Mrs. James and Mrs. Blaine remained with Mrs. Garfield. A *Tribune* correspondent met Secretaries Lincoln and Kirkwood and Post-master-General James at 1.30 A.M. as they were leaving the White House to snatch a few hours sleep. Mr. Lincoln said, "I have just talked with Dr. Woodward. He says the President's condition is critical, but there are still slight grounds for hope. The distention of the bowels is only slight, but it is, of course, a very unfavorable symptom. Our going home has no significance. The house is crowded, and if we remained we must have sat up. It is not expected by the physicians that any material change will take place before 7 o'clock. Certainly there is no probability of a fatal result during the next six hours."

The following postscript was attached to the bulletin issued at 12.30 A.M. : " In view of the fact that it is deemed best to keep the President perfectly quiet during the night no further examinations will be made and no other bulletins issued till 7.30 this morning."

1 A.M.—The President at this hour is sleeping quietly, and the hopes of the physicians in attendance are still good. All the members of the Cabinet left the Executive Mansion before midnight, and at that hour the doors of the White House were closed, and nobody has been allowed to enter since. Dr. Gunnell, a surgeon of the Navy, is watching the President. Drs. Bliss and Reyburn are sleeping in the surgeon's room, which adjoins the chamber of the President. Drs. Barnes and Woodward have gone home to get needed rest. If any unfavorable symptoms appear, Drs. Bliss and Reyburn will be called. Mrs. Blaine sits by the bedside of the President, and will remain there all night. Mrs. Garfield is sleeping in the room at the north-western corner of the Executive Mansion, and nobody is allowed on the portico for fear of disturbing her rest. The President has been out of his mind only once since the shooting. This afternoon, when nobody but his nurses and the doctors were in the room, he suddenly exclaimed : " Why don't you take all those people out of the way ?" He recovered himself almost instantly, however, and since then he has been himself. Dr. Bliss says that there is not the least danger of his dying to-night, and upon this assurance the crowd which had lingered around the White House all day dispersed. The condition of General Garfield is, however, very critical, and in all probability the next 24 hours will decide his fate.

July 4, 10 A.M.—Dr. D. Hayes Agnew, of Philadelphia, arrived here at 4 o'clock, and Dr. Frank H. Hamilton, of New York, at 6 o'clock this morning, in answer to the telegrams of yesterday summoning them to a consultation. At 7 o'clock they held a consultation, after examining the wounds of the

President, with Drs. D. W. Bliss, J. J. Woodward, Robert Rey-burn, and Surgeon-General Barnes, who are now attending General Garfield. The consultation lasted for an hour and a quarter, and at 9.40 its result was conveyed to the anxious public in a bulletin stating that the management and course of treatment of the attending physicians were approved in every particular by the consulting physicians. Drs. Agnew and Hamilton, while they admit that the wound is of a dangerous nature, continue to give encouraging hopes of the ultimate recovery of the President. At this hour, 10 A.M., the patient is resting easily and everybody in the White House is hopeful. The city is perfectly quiet and the day appears more like Sunday than the Fourth of July. Flags are hoisted over the Executive Mansion and public buildings, but beyond this the national significance of the day is ignored in the great anxiety for the life of the President.

11 A.M.—The surgeons have succeeded in alleviating the pain in the President's feet and ankles, and he now rests somewhat easier. The tympanitis which began to develop last night has been kept under control up to this time, and the physicians feel very confident that they can prevent its increase. Dr. Agnew has left for Philadelphia, and Dr. Hamilton will return to New York this afternoon. Mrs. Garfield is the only person, except the physicians and nurses, who is allowed to see the President. A great crowd is in front of the gates to the White House, and the streets are full of people, but everything is quiet. The day is very warm.

12.30 P.M.—There has been but little change in the President's condition since the last bulletin. He complains much less of the pain in his feet. Slight vomiting occasionally. Pulse, 110 ; temperature, 100° ; respiration, 24.

D. W. BLISS,   J. J. WOODWARD,
J. K. BARNES,   ROBERT REYBURN.

2 P.M.—Dr. Hayes Agnew, the eminent Philadelphia surgeon, who, with Dr. Hamilton, of New York, was summoned to Washington last night to consult with the President's attending physicians, said this morning before returning to Philadelphia that there were many marvellously favorable symptoms about

the President's case. He was quite certain that the abdomen has not been injured, and that the kidneys are not disturbed. He believes that the liver has been lacerated by the ball, but to what extent this organ has been injured cannot, of course, be determined until an examination of the course taken by the ball has been made. The tearing pains in the limbs are caused, Dr. Agnew said, by the laceration of the liver and the severing of certain nerves thrown out from the spinal column. Dr. Hamilton also takes a hopeful view of the President's symptoms. At noon Dr. Bliss said that the inflammation, when the last examination was made, was natural to the wound, and was really less, all things considered, than was expected. There is, he said, a liability to abscess and pus, but he has no apprehension from such formations, and says they can be readily treated. Dr. Bliss is quite hopeful for the President's recovery, but said no positive opinion could yet be formed as to what the result might be. Much would depend, he thought, upon the development of the current 24 hours.

2.25 P.M.—The President awaked from sleep a few moments ago and said to Dr. Bliss, who stood by his bed-side : "Doctor, I feel better than I have at any time since I was wounded."

2.45 P.M.—The attending physicians continue to express a hopeful opinion of the President's case. Peritonitis has not supervened as yet, and there are no more indications of it than there were this morning. The condition of the patient, therefore, although critical, is no worse than was to be expected.

4.30 P.M.—Dr. Woodward, in conversation with Secretary Hunt about fifteen minutes ago, said that there was no perceptible change in the President, and that the symptoms continued very favorable.

5.15 P.M.—The President partook of a quantity of chicken-broth a short time ago, and has retained it. He is resting about the same as when his condition was last reported.

6.30 P.M.—Colonel Rockwell has just sent a despatch saying: "The President is now resting. His symptoms at this hour are not considered so favorable as at the date of the last bulletin."

7.35 P.M.—The President this evening is not so comfortable. He does not suffer so much from pain in the feet. The tympanitis is again more noticeable. Pulse, 126; temperature, 101.9°; respiration, 24. Another bulletin will be issued at 10 P.M., after which, in order not to disturb the President unnecessarily, no further bulletins will be issued until to-morrow morning.

D. W. BLISS,   J. J. WOODWARD,

J. K. BARNES,   ROBERT REYBURN.

10 P.M.—There has been slight amelioration of symptoms during the past two hours. No vomiting during that period. Pulse, 124; temperature, 101°; respiration, 24. In order not to disturb the President unnecessarily no further bulletins will be issued until to-morrow morning.

D. W. BLISS,   J. J. WOODWARD,

J. K. BARNES,   ROBERT REYBURN.

11.30 P.M.—General Hazen, who has just come from the White House, reports that everything was very encouraging there; that the indications all were that the President would pass a quiet night, and that there was very much more cheerfulness in the Executive Mansion. General Hazen firmly believes the President will pull through.

MIDNIGHT.—The condition of the President has further improved since the date of the last official bulletin. His temperature and pulse have again fallen slightly, and he is at this hour sleeping quietly.

THE GLOOM AT THE CAPITAL.

A very quiet Fourth—Deep Anxiety manifested on every Hand— Admiration for the President's heroic Conduct—A suppressed Feeling of Anger against Guiteau.

WASHINGTON, July 4.—The Chief of Police of this city issued an order on Sunday evening, as the *Times* has already been informed, to prevent the setting off of fire-crackers and other explosives. It is only just, as it is creditable, to the people here to say that the order was altogether unnecessary, because of a peculiar sentiment everywhere observable. The city to-day has been unnaturally quiet. The pall of silence followed the startling act of the would-be assassin, and men have unconsciously fallen into the habit of suppressing sounds which would otherwise have been given free vent. No steam or other whistles have been heard in the city. Bells have ceased to toll; men walk about as though shod in soft slippers, and talk with bated breath. A correspondent of the *Times* has walked and ridden about this city for miles to-day and has not heard the sound of a fire-cracker or a torpedo. To fire a pistol would be almost as much as a man's life was worth. For very silence this day will be a memorable one in the history of the capital of the nation among the anniversaries of Independence Day. This homage of silence has been born of a sentiment, and there is no hypocrisy in its observance. An incident or two may perhaps serve to illustrate this. The *Times* correspondent was at Police Headquarters to-day, making inquiries as to Guiteau's condition. A policeman strode along and eagerly inquired about the latest bulletin. It happened to be unfavorable in some particulars. He heaved a deep sigh and a shadow fell over his rough and weather-beaten countenance. He fairly trembled, as men do who hang about the sick-room of a loved one and quiver as they ask the doctor, fresh from the bed-side, of the chances of recovery. Something about the correspondent's manner may perhaps have prompted an explanation of the evidences of emotion displayed by the officer, who said, in tones as though it had been wrung from him, " Why, I pray daily for the President's recovery. His name is in my devotions;" and tears stood in the eyes of the manly fellow as he said so.

A colored man stood waiting at the main entrance, just outside the grounds attached to the Executive Mansion. I could not help noticing him this morning as I passed in through the iron gates and by the sentries who guarded the opening. He was emphatically what they call here " a poor nigger." He was hatless, shoeless, shirtless. The few worn garments which invested his spare frame wanted only an apology for going to pieces. His frizzed hair and thin gray beard were dishevelled, but they seemed to gain a glory from the tints of the bright warm sunshine, whose heat was almost overpowering. Like an ancient servitor stood the old man close to the sentries and peered through the iron gates, whose portals he could not pass.

When any one came out of the grounds he would approach and eagerly listen for tidings. He kept his vigil well. When I told him that the doctors had great hopes of saving the President, he said, simply but with fervor, " Thank God for that." And so it is everywhere about the city. Men are tearful, prayerful, and quiet. High and low share in the feelings of sympathy and devotion. The Cabinet officers and their wives, men of mark who have won renown in battle, debate, or in the marts of trade, all have the sense of personal bereavement. It stirs one to see old army veterans, some of them battle-scarred, to whom wounds were mere child's play in war-time, actually cry outright at the present sad calamity.

HEROISM OF THE PRESIDENT AND HIS WIFE.

Devotional feelings have been called out to a surprising extent by the event. Attention has been already called to this. The prayer-meetings in the churches, including the Jewish synagogues, are evidences of it. But besides such public tokens, there are prayers at many family altars, and the President's is joined among the names of loved ones in the invocation at the hearth. There is also a manifestation of feeling of a different kind, which is noteworthy. Men speak constantly of the President's manliness, his gentleness, and courtesy. They are recalling and repeating incidents showing his kindness of heart and singleness of purpose. His chivalrous devotion to his wife and mother are remembered. The heroism he has shown under the present circumstances is descanted on, and coupled with it is the fact of the utter abnegation of self he has displayed. When first wounded his thought was of his loved wife and little ones, and how to spare them pain. His mother's anxiety was also uppermost in his mind, and by his direction care has been taken to send the old lady messages of cheer and hope. When those good, kind-hearted women, like Mrs. James, Mrs. Hunt, and others, sat up during the long watches of Saturday night, when all was gloom and not one bright ray of hope appeared, and when he was told he had only a single chance of life, he repeated that he was not afraid to die. During this time there was on his part the most tender consideration for others. He moved his arm while in a paroxysm of pain, and just touched a little rudely one of his kind-hearted watchers. Instantly he lost all

5

feeling for himself, and his lips parted with a heartfelt apology for having been guilty of brusqueness towards the lady, who had not even given the circumstance a thought, and would not have done so had it not been for the innate manliness of the one who lay on his bed of pain. His demeanor towards his noble-hearted wife has been chivalrous in its best sense. He has ever sought her ease and welfare, and to keep her from anxiety and suspense. When she first entered his room he met her with a smiling face, and he has had a smile and a word of cheer for her ever since, even though his sufferings have been at times very great. With true wifely devotion, too, has Mrs. Garfield borne herself, and her cheerful, hopeful demeanor has done much to free from care her husband's mind. He feared for her. She had just risen from a bed of sickness, and he was afraid that she would have a relapse. She, poor woman, knowing his fear, steeled herself by a mighty effort. To no one has she made a complaint; to no one has her husband said a word of aught except kindness. They have been a model husband and wife under circumstances most trying to their natures. Each has brought solace to the other, and the wife has ministered at the bedside of her liege, with an intelligence none the less powerful and efficient than the love she has shown. All these things leak out. It would be surprising, indeed, if they did not. The few persons who have been admitted to the chamber of pain— the doctors, the watchers, and the nearest of kin—bear unconscious testimony to the conduct of the first gentleman and first lady of the land. Words are let drop, kind expressions are repeated, and bit by bit comes out the heart history of the loving pair. Such stories spread. All are only too willing to help embalm in the memory of friends the ministry of love and gentleness, of kindness, and of devotion which the national Executive Mansion discloses. People have taken the stories to heart, and they are fashioning inwardly portraits of the President which would do no injustice to the kindest and best of men the earth ever saw. There is a hero worship here that is carried out to a surprising extent; but the people know and feel there is a good basis for much of what they believe, and the glamour of devotion adds bright and attractive colors to the picture and gives it a setting of love.

THE DASTARDLY ASSASSIN.

It is because of these things that men here speak as they do and act as has been shown. Their thoughts are all engrossed with the occupant of the White House, and they can scarcely spare a thought for the wretched miscreant who lies confined in the District jail and jabbers unto his jailors the delight he feels. Interviews have been published with Guiteau, but they are all untrue. He has been permitted to see no one, and he is strongly guarded lest an organized attempt should be made to rescue the prisoner and bring him before Judge Lynch. At present the precaution seems useless. Of course it would not be safe for the fellow to travel the streets of this city. He has too many personal enemies, men whom he has defrauded by petty swindles, and who would like nothing better than the chance of getting even with him. If a stray bullet should by chance happen to hit and kill the fellow there would be little sympathy, and few would care whether the murdered man had been in a condition in which he was not responsible for his acts. Fine-drawn distinctions about mental responsibility might come in the subsequent proceeding and be raised, but they would inure to the benefit of the assailant. But the first thoughts of lynching Guiteau are apparently stilled. It would not do to say that they are eradicated. There is now a condition of suspense. People have now neither the time nor the inclination to do more than watch the pulse of the President and listen to the utterances of his physicians. Will he recover, is their uppermost thought, and next in their minds is a recollection of his kindly qualities. When Mark Antony made his oration over Cæsar's corpse, he first told the Roman mob of the gentleness, kindness, and patriotism of the murdered man. The mob did the work of revenge afterwards. Some such thing might happen here. With suspense ended by the President's death, the people, whose minds have been filled with admiration for his services and his splendid bearing, might take it into their heads to lynch the murderer. No eagerness, except by newspaper men, is shown to see the prisoner. It is, perhaps, as well for him that the people have not shown an overmastering curiosity to see him. The thread of their conversation might be of hemp.

HISTORY OF THE ASSASSIN.

CHARLES JULIUS GUITEAU was born in Freeport, Ill., September 8, 1841. His height is about five feet five inches. He has a sandy complexion and is slight, weighing not more than 125 pounds. He wears a moustache and slight chin whiskers, slightly tinged with gray. His sunken cheeks and widely separated eyes give him a sullen, morose appearance. His father was L. W. Guiteau, who for many years before his death, which took place one year ago, was cashier of the Second National Bank of Freeport. Charles received an ordinary education in the schools of his native town. He was then sent to Ann Arbor, Mich., where his father lived in 1835, and where the son was to prepare to enter the University of Michigan. The eccentric young student ruthlessly discarded his father's plans for making him a useful man, and abandoned his studies. He conceived the idea of joining the Oneida Community and did so. He remained with these peculiar people for four or five years, when he became dissatisfied at the lack, rather than at the excess of, licence in social affairs under the rules of the Community. He was unable to go to the extremes his depraved nature desired to, and he accordingly severed his connection with the society. He became its bitter opponent, and threatened to write a book exposing the affairs of the community. He was checkmated in this by the head of the Oneida Society, who in turn exposed Guiteau's connection with the society in the society paper. This took place about 1869. Guiteau then went to Chicago and began studying law in his brother's office.

Soon after his arrival he became intimate with a young lady employed as librarian in the Young Men's Christian Association Rooms, and married her. It was not a happy union, and two or three years after he deserted her. From the religious people of Chicago he received much sympathy on account of his antagonism to the Oneida Community; but it was evident to those

CHARLES J. GUITEAU.

who knew him intimately that he was at best not rightly balanced, if not thoroughly vicious. He was admitted to the bar in Chicago, opened an office, and obtained a small practice in collecting bills, etc. He soon developed bad habits in failing to account for funds collected, and came to grief and disgrace to such an extent that he left Chicago. He next opened an office in New York, pursued the same methods, and finally landed in Ludlow Street Jail for improper appropriation of money. He was released through the efforts of his brother-in-law, George Scoville. He sued the New York *Herald* and *Times* repeatedly for libel. The New York and Chicago papers repeatedly posted him as a fraud, and he retorted by instituting libel suits for large amounts. None of these cases ever came to trial. This action is fully characteristic of the man, it being also a mania with him to gain notoriety in every conceivable way. He returned to Chicago about 1875 and attempted to resume the practice of law. He failed to get any business, because, as he said, of Heaven's desire to make known through him the truth about the second coming of Christ. He claimed that Christ's second coming was revealed to him as having actually transpired A.D. 70 at the destruction of Jerusalem.

The following is an extract from a letter dated March 30, 1873, from the father of the assassin to·John W. Guiteau, the brother in question, in which he writes referring to " his abominable and deceitful dealings" :

" I have been ready to believe him capable of almost any folly, stupidity, or rascality. The only possible excuse I can render for him is that he is insane. Indeed, if I was called as a witness upon the stand, I am inclined to think I should testify that he is absolutely insane and is hardly responsible for his acts. My own impression is that unless something shall stop him in his folly and mad career he will become hopelessly insane and a fit subject for the lunatic asylum. Before I finally gave him up I had exhausted all my powers of reason and persuasion, as well as other resources, in endeavoring to control his actions and thoughts, but without avail. I found he was deceitful and could not be depended upon in anything ; stubborn, wilful, conceited, and at all times outrageously wicked, apparently possessed with the devil. I saw him once or twice when it seemed to me he was willing to do almost any wicked thing. You will remember perhaps at the last conversation we had about him, I told you to keep clear of him and not have anything to do with him. Should anybody ask about him now, I should be compelled to say to them, I thought he was insane, or at least a monomaniac, and should there leave it and say no more about him. His insanity is of such a character that he is as likely to become a sly, cunning desperado as anything. Could I see him I might possibly make another and more vigorous effort to change the whole channel of his thoughts and feelings; if I could not do that I should have no hope whatever of being able to do him any good. I made up my mind long ago never to give him another dollar in money until I should be convinced he was thoroughly humbled and radically changed. I am sometimes afraid he would steal, rob, or do anything before his egotism and self-conceit shall be knocked out of him, and perhaps, even all that will not do it. So, you see, I regard his case as hopeless, or nearly so, and, of course, know no other way but to dismiss him entirely from my mind. I leave him entirely in the hands of his Maker, with a very faint hope that he can be changed either in this world or the next."

It was evident that although he thought he had some new truths to reveal, he was more or less crazy. He delivered a dictatorial aggressive lecture, full of assertion, but bare of argument, and entirely lacking in oratorical merit. His effort was, of course, a complete failure. He left town without paying the bills for printing and hall rent, and made a tour of some of the New England towns. Local papers posted him as a crazy fraud and dead "beat." In 1879 he republished an edition of a thousand volumes of his "Life of Christ," under D. Lockwood & Co.'s imprint, which he obtained the right to do surreptitiously. It was printed by Wright & Potter, who were never paid for their work. Failing to obtain any sales of his book, he advertised himself as an attorney-at-law, with an office in the Congregational House, and attempted to get collections. He had no license to practise in Massachusetts, and soon after left for parts unknown. Before his departure he had one or two stormy interviews with his brother, John W. Guiteau. A number of persons, boarding-house keepers and others, whom Charles had swindled, had inquired of John W. Guiteau about the fellow, and he had told them that his brother was irresponsible. Charles was highly indignant at this action of his brother, and upbraided him for it, even to the extent of showing personal violence, so that on one or two occasions Mr. Guiteau was compelled to forcibly eject him from his office. John W. Guiteau describes his brother as possessed of very peculiar moral qualities. He does not believe he would intentionally lie, but he will contract debts without limit which he knows he will be unable to pay. For instance, he once borrowed $200 from Mr. Scoville, giving his promissory note for the amount, and when urged to pay the obligation exclaimed: "Why he knows I paid him; he can go to any bank and get the money on my note."

After leaving Boston in 1879 he was next heard of as being among the victims of the Narragansett disaster. He turned up, however, with a graphic description of his experiences on board that unfortunate vessel, given in one of the New York papers. He has since roamed about the country from Maine to California, living by his wits. His father was compelled years before he died, on account of his irregularities and dishonesty, to discard him.

Describing his brother's personal and mental characteristics, Mr. Guiteau said that Charles was the personification of egotism and obstinacy. He was lazy beyond degree. When remonstrated with by his brother for some dishonest proceeding, he exclaimed petulantly: "You talk to me just like father; you assume that I am all wrong." He is a great reader of daily literature, and Mr. Guiteau thinks it quite probable that after the assassination of the Czar he put himself in communication with European Nihilists, and has tried to organize a society in this country. He was a man of incomparable "cheek" and claimed to be the personal friend of many prominent officials. He has always been a Republican in politics, but has not been a monomaniac on the subject as on religion, until probably the beginning of the New York quarrel. Personally he is a perfect coward, and has often refused to go into a dark part of the house at night, without first arming himself with a revolver.

STORY OF ONE WHO HAS KNOWN HIM FROM THE CRADLE TO THE CRIME.

Colonel Burnside, the disbursing officer at the Post-Office Department, Washington, says he knew Guiteau when he was a baby in his mother's arms. His father, J. W. Guiteau, was an old resident and respected citizen of Freeport, Ill., where he held many offices of trust. Some years ago he became deranged on the subject of " Perfection," and lectured extensively through the North and West on that subject. He married a very beautiful woman, with whom and the younger children he joined the Oneida Community. He afterwards returned to Freeport, where from 1864 up to last September, the time of his death, he served as cashier of the Second National Bank. There were three children. An older brother, Wilkes Guiteau, for a long time practised law at Davenport, Iowa, but is now practising his profession in Boston, Mass., where also he is at the head of large insurance interests. A younger sister, Flora, was a very promising girl, having a decided talent for music. Charles Julius Guiteau, who to-day is in jail for the murder of the President, was an odd boy. He appears to have been the only one of the children tainted with his father's eccentricities. When the family left the Oneida Community, Charles, then fifteen or sixteen years old, was left behind. He afterwards went to Chicago, where he studied law, being cared for and supplied with money by his father. After completing his studies Guiteau went to Europe, where he travelled several years, imbibing socialistic and other eccentric doctrines. A few years ago he returned to this country and lectured on the second advent of Christ. He published a pamphlet on the subject, in which the egotism of the man was plainly shown. He spoke of himself as a messenger of God to announce his coming. His lecture here in Lincoln Hall on this subject was a failure. Julius—we used to call him Julius, but I see he has dropped that part of his name—is now about forty or forty-two years old. From what I knew of the boy, his education in the Oneida Community, and his utterances on religion, I was not at all surprised at his committing the act this morning. I understand from people employed at the White House that Guiteau had forced himself upon the President before. He was an applicant for the consulship at Marseilles, and a few days ago obtained access to the President, and acted so rudely that the President had him removed. I have no doubt that, feeling offended by this act, he determined on the course which culminated in the terrible tragedy of this morning. Guiteau was hanging around the Republican headquarters, No. 241 Fifth Avenue, New York, during the campaign last fall. He made a few speeches, but his efforts did not seem to be appreciated by the committee. He was poor and seedy looking, and borrowed some money from Mr. Jewell after the election, and a few days before the committee broke up he asked Governor Jewell for a recommendation for a consulate. He specially urged that if he could secure a consulate a certain rich lady would marry him. It is not known whether the Governor recommended him or not, but one thing is certain—he was looked upon as a person who was not exactly right in the upper story.

PREPARING FOR THE DEED.

John J. Rae, one of the clerks at the Riggs House, made the following statement: "This man Guiteau came here Thursday night, registered, and was assigned to room No. 222, which, by a strange coincidence, was the very number of the Pullman palace car that was to take the Presidental party to-day from Washington. Ever since the Inauguration he has had his letters addressed here and called regularly for them. I noticed that most of his letters were postmarked Chicago. It was his custom to present his card and inquire for his mail. He seemed very polite, but there was something about him that appeared strange. He often seated himself in the waiting-room, but rarely engaged in conversation with any one. He was out much of the time, and I have not seen him since he registered. I understand, however, that he came here this morning, got a satchel which he had checked, took something out of it, and returned the same. It must have been about a half an hour before he committed the deed, and he must have gone directly from the house to the depot."

A boarder at Mrs. Grant's said that Guiteau had been a boarder there for the past six weeks; he was prompt at meals, but when he came in too early he walked up and down the halls and parlors in a cat-like manner. The boarders never took to him on account of his odd actions, and we all thought there was something wrong about him. He left the house day before yesterday, owing six weeks' board. A Mr. Barstow overheard a conversation in the Baltimore and Potomac Railroad ticket-office, last evening, which clearly showed the action contemplated by Guiteau. He says that Guiteau came into the office, and inquired in relation to the train that the President proposed taking to-day. He was told that it left at half-past nine A.M. Thereupon he started out hurriedly, remarking as he neared the door,

5*

" I'll give him a Russian bomb."   Mr. Barstow said he was surprised at this remark, and said to a gentleman, who stood near him, that such an assertion from an insane man was intolerable, let alone from one who appeared to be sound in mind; that he thought such an assertion would justify his going to the Attorney-General and laying the matter before him.

HIS FIRST MONTHS AT THE CAPITAL.

In March Guiteau went to the well-known boarding-house of Mrs. Lockwood (formerly Mrs. Rines), No. 810 Twelfth Street, and tried to secure board.   Mrs. Lockwood did not like his appearance, and gave him an out-of-the-way room in the house in the hope of getting rid of him.   He pretended to know General Logan and others then boarding there.

PERSONAL PECULIARITIES.

He did not appear to get along very well with the boarders, who avoided him as much as possible.   " He appeared to have a cat-like tread," said one of the boarders, " and walked so easily that he was always up alongside persons before they knew it."   He was said to be rude at the table, too, so much so that a gentleman and his wife stopping there would not sit alongside of him.   Mrs. Lockwood states that he acted strangely at times, and about the middle of the month when she presented his bill he could not pay it.   He afterwards left the house and sent Mrs. Lockwood a note, stating that he was expecting a $6,000 position and would soon pay his bill.   Mrs. Lockwood showed this note to General Logan, who said the man was crazy.   Three weeks ago he met Mrs. Ricksford, of Mrs. Lockwood's boarding-house, on the street, and requested her not to say anything about the bill he owed, as it would injure him in his efforts to secure a position.   He expressed great pleasure at the fact that Mrs. Lockwood had treated him very kindly while he was at her house.   Mrs. Lockwood said that Guiteau was a great bother to General Logan, so persistent was he in his attempts to secure that gentleman's efforts in his behalf.   Since leaving Mrs. Lockwood's house he has been stopping at various places, but never for a great length of time, for the reason that he appeared to have no funds.   He told one of the boarders at Mrs. Lockwood's that he expected to be appointed Minister to France, but he did not desire it to be known. Up to the day before yesterday, when he registered at the Riggs House, Guiteau had been stopping for the last six weeks, with no baggage but a paper box, at No. 920 Fourteenth Street.

AT THE CHICAGO CONVENTION.

The librarian of the Navy Department appeared this afternoon before the Attorney-General. He says that Guiteau was one of Farwell's supporters in the effort to break the unit rule in the Chicago Convention, and says that Guiteau was in the habit of calling at the librarian's room and telling how he had been treated by Secretary Blaine.

GUITEAU IN GOTHAM.

According to the statement of some gentlemen who had personal dealings with Guiteau, he came to this city in 1871, shortly after the Chicago fire, and hiring an office carried on the practice of the law. According to statements made by him afterwards, he arrived in New York a perfect stranger and with only $10 in money. The first year, however, he made $1,500 from his professional work and the second year $2,500. He had cards issued on which was printed "Charles J. Guiteau, attorney and counsellor-at-law of the Supreme Court." Notwithstanding the above-mentioned sums of money which he claimed to have earned in the practice of the law he became known in many boarding-houses of this city as a swindler. In the fall of 1873 he was arraigned before Justice Sherman Smith in Jefferson Market Police Court on a charge of false pretence. The complainant was the proprietor of the St. Nicholas Hotel. Guiteau had been stopping at the hotel for some time, and avoided payment of his bill by tendering many plausible excuses. When the amount he owed had become quite large he disappeared suddenly. Detective Kealy, of the hotel, got upon his track and finally ran him down. The proprietor of the St. Nicholas was only one of a number of people who turned up in court against Guiteau as soon as the news of his arrest became known. Mrs. Simonson, who kept a large boarding-house at No. 31 East Twenty-second Street, testified before Justice Smith that Guiteau had been a guest in her house, and that in settlement of his board bill he had given her a check for $21 on the Leather Manufacturers' Bank. She believed the check to be genuine, but when it was presented for payment at the bank the cashier said that Guiteau not only did not have an account there but had never had one. The check was obtained by Mrs. Simonson only after she had become possessed of Guiteau's baggage, and held it as security for his indebtedness. He asked her to give him the baggage, which she refused to do unless he settled with her. He then presented her with the check, received his property, and disappeared. Other complainants against him were Stephen Thorne, of No. 19 West Twenty-fourth Street; John P. Worstell, of No. 208 Fifth Avenue; Mrs. Bishop, of No. 31 Madison Avenue, and Mrs. Stahl, of No. 26 East Twenty-third Street, who testified that they had been similarly victimized. Guiteau had boarded at different times with each of these parties, run up bills, and in some instances absconded at night with his baggage. When he was prevented from carrying out this plan he resorted to the passing of worthless checks, as in the case of Mrs. Simonson. Guiteau denounced the charges made against him as malicious and false. In explanation of the check he had given on the Leather Manufacturers' Bank, he said that he had kept an account with the institution for several months, and had placed in it as much as $1,000. He claimed that not one of the complainants had a lien on his baggage, as they were not boarding-house-keepers under the law, and he had a right to remove it. He acknowledged that he owed each of the persons named small balance for board: To Mr. Thorne, $20; to Mr. Worstell, $15; to Mrs. Bishop, $12; to Mrs. Stahl, $6, and $16 to Mrs. Simonson. Mrs. Simonson, he went on to say, kept a boarding-house near the Fifth Avenue Hotel, and he boarded with her two months. He paid her promptly every two weeks, but ran $21 in her debt toward the latter part of his stay there. He gave her the check for this amount. At that time he had an account with the Leather Manufacturers' Bank, but she withheld presentation of the check until it was three weeks overdue, when she returned it to him, saying it was worthless. He gave her $5, and promised to pay the remainder in a short time afterwards. Justice Smith, having heard the testimony on both sides, committed Guiteau to the Tombs Prison in default of $1,000 bail. Guiteau described his feelings at this time in the following words: "I had no money and no relatives in the city, and I languished in prison for over five long and dreary weeks, hourly and daily expecting and hoping and praying for my release, as I knew my detention was wholly illegal. Finally it came, thank God! I was free again. Free to breathe the sweet air of heaven; free to go and come; free to do my own will; free to eat, drink, and sleep like decent people, and to associate with them. No one never imprisoned can realize the horrors of confinement. It is a lingering death. 'A man who can't buy bread is no man at all,' people have thought when I asked them to aid me, and they were right."

SUED FOR MISAPPROPRIATION.

On the 21st of April, 1874, Guiteau was defendant in an application in the Supreme Court, Chambers, for an attachment to compel him to pay certain moneys collected by him for the Reis Brothers, wholesale grocers, of Cincinnati. The application was made to Judge Donohue by Reis Brothers' counsel, General Sandford, who stated that the firm had placed in Guiteau's hands a note for collection, and that Guiteau had collected $175. They wrote for the money. Guiteau's answer was, "All respectable lawyers retain a half for collections. I have collected my half, and therefore nothing is due to you!" Reis Brothers were owed $275 by a Chicago firm who failed in 1870. Guiteau, then in Chicago, wrote to Reis Brothers asking if they would accept fifteen cents on the dollar. Reis Brothers, supposing he was acting on behalf of the firm that had failed, replied that they would accept not less than fifty cents on the dollar. The next they heard of this matter was that the bankrupt firm had settled with Guiteau for $175. Guiteau's claim was that the $175 was his for the trouble he had taken in settling the matter, that this bankrupt firm had promised to settle the amount in full, and that when they did so Reis Brothers would receive their share, which he figured at $82. The application was denied by Judge Donohue. At that time Guiteau had his office at No. 170 Broadway. Afterwards his office was at No. 51 Chambers Street and No. 57 Liberty Street. He next turned up at No. 144 Dearborn Street, Chicago.

HIS ADVENTURES IN NEW YORK.

ALBANY, July 2, 1881.

During the campaign last fall he turned up at various places in this State.

Thurlow Weed Barnes, of the Albany *Evening Journal*, a grandson of Thurlow Weed, says that Guiteau called upon him last October, and asked for a chance to speak on the stump for the Republican national ticket. Guiteau said he had been employed by the Republican State Committee to do work at their rooms in New York and that he was on his way there. Mr. Barnes questioned him closely at the time, and, not liking his looks, told E. M. Johnson, secretary of the State Committee, that he believed Guiteau to be a fraud. Mr. Johnson made a memorandum, and said he would look into the case. Mr. Barnes was chairman of the County Committee. Guiteau said he came from Chicago. He was in Poughkeepsie in July last, and advertised a lecture on the political situation on the evening of July 2, one year ago to-day. An admission fee was to be charged, and as people would not pay to go to a political meeting the lecture was not delivered. He afterwards wanted to be engaged as a speaker by the Republican Committee, but leading Republicans then thought his mind was unsound and they would have nothing to do with him. He afterwards was announced to speak at other places in the State.

A SARATOGA REMINISCENCE.

A special despatch to the *Herald* from Saratoga Springs says: Guiteau came to Saratoga Springs in July, 1880, and stopped at C. R. Brown's boarding-house. When his week was up he failed to pay and left for the Columbia Hotel, registering there on Saturday evening, July 3. He had announced himself to deliver a political lecture, entitled "Hancock *vs.* Garfield," at the Town Hall, on the previous Thursday evening, charging an admission fee. Nobody attended, as there were too many political harangues to be heard without price at that time. His announcement was a curious piece of bombastic nonsense, in which he styled himself "The celebrated orator of the West." He made another attempt on Saturday evening,

July 10, but even the doorkeeper failed to put in an appearance. He left Saratoga on the following morning, again leaving his bill unpaid, but stating in a note that he would remit from New York, which he never did. He was not particularly loud, and betrayed no evidences of insanity in his general conduct. On August 6, following, he delivered in New York city the speech to be found subjoined :

GUITEAU'S LAST CAMPAIGN SPEECH.

The appended speech was delivered by Guiteau in New York, August 6 last, and issued in pamphlet form by the Republican National Committee :

GARFIELD AGAINST HANCOCK.

A SPEECH BY CHARLES GUITEAU, OF CHICAGO, ILL., DELIVERED IN NEW YORK, AUGUST 6, 1880.

New York Address, Republican National Committee, 241 Fifth Avenue.

THE PAST REVIEWED.

In 1861 this nation was convulsed by one of the most gigantic wars on record. For generations America had been cursed by human slavery, and the conviction had been growing among all classes that no nation could always continue half free and half slave. In 1834 William Lloyd Garrison, backed by Wendell Phillips, the silver-tongued orator of Boston, assaulted American slavery as in league with the lower regions. They denounced it in season and out of season, by voice and pen. Little by little they were backed by Horace Greeley, the great, good Horace; Henry Ward Beecher; Harriet Beecher Stowe, with her "Uncle Tom's Cabin" (a matchless work of fiction); Charles Sumner, who was stricken down in the United States Senate by Bully Brooks, of South Carolina, and scores of like-minded compatriots. In 1856 the Republican party was organized. It was an offshoot of the old Whig party, founded by Henry Clay, he of matchless eloquence, and by Daniel Webster, the favorite and gifted son of New England and the great defender of our national Constitution. In 1856 Fremont, the standard-bearer of the young Republicans, was defeated for the Presidency by Buchanan, backed by the slave oligarchy. In 1861 the Republicans elected to the Presidency Abraham Lincoln—the immortal Lincoln. This was the signal for a grand onslaught by the slave oligarchy on the principles of liberty and progress. In 1861, after years of agitation for and against American slavery, the cannons were heard booming around Sumter, and our national existence was in peril. Jeff Davis and his cotraitors had seceded. They had stolen some of our forts and implements of war, and were trying to run a government on their own account. They had trampled under foot our national flag—that grand old ensign of our Republic. When the rebels assaulted Sumter it stirred the North to its depth. "To arms! To arms!" resounded all over this broad land. Thousands of brave boys went to battle—to victory or to death. They left their homes and loved ones—many never to return. Their mangled remains lie buried in many a grave. After years of war came peace. Our national flag again waved in triumph from every fort and battlement in the Republic, and slavery was no more. In 1861 there lived at Galena, in my own native State of Illinois, a quiet, modest man. He had graduated at West Point. He had seen service in California and Oregon. He had tasted poverty and distress in St. Louis and Galena. When President Lincoln called for 75,000 troops to suppress the incipient rebellion, Captain Grant determined to offer his services to the Government, and went to Springfield and interviewed Governor Yates. After some delay he was given a position, and finally was sent into the field as colonel. Little by little he arose till he became general of the national arms. From Galena through the war to the White House was but a step. From the White House around the globe, the recipient of the greatest ovations ever given to mortal man, was but another. Such prosperity would have crazed most men, but it did not Grant. The great, silent man's head is just as level to-day as when he sold cowhides in the streets of Galena. The military genius of Grant is not surpassed by that of Alexander, Julius Cæsar, or the great Napoleon. Originally a Grant man, I am well satisfied with Garfield's nomination. "Nothing but an act of God," said the great senator from New York, "can prevent Grant's nomination." General Garfield was born in poverty and obscurity, and has attained his present position under Providence by his own efforts. When the war came he was president of a small college in Ohio, and promptly offered his services to the govern ment in suppressing the rebellion. After nearly three years' service he was made a major-general. He was then elected to Congress and has held the position ever since. His long service on some of the most important committees shows that he is a square man and can be implicitly trusted. Some people say he got badly soiled in that Credit Mobilier transaction, but I guess he is clean-handed. Last winter he was elected to the United States Senate in place of Senator Thurman, and to-day he is the Republican nominee for the Presidency, with every prospect of success. He is a high-toned, conscientious, Christian gentleman. Some persons are down on General Arthur because he was removed from the New York Collectorship by President Hayes. General Arthur was appointed Collector by General Grant, and held that important office for several years, and gave unbounded satisfaction to the merchants of New York by his able and careful administration of his office, and he is supposed to have been removed without cause. General Arthur is a lawyer of marked ability, great culture, wide experience, and would be an ornament in the Vice-President's chair. When I was a boy Washburne represented the Galena and Freeport district in Congress. I was born in Freeport, Ill., and I have watched with marked pride the brilliant career of Grant and Washburne. Grant, Washburne, Garfield—these names go together. Grant, renowned in war and in peace; Washburne, distinguished for his civil service at home and abroad; Garfield, the scholar, soldier, and statesman. In October last, in old Faneuil Hall, in Boston, I heard Senator Chandler, who was the keenest Roman of us all, say that the rebel spirit then was the same that it was twenty years ago, just prior to the breaking out of the rebellion, and he was right. The Democrats now in majority in Congress would precipitate this action into another war had they power, and they would have the power save for President Hayes and his stalwart Cabinet. The Democratic majority now in Congress makes it imperative that the President and Cabinet be Republican, otherwise the national Government will be entirely controlled by ex-rebels and their Northern friends. The Democratic party are panting for the national Treasury. They have been starving since Buchanan retired, in 1861, and they are dreadfully hungry. They will make a

desperate effort to get in this time under the lead of that
gallant soldier General Hancock. Hancock's nomination was a
godsend to the Democratic party, and they will make the most
of it.   They are trying to run him as they did Horace Greeley
in 1872.   Poor Horace went down in that combination, and the
chances are that Hancock will do likewise.   This is the issue—
a solid North against a solid South.   The North conquered the
South on the field of battle, and now they must do it at the
polls in November, or they may have to fight another war.   Ye
men whose sons perished in the war what say you to the issue?
Shall we have another war?   Shall our national Treasury be
controlled by ex-rebels and their Northern allies, to the end
that millions of dollars of Southern war claims be liquidated?
If you want the Republic bankrupted, with the prospect of
another war, make Hancock President.   If you want prosperity
and peace, make Garfield President, and the Republic will
develop till it becomes the greatest and wealthiest nation on the
globe.

GUITEAU'S BOOK.

In 1879 the Chicago firm of Donelly, Gassette & Loyd published a small volume of religious essays and lectures by the
assassin of the President.   The title, which is headed " A Book
for Every One to Read," is "The Truth, a Companion to the
Bible.   By Charles J. Guiteau, lawyer, theologian, and lecturer."   The short preface is, " A new line of thought runs
through this book, and the author asks for it careful attention
to the end that many souls may find the Saviour."   Under five
different heads infidels are answered, St. Paul is eulogized, the
second coming of Christ is asserted to have occurred at the
destruction of Jerusalem, Christianity is reviewed, and Hades
described.   In the opening essay, "A Reply to Recent Attacks
on the Bible," the author, by quotation from the Bible and
learned divines, argues the existence of hell, defends the doctrine
of the immortality of the soul, and the Holy Book which he
insists is God's word.   In speaking of the atonement he con-
cludes : "' But,' says a noted infidel, and this is his great point,
' hell being such a terrible, awful place, and God being so very
good, He won't send any one there.'   We answer, God must
sustain his government.   Heaven is for the righteous.   Hell is
for the wicked.   Heaven would be a hell, if the wicked could

get into it. Hell is for the devil's seed; heaven is for Christ's seed." Further on he speaks of the infidel's end. "When the cold hand of death comes you will curse the day of your birth, you will flee to the mountains and say, Fall on me! fall on me! for I have crucified the Son of God. Henceforth there is nothing for me but eternal remorse. This remorse is the 'worm' that burns forever and ever." The reply to infidel statements is followed by a short essay on the life of "Paul, the Apostle." In opening this he says of Christ: "This wonderful creature had no where to lay his head. He had no money, He had no friends. He never travelled. He never wrote a book. He was hated, despised, and finally crucified as a vile impostor. Then back he went to the bosom of his Father." In opening his talk about Paul, he says: "When God wants anything done, he sends a man to do it." Further on we quote: "'The powers that be,' said Paul, in the midst of pagan Rome, 'are ordained of God!' A strange statement for an ambassador of Christ to make, and explained on the ground that Christ's kingdom is not of this world." At the end of this essay the writer makes the curious statement, "Yes, yes; thou Paul waited only two years for thy 'crown.' Thou wert executed A.D. 68, and thy Master came at the destruction of Jerusalem A.D. 70, and gavest thee thy 'crown.'"

CHRIST ALREADY COME.

The third portion of the book is devoted to a lecture embodying the author's peculiar views as to this alleged second coming of Christ. It is headed "Christ's Second Coming. At the Destruction of Jerusalem, A.D. 70. This lecture is a key to the Bible; study it and get some new and important ideas." The reason that the expectation of eighteen centuries as to the second coming of Christ has not been fulfilled is because "He came at the siege of Jerusalem, A.D. 70, 'in the clouds of heaven, with power and great glory,' and judged 'the quick and the dead,' the righteous and wicked of the primitive Church and Jewish nation. This is the proposition we propose to establish by a careful review of the New Testament." The great value of his "discovery" is, he claims, that no one can understand the Bible without it.

Many ingenious quotations and applications of Scripture are resorted to to prove his theory that all Christ's predictions relative to his second coming were fulfilled prior to the destruction of that city, and that immediately thereafter he " snatched the righteous part of the primitive Church and the righteous dead of past ages and hurried with them into glory." " This was the first resurrection and first judgment corresponding to the Jewish and Gentile dispensations. The Jews as a nation had their judgment at the destruction of Jerusalem, and the Gentiles will have theirs at the end of the world." He rejects Peter's idea about the burning up of the physical universe as simultaneous with Christ's second coming, stating that God allowed it to go into the Bible because " God wanted to curse the Antichrist part of the primitive Church on account of their unbelief concerning the coming of Christ then at hand." His doctrine, he contends, abolishes the communion which was to be celebrated " In remembrance of me till I come."

He tells us in the next lecture, which " reviews Christianity from the destruction of Jerusalem to the present time," that Josephus and other historians make no mention of Christ's appearing at the destruction of Jerusalem, because it happened " in the clouds of heaven," directly over that city, and besides that they were too busy recording what happened on earth. The " terrible record of Christianity during the dark ages" was because Christ had left behind the unrighteous part of the primitive Church. During the fifteen centuries to the time of Luther " the Almighty seems to have withdrawn all interest in human affairs." The Roman Catholic Church had its origin in " the apostates whom Christ left on earth," and Luther was used as the instrument of reformation. Since then Christianity has been cursed by the thousand subdivisions among Protestants.

The conclusion, which is devoted to " Hades," informs us that all who died before A.D. 70 went to Hades, and remained there until that time, when they were resurrected and judged, the " sheep" passing into heaven and the " goats" into hell. Hades the author defines as a " resting place of the dead," " neither heaven nor hell." Its inhabitants are in a state of sleep, but not necessarily of unconsciousness. All who have died since A.D. 70 " have been detained in Hades," where they will remain until the final judgment. Paul, who was executed A.D. 68, only waited two years in Hades, while Abraham was there 2,000 years. " The judgment of the Gentiles and the

destruction of this physical universe will be simultaneous."
The world " is rapidly ripening for its final end."

MORE ABOUT THE ASSASSIN.

" I know Charles J. Guiteau very well," said Mr. Stephen
English, the editor of the *Insurance Times*, to a *Herald*
reporter. " He is an old offender, and there are many in this
city who have good cause to complain of his fraudulent conduct, myself among the number. Some time ago I retained
him as my lawyer in a case and intrusted him with a check for
$300 to pay certain parties for services rendered. He drew the
money and, instead of paying it out as I directed, he appro-
priated it to his own purposes. Now, he had not the slightest
excuse for this breach of trust, as I paid him liberally for his
legal services. I had to pay the $300 a second time and
brought an action in the courts against him to recover the sum.
A judgment was obtained against him, but when Guiteau
heard of it he fled the city. If you turn to the files of the
Herald for the autumn of 1873 you will find that he there
figured in police courts, where he was charged with what is
vulgarly known as " bilking" hotel and boarding-house keepers.
The reason I employed him was that I knew his brother, John
J. Guiteau, who was then and is now connected with a life
insurance agency in Boston. His brother is a very pleasant
man and bore a good reputation. As soon as I ascertained
Guiteau's real character from the *Herald* police reports I
determined to secure his criminal indictment, but was dissuaded
from my purpose by my lawyer, Mr. Darlington. He subsequently went on the lecture platform and expatiated on religious
topics, but did not venture nearer to New York than Jersey
City, as he knew I was anxious to secure his arrest. I have
always held that he was a disgrace to the legal profession, and
I have been told that he was debarred in Illinois."

" Do you think it likely that he was insane when he shot the
President, as is intimated in the Washington despatches?"

" Insane? Not at all. He was a cool, calculating villain, and
has always borne that character. There was nothing of the fool
about him. He was a rascally knave, who dressed well, talked
well, and cheated everybody he came in contact with. He

would accept a case and talk very favorably about it until he had secured all the money from his client that he could. After months of procrastination and promises the client would wake up to find that he had been gulled and that nothing had been done in the case at all. Whoever takes Charles J. Guiteau for a fool is mistaken. He is an innate rascal. I never would have suspected him of assassination though; he was not the style of a man who would ordinarily be capable of that kind of crime."

" Did you know of his aspirations for office ?"

"I know that he was looking for a United States Consulship, and there never was a man more unfit for such a position. The President showed his wisdom by refusing to have anything to do with him. I suppose he must have made an investigation into his record and then dropped him from his consideration. If Mr. Garfield had appointed him as a consul I would have written to the Senate and taken every means in my power to denounce him. This is a fit ending to the life of such a man as Guiteau was."

" Was he a good lawyer ?"

" No, I don't think he was. At least he never showed any legal cleverness or tact here. The man simply got all the money he could before his client found out who he was. As to his being debarred in Illindis I got that information through another person; but I have every reason to believe that it is true. He was, I think, readmitted to the bar in this State. His brother is an entirely different kind of a person. He used to be in the employ of an insurance company in this city. I had close business relations with him several times, and came to think of Charles J. Guiteau as a good lawyer, because he was talked of frequently."

General Ramsey, of New Jersey, was very emphatic in his denunciation of the outrage. He said : " It is a most terrible affair, and I cannot fully realize it as yet. My opinion is that the crime was committed by some political enemy, who saw that General Garfield was a man of nerve and courage, and could not be swayed by the clamor of one faction or another. I am at a loss to think what the event may mean. Events can only determine that. My impression is, however, that the design was well thought over and that the work was done by a cold-blooded villain. I do not believe in his insanity, although he may have had this affliction. The country is not in the best possible condition when our President cannot go on the streets of the capital with safety."

On the register of the librarian's department of the Young Men's Christian Association, at Twenty-third Street and Fourth Avenue, is written in a bold, round hand, under date of October 20, 1873, in the handwriting of President Garfield's assassin :— "Guiteau, Charles J., 31 East Twenty-second Street, city."

The librarian of the institution, Mr. R. B. Poole, when questioned concerning the would-be murderer by a *Herald* reporter, said: "Since he first registered his name in that book Guiteau was in the habit of coming here on and off. Sometimes I would see nothing of him for months together, and he has remained away as long as six months and a year. About six years ago he went to Chicago to study law and remained there a long while. Then he came back here again. He told me he was a passenger on the steamer *Narragansett* at the time she was wrecked by colliding with the *Stonington* on the Sound. I remember he came up here the next day, and occupied several hours writing what he said was an account of that terrible disaster for the *Herald*. After this he disappeared again, and I next saw him last fall when he went off to work, as he said, for Garfield. Shortly afterwards I met him on the street, and he was then certainly better dressed than usual. To me he always appeared like a person floating round taking it easy. I should certainly say his mind was not evenly balanced, and I took him to be a man of indolent habits. At different times when he came up here he would write for hours together, and frequently consulted numerous books. As far as I know he never used intoxicating drinks, and in fact I understood he used to lecture on temperance. Sometimes he would borrow small amounts of me, but these he invariably repaid. I learned from him that he belonged to a free love community, but that was prior to October, 1873. I can't remember what sect it was."

Mr. McBurney, the secretary of the association, who was found at his desk, said to the reporter: "I am certain Guiteau's mind was not properly balanced. I was astonished one day on opening a book which was sent to me to find his name attached to it as author. It was on religious subjects, but it was such a half-crazy medley that I threw it aside, and to-day when I looked for it failed to find it, so I cannot tell you its title. He was never a member of the association, but used our library, just as you or anybody else might do who conforms to our rules."

The lady who occupied the house No. 31 East Twenty-second Street, where Guiteau claims to have lived in 1873, has removed to the country, and therefore no information could be obtained respecting him from that source. The list of the saved from the wreck of the ill-fated steamer *Narragansett* does not include the name of Guiteau.

A member of Calvary Baptist Church said of him:

"When I read the first despatches this morning, I doubted whether I knew the assassin; but subsequent despatches assured me. He is the same Charles Guiteau who came to this city in the summer of 1871 with strong letters of recommendation from the pastor of the First Baptist Church in Chicago introducing and recommending him to our church. On the strength of these he was received into fellowship. He said that he had lived in New York, and been a member of the Rev. Henry Ward Beecher's church, but that on taking a wife in Chicago he became a member of her church. After Guiteau had been some time in this city his wife called upon our pastor, the Rev. Dr. Robert S. MacArthur, and said that her husband was a practising lawyer, and needed $100 pending the decision in an important case. Mr. MacArthur lent the $100, and that's the last he ever saw of it. Guiteau moved to Brooklyn that autumn, but continued to attend our church and to have a sitting in it, and occasionally he attended our social meetings. Then he moved back to this city, and in 1876 or 1877 his wife visited our pastor and recited a story of wrongs that satisfied us that her husband was a thoroughly disreputable, bad man. The story of his immoralities is about as bad as such a tale could be. His licentiousness and his brutality had driven Mrs. Guiteau to institute proceedings for divorce. She is a good, true woman, and had borne all that a human being could bear, and then she appealed to the courts. A decree of divorce was granted. We cited him to appear before a committee of discipline, and he appeared in response to the citation. He acknowledged his gross immorality and professed penitence, at the same time beseeching us not to discipline him publicly, as such an act might ruin him. But his penitence seemed to be feigned: we more than doubted his sincerity. Therefore we summoned him to answer a charge of gross immorality, but on the evening set down for the hearing he did not appear, and he was unanimously expelled from Calvary Baptist Church.

"But notwithstanding he had proved himself an incorrigibly bad man Guiteau had the effrontery not long after his ignominious expulsion from our church to send for Dr. MacArthur to intercede for him in Jefferson Market Police Court. Guiteau had been arrested for obtaining money under false pretences. The magistrate was willing to deal leniently with the prisoner if our pastor desired it; but Mr. MacArthur said that Guiteau's career had been such that he could not conscientiously interfere to save him from prison.

"The next I heard of Guiteau was last fall, when he was advertised as one of the speakers at the political meetings. As long ago as when he was expelled from our church we had doubts as to his sanity, and I can readily believe, in view of the life he has led, that he is insane."

NEVER A CONSUL.

Frank W. Potter, late United States Consul at Marseilles, said: "No such person as Guiteau ever was United States Consul at Marseilles. The only consuls at that port now living are George W. Van Horn, of Wisconsin, from 1861 to 1867; Martin F. Conway, of Kansas, from 1867 to 1869; Milton M. Price, of Iowa, from 1869 to 1873; Frank W. Potter, of New Jersey, from 1873 to 1878, and J. B. Gould, of Massachusetts, from 1878 to 1881. Horace N. Taylor, of Michigan, was recently appointed to succeed Gould. It is more likely that the assassin was applicant for instead of an occupant of the Marseilles consulate."

Some explicit and reliable information concerning what the police would called the "pedigree" of the would-be assassin of President Garfield was furnished by Mr. S. D. Phelps, of No. 112 East Thirty-seventh Street, New York city. Mr. Phelps, whose office is in the *Evening Post* building, and who is well known as a business man in this city, was formerly Charles J. Guiteau's employer, and tells his story as follows:

"Guiteau—Charles J. Guiteau, I mean"—said Mr. Phelps, "was formerly a clerk in the employ of the law firm of Reynolds & Phelps, of which I was the junior member. We had our office in the Mercantile Building, so called, in La Salle Street,

6

Chicago, just opposite to the Chamber of Commerce Building, in 1867–68. Guiteau was a clerk in our employ during a part of those years, though I am unable now to say whether he was employed by General Reynolds or myself. I don't remember now what his references were or how we came to employ him. All I know is that he was engaged either by my partner or myself, and that he had a desk in our office. He was employed in the usual duties of a law clerk. After he had been in our employ for a considerable time—I cannot say just how long, though it was in the years I have mentioned—I came to know something of his past history, though not very much, by the fact that he consulted me in regard to the possibility of his recovering a considerable sum of money that he had invested or placed in the Oneida Community.

" I learned by the facts that he disclosed to me in this consultation that he had been a member of the Oneida Community for a considerable time, and that he had, as I understood the case, invested some $16,000 in the funds of the Community. That is the amount as I recollect it, though I can't say that I am certain about the amount.

" He told me that the male novitiate in that Community, that is to say the younger male members, had to serve a term of two or three years of pupilage before they could have any communication with the female members, and that it was during this novitiate that he had invested money that he had in the Community. He was enthusiastic about the matter at first and he remained with the Community, as he stated the circumstances to me, some two or three years; but not being advanced as rapidly as he thought he ought to be in consideration of his individual merits he left and started into the legal profession in his own fashion. After he had deserted the Community he made some effort to get his money back, but on his own statement of the transactions as he made it to me I advised him that he would never be able to recover the money under the terms of the agreement he made in paying it, and so far as I know he never did recover the money or any part of it.

" When he came into our office he knew but little law, although he had read some text books. If I remember right he was tolerably well informed concerning a part of Blackstone. While he was with us he performed the ordinary duties that fall to the lot of the clerk of a law firm, such as copying papers, etc.

He had not been with us long, however, before it was observed —aud it was a significant circumstance—that he never could apply himself properly to anything that was put in his charge. He was always unreliable. I cannot say, even now, that he was a lunatic or an idiot, but there was something wrong about him, and I don't know that I can express it any better than by saying that there was a screw loose somewhere, or perhaps I ought to say that he was weakminded. I wouldn't undertake to make a diagnosis of his case, but it was certain that, as the Scotch say, he was 'not all there.'

"After he had been with us about one and a half or two years his services were dispensed with. I don't think you had better say that he was discharged—his services were dispensed with is a better phrase. We didn't care to keep him in the office any longer. In short he wasn't worth a ——. After he left us I saw him occasionally at intervals for several years. I was connected with the Chicago *Inter-Ocean*, and during the time that I was on that paper he came to see me on a number of different occasions, telling me that he had concocted a scheme to buy out the *Inter-Ocean* for $500,000, and by controlling the policy of that paper to run the politics of the entire country. I paid only a little heed to his stories, for I had reason, from my previous knowledge of him, to believe that he was weakminded, and that what he said was not to be relied upon. I got that impression in the law office, and his conversation when he called on me in the office of the *Inter-Ocean* confirmed it. His visits after a time became so annoying that I instructed the office boy to say to him whenever he should call that I was not in. I don't know that I can say why I thought he was unreliable, excepting that there was a certain look about his eye that suggested it, and the general impression that one obtained by talking with him was that of a man who was *non compos mentis*. I can't describe it any better, but everybody will understand the matter if you state it in that way.

"During the years 1874–75 he was connected, I believe, with the Chicago press in some capacity, though I cannot say with what paper or in what capacity he worked. I can't exactly locate him, but I'm certain he was at that time a newspaper man. After that I never saw him until I met him two or three years ago in Newport. I met him afterwards in the Fifth Avenue Hotel in this city, and he told me that he had either just received, or was just about to receive, a government appointment to some position in France. I do not know certainly whether he ever had such a position or not, but I have the impression that he did. He said he had been taking considerable part in political matters, and that this was the reward he had received or was about to receive from President Hayes, or the administration under President Hayes. I had known before that, and I told him so, that he had been prominent in stumping the State of Illinois for Hayes, and that he had taken considerable part in the canvass outside of the State of Illinois. I did not prolong the conversation because I had no confidence in his prospects as he had stated them to me. I really thought that he did not know what he was talking about, though I have the impression that he did get some such appointment as he talked about, and, if I am not wrong, he was Consul at Marseilles.

"Two or three years after this I met him several times on the streets of New York. Perhaps this was three or four years ago, but I didn't care to talk with him when I met him, because I did not think his talk was worthy of any attention. Since then I haven't heard from him, and I think it must have been as long ago as 1878 or 1877 that I saw him last."

Being asked for a personal description of Guiteau, Mr. Phelps said that he was now about thirty-three or thirty-four years old, and about five feet eight inches in height. Judging from his appearance when he last saw him he was probably about 145 pounds in weight. When Mr. Phelps last saw him he had a short cropped black beard. His mouth was large and his eyes were large and dark and very restless. He had the trick, so often associated with guilt, of never looking an interlocutor in the eye, and was extraordinarily nervous in all his movements. In manner he was preoccupied and was never able to confine himself to a single subject in conversation, but jumped from one subject to another in an erratic manner. He was a single man and it was understood belonged to a good family in Baltimore. While he was in the office of Reynolds & Phelps he was constantly in receipt of remittances from Baltimore.

Guiteau was well known to many persons who frequented the various Republican headquarters in this city during the last campaign. He came to this city at that time from Chicago, and registered at the Coleman House. He claimed to be employed in the State Committee rooms, and secured credit in a number of places on the strength of that claim. He vainly endeavored to get Chairman Jewell, of the National Committee, Chairman Arthur, of the State Committee, or President Manierre, of the Republican Central Campaign Club, to send him out as a campaign speaker. He wrote two or three speeches as specimens of what he could do. They were wild and disjointed and showed the man to be incapable of making a speech, so he was not employed. He was a frequent visitor at the various headquarters, and although somewhat wild in his appearance, no one regarded him as anything but a man who hoped to get office. "If he is insane," said a gentleman last night, who knows him well, "there is a good deal of method in his madness; about too much for belief."

In the course of the campaign, Mr. Gildersleeve, a printer of this city, who was doing much work for the Republican National Committee, was called upon by Guiteau with letters of introduction and recommendation from some persons at the National Committee rooms. He had a speech in manuscript which he desired put in type, and represented that the committee would meet the expense. Mr. Gildersleeve not finding in the letters definite authorization for the publication hesitated and examined the speech. He found it a very extravagant eulogy of General Grant and his friends, but Guiteau said that it was his aim by that means to draw the friends of Grant to the support of General Garfield. The same speech, though not printed by Mr. Gildersleeve, was, it is believed, delivered more than once during the campaign.

About the middle of March last, Guiteau wrote to a man in this city, who is a prominent member of the Republican Central Campaign Club, and who took an active part in the campaign of last year, saying that he had been promised the position of Consul at one of the Austrian ports; that his claims were being pressed by Senators Logan and Conkling, and there was no doubt of his appointment. He added that if he received the position he would appoint the man to whom the letter was addressed as his secretary. The recipient of the letter was congratulating himself on his good luck, when he received another from Guiteau asking for the loan of twenty dollars, promising to repay it when he received his appointment as Consul. This was too transparent a fraud to be successful, and the man from whom the loan was solicited was conveniently "short" at that time.

Guiteau afterwards sent several letters and postal cards denouncing this man as "no gentleman" for declining to advance him so small a sum.

H. B. Pool, Librarian of the Young Men's Christian Association, told a *Tribune* reporter last evening that he had known Guiteau for nearly eight years. He was never a member of the Association, but often went there to read. In the readers' register is his signature with his address, "Guiteau, Chas. J., No. 31 East Twenty-second Street, October 20, 1879." The day after the disaster to the steamer Narragansett last summer, he visited the library and told Mr. Pool that he had been on the steamer that was struck, but that he was not afraid for he was a Christian, and knew that if the steamer had sunk he was prepared to die.

A few weeks before the last November election Guiteau stated that he was going to work for Garfield with all his soul. He did not go to the Association building until after the election, when he had a new suit of clothes and seemed to have plenty of money. He then said he was going to Chicago to study law; and he has not been there since.

When asked as to Guiteau's sanity, Mr. Pool stated that he did not think the man had a well-balanced mind; he always was just going to do something wonderful, but never seemed to do it. He was very quiet, but never seemed to have any purpose in life. Previous to his coming to New York, he had belonged to a Free-love community, but had left that sect, and did not belong to any church. Inquiry at Guiteau's former boarding-house in Twenty-second Street revealed nothing, as the present family has lived there only a short time, and knew nothing of the persons who had previously occupied the house.

When Guiteau came to this city several years ago from Chicago, his wife, whom he married there, was with him. She is described as an estimable woman. Both of them brought letters from a prominent pastor of a Baptist Church in Chicago, and were admitted to membership in the Calvary Baptist Church in Twenty-third Street, of which the Rev. Robert S. MacArthur is pastor. A short time after his admission to the church it was discovered that Guiteau was grossly immoral, and was at once publicly expelled from the society. It is believed by those who knew him that his professions of religion were made in order to advance his ends. He pretended to practise law, but was never known to have clients except such as he could pick up at the police courts. A man who knew him at that time said last night that Guiteau was nothing more than a confidence man, and that he was once arrested on a charge of obtaining money under false pretences. After his release from confinement in the old Jefferson Market Police Court prison, he brought suit against one of the daily newspapers for defamation of character. By this suit he anticipated making a large fortune. Meanwhile he did nothing for his wife's support, and cruelty being added to neglect, she obtained a divorce from him on the ground of abandonment and infidelity. Some time after his arrest Guiteau removed to Brooklyn, where he had lived before going to Chicago.

HIS BAD NAME AT SARATOGA.

SARATOGA, N. Y., July 2.—Guiteau was in Saratoga early in the Presidential campaign, and advertised as follows in the *Saratogian*: "Garfield against Hancock. Charles Guiteau, of Illinois, the orator from the West, will speak at the Town Hall, Saratoga, Saturday, July 10, at eight P.M. Admission twenty-five cents. Let the people turn out and hear an able, eloquent and patriotic address."

The meeting never came off. Guiteau was present without an audience. He therefore "skipped" his board bill and the town without paying for the hall or for the advertising. The books of the *Saratogian* opened this account at the time: "Charles Guiteau, July 1, 1880, to advertising lecture of Garfield-Hancock daily, three dollars." Across the face of this the bookkeeper had long ago written "fraud."

Judge Anthony, of Chicago, is here, and states that Guiteau is "a rattle-headed" fellow, who was a laughing stock in Chicago. His explanation of the action is that Guiteau became crazy on the subject of office, and not getting one was soured, listened to the loud talk of the Stalwarts during the present controversy, and acted out his own inclinations.

GUITEAU KNOWN AT POUGHKEEPSIE.

POUGHKEEPSIE, N. Y., July 2.—The assassin of the President, Charles Guiteau, was in this city in July last, and advertised a lecture on the political situation, on the evening of July 2, one year ago to-day. An admission fee was to be charged, and as people would not pay to go to a political meeting the lecture was not delivered. He afterwards wanted to be engaged as a speaker by the Republican Committee, but the leading Republicans here thought his mind was unsound and would have nothing to do with him. He afterwards was announced to speak at other places in this State.

GUITEAU'S SERVICES REJECTED.

ALBANY, July 2.—Thurlow Weed Barnes, of the Albany *Evening Journal*, who was chairman of the County Committee, says that Guiteau called upon him last October, and asked for a chance to speak on the stump for the Republican National ticket. Mr. Barnes questioned him closely at the time, and not liking his looks, told E. M. Johnson, secretary of the State Committee, that he believed Guiteau to be a fraud.

GENERAL GRANT'S RECOLLECTIONS.

Guiteau an Applicant for the Austrian Mission—Soliciting Grant's Influence.

"I met Guiteau in the Fifth Avenue Hotel at the close of the last Presidential campaign. He wanted me to sign a paper recommending him as a proper person to appoint as Minister to Austria. I knew nothing about him; but Col. Frederick Grant, my son, told me that Guiteau was a lawyer in Chicago, and was supposed to be half crazy. I subsequently heard that he had delivered some speeches in favor of the election of Presidents Hayes and Garfield. He was no doubt crazy when he shot the President, and I attach no political importance to his act under these circumstances. It was the act of a cowardly assassin who had been disappointed in his search for office. Guiteau evidently believed that he was a man of great importance to the Republican party, and the defeat of his aims must have unbalanced his mind. He told me that he was engaged to a young woman worth one million dollars, and that he should obtain the appointment he was looking for if I would join Henry Ward Beecher and others in seeking it for him. I refused to sign his paper. I told my servant not to allow him to enter my parlors. He sub-sequently forced his way in one day, but I refused to talk with him and dismissed him speedily. I regret this sad occurrence from the bottom of my heart."

A SPECIMEN DEAD-BEAT LECTURE.

Newark, N. J., also furnishes a characteristic reminiscence of the assassin, Charles J. Guiteau. He visited there in March, 1878, announcing himself as a lawyer, an orator, and a lecturer. He advertised in the local papers as follows:

NEWARK OPERA HOUSE.
"Is There a Hell?"
CHARLES J. GUITEAU,
A Chicago lawyer and orator of great power, will answer this question, and review
ROBERT G. INGERSOLL,
AT THE
Newark Opera House, Friday, March 8, at eight o'clock.

Admission, 10 cents; reserved seats, 15 cents. For sale at Dennis & Co.'s.

☞ The Boston papers speak of this lecture as a masterly effort full of ideas.

On the day after the "lecture" the Newark *Daily Journal* gave the following account of it and the lecturer:

"IS THERE A HELL?"

Fifty deceived people of the opinion that there ought to be.

The man Charles J. Guiteau, if such really is his name, who calls himself an eminent Chicago lawyer, has fraud and imbecility plainly stamped upon his countenance, and it is not surprising that his "lecture" in the Opera House last evening did not leave a pleasant impression on the minds of the fifty people who assembled to hear him reply to Bob Ingersoll's talk on hell.

His lecture was a wonderful production of genius. It consisted of the averment that the second coming of Christ occurred in the year 70, when Jerusalem was destroyed; interesting readings

6*

from the book of Genesis, and the prediction that the world would soon come to an end.

Although the impudent scoundrel had talked only fifteen minutes, he suddenly perorated brilliantly by thanking the audience for their attention and bidding them good night. Before the astounded fifty had recovered from their amazement, or the half dozen bill collectors who were waiting for an interview with the lecturer had comprehended the situation, the latter had fled from the building and escaped. He is supposed to be a first cousin of the spiritualistic fraud who played the same game in New Institute Hall last spring.

It was ascertained that the notices Guiteau exhibited as having appeared in the Boston papers were fabrications.

THE FEELING THROUGHOUT THE COUNTRY.

IN NEW YORK CITY.

THE STORY OF THE SHOOTING RECEIVED WITH HORROR AND SADNESS—SCENES ON THE STREETS AND IN HOTEL CORRIDORS—HOW THE PARTICULARS OF THE AFFAIR WERE GIVEN TO THE PUBLIC.

NOT since the gloomy 15th of April, 1865, when the news of the death of the martyred President, Abraham Lincoln, was received, has this city been the scene of so much excitement, mingled with heartfelt mourning, as yesterday. At 10 o'clock in the morning, just when the active business of the day was beginning, and when the down-town streets were filled with merchants and business men, the first despatch announcing that President Garfield had been shot in the depot at Washington was received. It was a somewhat indefinite message, but gave the impression that the President had been killed. In an incredibly short time the terrible news had spread throughout the business part of the community down town, and alarm and consternation were stamped on every face. The story seemed so preposterous at first that those who heard it refused to believe it, and set it down as a canard. President Garfield's life had been of such a character that it seemed almost impossible for him to have made any personal enemies, and the notion that he had been murdered as a political measure could not be entertained for a moment. Scores of men hurried to the Western Union Telegraph office, hoping that the news would be found false. They were met there by a sad confirmation of the despatch, although they learned that the President was not dead, and that hopes of his recovery were entertained by Surgeon-General Bliss and the other physicians in attendance upon him. These hopes were something to lean upon for a while, and men went about their business as usual; but faces were clouded with fear, and there were no smiles to be seen among the thousands of persons who thronged the lower part of Broadway.

Meantime the news had spread with remarkable rapidity throughout the length and breadth of the city. The telegraph carried it to all the principal hotels, and from these common centres of information it radiated to the smallest side streets in the crowded tenement-house districts. Before noon there was scarcely a man, woman, or child on Manhattan Island who did not know that the Chief Magistrate of the nation had been shot and probably killed. Groups formed on the sidewalks and discussed the terrible news excitedly. In the hotels and the clubs, in the parks and in the saloons, wherever there was room and opportunity for men to gather together, they assembled in crowds and talked over the tragedy which had been enacted at the capital of the nation. But little of the details of the terrible crime were known at this time, and speculation had full swing, not only in debating upon the probable result of the attack on the President, but in seeking some plausible motive for the act of the assassin. If President Garfield should die, Vice-President Arthur would become the executive of the nation, and the effect of his accession to the power and patronage of the executive office was the subject of grave discussion among the business men of the community. Merchants were alarmed at the possibilities involved in the death of President Garfield. On the whole, however, great confidence was displayed in the innate strength of our popular institutions. "It seems," said one prominent merchant, "that we are adopting the system of the Russian Nihilists in America, but it won't work here. If President Garfield dies we shall go on the same as before, only we shall mourn the loss of a pure and good patriot at the head of the state." This sentiment, after the first shock was passed, was echoed on all sides, and men went about their business with sad faces, but still hopeful that the worst to be feared might not be realized.

At 11 o'clock the news of the assault upon the President came slightly more in detail, and with the absolute knowledge that President Garfield was still living, and that Dr. Bliss gave great hopes of his recovery, men breathed more freely; but still there was a sad and subdued look upon the faces of all as they passed in the street or met in the public places. The newspapers were receiving despatches every few minutes, and as fast as they came from Washington they were posted on the bulletin boards, so as to give the earliest possible information of any change in the President's condition to the anxious people. Park Row became the centre of attraction, and the sidewalks and streets in front of the different newspaper offices were soon crowded with men, who stood in the broiling sun and forgot the heat in their eagerness to hear the latest news from Washington. The throngs became so great between 11 and 12 o'clock that six policemen were stationed at each office to keep the passage-way clear for pedestrians. The men were very quiet and orderly, and talked in low tones of the tragedy and its probable and possible effects. The excitement was too deep to display itself in the ordinary noisy way, and the sadness of the people too genuine and heartfelt to expend itself in loud talk. There were men of all shades of political opinion in the crowds which surged round the bulletins; but they all had one sentiment in common upon the great crime which had been committed, and the invectives heaped upon the murderer were bitter and terrible. Broadway at its junction with Park Row was filled with a crowd so dense that a dozen policemen were required to furnish a passage for vehicles, and there was momentary danger of somebody being run over and killed. Drug stores and hotels also had their bulletins, and those, too, were crowded with men anxious to hear the latest news from the President.

At noon extras appeared, and the newsboys and girls pushed their way into the throngs around the bulletin boards, and flew up town as fast as the elevated trains could carry them. The demand for the papers was greater than the supply, and the boys sold out their stock as fast as they could peddle the papers out. Very little change was made, as people were too anxious to read the news to bother the boys for the change of a nickel or a dime. The papers were soon in everybody's hand, and the whole city was reading the meagre details of the tragedy which had been telegraphed up to noon. Nearly every passenger in the horse-cars had a paper, and men edged their way through the crowds in the street reading the few lines which had come from Washington. The information given in these early despatches was very brief, but it was of a reassuring nature. The President had been removed to the White House, was conscious, and the doctors thought that he might survive, while Guiteau, the assassin, was in jail under a strong guard. The hopes held forth by this news were eagerly grasped at by the excited multitude, and all began to feel somewhat reassured. Despatches continued to be received every few minutes, and the news which they contained was posted on the bulletins and issued in extras during the entire afternoon. Up to three o'clock they were favorable to the recovery of the President. Postmaster-General James telegraphed to the *Times* that Dr. Bliss gave great hopes of saving the life of President Garfield, and this despatch, when posted on the bulletin board, was accepted by the throng as almost decisive that the assassin's bullet had not reached a vital point.

CALUMNY BURIED.

It is needless to say that all the calumnies of the campaign last year were utterly buried and forgotten, and a warm feeling of affection for the man was cherished in every breast animated with the common instincts of humanity. As the afternoon wore on the crowds about the bulletin boards increased in force and eagerness, until it became necessary to send several details of policemen to keep the sidewalks clear and unobstructed. Even then there was some difficulty in making way for pedestrians, so intensely anxious were the people to get at and read the bulletins as they came thick and fast from Washington. A little after two o'clock despatches leaving no further hopes of the President's recovery were received, and the excitement rose to fever heat. In the rotunda of the Astor House several groups of politicians were assembled, and as a rule their criticism of the affair in Washington was confined to the emphatic expression, "D——dest outrage that ever was." Here and there some asinine specimen of the human breed attributed the catastrophe to the political agitation at Albany in the election of United States senators, and went so far as to hold Conkling and Platt responsible for the deed; but the great mass of citizens, when they learned the full particulars, which came along from Washington between four and five in the afternoon, indicating that the assassin had no political or pertinent motive whatever—that he was simply a plain and unadulterated lunatic, who in a particular mood of mind would shoot any man who was the occupant of the same high station that Garfield filled—felt that there was nothing left to criticise; that all it resolved itself into was, that a crazy man met the President of the United States at a favorable opportunity, and shot him in his unreasoning delirium. All along Broadway and other leading streets bulletins announcing the tragic occurrence were hung up outside business stores, and the whole city was soon aware of the direful proceeding. Men in the rotunda of the Astor House, who were political opponents of Garfield, spoke in the most kindly possible strain about him. One who formerly held a prominent position in the city government said, "This thing makes my heart bleed. No matter what Garfield was politically or any other way, he was a splendid specimen of American manhood. He was in the prime of life and health, and married to a most superior woman. Think of that woman's grief; think of her children's grief; think of the grief of a whole nation, who hoped, despite all the low, sneering twaddle of the politicians, to enjoy four years of unexampled prosperity under his administration. It is the saddest tragedy, every way you take it, that was ever perpetrated on American soil." Much talk like this prevailed in the Astor House.

WHAT MAYOR GRACE SAID.

Mayor Grace felt profoundly shocked on receipt of the news from Washington. He said: "I found it difficult to account for the motive that could have induced such a crime. Certainly President Garfield was not the type of man to provoke such a vindictive outrage. He was popular with men of both parties, and his death will be universally deplored. Yet, from the strange political happenings that have been recently occurring in Albany and elsewhere, nothing is apt to surprise people. The late event at the State capital is quite as bewildering as the news just received from Washington, and indicates that there is something rotten in the political and moral system of the whole country. God has conferred great blessings on this country, but there appears to be little disposition to thank him for the fact. The rush in every direction appears to be entirely after material things, to the total neglect of the higher and more spiritual necessities of men, and no wonder that the country is visited with disasters like this."

EXCITED THRONGS AT THE BULLETIN BOARDS.

Excited throngs congregated up to a late hour in the evening in front of the bulletin boards, anxiously scanning the despatches as they were received and placed in a conspicuous position. These despatches were sufficiently contradictory to be confusing and exasperating. At one time it was confidently announced that the President's injuries were not serious, and that his pulse and temperature were normal, that the doctor was in attendance, and that the balls would soon be extracted without danger to the patient. Another account stated that he was suffering from collapse, and no hopes were entertained of his recovery. These conflicting reports produced alternate feelings of hope and despondency in the breasts of the anxious and expectant multitude. At one time the crowds would look reassured and confident, words of encouragement and hope would be interchanged, and the deep-seated gloom that rested on every face would be temporarily dispelled. Yes, the President would be spared to the country after all; the sanguinary and cowardly designs of the would-be assassin would be frustrated. Congratulations thereupon would be interchanged, and the restless assemblage would begin to melt away. The next moment a heated-looking courier would make his appearance bearing a sheet of paper. That was the signal for those in the street to crowd forward those who held a closer and more advantageous position on the sidewalk. Every one wanted to ascertain without a moment's loss of time the latest change in the President's condition. A low murmur of pent-up passion and indignatión greeted the posting of the despatch, which contained the information that the President was in a precarious condition. Men could not believe that he would die. Why should the Chief Executive of the nation—a man, too, of amiable traits—be ruthlessly shot down and slain, without warning or provocation, in the honeymoon of his administration, so to speak, and at a time when the country was enjoying profound peace and the greatest prosperity? While these feelings were predominant, the general excitement would be increased to the straining point by another bulletin setting forth that death had actually put an end to his sufferings. Then the fierce denunciation that honest citizens heaped upon the head of the assassin would find vent in a vehement shout of rage, and men would walk away with darkened brows and clinched teeth, muttering threats of vengeance.

SCANNING THE DESPATCHES.

A group of excited persons drew a large audience in front of the bulletin boards, while they eagerly commented upon the character of the despatches received. "It has come to a pretty pass," said one, who, by common consent, seemed to be regarded as spokesman, "when the chosen Chief Magistrate of the nation is shot down by the hand of an assassin! Is it not enough that in our day and generation, in this boasted nineteenth century civilization, we should have one martyred President? Is this country to become Cossack in its methods of political warfare? It will not be long until it can be said of us, as it has been of Russia, that ours is a government tempered with assassination. We must stamp out such miscreants, if any exist. Whoever is guilty of this terrible deed must pay the penalty for it with his life. No mercy must be shown to traitors or assassins; a terrible example must be made of the miscreant, whether the President live or die, who has produced such a shock to the moral and humane conscience of every honest, self-respecting and God-fearing man."

These remarks, delivered with vehement declamation, were applauded by all present. The popular mind was worked up to the highest pitch of frenzy. The news of the shooting, so wanton, so deliberate, and so atrocious, for the time being appalled and terrified the nation. All classes and conditions of men, without regard to party proclivities, Democrats and Republicans, Secessionists and Federalists alike, were equally concerned in the tragedy, and all freely and vehemently denounced the act.

"Thirteen of my family," remarked a man as he scanned the bulletin board, "served in the Confederate army, and only five of them escaped death on the field of battle, and when I heard of the assassination of Lincoln I regarded it as a political blunder, if nothing worse; but this is past human comprehension; it prostrates one's judgment and conscience; it is the greatest of all recorded crimes; it is a reproach to our age and a disgrace to our institutions."

Another absorbing phase of the tragedy, scarcely subordinate in public interest to the question of the death or recovery of the victim was, "Who was the perpetrator of the savage deed, and what the motive of the crime?" The wildest reports were in circulation during a portion of the day on these heads. One was that the slayer was actuated by jealous motives, another that lunacy was the prevailing cause. Others, again, urged that the Stalwart fight was responsible for it all; that, in fact, it was the result of a deep-laid conspiracy. The few foolish people who took the latter view of the case reluctantly relinquished their prejudiced theory only when later and fuller despatches showed that in all probability the assassin was demented, and not morally responsible for his awful crime.

When the announcement was made that Mrs. Garfield had arrived in Washington and conversed with her husband, who was said to be "rapidly sinking," a groan of sorrow and despair escaped from the bulletin gazers. At half-past eight in the evening a cheer rent the air in front of the *Herald* office, where thousands had congregated in feverish expectation to catch the very latest information from Washington. This expression of gratitude and approval was occasioned by the public display of the following despatch: "The President's voice is stronger and unimpaired. He converses freely with those near him."

AT THE HOTELS AND CLUB-ROOMS.

The scenes in and around the leading hotels were scarcely less exciting. Many persons who, during the warmest portions of the day, had stood in the streets anxiously scanning the bulletin boards, late in the afternoon could be seen in the corridor or reading-room of some hotel still discussing the tragical situation. The Fifth Avenue, the Brunswick, the Windsor, Delmonico's, and other similar resorts were frequented by groups of excited citizens, all eagerly discussing the one overwhelming and absorbing subject. It is safe to say that every person—man, woman, and child—in the city talked hardly of anything else. People who had read their morning paper in mental quietude and proceeded to their daily avocations untroubled and undisturbed, a few hours later were thrown into the profoundest state of excitement. The news, in fact, for the time being, brought all sorts of business to a standstill, and men otherwise filled with personal and political cares and responsibilities at once left their offices and homes, and sought for further particulars of the tragedy at some club-house or hotel. The smallest gossip or rumor was received with the greatest interest. The man who had talked with any leading political celebrity was sought out that his views and opinions might be received, while the evening papers were read with eagerness.

At the Fifth Avenue Hotel several gentlemen were engaged in an animated conversation. One ventured to remark that he thought the dastardly deed would be the means of cementing the Republican party. Another scouted the insinuation that politics had anything to do with the tragedy, and that if the victim survived his injuries party lines would remain unchanged. At the height of the debate a man, wearing a check jumper, pushed himself eagerly, to the front. In an instant all eyes were turned upon him. "Say, mister," said he to the central figure of the group, "what was the man's—I mean the scoundrel's name that did it? It wasn't Doty, was it?" There was something almost grotesque in the wistful expression of the man's face as he waited for an answer.

"No," said the gentleman addressed, "the papers say his name is Guiteau." "Thank God for that!" said the other rapturously, "for my own name is Doty, and I heard that the fellow who shot the President was called Doty, too. If he was I'd never own my name for the rest of my life. Thank you, gentlemen," and the honest fellow walked away, looking happy.

An almost similar incident occurred in the rotunda of the Astor House. A gentleman was scanning the *Telegram*, and standing close to the cashier's desk, when a thick-set citizen with a scowling face approached and asked:

"What's the news, boss? Is it true what they tell me about the President?"

"If you have reference to his being shot, I am afraid it is," was the answer. The gentleman bent his gaze upon the paper, when his interlocutor again inquired:

"They say that he was shot by a man of the name of Dougherty; is that true, also?"

"I think not; the papers don't state so; the assassin's name is said to be Guiteau."

"That's good news for me," said the other thankfully.

"Why so; how can it be good news for you?" asked the gentleman, regarding his questioner attentively.

" Oh, Dougherty's my name, and I wouldn't like to have it disgraced like that."

" But what made you think that Dougherty was the name of the assassin ?" was the next inquiry.

" I was told so by a man who said he read it in the papers," was the reply, as the man turned and walked away.

WALL STREET IN A FERMENT.

The news created much excitement in Wall Street and the neighborhood, and expressions of sympathy, regret, vengeance, consternation, disgust, and general sorrow were heard on all sides in the throngs that crowded the different exchanges and other public institutions of business. An atmosphere of gloom pervaded the Custom House.

Collector Merritt was deeply agitated, and when a telegram came announcing that the President was sinking, tears started in his eyes. He said that he had received many callers, all tendering the sincerest sympathy for the afflicted family in Washington. Consul-General Archibald, of England, called very soon after the news of the assassination had arrived, and expressed his own personal sorrow and that of his government, and he begged to extend the sympathy of the entire English nation to the American people in their great affliction. Among others who called during the day were Lieutenant Mitchell, of the staff of the Khedive in Egypt; General Anson G. McCook, and Congressman A. A. Parker. The Collector said that he did not know what would happen in the case of President Garfield's death; it was sad enough to think of his present suffering. He had not been invited to attend Mr. Field's reception to the President, and he knew nothing about Senator Robertson's future plans.

Mr. Thomas C. Acton, chief of the Assay Office, was found reading a telegram announcing the President sinking. " This is an hour," he said, " when political intrigue and ambition for office should cease."

" But if the President dies his place must be filled," said a reporter of the *Herald*.

" Yes; General Arthur will go in. He has a good head, and if he be wise, as I think he is, he will not make many removals. The Cabinet will undoubtedly be changed, and Conkling may be placed at the head of the State Department and General Grant be made Secretary of War. With Grant in the War Office Europe would need no hint to let us alone and treat us with unusual courtesy. With Grant as our Minister of War his name would command the respect of all the fighting nations of Europe. When Grant spoke they would know what was meant, and his wishes would be respected. The time for a great statesman has arrived, and a real statesman will be very careful about making any serious changes in the government. Blaine will have to go out; that is certain. His race at the White House is run. The thing to do now is to heal the wounds of the past, and leave political feuds to be buried with the politicians."

AMONG THE BROKERS.

Rufus Hatch said that the market was necessarily affected by the news, but a change would be of benefit to the country. Stocks were from forty to one hundred per cent too high. The death of one or twenty men would not seriously affect the country, for it was prosperous. "The people and the country," he said, "are all right, but these great and sad events teach us a great lesson. It is better to be a private citizen than to be Vanderbilt or Jay Gould. We will survive in spite of Communistic assassinations. There will be just as much corn and wheat raised as there was last year. The effects of the calamity in Wall Street cannot be fully known before next week, when we shall have returns from Europe. One thing is plainly shown by this assassination, and that is that our immigration system needs radically changing. So long as the Communists and criminals of Europe are allowed to swarm over into this country somebody will be sure to get hurt. There should be a change. We need to 'bull' the country and 'bear' the politicians and swindlers at large. Then we shall be all right. In regard to the situation in Washington, if the President dies it is safe to say that Vice-President Arthur will not slop over. He is not that kind of a man, and I am sure he will do about the wise thing. The effect of this great event will be to clean out the political stables at Albany, and give the country a new 'deal' all around. Windom is in the right place. He has done his work well, and it cannot be changed, for the country has already reaped the benefit. Sherman will never be put into his place. If any more men are assassinated in this country it will be the railway kings, and I am sure that all of them will not die in their beds."

Mr. Washington Connor was found in his office adjoining that of Jay Gould. He said : " The result of this calamity will be what Mr. Vanderbilt and other leading operators have been striving to accomplish—a decline in the market. They want to buy stocks at lower rates; now they will get them. The only change in the government that will affect Wall Street will be a change in the Treasury, and I do not believe that General Arthur will interfere in that department. The administration will probably be controlled by Conkling. The country is prosperous, and the present excitement will not affect the market very long. At the end of thirty days fifty million people will forget that there has been a change, even if Arthur comes in."

Mr. A. S. Davis said that while this event may have no political significance—as being the result of the act of a crazy man —yet it is a blow at the security of investments. Investors have a vivid realization of how quickly their money is liable to melt away in case of any unforeseen catastrophe.

Another prominent broker said that a striking feature of the day was the unexpectedness of the terrible news from Washington. Its effect on the London market was yet to be determined. The general feeling in the street was that it was exceedingly fortunate that the sad event occurred when the London market was closing, for it would give the people time to recover from the paralyzing effects of the first shock, and prepare them to meet emergencies. It was regarded as peculiarly fortunate that the depression would be followed by holidays, so that when the New York market should open on Tuesday it would be one day after the opening of the London market, and the worst would be known. The holidays would prevent American stocks from being returned by cable to depress the American markets.

ALBANY, N. Y., AND ELSEWHERE.

THE STATE LAW-MAKERS STUPEFIED AND DAZED.

Senators and Assemblymen Filled with Sorrow and Indignation —Speculations upon Changes which may Follow the President's Death.

ALBANY.—Like a thunderbolt out of a clear sky fell this morning upon the capital the news of the shooting of the President. Like a thunderbolt, because for a time it stupefied and dazed and then left prostrate in grief all who heard the horrible report. Not since that bitter morning in April, 1865, when the country was shocked with the news of the death of Lincoln, have the people of this city been so aroused or pained. It was about 9.30 o'clock when a telegraphic despatch was handed to Judge Robertson at the Kenmore Hotel announcing that the President had been shot. So incredible was the report to him that he could not believe it true. At the same time, however, a similar despatch was received at the Western Union office, and was immediately posted on a bulletin. With marvellous speed the report was carried from point to point, and before the later despatches confirming the first had been received the city was in a state of painful excitement. Men ran here and there inquiring for the news. "Is he dead?" was the question asked a hundred times a minute by men and women with blanched faces and wet eyes. No one could tell more than the telegraph wires would bring, and so the expectancy increased. Throngs surrounded the bulletins and lingered along State Street and Broadway in the neighborhood of the telegraph office.

At the hotels, among the politicians, the effect of the report was to paralyze and strike dumb. It could not be true—there must be some mistake—it was a stock-jobbing story the brief despatches that came at 10 o'clock, and after dashing hope to the ground filled every heart with irrepressible grief. Senator Robertson, leaving his wife, who was terribly affected by the news, at the Kenmore, went to room No. 450, at the Delavan, occupied by Senators Woodin and Wagner. Into this room flocked everybody in search of news, to find it filled with men speechless with grief and indignation. Senator Woodin, too much broken to converse, sat with bowed head, looking upon the floor.   Senator Robertson, calm, yet anxious, conversed with Senator Wagner in a hopeful strain, which was scarcely encouraged by the despatches which came from time to time.   About 10.30, when the news came that Dr. Bliss had pronounced the President's wounds not fatal, and Senator Robertson read the despatch, it affected Senator Woodin so deeply, causing a reaction, that he jumped from his seat and then fell in convulsions, while others in the room were violently ill, and many strong men wept like children.   As the minutes slowly passed in the anticipation of good or bad news the excitement became more intense.   No one could think of anything else.   Business was practically suspended.   At the Kenmore the room of Mrs. Robertson was filled with weeping women.   The daughter of Senator Sessions, who had been much excited by the news, swooned several times, and had to be carried away.   The sorrow and indignation was not confined to Republicans.   Democrats joined in the general declaration of grief and horror at the assassination.   Ex-Senator Hughes, stopping here for the day, abandoned his business and waited excitedly to hear further tidings· He could not find words strong enough to express his indignation, and declared that he would have cheerfully put himself in the way of the assassin's pistol to shield the country from so terrible a calamity.

With reluctance the members tore themselves away from the bulletins and telegraph stands to go to the Capitol at 11 o'clock, where they were unable to attend to business.   In the Senate, Chaplain Halley alluded to the shooting of the President in his opening prayer in very tender words, and the body took a recess.   The Chaplain of the Assembly also alluded to the horrible crime that had been committed, and then, at the instance of Col. M. C. Murphy, of New York, who denounced the atrocity in earnest words, the Assembly took a recess.   In both houses all despatches received from Washington were read aloud from the Clerk's desk.   When the two houses dispersed there was again a rush to the telegraph office.   The bulletins were scanned eagerly, yet with dread, for the report was constantly abroad, and traceable to no authoritative source, that the President was dead.   Instead of abating as the day grew, the excitement and anxiety to learn the best and the worst increased.   From time to time extras were issued, and the brief and unsatisfactory .

tidings they contained were read eagerly. The State offices were deserted, and the office-holders crowded the hotels to gather up the last information. The crowds in the streets talked of nothing else. As the matter became a subject of conversation, it was found that some of the Stalwarts here were not receiving the news with the same spontaneous indignation that it created among other Republicans and Democrats. Senator Hogan, sitting at breakfast with a man whom he describes as a prominent Republican politician, spoke of the shooting to the Republican, who said, "I don't believe a word of it; it's too good to be true." The Senator absolutely refused, when he repeated his statement, to say who made it. His refusal was prudent, for in the hot condition of the blood of most men here it is altogether probable the man would have been treated roughly if he could have been found.

Gov. Cornell heard of the shooting about 10 o'clock, when he reached his office in the old Capitol. He was profoundly moved by it, and unable to devote himself to the ordinary business of his office. Gen. Townsend joined him later, with Private Secretary Abell. The despatches sent from time to time from the Western Union office were anxiously examined. The Governor's detestation of the assassin and his sorrow for the deplorable calamity which had befallen the country were expressed calmly and with great sincerity. He saw that its effects were to be far-reaching, more serious than could be supposed by those who merely regarded the loss to the country of its President. At noon he sent the following despatch:

ALBANY, July 2, 12 M.

To the Hon. James G. Blaine, Secretary of State, Washington, D. C.:

Please accept for the President my prayerful sympathy and earnest hope for his early restoration. Intense feeling exists throughout the State, mingled with indignation.

ALONZO B. CORNELL.

Senator Robertson continued to receive despatches from Washington direct and by way of New York through Chauncey M. Depew. The senator, while apparently calm, was deeply moved. He had made arrangements to meet President Garfield

7

to-night at Dobbs Ferry on his way to dine with Cyrus W. Field. He had not seen him since he was appointed Collector, and looked forward to the meeting with great expectations of pleasure. He had sent his trunk down the river, and was to follow this afternoon. He has now determined to remain in Albany.

About 5.30 o'clock a report was circulated that the President was dead. Without waiting to verify the report, preparations were made all over the city for draping stores and houses in mourning. The Grant Club arranged black and white streamers across the front of its rooms, and raised its flag half-mast. Several shops in Pearl Street were draped, and flags appeared at half-mast on the old Capitol and other buildings. At 6 o'clock a despatch from the railroad telegraph office, from which the news was said to have originated, was posted in the Delavan, and the mourning bands and flags soon after disappeared.

When the Assembly was called to order at 11 o'clock this morning, a painful stillness prevailed in the chamber. A gloomy sensation of foreboding and anxiety seemed to hang over the scanty throng of representatives present. In the opening prayer, offered by the clergyman present, a slight allusion was made to the attack upon the President, and a fervent wish expressed that his wounds would not prove fatal. Then, after the reading of the journal, Mr. M. C. Murphy, Democrat, of New York, rose and said:

" Mr. SPEAKER.—I move you this house take a recess until five minutes before twelve o'clock. I make this motion because of the deplorable news that has reached the city of Albany in regard to the assassination of the gentleman from Ohio, the President of the United States. Mr. Speaker, when we see a boy driving two horses on the canal; when we see that boy going along the towpath; when we see that boy sawing wood in college and doing chores for his education; when we see that boy graduating with distinguished honor; when we see him become a professor; when we see him go to the defense of his country and command a division of troops; when we see that man go to Congress and serve twenty years, a bright star among brilliant men; when we see that man elected to the office that is the highest in existence to-day, the President of the United States; when we see that man shot down by the hand of an assassin, there is no condemnation too great by Democrats, as well as the majority of this house, to give utterance. When we see that office disgraced, not the man, because it is the office that is disgraced, I say, sir, on the part of the minority of this house, that there is nothing at our hands that we are not prepared to acknowledge and condemn on the part of the vagabond that was incited or the maniac who attempted it."

RICHMOND, VA., July 2, 1881.

The most intense excitement has prevailed here during the day over the intelligence of the attempted assassination of President Garfield. When first the rumor was reported it was generally discredited; but on confirmatory despatches being read, the public mind began to realize the shocking news, and in a short time the whole city seemed moved. Crowds gathered rapidly at news centers anxious for particulars, and expressions of deep regret at the dire calamity which has befallen the nation and condemnations of the dastardly act are general.

HARRISONBURG, VA., July 2, 1881.

The intelligence of the attempted assassination of the President creates universal indignation and regret here among all classes.

MONTGOMERY, ALA., July 2, 1881.

The attempted assassination of the President causes universal sorrow and indignation here. A call has been made for an indignation meeting, to be held on Monday night.

SELMA, ALA., July 2, 1881.

The news of the attempt to assassinate the President was received here with the most profound regret. A mass meeting called by the chairman of the Democratic Executive Committee, the Mayor of the city, our member of Congress, and other prominent citizens, was held at 6 P.M., and was largely attended. Resolutions were passed by a unanimous rising vote, denouncing the dastardly act, and expressing the most sincere grief at the nation's calamity.

ATLANTA, July 2.—In response to a call issued at noon today by the Mayor, a large number of the best citizens assembled at the Opera House this evening at 4.30 o'clock, to consider appropriate resolutions concerning the assassination of President Garfield. Appropriate resolutions were adopted by a rising vote. Speeches were made by Congressman Hammond, General John B. Gordon, Senator Brown, Chief-Justice James Jackson, and ex-Governor Bullock.

NEW ORLEANS, July 2.—The shooting of President Garfield created intense excitement in this city to-day, and was almost the only subject discussed. All people condemn the act in the strongest terms, and express regret for the President.

AUGUSTA, GA., July 2.—This community was thrilled with horror, indignation, and disgust on hearing of the shooting of President Garfield. All classes bemoan his fate, and express the most profound sympathy with the illustrious victim of a cowardly crime.

NASHVILLE, TENN., July 2.—The community here was shocked with news of the shooting of the President, and popular indignation and abhorrence at the act were universal. Crowds gathered about the newspaper offices, and inquiries for news were despatched from all parts of the State.

RALEIGH, N. C., July 2.—A public meeting of the citizens has been called here to denounce the crime.

THE SENTIMENT IN BROOKLYN.

The assassination of Abraham Lincoln did not cause a greater thrill through the hearts of the community of the City of Churches and homes than was sent from one end of Brooklyn to the other upon the announcement of the assassination of President Garfield. All factional, all partisan feeling and animosities were covered up and lost sight of in the one great appalling fact that the Chief Magistrate of the United States had again fallen at the hands of an assassin. The telegraph offices and the local newspaper sanctums were besieged by pale-faced, anxious-visaged men of every shade of party complexion and diversity of opinion, who could hardly believe the astonishing announcement and who sought verification from the best available sources. The streets were filled with newsboys selling extra *Telegrams* and other evening papers, and the venders of the extras realized exorbitant profits in satiating the thirst for further details of the national tragedy among the people.

"I don't know what we are coming to. This is really terrible," said Mayor Howell. "I opposed the election of Mr. Garfield, but as he was duly elected by the majority I respect him as the Chief Magistrate and President of the United States. I deeply deplore this terrible occurrence. I have given orders to the keeper of the City Hall in the event of the death of the President to drape the building with mourning." The Mayor also told Captain Dick, Chief of the Bureau of Supplies of the Department of City Works, who has immediate supervision of the fireworks ordered for the celebration of the Fourth of July, to have the public exhibitions postponed until some future occasion should the President die. The Mayor said the assassin should be hanged. If he was crazy they should hang him twice.

"It's shocking," said General Jourdan, Commissioner of Police and Excise and major general commanding the Second division of the National Guard. "I can think of no other means of expressing what I feel. Garfield would have made a good President. Should the President die Arthur would make a good President. The country would go on the same."

Collector of Taxes and Assessments, "Corporal" James Tanner, said: "It is terrible! It is terrible! It is the act of a lunatic."

General Isaac Catlin, the District Attorney of Kings county, said he was thoroughly overcome by the news of the shooting.

Commissioner of City Works, John French, said that no sane person would, he thought, recklessly shoot so good a man as President Garfield.

Police Justice Walsh, democrat, said: "Garfield was a better man for the business interests of the nation than Arthur, who will succeed him, ever can be."

A few minutes before five o'clock mourning streamers were displayed from the half-masted flags on the roof of the City Hall.

The keepers of the County Court House and Municipal Building displayed flags at half-mast. Ex-Sheriff Dagget's headquarters, corner of Montague and Court Streets, displayed the flag looped with crape. From many private residences throughout the city the colors were also half-masted.

Mayor Howell sent the following communication to General Jourdan :

General James Jourdan, Commissioner of Police and Excise :

Dear Sir—The murderous assault upon the President of the United States has deeply excited the public mind, and to such an extent that it is not improbable that disturbances of the peace of this community may ensue.   In view of the condition of things I have to request that you direct instructions to the captains of the several police precincts to exercise the greatest vigilance, and the whole force of the department be held in readiness in case of any outbreak.   I would also suggest that the military under your command be notified and be prepared to execute your orders at any moment.   Very respectfully yours,   JAMES HOWELL,
Mayor.

Police Superintendent Campbell, in accordance with instructions from the Commissioner, issued an order to the captains impressing them with the necessity of exercising the utmost vigilance.

THE NEWS IN PHILADELPHIA.

Philadelphia, July 2, 1881.—The first intimation of the shooting of President Garfield was received over the private wire of a Third Street banking house about ten o'clock, but it was only a few minutes until bulletins were posted at all the newspaper offices on Chestnut Street, and for a time all business was practically suspended.   The news spread with the wind, as it seemed, and long before any extra editions of the afternoon journals were on the street the terrible intelligence had reached the extreme limits of the business portion of Philadelphia.   Great crowds at once gathered about the newspaper offices, and the bulletins there displayed were eagerly scanned and commented upon.   When, about two o'clock, the bulletins began to indicate unfavorable symptoms the effect upon the crowds of people was to greatly increase the growing horror.   All the previously wild discussion as to the instigators, or the criminal's motive, were hushed, and the people stood, with painful anxiety evident on every face, waiting to read the half-hourly bulletins which were sent out from the dying (?) President's chamber at the White House.   The expression, "Isn't it horrible ?" was heard on every hand. One man in the crowd in front of the *Times* office said solemnly, "The scarlet circle of the king killers has been extended to the United States." This was anent the announcement that Guiteau was known to be a prominent member of the socialist societies in Chicago. "Yes," said a prominent judge as he read the latest bulletin, while hearing the words of the man at his elbow, "yes, the revolt of the Proletariat has begun among us." It would be worse than idle and unjust to repeat the gossip and the violent opinions expressed by the thousands of people who jostled each other about the various news centres.

SORROW AT TRENTON.

TRENTON, N. J., July 2, 1881.—The attempted assassination of President Garfield has caused a feeling of consternation, horror, and sorrow among all classes here, and the city is over shadowed with gloom. Excitement runs high and the streets are crowded with people, the telegraph bulletin boards being besieged. Every one prays that the President may recover.

HE NEWS IN THE SENATE.

The Senate met at half-past eleven o'clock, and was called to order by president *pro tem.* Robertson amid manifestations of deep feeling.

Rev. Dr. Halley offered up the following pathetic prayer:

"Almighty God! We have been summoned to this Senate chamber after hearing the startling and melancholy intelligence that the President of the United States has been shot by the hand of an assassin. But a few months have elapsed since we read of the ceremonies of his inauguration to this high office and of the interesting scenes connected with his installation, surrounded by the great men of the country, and the foreign ambassadors, in emblazoned robes, cheerfully paying to him their homage of respect and love. The lesson teaches us of the insecurity of human life, and we pray Thee, Almighty God, that Thou wilt spare him, that he may recover his health, that his sun may not yet go down, that those who may have been instrumental in concocting so diabolical a crime may be frustrated in their hopes, and that the stability of our institutions may be preserved. We know that the best medical staff will be called into exercise in order to afford every remedy whereby this calamity may be remedied. Forbid, Almighty God, that the President should be thus cut down in the maturity of his manhood, and we pray Thee that whilst thou didst bring him so near the gates of death that Thou wilt raise him up and make him an instrument of blessing to thousands; and we pray Thee that Thou wilt arrest the progress of vice and crime in our midst. We pray Thee that we will not be further compelled to read in the public prints of unholy familiarity with crime, and we pray that stringent measures may be employed to support the dignity of the law and prevent a repetition of these crimes that are every day startling the public, wounding the heart, and carrying grief and desolation into families. Do Thou ever watch over us, and may all these dispensations of Providence teach us to lean more and more upon Thee. Pardon our sins and bless us for Christ's sake. Amen."

Immediately after the reading of the journal the Clerk read from the desk an Associated Press despatch and a private despatch to Senator Wagner, briefly conveying the latest information obtainable.

Senator Halbert then offered the following:

Whereas, the Senate of the State of New York has learned with profound sorrow of the attempted assassination of the President of the United States; therefore

Resolved, that we tender our heartfelt sympathy to the President and his family, and at the same time express our horror and indignation at the atrocious attempt made upon his life.

Senator McCarthy said:

Mr. PRESIDENT—While I agree in much of that resolution, and am willing to express indignation and horror and all the feeling that the heart is capable of expressing on a matter of this kind, I hardly feel at liberty to offer condolence or sympathy until I learn what the result of this shall be. I have no idea of objecting to this resolution. I hope that nothing will occur at the White House, at any time in the near future, that will make it necessary to offer any further resolution on this subject.

The resolution was agreed to.

Senator Mills, in view of the great calamity that had fallen on the country, moved a recess until five minutes of twelve o'clock. A recess was taken.

During the intermission the senators gathered in an excited group in front of the Clerk's desk and listened to the reading of the Associated Press despatches, in which they manifested intense interest.

Immediately on returning from the joint assembly the Senate adjourned to ten minutes before twelve o'clock on Monday morning.

Despatches having been received here at about half-past four P.M. announcing the death of the President, Mayor Nolan ordered the fire-alarm bells tolled. The cathedral chimes were also tolled on the minor chords. All the public buildings had their flags lowered to half-mast, and a number of stores were draped in mourning. An air of sadness pervades the entire city, and there is a strong feeling among all classes. Both political parties join in reprobation of the act.

NEWPORT, R. I.

The attempt to assassinate the President has been the absorbing topic of conversation throughout this city and State. As previously stated in the *Herald*, a monster celebration of the Fourth of July had been determined upon by this municipality. It has now been decided, notwithstanding the expense to which the city has been put, to forego the festivities of the day in view of the probable death of the President. The celebration at Bristol will also be postponed. Newport's celebration, with the aid of the summer residents, promised to be one of the finest ever held in the State.

LOUISVILLE, KY.

There is considerable excitement here over the news of the attempted assassination of President Garfield, and great anxiety is manifested to hear from Washington and New York. The impression is that the outlook for the country, and for the South especially, would be very much less bright with Arthur than with Garfield in the Presidential chair; but there is no anticipation of any serious trouble in any event. Much sympathy is expressed for President Garfield and his family. At the Board of Trade a resolution was adopted expressing abhorrence of the attempted murder, and proffering the sympathy of the Board to President Garfield's family and to the country. The

7*

resolution was telegraphed to the Secretary of State at Washington.

RALEIGH, N. C.

There is great indignation here at the attempted assassination of the President. A public meeting of the citizens has been called to denounce it.

CHARLESTON, S. C.

The news of the assassination of President Garfield excited universal grief and horror in Charleston. The sorrow felt by the community is seen on the faces of all classes. Hope is everywhere expressed that he will soon recover. The Chamber of Commerce held a large meeting at two o'clock. Addresses were made declaring sentiments of sorrow, condemning the act of the assassin as the deepest crime, expressing the wish that the President will soon be restored to the people of the United States, to whom he is so dear, without regard to political opinions, and declaring to the President and his family the sympathy of the people of Charleston with them in their affliction.

NASHVILLE, TENN.

The community was shocked at the news of the attempted assassination of the President, and popular indignation and abhorrence at the act are universal. Great anxiety is felt to hear tidings of the wounded President's condition, and expressions of sympathy and hope for his ultimate recovery are heard everywhere. Crowds are gathered about the newspaper offices, and inquiries for news are despatched from all parts of the State.

BALTIMORE, MD.

The most intense excitement prevails throughout this city at the attempted assassination of President Garfield. All business is suspended, and groups of men are assembled on every street dumbfounded, anxiously and fearfully awaiting the result. Around the newspaper offices, about Baltimore and South streets, the sidewalks and streets are blocked by crowds of men. The papers are issuing bulletins every half hour. There is a universal expression of sorrow and indignation.

LITTLE ROCK, ARK.

The news of the assassination of President Garfield created intense excitement, and a feeling of universal horror was expressed for the atrocious act. The greatest sympathy is expressed for the President. Mayor Kramer called a meeting of citizens this evening to take suitable action in reference to the calamity.

CHARLOTTESVILLE, VA.

There was intense indignation here this morning upon the receipt of the news of the attempted assassination of President Garfield. A call is out for an indignation meeting to-night, and is signed mostly by Confederate soldiers.

WILMINGTON, N. C.

The news of the shooting of President Garfield was received here with a universal expression of horror and regret. The act is severely denounced, and the President's early recovery is earnestly hoped for by all classes.

NEW ORLEANS, LA.

The news of the attempted assassination of President Garfield created intense excitement in this city, and is almost the only subject discussed. All condemn the act in the strongest terms, and express sympathy for the President and hope for his speedy recovery.

BUFFALO, N. Y., July 2.—The reported assassination of President Garfield created the most intense excitement in this city this morning. All political differences are for the time forgotten, and a universal expression of sorrow, coupled with a loud call for vengeance upon his would-be murderer, prevails everywhere. All business for a time was almost entirely suspended, and the people were gathered upon the street corners discussing the affair.

The *Commercial Advertiser* (Republican), alludes to the assassination, in substance, as follows: " In the height of a crisis like this the pen falters, and it is hard to describe the effect of such startling news upon the people of a great nation. The despatches from every part of the country report that the excitement has been without precedent or parallel since the hour when the name of Lincoln was placed upon the roll of the martyred dead. Business is suspended. Men have little thought or care for the affairs of every-day life when they know that an assassin has aimed at the head of the national Government. But the calamity has revealed the firm hold that President Garfield has upon the esteem and affection of his fellow-citizens. That he may be spared and restored to the vigorous health that has been his blessing is the prayer that ascends to the great Ruler of nations from the millions of people in this vast Republic. James A. Garfield, if he lives, will learn, after the trial to which he is now subjected, how sincerely he is respected by the people who so recently placed him in the highest office of their Government. There are no political lines now when a nation is shocked by the reports of assassination, and mourns, with loved ones and loving wife, who are gathered by the beside of a wise father, a kind husband, and a faithful son. There are distinctions of persons in this great nation at such a time for all who are Americans by birth, or by adoption, who cry out against a crime so heinous, and their hearts turn towards the victim of so foul a wrong."

THE NEWS IN PITTSBURG.

PITTSBURG, PENN., July 2.—The news of the attempted assassination of President Garfield has paralyzed business. Intense excitement prevails, and the streets are crowded with people waiting anxiously for news.

LANSING, MICH., July 2.—On receiving the news of the attempted assassination of President Garfield the Greenback camp-meeting, now in session here, unanimously adopted the following declaration:

Whereas, The telegraph informs us that an assassin has this day made an attempt on the life of the President of the United States, therefore we, representatives of the National Greenback party of the Union, take this occasion to deplore and condemn the second attempt to deprive our Republic of its legitimate head, and we demand that all the power of the Government be put in force to punish this and all such acts of violence and violations of law.

DENOUNCING AN ATROCIOUS DEED.

LITTLE ROCK, July 2.—The news of the assassination of President Garfield created intense excitement, and a feeling of universal horror was expressed for the atrocious act. The greatest sympathy is manifested for the President. Mayor Kramer called a meeting of citizens this evening to take suitable action in reference to the calamity.

EXECRATION FOR THE ASSASSIN.

SAVANNAH, GA., July 2.—Despatches briefly announcing that President Garfield had been shot, but giving no particulars, were received here at 10.30 o'clock this morning. The news created a profound sensation throughout the city, and words of execration for the assassin and deep sympathy for the victim were on every lip. In its first extra edition containing the sad intelligence, the *News* said : " The event in itself is astounding and deplorable in the extreme, but its significance depends much upon the character of the assassin and the motive which prompted the murderous act. If it should prove to be like the attempt on the life of President Jackson in 1834—merely the irresponsible act of a madman—it will be deplored as a national calamity.

WILLIAMSTOWN, MASS., July 2.—The news of the attempted assassination of President Garfield created high excitement here, not only because of his being a Williams alumnus, but particularly from his intention of attending commencement exercises. Every arrangement had been made for his coming, and when first the news reached here the telegraph office was crowded with excited students and professors, with President Chadbourne at their head. The report has got out that there will be no commencement in consequence of the shooting. President Chadbourne says that unless Mr. Garfield dies the exercises will proceed in regular order. No changes are to be made until the trustees' meeting on Monday. Meanwhile a feeling of deep sadness prevails in the town and college.

CINCINNATI, July 2.—The feeling in Cincinnati is one of mingled grief and rage in reference to the shooting of President Garfield. The cooler heads counsel moderation. Groups of people gather everywhere and make the awful event the only topic of conversation. The outcry against the leniency of communities towards crimes against persons as breeding the spirit of murder is everywhere emphatic and outspoken. The hope that the President will survive, coupled with the fear that he will not, adds suspense to the excitement and intensifies it.

INDIANAPOLIS, July 2, 1881.

The news of the attempted assassination of President Garfield created intense excitement, and for a time business was suspended and crowds thronged about the telegraph and newspaper offices. As the news comes in this afternoon of the President's unfavorable condition, expressions of sorrow are heard from all. Telegrams from all parts of the State are coming in rapidly, asking for the latest news from the President, and indicate great anxiety all over the State.

CHICAGO, ILL., July 2, 1881.

The excitement here caused by the news of the attempted murder of the President is very intense. Nothing since the death of Lincoln has so stirred the populace. On its first announcement, business was at once suspended, and everybody hurried into the street to learn the latest particulars.

BOSTON, MASS., July 2, 1881.

The news of the attempted assassination of the President caused the most intense excitement in this city, and crowds surrounded the newspaper offices, all of which have issued extras. In the early part of the morning, business was temporarily suspended on every hand. The later favorable news that the President was not dead in a measure quelled the excitement.

PITTSBURG, PA., July 2, 1881.

The news of the attempted assassination of President Garfield has paralyzed business. Intense excitement prevails, and the streets are crowded with people waiting anxiously for news.

BRIDGEPORT, CONN., July 2, 1881.

The assassination of President Garfield has cast a gloom over the city. Business is entirely suspended, and the telegraph and newspaper offices are surrounded by crowds of excited people.

PORTLAND, ME., July 2, 1881.

Mayor Senter telegraphs to Secretary Blaine as follows: "Grief is felt here at the President's condition, and all citizens unite in earnest hopes for his recovery. They would regard his death as a most grievous public calamity."

Great excitement and feeling prevail, and business is almost suspended. Crowds of people hang about the bulletin boards.

ST. ALBANS, July 2, 1881.

Perhaps in no place in New England could the news of the attempted assassination of President Garfield have created a more profound impression than at St. Albans. The anticipated visit of the President during the meeting of the Teachers' Institute has been looked forward to by our people with cordial satisfaction, and the most extensive preparations had been made for the entertainment of himself and the party who were to accompany him. The announcement of the dastardly attempt upon his life was received with universal expressions of incredulity. The confirmation of the report created most profound indignation. Business was entirely suspended, and the utmost bewilderment pervaded the community. Governor Farnham has been in constant communication with Colonel Childs, chief of staff, under whose supervision the arrangements for the reception of the President were made, and this evening orders were issued revoking former instructions to the staff. The Governor has also forwarded to the Secretary of State at Washington the expression of his profound sympathy and regret.

LOUISVILLE, Ky., July 2.—There is much excitement here over the news of the attempted assassination of President Garfield, and great anxiety is manifested to hear from Washington and New York. The impression is that the outlook for the country, and for the South especially, would be very much less bright with Arthur than with Garfield in the presidential chair, but there is no anticipation of any serious trouble in any event. Much sympathy is expressed for President Garfield and his family. Business to-day is rather more quiet, but not to any extent disturbed. At the meeting on 'Change at the Board of Trade to-day the following was adopted and telegraphed to Washington:

LOUISVILLE, July 2.

Secretary of State, Washington:

The Board of Trade of Louisville expresses its abhorrence of the attempted assassination of the President, and proffers its sympathy to his family and the country, with the earnest hope for his recovery.   JOHN E. GREEN,
President.

SORROW IN INDIANAPOLIS.

INDIANAPOLIS, July 2.—The news of the attempted assassination of President Garfield created intense excitement, and for a time business was suspended and crowds thronged about the telegraph and newspaper offices. As the news comes in this afternoon of the President's unfavorable condition, expressions of sorrow are heard from all. Telegrams from all parts of the State are coming in rapidly, asking for the latest news from the President, and indicate great anxiety all over the State.

WILLIAMSTOWN, Mass., July 2.—The news of the attempted assassination of President Garfield created high excitement here, not only because of his being a Williams alumnus, but particularly from his intention of attending commencement exercises. Every arrangement had been made for his coming, and when first the news reached here the telegraph office was crowded with excited students and professors, with President Chadbourne at their head. The report has got out that there will be no commencement in consequence of the shooting. President Chadbourne says that, unless the President should die, the exercises will proceed in regular order. No changes are to be made until the trustee meeting, on Monday. Meanwhile a feeling of deep sadness prevails in the town and college.

NASHVILLE DEEPLY SHOCKED.

NASHVILLE, Tenn., July 2.—The community was shocked at the news of the attempted assassination of the President, and popular indignation and abhorrence at the act are universal. Great anxiety is felt to hear tidings of the wounded President's condition, and expressions of sympathy and hope for his ultimate recovery are heard everywhere. Crowds are gathered about the newspaper offices, and inquiries for news are despatched from all parts of the State.

ROCHESTER, July 2.—The feeling in this city over the attempt on the President's life is intense in the highest degree, recalling the sad scenes of the death of Lincoln. There is no thought uppermost in the public mind except the one of the immeasurable injury that has been done public security by such an outrageous violation of the rights of official life. There is no disposition among decent and common-sense thinkers to attach any political significance to the inception and execution of the deed, although no one denies that the consequential political circumstances are somewhat uncertain and unsettling. Mr. Garfield was exceedingly popular in western New York, and the best that can be hoped for the land if he shall die is that power and responsibility will make his constitutional successor fit to wear his mantle. At this writing the fate of the Executive is still undecided, but the people are hoping faintly against strong fears. The Rochester *Union* (Democrat), commenting, says: "While the life of no man is necessary to the administration of our Government or the stability of our institutions, the taking off of the Chief Magistrate by violence at any time or under any circumstances would be a great public calamity. More especially would that be the case now, in the anomalous political situation that exists. Ordinarily, the country is the witness of party feeling between the two great parties running high. Now it is a feud in the party of the Administration, the President at the head of one faction, and the Vice-President at the head of another, that forces itself upon the unwilling attention of the people. The succession of the latter to the Presidency in case of the decease of the former would produce more of a jar than a change of Administration as the result of a regular party contest, and is not to be desired. President Garfield's recovery is devoutly to be wished."

The Rochester *Express* (Republican) says: "The political consequences that would result from President Garfield's decease would be serious, but need not now be considered. The inexcusable neglect of Congress in not providing, as usual, for the succession if both President and Vice-President should die, will now be forcibly brought to mind. Our approaching national anniversary will be spent in despondency and sadness, unless encouraging intelligence from Washington shall before then roll over the land like a wave of gladness. To-morrow will be the most remarkable Sabbath that our people have ever known. It will be most emphatically a day of prayer. Persons who have never believed in Providential interference will hope now that there is something in the doctrine, and that an arm stronger than that of man may be outstretched for our deliverance from this impending disaster."

HARTFORD, CONN.

The first news of the shooting of President Garfield caused an excitement like that which followed the news of the assassination of Lincoln, sixteen years ago. Small groups of men gathered around the bulletins, and, as if blown by the wind, the news spread far and wide, and the little groups grew to thousands of people that, upon busy corners and near the mercantile marts, blocked the way and left no thoroughfares. There was a pretence of carrying on business as usual, but it was done only in a half-hearted way, for the people were completely absorbed in the unusual event of the morning, and trade and commerce were ignored for the time. The news was at first generally disbelieved, and it was only when the second and third despatches were bulletined that the first incredulity gave way to reluctant belief. On a corner a group of men were discussing the news, and one suggested that there was one important omission, and that there should have been a despatch announcing the death of the assassin soon after the shooting. Among the brokers there was no special disturbance. Stocks were slightly affected, but there were no orders to sell, and the recovery in quotations was prompt. Several persons here, among them ex-Gov. Jewell, have known the assassin thoroughly, and speak of him as a man of unsound mind. They agree in his craving for notoriety at any price, and as to the extravagant claims he made for himself, and his greed for office that was absurdly beyond his powers.

RALEIGH, N. C.

There is great excitement here over the news of the shooting of President Garfield. An indignation meeting has been called for 8.30 o'clock to-night, and will be addressed by leading men without regard to party.

The news of the shooting of President Garfield was received here with incredulity at first, but when the intelligence was confirmed there was a profound feeling of sorrow and shame that this disgrace and misfortune should for a second time fall upon the nation. The city had been preparing for the coming celebration of the national holiday, and the sudden change from buoyant hope and confidence in the general prosperity and happiness of the country caused a deep revulsion in the popular mind. Everywhere people go about with lengthened faces, anxiously inquiring as to the latest reported condition of the President, and sadly speculating at the probable outcome of this terrible affair. Republicans and Democrats alike are profoundly disturbed at the probable accession to the Presidency of Vice-President Arthur, with the consequence that Conkling shall be the President *de facto*, and a general revolution in every department of the Administration. People of all parties were just looking forward to an era of prosperity and of sound administration under President Garfield, and the disaster has produced a terrible shock to all. There were many who felt intensely dissatisfied that the indignant crowd in Washington was not permitted to wreak summary vengeance on the assassin of the President. Many declared that the proper disposition of him would have been to have held him under the grinding wheels of the railroad train which was to have carried President Garfield away, and to have thus ground him to mince-meat. While it seems incredible that a sane man could have done so desperate and utterly inexcusable a deed, the feeling is quite general that it would be best to execute him first, and try the question of his sanity afterwards.

Gen. Toombs was in the telegraph office when the first telegram of the shooting of President Garfield came. He walked to the hotel and spread the news, which created a sensation such as has been seldom known in the history of Atlanta. All deeply deplored the sad intelligence. Mayor English called a meeting, and, on two hours' notice, over a thousand of the best people in the city had gathered. Gov. Colquitt presided, and spoke feel-

ingly of the public calamity.   Congressman Hammond presented
the following resolutions in a speech expressing the sympathy of
the people :

Resolved, That we, as citizens of Atlanta, received the telegraphic announcement of the shooting of James A. Garfield,
President of the United States, this morning, with the profoundest regret and horror.

Resolved, That to him and his family we tender our deepest
sympathy in their affliction.

Resolved, That we join with all in the prayer that his life
may be spared for the discharge of the duties of the high office
to which he was elected.

Ex-Senator Gordon, Senator Brown, ex-Governor Bullock,
Chief-Justice Jackson, and others spoke, and the resolutions
were adopted by a unanimous rising vote.   Gov. Colquitt sent a
telegram in behalf of the people of Georgia, expressing their
sympathy and prayers for the President's recovery.   Senator
Hill was kept from the meeting by sickness, but says he heartily
sympathized with it and is deeply saddened at the news.   Justice
Woods, of the Supreme Court, says he is thankful it cannot
be contorted into political significance.   Bob Toombs says it is
a great calamity, and will degrade the morals of the people.

VICKSBURG, MISS.

The first news of the President's assassination was received by
way of New Orleans, the *Commercial* announcing on its bulletin
board that such a report had been received by the New Orleans
press.   No credence was at first given to the report, and its confirmation by a special to the *Herald* from Washington was
received with horror.   The noon despatches, which gave an idea
of slight danger, were joyfully received, and not until the later
despatches announced the President's almost hopeless condition
did people realize the terrible extent of the crime.   The call,
through the *Evening Commercial*, for a mass meeting was nobly
responded to.   The Rev. C. K. Marshall was called to the chair.
A short prayer was then offered by the Rev. C. B. Galloway for
the recovery of the President, and invoking the aid of God to
quell the passions of the people in this enlightened age, and
render the value of human life greater than it now seems to be.
Mr. Marshall addressed the meeting, and in a very affecting

manner reflected the sorrow of the whole community. The following resolutions were adopted:

Whereas, Our free Government, resting on the consent of the governed, was founded by our fathers to maintain life, liberty, and the pursuit of happiness;

Whereas, The peace, safety, and life of our Government, our families, ourselves, and all we hold sacred and dear depend on the preservation of law and order;

Whereas, Murder in its most vicious form is that which is committed by the assassin's hand, and

Whereas, We have heard with horror that a cowardly assassin has attempted to take the life of the President of the United States—therefore, be it

Resolved, That we, the people of Vicksburg, Miss., without regard to race, color, or condition, condemn the act of the assassin who attempted to-day to take the life of James A. Garfield, President of the United States, as a base and cowardly deed, subversive of our Government, destructive to the peace and order of society, repugnant to the laws and to the sense of the whole civilized world.

Resolved, That we offer our condolence to the nation for the calamity which has befallen us, and our heartfelt sympathies to the stricken members of his family.

THE FEELING IN OHIO.

INTENSE EXCITEMENT THROUGHOUT THE STATE—COMMENTS OF THE PRESS.

COLUMBUS, O., July 3.—The intense excitement throughout the State has not diminished in the least, and thousands have crowded around the bulletin boards and telegraph offices during the entire day. Governor Foster has been in the Executive office during the day receiving and sending despatches to nearly every part of the State. In accordance with the proclamation of the Governor, Mayor Peters has issued a request that the recommendations be fully carried out. The proclamation was read from the pulpits to-night in all the principal cities and towns in the State, and it is probable that divine service will be held in the morning by all denominations. The following is a double-leaded editorial from the *Times*, Democratic organ, and receives the unqualified approval of every one:

It would be too monstrous for human belief to think that any sane man could have a possible motive, either political or personal, for the murder of James A. Garfield, a man of noble and lofty character, of broad and liberal views, of the most genial personal deportment and bearing. His very warmest personal friends were his most radical political opponents. His political antagonism bred no personal animosities. If disappointment in search of office led to this diabolical crime, then, indeed, the country needs a cessation of professional office-holding. The attempted assassination of President Jackson years ago by a lunatic had been forgotten, when the villainous hand of John Wilkes Booth sent President Lincoln to a premature grave. Nothing since the death of Lincoln has so shocked and amazed the country as the assault upon President Garfield. It is a crime too monstrous to discuss with moderation so soon after its perpetration. The speedy arrest of the assassin but ill compensates for the blow struck at the public welfare. The country hoped much and had reason to hope much from President Garfield's great natural ability and acknowledged statesmanship. The factional fight in his party boded no evil to the country, but rather good. The fate of the Republic does not depend upon parties; it will survive them all, and still stand the wonder and admiration of the world. Its fate will not depend upon the life of President Garfield, although the country will sadly miss his services, now that it is entering upon the road to prosperity which he did his share in shaping. Many foolish persons on the streets insist that the empire alone would save the country. Shame! shame! Sacrilege at the very doors of death, and in the vestibule of the nation's temple of woe! If the assassin would seek the life of a man of such grand human traits as James A. Garfield, a thousand assassins would stand ready to slay a tyrant. No, no, the empire will not come. The death of the President will not take the life of the Republic. It will live on, supported by the love and the loyalty of the people; and while the people mourn for the dead, they will remember and emulate his many virtues, while they will bury in oblivion whatever of faults he may have had. Twice have we been called upon to write of the assassination of the nation's Chief Magistrate. We are too heart-sick to follow up the subject, to comment upon this most unprovoked and most unexpected atrocity. We refer our readers to the terrible details elsewhere. To Mrs. Garfield a nation's deep sympathy will be unstintingly extended.

The Ohio *State Journal,* in a carefully considered article, will say:

We have neither time, space, nor inclination to speak at length of these causes at present. Suffice it to say that they are almost wholly un-American and must be destroyed, root and branch, if this Republic is to live, and if liberty is to have an abiding place on the footstool of the Creator. We are unprepared to adopt any of the theories which have been advanced to account for Guiteau's crime. We prefer to wait for the facts. It may be the result of a conspiracy on the part of a faction to seize the control of the Government, for the purpose of rewarding its friends and punishing its enemies; but we are constrained to say that that theory strikes us as incredible, and the evidences to support it are insufficient. It may be that criminals, driven to the wall, driven to desperation, and seeing no hope of escape save through a change of administration, conspired together to compass the death of the President, and furnished this medium with the means and fortified him with the motives of gaining an infamous immortality. No one, however, should jump to that conclusion, for the proofs are lacking. It may be that men in office and men who expect office in certain contingencies, men who expected to be dismissed by the present Administration, or installed in office in the event of a change, have egged on this crazy villain to murder the President, but up to this writing there are not sufficient facts upon which to base such a conclusion. In our judgment, too much stress is laid on Guiteau's alleged insanity. If insane at all he is insane in the sense that murderers are and thousands of enthusiasts who can entertain but one idea at a time are insane. In that sense no sane man ever committed murder. A man who can plan a murder, provide himself with implements of death, and so time his movements as to make sure of his work and probably escape, is sane enough to be put to death, and the law is sadly defective in that it does not prescribe the same penalty for an attempt to kill that it does in the event of success. This plea of insanity has been pressed too far, and lawyers and courts ought to understand by this time that the people are growing wonderfully restive and impatient because of it. The successful interposition of that plea is the cause of more lawlessness, mobs, lynchings, and murders than any other one thing known in America.   Though necessarily alarmed and indignant, the American people can afford to keep cool, for in the language of President Garfield, used upon the occasion of the murder of one of his predecessors, "God reigns and the Government at Washington still exists.   No assassin can destroy the Government so long as the love of liberty and law has a home in the hearts of the American people."

Boston, Mass., July 4, 1881.

The following despatch was sent from the Israelites of Boston to-day :

New Era Hall, July 4, 1881.

Hon. James G. Blaine, Secretary of State, Washington, D. C.:

The Israelites of Boston, in convention assembled, extend their heartfelt sympathy for President Garfield and their intense indignation at the outrage committed on our honored Executive. Convey our profound sorrow and tenderest sympathy to Mrs. Garfield and family.   Our prayers are fervently offered that the President may recover and live to fulfil the promise of his grand career at the helm of our beloved country.

Edward S. Goulston, chairman ; Charles Morse, Israel Cohn and Isaac Rosnosky, committee.

Cincinnati, Ohio, July 4, 1881.

A Sabbath stillness characterized the city to-day.   Prayer-meetings were held at noon in several churches, and many prayer-meetings will be held to-night.   The Western Union Telegraph Company is using its wires without intermission both night and day, the entire force of operators being employed to the extent of their endurance in working extra time.   The old men and women of the Cincinnati Pioneer Association to-day sent a letter of condolence to Mrs. Eliza Garfield, mother of the President, and a similar message to the wife of the President.

Newport, R. I., July 4, 1881.

A public meeting to express sympathy for the President and his wife was held here to-day in Zion Episcopal Church, where the leading citizens of the place assembled.   Stirring addresses were made.

SPRINGFIELD, ILL., July 4, 1881.

Governor Cullom had an appointment to address the people of Lake county to-day, but in view of the condition of the President he instead issued a letter, in which he says: "While the Chief Magistrate of the nation lies upon a bed of pain, and per- haps of death, it seems to me befitting the seriousness of the hour, and in conformity with suggestive obligations of duty, that your Governor should not absent himself from the capita' of the State, and that the public rejoicing with which I hope(to greet you should, in our joint sorrow, be changed into and concentrated in a heartfelt prayer for the speedy recovery of our honored and beloved President. The occasion is more eloquent than language, and I need hardly commend to you and all others commemorating our nation's birth an obvious thought— even this sorrowful incident is a fervid witness to personal free- dom under the government of the United States—to its per- petuity, which hangs not upon any single life, either of citizen or President, and to its strength—before which all the provision of liberty shall remain fertile—and through which all offences against law shall meet just punishment.

WORCESTER, MASS., July 4, 1881.

A union prayer-meeting was held here in Mechanics' Hall at noon to-day. Fifteen hundred persons were present. Prayers were offered by the leading clergymen. Senator Hoar address- ed the meeting at considerable length. He said: "All the citi- zens here feel as though their first-born was lying at the point of death. There are times when we realize most deeply what we owe to our country. This is such an occasion, and no courage, no comfort except that which comes to Christian hearts from God's Word, can meet our wants. All pain must find relief in some articulate cry, but the only cry that can alleviate our pain is that cry to God which His ministers can best utter. The love of the people for the President is not misplaced. He has a great, brave, affectionate heart. He loves his country. He has a high conception of a pure administration; and if we are to lose him it will be the greatest single calamity except the death of Lincoln that has ever fallen upon this country.

Senator Hoar spoke of his own close personal relations with the President and of his glorious New England ancestry who participated in the first struggle of the Revolution. "Their

8

noble qualities," said Senator Hoar, "have descended to him. God grant that this precious life, this brave soul, this teeming brain may be spared. God grant that in this hour of peril all may share the faith and courage which fill his own soul."

CHEYENNE, W. T., July 4, 1881.

A mass-meeting of citizens was held to-day and passed resolutions expressing sorrow and sincere sympathy with President Garfield and condoling with Mrs. Garfield. The resolutions were telegraphed to Secretary Blaine, by Delegate Post. Speeches were made by Governor Hoyt, Secretary Morgan, Chief Justice Sener, Associate Justice Peck, General A. G. Brackett and a number of clergymen. The city had been decorated gayly for the Fourth, but the decorations were all taken down. The people are bowed in sorrow.

WILKESBARRE, PA., July 4, 1881.

Owing to the great calamity which has befallen the whole nation no demonstration was made here to-day. The excitement at the various bulletins concerning the welfare of the President is increasing.

LANCASTER, OHIO, July 4, 1881.

All the churches united in a prayer-meeting for the imperilled life of the beloved President to-day, and to-night a pall has settled over the city. Hundreds of people are in the streets feverishly awaiting the woeful intelligence that is momentarily expected.

ELBERON, LONG BRANCH, N. J., July 4, 1881.

The bulletins received this afternoon from Washington made everybody here joyful. The less favorable bulletins to-night have caused a revulsion of feeling, and sad and anxious faces are seen everywhere. Especially are the evidences of grief noticeable among the guests of the Elberon Hotel, where President Garfield had lately stopped. There were no festive demonstrations at all here to-day, the Mayor having prohibited the explosion of fireworks or powder, because of the nation's impending calamity.

SOUTHERN GRIEF AND ANXIETY.

COLUMBUS, GA., July 4, 1881.

At a public meeting of the citizens of this city, held in the Opera House to-day, the following resolution was unanimously adopted :

Resolved, That the chairman of this meeting be requested to send the following by telegraph to the Hon. James G. Blaine, as expressive of the unanimous sentiment of this community.

COLUMBUS, GA., July 4, 1881.

To the Hon. James G. Blaine, Secretary of State :

The people of Columbus, Ga., at a public meeting assembled, express their great abhorrence at the attempted assassination of the President of the United States. They deplore the act as a public calamity and resent it as a national outrage. Please signify these sentiments to the President, and assure him of our earnest wish for his recovery; also express to Mrs. Garfield our warmest sympathies in her great affliction.

MARTIN J. CRAWFORD, *Chairman.*

WALTER H. JOHNSON, *Secretary.*

RICHMOND, VA., July 4, 1881.

It is suggested here that Dr. Hunter Maguire, of this city, who was medical director of Stonewall Jackson's corps and is noted as a surgeon, be invited to Washington for the purpose of examining the President's wounds. He has made the treatment of gunshot wounds a specialty. It is said that Dr. Maguire has expressed an urgent wish to examine the President's case, and, if possible, to give the distinguished patient the benefit of his experience. Of course Dr. Maguire, observing professional etiquette, would not go to Washington unless specially invited to do so.

AUGUSTA, GA., July 4, 1881.

The City Council of Augusta has adopted resolutions expressing sorrow and indignation at the attempt to assassinate President Garfield, extending sympathy to his family and expressing the hope that the President would be spared to discharge for the good of the country the important duties of his exalted office.   Mayor May was instructed to telegraph the resolutions to the Department of State.

STAUNTON, VA., July 4, 1881.

The most intense sorrow prevails in this city in consequence of the President's condition.   Business is almost entirely suspended, and crowds gather around the bulletin boards.   A large meeting of the citizens was held to-night, and resolutions of sympathy for President Garfield were adopted.   A. H. H. Stuart, Secretary of the Interior under President Fillmore, presided, and a number of addresses appropriate to the occasion were delivered.

LYNCHBURG, VA., July 4, 1881.

The most intense solicitude is manifested here by men of all politicial parties in the fate of the President, and nothing but a sense of horror and indignation is expressed at the great crime against him and against the Republic.   Prayers were offered yesterday in all the churches for his speedy recovery.

MOBILE, ALA., July 4, 1881.

Great excitement still prevails in the city, and the universal expression is one of horror at the crime.   Crowds congregate around the telegraph office and deep sympathy is being felt. Bulletins are anxiously expected.

CHARLESTON, S. C., July.4, 1881.

The State Society of Cincinnati to-day adopted unanimously resolutions of indignation at and sorrow for the attempted assassination of President Garfield, which is aggravated by the fact of its commission almost on the eve of the anniversary of American independence.   They express their sympathy with their fellow-citizen, the President, who has been exposed to the weapon of the assassin because he was conscientiously discharging his duty to his countrymen in the exalted office to which he was called by the suffrages of a free people.

FREDERICKSBURG, VA., July 4, 1881.

The attempted assassination of the President has excited feelings of the most intense indignation here.   Resolutions of the Mayor and Council expressing detestation of the crime and solicitude for the President's wife were telegraphed to the Secretary of State on Saturday night, and yesterday prayers were offered in all the churches for his recovery. Telegrams from Washington are awaited anxiously to a late hour by all classes to learn the latest bulletins from the physicians in attendance upon the Chief Magistrate.

GALVESTON, TEXAS, July 4, 1881.

Specials to the *News* from all over this State report that the people everywhere in the State condemn, in the strongest terms, the attempted assassination of the President. Expressions of the most profound sympathy and deepest sorrow are pouring in from all points. The prevailing opinion is that it was the work of a madman.

NEW ORLEANS, LA., July 4, 1881.

Business is suspended, and eager crowds constantly surround the bulletin boards seeking news as to the condition of the President. A meeting of colored people, called to dedicate St. James's Hall, an institution of learning, adopted resolutions of sympathy and condolence in behalf of President Garfield, and forwarded them to his family through the Secretary of State. The Hancock Club adopted resolutions of profound regret and indignation at the dastardly attempt on the life of the President, praying that his life may be spared, to the end that the honor and integrity of American institutions may be sustained, and the administration of the Government continued under his conservative, wise, and just control.

COMMENTS OF THE PRESS.

PROBABLY no event in the history of our nation has caused such deep and widespread feeling among all classes, and we here present the feelings as expressed by the leading papers in the land.

From N. Y. Herald, July 3, 1881.

ATTEMPTED MURDER OF THE PRESIDENT.

Another President of the United States has fallen at the hands of an assassin in but little more than sixteen years from the time of the death of Abraham Lincoln. But, happily, the murderously intended blow has fallen short of its desperate purpose; for, though Mr. Garfield's present condition is one of great and pre-eminent danger, he still lives and has so far rallied from the first two perils of his position—shock and hemorrhage —as to afford some ground for the hope that he may survive his wounds.

Should he die his fate would be a national calamity; for where a man, called by the voice of the people to the highest office in their gift, is thus forcibly assailed by violence and crime—where the will of one wild ruffian is put against the predilection of the nation—the victim of his assault is entirely lifted out of his individual character and attains in an especial and peculiar sense a supremely representative quality; and every man of right mind feels that he is personally wronged by such a wrong against the head of the Government. Fortunately there seems to be the deepest possible distinction perceptible to all between this crime and that of the murder of President Lincoln, with which it is spontaneously compared in every man's thought. That was the outcome of fierce political passions; an expression of the final and desperate rage with which the less heroic elements of a conquered people regarded the man whom the conquerors delighted to honor. This, on the contrary, appears to be only the wild act of a madman. Demonstration could hardly make a fact plainer than it now is that the assassin was crazy, and that he acted under an insane impulse in his conception that to have refused him an office was an outrage that called for the sacrifice of life.

Within a few years the attempt to murder men at the head of governments has become a common crime; but we have generally assumed that this was a vice of the European system. The Kings of Spain and Italy and the Emperors of Germany and Russia have in turn been assailed by these desperate and savage attempts, and our people have seen in this only the frenzy of the down-trodden masses of the Old World driven to conspiracy as the one resort for protest against a dominion they could not otherwise control. But how can that too lenient view of this dreadful sort of butchery be reconciled with the fact that ours is the only country in the world in which in our time two Chief Magistrates have thus been stricken down. In Russia they recently murdered a Czar, and if now they should murder another we would be apt to regard that country as given over to desperate chances, and society there as standing in permanent peril of the assassin's plans. Yet in the United States one President, as near to the hearts of the people as ever was any ruler in human history, was ruthlessly shot down in a public place; and now a second, also a great popular favorite, a man of those large-hearted, amiable, manly traits that captivate and hold the admiration of the people, is brought low by the assassin's pistol, and lies upon a bed from which he may never arise. If it be not demonstrated that this murder is the mere irresponsible act of a lunatic we must revise entirely our ideas of this kind of crime; for it cannot be regarded as the necessary product of tyranny if it occurs oftener than elsewhere in the freest country in the world.

If there ever was a man in high station who might have been thought absolutely safe from a fate like this it was certainly the man who has now fallen, for he stood in the way of no man, and no men who could in any contingency whatever have been supposed capable of reasoning that his removal by this method would be to their advantage. In even the recriminations of recent political agitation the only word said against him personally was that he was of a too gentle temper. Only madness it might well be thought could conceive of the assassination of

the President as a remedy for any imagined evil under a system
of government like ours; but it must be a madness more than
ordinarily removed from all the paths of ratiocination that
could lead to the fancy that if great abuses were possible under
our government they could be practised by this fair, easy, open-
minded man, whose whole nature and character were as well
known to the people as their own faces in the glass.   It may be
a poor solace to the stricken ones of the President's family to
consider that the blow which bids fair to blight the life in
which they so naturally feel the most honorable pride comes
from a source of this nature, and yet there should be some
slight consolation in the thought that no rational enemy's will
was behind this dreadful blow.   For that venerable lady who
lately reflected that she was the only President's mother who
ever lived in the White House; for the dear wife to whom the
chivalrous gentleman sent his love as the tender remembrance
of the first moment of his recovery from the consternation of
the tragic assault; for the fine boys, full of the proud regard
that sons must feel for such a father, there cannot but be some
satisfaction in the thought that no man of the American people
possessed of his reason could feel towards the son, husband, and
father a murderous hate that could strike at his life; and they
may well feel comforted and helped by a national sympathy
deep and tender which desires the recovery of their beloved one
with an earnestness and ardor that can yield only to their own.

By the regular gradation of our constitutional law, familiar
to the whole people, Vice-President Arthur will succeed to the
position of Mr. Garfield in case he should die, and thus for the
fourth time in forty years the great importance of this secondary office has been shown.   But for this change of persons the
President's death can cause no political changes in a national
sense, whatever may happen in a party sense.   Those whom a
hasty generalization is likely to put into the position of men to
be benefited in party respects by this change are wise and just
to act in any way save one likely to impress deeply and certainly upon the minds of the people the conviction that they do
not want to be held responsible for any such view of this tragic
and most lamentable event, and that they would be the last of
all men to desire such advantage.

It is plain and clear enough to our own people that the tragedy has no political relations and is only an expression of the

insane impulse of an individual. But abroad, where they imagine us from late agitations to be in a fever of revolution, and where they do not know that the limit of party passion never rises to this height, the event will be misunderstood and misinterpreted and commented upon as one of the growing evils of our system.

From New York Times, July 3, 1881.

THE ASSASSINATION.

In the crime which was committed at Washington yesterday there is the very irony of fate. Considering his origin and the circumstances of his youth, no man has passed a career more remarkable or attained a dignity more striking than that of President Garfield. Beginning life the son of an almost penniless widow, forced to struggle as few men must for the bare maintenance of an equality with his fellow-men, he has risen step by step to one of the most honorable positions offered by the government of any nation. It was his fortune to fall upon a time when great opportunities awaited great qualities, and to all occasions he presented qualities not unworthy of them. He entered manhood as the political contest with slavery approached its crisis, and he threw all the energies of a strong nature on the side of freedom. From the field of discussion and the ballot the conflict with slavery was taken to the field of war, and without hesitation, with absolute devotion, with a courage which knew no fear, he entered on this new and terrible task. In all the tests of fitness for the citizenship of a free Republic to which he was subjected he won high distinction, until at last his country called him to the greatest office within its gift. And this President, to whom Americans had pointed proudly and justly as a splendid example of what our country and its cherished principles were able to do for manhood—simple manhood, unfavored of fortune and unaided by any inheritance of title or precedence —is shot down without a moment's warning by an assassin whose hatred was directed not to the man but to the President.

The whole country is bowed with deep grief and indignation at this event. It is inevitable that it should be. There are few men who enjoy, and none who deserve to enjoy, the name of American citizen to whom this crime does not bring a sense of personal sorrow and a profound feeling of patriotic humiliation.

8*

Whatever may have been the criticisms which they have passed upon the President, all American citizens must feel the " deep damnation " of this attempted " taking off." He was an obscure son of the Republic who had brought to its most distinguished post gifts of mind and character which conferred credit on the office, and almost at the outset of his term his life is assailed by a wretch who represents as distinctly the evil in our system as President Garfield represents the good. For, though the murderer was obviously of disordered mind, it is impossible to ignore the causes which led immediately to this act—which directed his ill-regulated will to its final aim. He was a disappointed office-seeker, and he linked the bitterness of his personal disappointment with the passionate animosity of a faction. His resentment was inflamed and intensified by the assaults upon the President which have been common in too many circles for the past few months. Certainly, we are far from holding any party or any section of a party responsible for this murderous act, but we believe it our duty to point out that the act was an exaggerated expression of a sentiment of narrow and bitter hatred which has been only too freely indulged. It is not too much to say, in the first place, that if Mr. Garfield had not been the chief of a service in which offices are held out as prizes to men of much the same merit and much the same career as this murderer he would not have been exposed to this attack. And while this is beyond dispute, it is also probable that the murderer's mad spite would not have been "screwed to the sticking point " if it had not been stirred by the license that has prevailed in certain quarters with reference to the President. The event, therefore, is one which may and ought to convey a lesson, which should teach us the folly and the wrong of the insane pursuit of office which our methods of public employment invite, which should show us the danger and disgrace of the unbridled political passion aroused by these methods. In a certain sense the act of Guiteau was an accident, for it was entirely out of the range of any ordinary motives, but it is not inexplicable; it is clearly of those accidents which bring more vividly to the mind the forces that create them.

From N. Y. Sun, July 3, 1881.

PRESIDENT GARFIELD—THE LAND PLUNGED IN MOURNING.

James A. Garfield, President of the United States, was shot and mortally wounded, by an insane assassin, at the Baltimore Depot in Washington, at about ten o'clock yesterday morning. He was removed to the White House, where he remains at the point of death.

The President had gone to the depot to take the train for New York, where, with several members of the Cabinet, he had an engagement to dine in the evening.

No event since the assassination of Abraham Lincoln has created such a shock. The sensation of profound sorrow is universal. The American people have but one heart to-day, and it is overwhelmed with grief at this sudden, unexpected, and tragic striking down of their Chief Executive Magistrate.

Fortunately, deplorable as this terrible event is, and although it will be attended by important personal consequences, the death of General Garfield will have no political significance. It was not the work of a party or of a faction, but was perpetrated by one man, who is understood to have been in a state of mental aberration at the time.

Our great holiday—the anniversary of the nation's birth—to-morrow will be converted into a day of universal sorrow over one of the saddest events in our whole national history.

The paths of glory lead but to the grave.

From N. Y. Tribune, July 3, 1881.

FACTION'S LATEST CRIME.

A second President lies stricken down by assassination. President Lincoln was murdered, not by the rebellion, but by the spirit which gave the rebellion life and force. President Garfield has been shot down, not by a political faction, but by the spirit which a political faction has begotten and nursed. But for that spirit, there was hardly a man in this country who seemed at sunrise yesterday more safe from murderous assault. A great-hearted, loving, kindly man, whose warm and genial nature had made fifty millions of people his personal friends,

President Garfield was immeasurably more popular yesterday than he was when the ballots of the nation made him its President. The party which he had defeated had learned to admire and love him. His political friends were thrilled with pride when they saw that he had already accomplished, in only four months, more than other Presidents in four years of service. It was felt by friends and foes that he was one of the ablest Presidents ever chosen, and the country looked forward with great hope to the grand work to be done by such a President during the rest of a term but just begun. And yet to-day the whole nation bows in sorrow. The noble President, the statesman whose deeds have already honored the nation throughout the world, the genial friend, the tender husband and loving father, has fallen by the shot of an assassin. There was no personal quarrel. It does not appear that the victim had ever known or seen his assailant. There is absolutely nothing to account for this horrible deed, which to a great nation is a terrible calamity, except a crazy spirit of faction.

Every true American will rejoice if it shall appear that the murderer was insane. Yet did not men call Booth a madman? Both were sane enough in all the ordinary walks of life; both had passed without question as men of sound minds, ill-balanced indeed, but entirely responsible; and both were sane enough to prepare with caution, thoroughness, and precision as to detail, for a deed towards which they were moved by a spirit shared by many others. It does not appear that the assassin of yesterday had ever been thought a lunatic, by any associate or acquaintance, until the deadly shots were fired. Was he "crazed by political excitement," then, as many say? At what point, if ever, did the madness of faction become the madness of irresponsibility? Do the leaders of faction ever intend all the mischief which grows from the wild and desperate spirit which they create, feed, and stimulate, week after week? Is it not their constant crime against self-government that, by kindling such a spirit, they send weak or reckless men beyond the bounds of right or reason? This assassin, it seems, was not ignorant that he was trying to kill one President and to make another. His language and letters prove that he knew what he was doing only too well. As "a Stalwart of the Stalwarts," his passion was intense enough to do the thing which other reckless men had wished were done. So the assassin Booth put into a bloody deed the malignant spite of thousands of beaten rebels. His deed stands in history as the cap-sheaf of the rebellion. So the spirit of faction which fired the shots of yesterday gave in that act the most complete revelation of its real character.

That political fanaticism has been showing itself before us all in many phases little short of madness. The country has seen the wildest ravings of abuse about the President, and has paid little attention—but not because it thought the men who uttered them insane. It has listened to malignant scandals which it has seemed impossible that sane citizens would utter regarding the Chief Magistrate of their country; but has listened with contempt, fancying that the fanaticism of faction would go no further. But curses and threats are followed at last by murderous shots, and the country starts with horror. Never again will any sane man cry, " I am a Stalwart of the Stalwarts !" Never again will a blind and furious fanaticism of faction seem to sane men a thing to boast of. As Booth ended the rebellion by showing what its real spirit was, so this horrid flash of light, which shows how narrow is the dividing line between faction's frenzy and Mexican assassination, will bring an end, let us hope, to a most shameful phase of partisanship in this country.

Truly, the ways of Providence are inscrutable. That this grand President, so great and good, so kindly and so true, whose life seemed so full of promise for the land, should be stricken down, seems beyond human understanding. And yet, the Infinite Father has been too good to this people for us to doubt that his care is over us still. Perhaps this nation needed to be taught some things which only a great affliction and shame could teach. Perhaps it needed to be taught that the worship of men had gone too far. Perhaps it was necessary in order to save this country from gradual Mexicanization, to force home the conviction that the spirit of faction is at war with the very existence of free institutions. Must we not realize, in the light of the dreadful calamity at Washington, that those who breed and nurse this malignant, selfish, grasping, and desperate spirit are aiming a blow at the life of the Republic ?

A BLOW AT REPUBLICANISM.

The bullet of the assassin who lurked in the Washington railway station to take the life of President Garfield shattered the simple Republican manner of life which the custom of nearly a century has prescribed for the Chief Magistrate of the United States. Our Presidents have been the first citizens of the Republic—nothing more. With a measure of power in their hands far greater than is wielded by the ruler of any limited monarchy in Europe, they have never surrounded themselves with the forms and safeguards of courts. The White House has been a business office open to everybody. Its occupant has always been more accessible than the heads of great commercial establishments. When the passions of the war were at fever heat, Mr. Lincoln used to have a small guard of cavalry when he rode out to his summer residence at the Soldiers' Home; but at no other time in our history has it been thought needful for a President to have any special protection against violence when inside or outside the White House. Presidents have driven about Washington like other people, and travelled over the country as unguarded and unconstrained as any private citizen.

All this, we fear, must come to an end now. The assassination of Mr. Lincoln was regarded as the outcome of the rage of the beaten rebellion. When the war was fully closed, and its fierce anger died away under the softening influences of peace, no one thought there could be any personal danger attaching to the Executive office. Strangers went every day to the President's room to prefer their requests, or stopped him in the street to shake his hand. He came in contact with multitudes of unknown people, any one of whom could have shot him had he chosen. We were proud of the freedom and simplicity of our President's way of living. Now General Garfield is stricken down by two cruel wounds from a murderous weapon, in a time of profound peace, when there is nothing to stir the passions of men save a pitiful contest over a few offices in a single State. Henceforth, alas, the President must be the slave of his office, the prisoner of forms and restrictions, for he will have reason to fear an assassin in every crowd that presses about him, and in every stranger who seeks to approach him. Who can blame him if he throws aside all the traditional ease, familiarity, and accessibility which have lightened the labors of the place in times past, and hedges himself in with ceremonials, soldiers, and official restrictions? Will not the country insist that he should do so? A President's life is the most valuable life in all the land, for it touches the interests of every citizen. It is far too precious to be left open to assault by any conspirator or madman who wishes to cut it short.

From the Philadelphia Press.

It is a strange and hideous mockery of reason that twice within the span of two decades our Government—the freest and best republic on earth—should be stained with the blood of its highest ruler. The tragic death of the beloved Lincoln was the dar:est page in our annals; and now we are startled with the swift and sudden repetition of that desperate and execrable deed which seemed to tower over all infamies as the unapproachable crime of the century. The country stands with bated breath to-day, as it did on that sad day sixteen years ago, not paralyzed, not trembling, not surrendering trust or hope, not doubtful that our institutions are equal to the severest strain; but wondering at the cruel fate which prostrates our cherished leader, and which casts over our enlightened liberty the shadow that we are accustomed to associate only with the dark despotisms of the Old World. No President since Lincoln has been more beloved than Gen. Garfield. None has commanded a greater degree of public confidence. . . . In the universal and profound horror which it excites, deep feeling and passion may associate with some political cause or inspiration, but such a thought is too monstrous to be entertained. No portion of the American people has yet descended to that depravity. We have not yet become so Mexicanized that assassination is employed as a political weapon. This crime, which plunges a whole nation into sorrow, is the deed of one maddened fanatic, crazed, it may be, by political excitement, and wrought into a morbid state by imaginary wrongs, but representing nothing but his own insanity.

From the Baltimore Sun.

In this community all personal, all partisan feeling seemed buried in the common sentiment of sorrow. While justly, perhaps, no political significance could possibly be attached to the act of a half-crazed assassin, the nation yet felt itself struck at and wounded in the person of its Chief Magistrate. It was the President as well the man who lay dying all day yesterday in the White House, and the whole country felt that the threatened loss and sorrow were its own. . . . Whatever the merits and qualifications of Vice-President Arthur may be, it is very certain that he was never seriously thought of by the American people in connection with the Presidential office. He was never named in the list of those upon whom the choice of the Chicago Convention might possibly fall. He was nominated for the second place, not the first. Although elected upon the same ticket, and by the same support, as President Garfield, he has been recognized as belonging to that wing of the Republican party which has arrayed itself in open and pronounced opposition to the President. His unexpected accession to the Presidency would signalize, therefore, a change of policy presumably almost as great as would follow from the election of a President of opposite politics.

From the Boston Traveller.

It is unutterably shameful and inexpressibly sad. Every friend of reaction, every enemy of liberty, every champion of strong, absolute government will take encouragement from this iniquitous deed. It is a plea for the rule of the Romanoffs and the Bonapartes, presented at the bar of history from the land of George Washington. Every citizen of the Republic will feel to-day the hot blush of shame on his face and a deep sen ʼf irreparable wrong at his heart. It is a crime utterly without excuse, evil, base, and damnable. Words will wholly fail to give expression to the feelings that will crowd for utterance from every honest heart. As the news of this outrage upon the human race speeds from one branch to another of the family of nations, they can but sit in silence and nurse the bitter wrath which they cannot hope to adequately express.

From the Albany Argus.

UNITED IN ABHORRENCE OF THE DEED.

In the abhorrence of the assassination, in the purpose never to let it be naturalized here as a means to vacate offices or to wreak the revenges of displaced men, in respect for the rights and persons of our rulers, in the resolve that murder shall be made as unprofitable as it is infamous, in adherence to the law and to the officials chosen by the law, we are all Democrats and we are all Republicans.

From the Albany Evening Journal.

A CHILD OF THE REPUBLIC.

No man ever deserved better of the Republic. He had conspicuously illustrated in his career the genius of our institutions; of the magnificent opportunity which it offers to wealth and intelligence. Every poor boy in the country had hope put in his bosom by reading his life. He was, in the best sense, a child of the Republic, the offspring of its distinctive ideas, and as such, the people, who so lately chose him as their Chief Magistrate, held him in the most respectful and affectionate regard.

From the New Orleans Times.

THE MOTIVE PECULIARLY MYSTERIOUS.

Inasmuch as the general feeling throughout the country towards President Garfield has been more kindly than has been known for many years past, the motive for the attempted assassination is peculiarly mysterious. Whether the wounds are fatal or not, the event must excite universal condemnation and regret.

From the Baltimore Sun (Dem.).

THE NATION WOUNDED.

In this community all personal, all partisan feeling seems buried in the common sentiment of sorrow. While justly, perhaps, no political significance could possibly be attached to the act of a half-crazed assassin, the nation yet felt itself struck at and wounded in the person of its Chief Magistrate. It was the President as well as the man who lay dying all day yesterday in the White House, and the whole country felt that the threatened loss and sorrow were its own.

From the Columbus (Ga.) Enquirer-Sun (Dem).

THE SOUTH HAS CAUSE FOR SADNESS.

The news of the attempt to take the life of the President caused intense excitement in this city. The deepest interest is felt throughout the entire community, and we but utter the sentiments of our citizens and of the whole people in this section when we express a sincere wish for his speedy recovery. Ilis death will be looked upon by our people as a public calamity. Business security, public progress, and civilization receive this blow of the assassin. The South has cause for sadness, the Union for tears.

From the Augusta (Ga.) Chronicle (Dem.).

A WAIL OF RIGHTEOUS INDIGNATION.

Because this is the American Union, and because our President is the fit ruler of a free people, a wail of righteous indignation swells in unbroken chorus over this whole land, protesting against the gigantic wrong, and demanding justice against the villain who horrified the Republic and disgraced the image of his Maker.

From the Richmond Dispatch (Dem.).

Though nations may swell the cry of indignation called forth by the attempt to assassinate the President of the United States, there will, in all the earth, be no sincerer mourners than the people of the Southern section of this Union. The true Southerner is a true man, and he despises treachery and cruelty and assassination. Well is it for the man who sped the bullet of the assassin that he did not do it in a Southern city; for hot Southern blood would have terminated his life without waiting to learn whether he was a maniac or not—as he was, we take it for granted. We all feel as if a personal wrong had been done to us—as if he were bone of our bone, and flesh of our flesh, who was basely assaulted in Washington yesterday. We claim him at once as our President, and if—which Heaven forbid—he should die in consequence of his wounds, every Southern house will go in mourning and every Southern heart will bleed, as every Southern tongue claims the martyr as its own.

From the Baltimore American (*Rep*).

A BLOW AT REPUBLICAN INSTITUTIONS.

The assassination of President Garfield is the most serious calamity that has befallen this country since the birth of the Republic. The death of Abraham Lincoln by the hand of Wilkes Booth, though not less terrible, was so plainly traceable to the malignant influences of the rebellion that it excited profound grief rather than actual alarm, and it did not for a moment raise a question as to the stability of the Government. The assassination of President Garfield, on the contrary, occurring at a time when the country is peaceful and prosperous, and the loyalty of the South has ceased to be a cause of apprehension, is in the nature of a blow struck at the very life of republican institutions.

Whether the assassin had accomplices or not—whether his design was known to those who were to profit by his crime or not—the fact stands out in startling prominence that the murderer was, by his own confession, inspired with the same motives that have actuated the third-term conspirators from the very beginning, and that he fired the fatal shot for the distinct purpose of accomplishing their plots by the succession of Mr. Arthur to the Presidency. He may be, as there is some reason to believe, a monomaniac; but his monomania is identical, except as to its practical result, with that of Conkling and Cameron, and Logan and Grant. If he was not the selected instrument of others, it will at least be admitted that a man better fitted for the work of an assassin could not well have been procured. Whatever may have been the part that this miserable wretch played, it is unhappily but too certain that the assassination of President Garfield is the logical outcome of the third-term conspiracy. The Stalwarts have indeed destroyed the President at last. What the ultimate consequences of this *coup d'état* will be it is impossible at the moment to predict. The event is still too recent to be looked at calmly.

From the Montgomery Advertiser

THE VOICE OF THE PRESS.

A gloom rests on the hearts of patriots in every section of the country. Its shadow already settles upon all the festivities of the Fourth of July, and the voice of sorrow rises above the song of joy and gladness. For the second time in the history of the Republic, the deadly bullet has been aimed at the life of the chief Executive. The murder of the lamented Lincoln remains a monument of shame and grief to the American people ; but it seems that even so ghastly a picture does not suffice for that brutal spirit whose satanic insanity defies the Ruler of the universe and feasts its savage revenge on human suffering. President Garfield is the second victim the assassin has sought in the person of the chief Executive of the millions whose glory has been that theirs is "the land of the free and the home of the brave." It is a most melancholy and humiliating reflection —the first officer of the Government shot down as though he were a culprit fleeing from justice ; it is a fact that sends a gloom over the whole land. It is the saddest sound that has ever fallen on the hearts of the oppressed millions of other lands, who would fain believe the American Republic the best and safest asylum on earth.

From the Buffalo Commercial Advertiser (Rep.).

A FOUL WRONG.

The calamity has revealed the firm hold that President Garfield has upon the esteem and affection of his fellow-citizens. That he may be spared and restored to the vigorous health that has been his blessing is the prayer that ascends to the Great Ruler of nations from the millions of people in this vast Republic. James A. Garfield, if he lives, will learn, after the trial to which he is now subjected, how sincerely he is respected by the people who so recently placed him in the highest office of their Government. There are no political lines now, when a nation is shocked by the reports of assassination, and mourns with the loved ones and loving wife who are gathered by the bedside of a wise father, a kind husband, and a faithful son. There are no distinctions of persons in this great nation at such a time, for all who are Americans by birth or by adoption cry out against a crime so heinous, and their hearts turn towards the victim of so foul a wrong.

From the Portland Advertiser.

The spoils system is directly responsible for the infamous outrage. It was because the appointing power is now vested in the arbitrary will of a President that Guiteau's malevolence was directed towards Garfield.

From the Boston Journal.

It was so impossible to conceive of any provocation for an attack upon the President, and it seemed so incredible that a career like his, as the honorably-elected leader of a great and free people, could be cut short by such weapons as are directed against kings and despots in Europe, that the first reports of the awful tragedy found few to accept them.

From the St. Paul Pioneer Press.

The half-crazy miscreant who committed this deed of horror struck to kill and rejoices in his infernal triumph. He claims himself a Stalwart of the Stalwarts, and a Conkling man, and boasts that he murdered the President as a political necessity to make Arthur President and reunite the Republican party. Doubtless he is crazy—the fact is duly certified to by his antecedents—but nothing but the most consummate craft could have planned a political assassination so opportunely for the purposes of the Stalwart chiefs who are benefited by it. The blow was struck just in the nick of time to save them from utter overthrow. A single life lay between them and the full possession of that power and patronage which they counted as the chiefest of earthly goods, and for which they had struggled with the firm disposition of hungry wolves, and that life has been snuffed by a murderer.

From the Boston Herald.

Sad and lamentable and far-reaching in its possible consequences as is this act of frenzy, it loses all sinister political significance when it appears as the deed of a disappointed office-seeker, who, through his disappointment, has lost his wits. Assassination has no place in our political system, if ever justifiable in a land of free speech and universal suffrage.

From the Hartford Courant.

There is probably no Government elsewhere that would be so little disturbed by such a crime.   The complicated wheels of the Executive machinery will hardly be checked for an instant if Garfield leaves us.   Should General Arthur become President there would be changes, but they would be chiefly in the mere *personnelle*.   In matters of general policy—notably in affairs of finance—he is in total accord with the present Administration. · · · · He calls himself a "Stalwart," whatever that may be; but it is a lie to give him only a political significance which he never possessed.

From the Buffalo Morning Courier.

In the face of such a calamity as the assassination of the President, it behooves us to remember that the man struck down in the prime of his glory was the representative and chief ruler of us all; that in him was personified the majority of the Republic; that to him was due the hearty allegiance of every citizen during the term for which the majority had chosen him.   The Democrats opposed General Garfield's election, and were outspoken in their criticisms of what they deemed his faults; but he was their President, no less than the President of the men who voted for him, and they feel the shock of the pistol shot that struck him down no less than their Republican neighbors.   This is the essence of our nationality.   The attempted assassination seems to be the act of an irresponsible and isolated lunatic, and not the result of a conspiracy with its root striking down into some mysterious social organization, or nourished by bitter fruitfulness of some political grievance.   Every suspicion that any American politician, even in the heat of a struggle of parties or factions, would resort to assassination as a means of putting a rival out of the way, should be set aside resolutely.   In addition to our sense of the public calamity we are simply content to express our grief for the genial, kindly man, possibly to be snatched away from life in a moment when life had everything to promise for his enjoyment; our sympathy for the gentle wife, who all day yesterday ran a race with death on her dreary journey to Washington, and our sorrow for the fine old mother who has seen all the glories of her son suddenly darkened in death's eclipse.

From the Chicago Inter-Ocean.

Throughout the day and night people watched with the suffering President, and in this vigil there came to them thoughts that come only to a free people in great crises. There was in no quarter any excuse for the act or any expressed or implied sympathy for the murderer. There was no disposition, except among the shallow-pated and little-souled, to turn the tragedy to political account, and the maudlin mutterings of this class were promptly rebuked. The people, to their credit be it said, saw the attempt on the life of the President in the light of a menace against the Government, and a crime against our civilization. They were more than the friends of General Garfield; they were the champions of good government protesting against any philosophy, any fanaticism, any Nihilistic tendency, however slight, that would excuse such a crime anywhere or that would fail to condemn it. If President Garfield should live through this crisis all the people will be reverent in their thankfulness and as one man in their rejoicing. Should he die they will turn in their sorrow and wrath to crush out all the un-American mushroom sophistry that makes assassination possible.

From the Hartford Evening Post.

How far is the moral responsibility of men in their right minds, controlled purely by their own selfish interests and ambitions, affected in tracing the causes of this assassin's irresponsible act? How much has all the talk of the severely exercised Stalwart organs and apostles contributed to upset the balance of a weak mind, already disturbed by personal disappointment? If this poor, weak fellow has been about Washington, nursing his grief from day to day, he must have habitually read the daily diatribes of the so-called Washington organ of the Conkling faction and the star route gang.

From the New York Times, July 4.

THE FEELING TOWARDS THE PRESIDENT.

Most of our readers must have been struck during the past forty-eight hours by the peculiar tenderness and affection with which the public have spoken of the President. It was natural that there should have been grief and indignation and humiliation over the attempted assassination, but we think that the hearty and kindly tone which pervaded the general comments on the President himself was a grateful surprise to most. It was not with the people at large simply that the chief Executive had been so cruelly struck down, or that our national reputation had suffered a shock; this was inevitable and was deeply felt; but what, we think, most observers were not prepared for was the wide outburst of unreserved sympathy and admiration and downright love for Mr. Garfield. Nor was this confined to his own party by any means. It was even more marked among those who had been politically opposed to him, who belonged to the party which, in the late canvass, was most bitter and abusive towards the Republican candidate.

This is a feature of the terrible experience through which the nation is passing which is of most hopeful significance. It shows that however reckless and violent may be the demonstrations of passion and prejudice in our party contests, they do not express the real and abiding temper of the people. They necessarily attract great attention, and appear to be the outgrowth of general sentiment; but the quiet and sincere feeling of the great mass of citizens is not only out of sympathy with but opposed directly to these manifestations. In Mr. Garfield's case this is particularly gratifying, because, while he has been a man of unquestioned and deserved distinction in public life for many years, his reputation has only lately been really national, it has only been recently that he has really been known to the whole people. The sentiment that has been manifested towards him has been brought into existence within the past year, and is a remarkable proof of the sane and sound manner in which the people do, in fact, frame their judgments, however reserved they may be ordinarily in giving form to them. Undoubtedly the basis of the affection which has been so strikingly exhibited during the last two days is the conviction of the essential rectitude of the President's character. Following his course in its broad features, the people have thoroughly approved of it. They have seen him vindicated very promptly in the selection of his Cabinet by the undoubted ability and elevation of purpose which the most active members of it have shown. They have watched his relations with the Senate, and have seen him courageous yet discreet, firm and dignified without obstinacy, showing no ill temper, and bearing with cheerful patience the wickedest attacks upon his motives. There has been nothing heroic, or brilliant, or imposing in his course; but it has been sensible, sincere, practical, and honorable, and it had undoubtedly given rise to a very strong sentiment of respect and confidence in the public mind.

Suddenly came the attempted assassination. The hourly bulletins from Washington described Mr. Garfield as bearing himself, in the face of almost certain death and under the most poignant suffering, with perfect composure and fortitude. Then the popular regard was instantly intensified into fervid affection and admiration. Every heart felt a tender pride in hearing that the wounded and possibly dying President had preserved the bearing of a soldier in the presence of pain and peril as great as if he had fallen on the battle-field. Mr. Garfield's splendid nerve, his patient and chivalric abnegation of self, his unfaltering manliness, appealed powerfully to the best feelings of every nature. And there was no American heart so callous that it was not moved by the simple eloquence of the despatch he dictated to his absent wife. These incidents brought out the personal character, the nobility and simplicity and solid excellence of the President. The knowledge of them instantly made a place for him in the intimate affection of his fellow citizens. These felt that he was, in the saddest and severest trial to which a man could be subjected, showing himself every inch a man. There was a sense of deep satisfaction that if it was our fate to furnish the miserable assassin whose mad and cowardly cruelty must disgrace the nation, our President, the elected highest representative of the entire people, was redeeming our name by the magnificent qualities which he was manifesting. This capacity for instant recognition and admiration of manliness is of no small value to a people, for its basis is sympathy with the virtue to which it is directed; and in the hearty affection that has everywhere gone out towards Mr. Garfield is an evidence of the essential soundness of the popular heart—an evidence which

9

some conspicuous incidents in our recent political life have rendered peculiarly welcome.

New York Tribune, July 4.

A NATION IN SUSPENSE.

While the stricken President still struggles between life and death a great and unwonted anxiety fills the public mind. It arises from two sentiments which the shock of this terrible calamity has clearly revealed. One is the affection and confidence in which General Garfield is held by the people, and the other is the dread of what may come after him if the "Stalwart" assassin's bullet proves to have done its work effectively.

No one knew until Saturday how strong a hold our President had gained upon the hearts of the people of this country. His honest, open, noble nature, his genial friendliness, his quick sympathy with all classes and conditions of men, had as much endeared him to our affections as his genius and great services had commended him to our admiration. He was the people's President, one of them in his origin, in his early struggles, in his honorable success, in the sturdy national strain of his character and mind. While he had attained by his great talents and splendid industry a place beyond the reach of competition years ago, and had afterwards been raised to the highest station upon earth attainable through the free choice of a people, he never lost the popular qualities which rendered him less an object of envy than of hearty personal regard, not only among the thousands who knew him, but also among the millions to whom he was merely a name and a type of greatness due to merit and to labor. The controversy forced upon him at the very outset of his administration, the good-natured firmness, utterly devoid of arrogance and bluster, with which he pursued the course he thought required by his self-respect and the best interests of the country, resulted in a great increase of his popularity among a people who like firmness and courage, most especially when accompanied with sense and modesty and free from arrogance and selfishness. Just at the moment when his fellow-citizens had begun to appreciate him and love him most, the bullet of the assassin laid him low, and the tenderest compassion was added to their former regard. By the every-day miracles of the telegraph and the printing-press working together the whole mass of the people have been admitted to his bedside, and have scanned his every action and expression since the blow was struck. In these long hours of pain and mortal peril they learned anew how brave and true and tender a soul their great ruler possessed. His calm resignation to the will of heaven; his absence of all feeling of resentment against his assassin and his enemies; the knightly devotion with which his first care was given to breaking the news and sending his love to his faithful wife; his cheerful serenity, lightened even to jocularity, with his friends at his bedside; his words of comfort to his weeping children; the indomitable will and courage with which, when his physician informed him that he had one chance in a hundred of living, he replied, "Then we will go in on that chance"—all these things have touched the hearts of millions, and turned their admiration and regard to warm and anxious affection. Yesterday, from thousands of churches, prayers went up to Heaven for the safety of a life that had suddenly grown more precious than ever, and last night there were few family altars in the land that did not send up the same petition with passion and tears.

The pain of his loss, if it be the will of Heaven that the nation shall lose him, seems therefore a sorrow too great to be borne, at this hour, when the people seem first to have come to a full and adequate knowledge of him. But mingled with this sentiment of sorrow is another which it is our duty as chroniclers to record. It is a feeling everywhere expressed on Saturday, and yesterday as well, that what is known of the Vice-President is not of a nature to inspire that full measure of confidence which would afford the only consolation possible in a disaster like the present. General Arthur is a gentleman of many accomplishments and many amiable and engaging qualities. He is represented to us by those who know him well as one of the most upright of citizens, one of the most loyal and devoted of friends. It is precisely here that the public mind finds its cause of doubt and apprehension. It is feared that he is more devoted to his friends than to the public welfare; that he can see nothing but good in them, and nothing but evil in their opponents. If this be true, and if the grief and misfortune is in store for us of losing the noble, enlightened, placable and generous ruler, whom we chose in joy and hope last year, then the bitterness of the present sorrow and the weight of the present anxiety will be as nothing to what we shall have to endure in the four troubled years which are to come.

From the Philadelphia Times.

Had the assassin's deed been done in the tempest of revolution, there might have been something to plead in extenuation of the crime ; but the animating purpose and the circumstances which precipitated the act are, if possible, more terrible to contemplate than the murder itself. That assassination should become the weapon of inflamed faction, and that trembling political criminals should murder the President of the great Republic of the earth, with the boast of crime mingling with the groans of the murdered ruler, make the bitterest cup ever presented to the lips of our free people, and its consequences are beyond the power of man to measure. If one so beloved and respected as James A. Garfield can be murdered under the very shadow of the Capitol when peace and plenty abound throughout the land, when the passions of sectional strife have been stilled, when the waves of party conflict have been calmed, and when only the murmur of the spoilsman could be heard in discord with the general tranquillity, then indeed is the gloom that encircles the nation impenetrable.

From the St. Louis Post-Despatch.

A DEPLORABLE EVENT.

A more deplorable event than this could **hardly have happened.** Of all countries in the world this is the one in which the weapon of an assassin should never be directed against men in authority. Our political system affords a ready relief, and there is no grievance against a ruler which cannot be reached through peaceful methods. It is plain that the terrible act of this man Guiteau can have no political significance. Having given himself to office-seeking he probably brooded over his disappointment until his mind was overthrown.

From the Columbia (S. C.) Register.

THE SADDEST OF TIDINGS.

The whole country is overwhelmed with consternation and sorrow at the terrible tidings the wires bring us of the shooting of President Garfield. We all feel, in this section of the country, that no sadder tidings could come to us than the death of Garfield, the chosen Executive of the people of the whole country. It is true, we believe, that the unboughten voice of the people of the free States of the Union would have seated Winfield S. Hancock; yet James A. Garfield has been installed into office without one word of dispute as to his lawful election, and as such he sits in the seat of Washington and Adams, Jefferson and Jackson—as much the President of the whole country as ever they were. The people of the South, although they claimed nothing at the hands of President Garfield but a lawful administration of the country's affairs, had reached a well-defined hope that the whole country would enjoy under Garfield another administration of peace and rest and comfort, which would push us along the road to enduring peace and a well begun prosperity. If this is all to be dashed by the hand of an assassin, and Vice-President Arthur takes the seat as a declared partisan of the most declared Stalwart stripe, then indeed is there trouble enough in the land to cover it with thick mourning. To attribute this diabolical deed to any faction in the country without further evidence than we have would be manifestly unjust. Yet the whole country must open its eyes to the fact as to who the beneficiaries will be by the event of the untimely, brutal, and cowardly slaying of our President; and should any Administration coming into power attempt to put us back under the Grant policy, the whole country will know the reason why, and see the power behind the assassin's weapon that slew the man who made a third term impossible. If any man can take comfort in all this wide land at the terrible blow at the whole country's heart, we, of the South, at least, bend our heads in deep sorrow whilst the bloody work flourishes over us.

From the Springfield (Mass.) Republican.

CONSUMMATION OF THE SPOILS SYSTEM.

The assassination of an American President is an event so terrible that we are glad that it is not devoid of meaning and of political significance.   A railroad collision or a madman might have been the means of President Garfield's death, but if he must be taken off by violence, and particularly by crime, let us rejoice that his death means something.   The assassination of President Garfield by a disappointed office-seeker is the consummation of the spoils system.   Guiteau is a miserable ne'er-do-well, who shares the common feeling that all the offices are in the dispensation of the President of the United States, and that he has a claim on that functionary for patronage.   He is in sympathy with Arthur and Conkling in the struggle over the New York Custom House.   His wits have become only a degree more disordered than those of Conkling himself, and being a much weaker and feebler man his vengeance has taken the direct and vulgar form of a pistol shot, rather than the more refined form of resigning the seats of the Republican majority in the United States Senate and demanding a vindication from the State of New York.   The practice of centring all patronage in the President, making his will and the will of his favorites the supreme test whether civil servants shall be retained or dismissed, regardless of their efficiency and regardless of the terms for which they were appointed—this dictatorship of the offices can but have the effect to centre upon the President all the intrigue and hostility of those disappointed, the desperate political opposition of senators and men of high position, and the malignity, hatred and violence of men of low instincts.

From the Albany Express.

JUSTICE BAFFLED.

In the presence of such a dastardly deed justice stands baffled. "Life for life," indeed.   Scores of lives might well be offered up to save the life of the President; but the death of millions of Guiteaus cannot avenge the shocking crime which this wretch has committed, nor can it be adequately punished by man.   It is to be deeply deplored, not only because it may remove from office one whose abilities, acquirements and accomplishments adorned the position, but because it inspires profound distrust of the personal safety of the President of a free people, engaged in the discharge of the duty to which they called him, whenever he disappoints a desperado who may dare to seek office at his hands.

From the Chicago Tribune.

THE PEOPLE OVERWHELMED.

The assassination of President Garfield has naturally shocked the national mind, and for the time overwhelmed the hearts of the entire people. It has rarely been the fortune of any man to be elected to the Presidency and enter upon the duties of the office under such favorable circumstances. To his aid he had called a Cabinet of able and experienced statesmen, and during the four brief months of his administration he had won the confidence of the great mass of the American people. The action of the assassin was deliberate. To the credit of the country it must be borne in mind that there is nothing in his attempted deed of murder prompted by popular complaint of the government, of the laws, or of the President personally. It was the act of a man of crazed mind seeking infamous notoriety, and madly believing he would find some one to glorify him. The country will unquestionably and without a dissenting voice acquit those at political variance with General Garfield of all complicity or knowledge of this atrocious deed. At the same time it will be remembered that this crazy demon was in that mental condition to be influenced by current events of the day, and the fact that a faction in New York was striving to defeat the administration was just such an event as would suggest to the mind of this man seeking notoriety that the removal of the President would terminate the contest, unite the party, and perhaps win for himself the gratitude of the victors. While no sane man will admit a suspicion that this attempted assassination has any connection with the New York case, still, on the theory that this assassin was deranged in his mind, and taking his own letters as indicating the direction of his insanity, no one will question that had not that factious controversy taken place this attempted murder would not have suggested itself to this man Guiteau. Even this does not establish any responsibility on the part of any one besides Guiteau for the deed itself, but it will rise in men's minds, and whether the President shall die or recover it will survive as part of the history of the whole murderous transaction, even long after the present generation shall have passed away. If anything could add to the universal grief of the American people over the attempted assassination of President Garfield, the anticipation of three and a half years' government under Mr. Arthur, and all which that implies, will be by the American people generally accepted as a pending national calamity of the utmost magnitude.

From the Knoxville (Tenn.) Tribune.

NOT DUE TO NIHILISM.

The attempt upon the life of the President is deeply deplored by every one we have heard express themselves. It is a fortunate thing for us as a nation that the calamity has occurred at a time when the world may be shown that no spirit of Nihilism instigated the deed or directed the hand of the assassin, and that it may not be traced to the great party schism now assailing this government; that, in short, it can be traced to neither North nor South as an indicative sentiment.

From the Chicago Times.

THE ASSASSIN NOT A MADMAN.

The man who has attempted to take the life of the President is not a madman. He is a very rational office beggar. He is one of a large class of citizens who have been educated by American politics and politicians to regard public offices not as places of public trust to which no individual person could set up any claim, but as the spoils of success to be fairly claimed as rewards by persons who have contributed by their efforts to the success of those higher trustees who hold the power to bestow them. He is a disciple of the political gospel preached by William L. Marcy and practised by Andrew Jackson; preached by Roscoe Conkling and Chester A. Arthur and John A. Logan, and not practised to the pleasure of either the assassin or his illustrious preceptors by President Garfield. As the assassin of President Lincoln (whose name and place were not material) was a product of public disease, which manifested itself in the pro-slavery rebellion, so the intending assassin of President Garfield (whose name and place also are not material) is a product of a public disease called the "spoils system." More notable products of the same disease are Conkling and Arthur and Logan. Every citizen who is not at heart a political assassin will earnestly peti- tion Almighty God to spare the life of President Garfield and save this land from the impending national calamity, the succes- sion of Chester A. Arthur to the Presidential office. Is it not also a good time for all good men to supplement their petitions for help to the throne of Heaven with resolutions to make all possible exertions to enable the people to help themselves by eradicating the infamous spoils system and abolishing the super- fluous contrivance called the Vice-Presidency.

From the Buffalo Courier.

NOT THE RESULT OF A CONSPIRACY.

In the face of such a calamity as the assassination of the President it behooves us to remember that the man struck down in the prime of his glory was the representative and chief ruler of us all; that in him was personified the majority of the repub- lic; that to him was due the hearty allegiance of every citizen during the term for which the majority had chosen him. The Democrats opposed General Garfield's election, and were out- spoken in their criticisms of what they deemed his faults; but he was their President no less than the President of the men who voted for him, and they feel the shock of the pistol shot that struck him down no less than their Republican neighbors. This is the essence of our nationality. The attempted assassina- tion seems to be the act of an irresponsible and isolated lunatic, and not the result of a conspiracy with its roots striking down into some mysterious social organization or nourished by bitter fruitfulness of some political grievance. Every suspicion that any American politician, even in the heat of a struggle of par- ties or factions, would resort to assassination as a means of putting a rival out of the way should be set aside resolutely. In addi- tion to our sense of the public calamity, we are simply content to express our grief. Genial, kindly man, possibly to be snatched away from life in a moment when life had everything to promise for his enjoyment! Our sympathy for the gentle wife who all day yesterday ran a race with death on her dreary journey to Washington, and our sorrow for the fine old mother who has seen all the glories of her son suddenly darkened in death's eclipse!

9*

WORDS OF SYMPATHY.

LONDON, July 3, 1881.

THE news of the attempted assassination of President Garfield reached London this afternoon in time to be printed in the last editions of the evening papers; too late, however, to become known to the general public until a much later hour.   In fact, the people living at the West End and in the suburbs are yet, in many cases, unaware of the tragedy, owing to the fact that the special editions of the evening papers are not published later than six o'clock.   The news first obtained general circulation in the theatres—at Covent Garden, where Patti was singing, at Her Majesty's, where it was a Nilsson night, and at the Princess', where there was a revival of Bronson Howard's play, "The Old Love and the New."   A general exodus of Americans took place after the sad news became known, and their departure caused visible vacancies in the stalls and boxes. Thenceforward a stream of inquirers, among them many ladies in opera dress, poured into the *Herald* office, into Minister Lowell's private residence, and into the American Exchange, all anxious to learn the latest particulars.   At the hotels and the American Exchange numbers stayed up until daylight this morning waiting for the bulletins forwarded by you to the London office.   It is not too much to say that scarcely an American family in London retired to rest until they had received news of your latest bulletin telling of the almost hopeless condition of the sufferer.   Telegrams keep pouring in from all parts of the United Kingdom asking for detailed information.

OFFICIAL DESPATCHES.

The news was received at the Foreign Office a little before four o'clock, and a message was immediately forwarded to Lord Granville at his private residence.   He at once communicated it to the other members of the Cabinet and to the Queen at Windsor, who was deeply moved by the startling intelligence. During the afternoon Lord Granville called twice at the Legation to inquire after the condition of the President. Later in the evening Minister Lowell received the following despatch from Her Majesty :

" *Sir Henry Ponsonby, Windsor Castle, to His Excellency Mr. Lowell, United States Minister :—*

"The Queen has heard with the deepest concern the report of an attempt having been made on the life of the President, and sincerely trusts that the rumors of his having been seriously wounded are untrue. Her Majesty would be glad to learn any news you may be able to give her."

This despatch was immediately communicated to the Secretary of State at Washington.

COMMENTS OF THE "OBSERVER."

The following appears in this morning's *Observer* in double lead: "A most profound and sincere feeling of regret will be occasioned by the news we publish this morning of a dastardly crime of which the President of the United States has been the victim. There is no evidence as yet that the attempted assassination comes under the category of political crimes. Mr. Garfield owes the attempt upon his life, in as far as is known, to the fancied grievance sustained by some dismissed official. Regicide, however monstrous in itself, is still an intelligible crime—that is, a crime for which it is possible to assign a motive; but to kill one President with the view of making room for another is an act of insane folly, as well as wickedness, which is hardly likely to be committed by any man in his senses. It is too early yet to form any opinion as to the President's chances of recovery, but our American kinsmen may rest assured that the intelligence from Washington will be awaited almost as eagerly by Englishmen as by the President's own fellow countrymen."

Telegrams from far and near conveying Expressions of Sorrow, and the Answers sent.

SECRETARY BLAINE TO MINISTER LOWELL.

WASHINGTON, July 2.—The following has been forwarded by cable:

DEPARTMENT OF STATE,
WASHINGTON, D. C., July 2.

James Russell Lowell, Minister, etc., London:

The President of the United States was shot this morning by an assassin named Charles Guiteau. The weapon was a large-sized revolver. The President had just reached the Baltimore and Potomac station, at about 9.20, intending, with a portion of his Cabinet, to leave on the limited express for New York. I rode in the carriage with him from the Executive Mansion, and was walking by his side when he was shot. The assassin was immediately arrested, and the President was conveyed to a private room in the station building and surgical aid at once summoned. He has now, at 10.20, been removed to the Executive Mansion. The surgeons, on consultation, regard his wounds as very serious, though not necessarily fatal. His vigorous health gives strong hopes of his recovery. He has not lost consciousness for a moment. Inform our Ministers in Europe.   JAMES G. BLAINE,
Secretary of State.

MINISTER LOWELL TO SECRETARY BLAINE.

LONDON, July 2.

Blaine, Secretary, Washington:

Telegram received. Express to Mrs. Garfield the profound sympathy of this legation. Queen has sent to inquire and express solicitude.   LOWELL,
Minister.

EARL GRANVILLE TO MINISTER THORNTON.

LONDON, July 2, 5 P.M.

Thornton, Washington:

Is it true that President Garfield has been shot at? If so, express at once great concern of Her Majesty's Government and our hope that report that he has sustained serious injury is not true. GRANVILLE,

Foreign Office, London.

GENERAL HANCOCK TO GENERAL SHERMAN.

GOVERNOR'S ISLAND, N. Y., July 2.

To General W. T. Sherman, Washington :

I trust that the result of the assault upon the life of the President to-day may not have fatal consequences, and that in the interest of the country the act may be shown to have been that of a madman. Thanks for your despatch and for your promise of further information. W. S. HANCOCK.

GENERAL GRANT TO SECRETARY LINCOLN.

ELBERON, N. J., July 2.

To Secretary Lincoln, Washington :

Please despatch me the condition of the President. News received conflicts. I hope the most favorable may be confirmed. Express to the President my deep sympathy and hope that he may speedily recover. U. S. GRANT.

MINISTER LOWELL TO SECRETARY BLAINE.

LONDON, July 3, 1881.

To Blaine, Secretary, Washington :

Just received the following from the Queen : " I am most anxious to hear latest accounts of the President, and wish my horror and deep sympathy to be conveyed to him and Mrs. Garfield." LOWELL,

Minister.

SECRETARY BLAINE TO MINISTER LOWELL.

Sunday.

Lowell, Minister, London :

Please convey to her Majesty, the Queen, the thanks of the President and Mrs. Garfield for her repeated expressions of sympathy and interest. Inform her Majesty that at this hour, 12.30, the condition of the President is much improved, and his symptoms are regarded as favorable, or at least hopeful.

BLAINE,
Secretary.

MR. EVARTS AND OTHERS TO SECRETARY BLAINE.

PARIS, July 3.

Blaine, Secretary, Washington:

Our countrymen receive successive accounts of President's condition with profound sorrow and deepest sympathy with public and private affliction. We receive expressions of condolence and of horror at crime from representatives of other nations. We still cherish hopes of favorable issue, and desire to express our heartfelt sympathy in the grief that surrounds the President.

EVARTS.
THURMAN.
HOWE.
HORTON.

C. H. GROSVENOR TO COLONEL ROCKWELL.

ATHENS, OHIO, July 3, 1881.

Colonel A. F. Rockwell, Executive Mansion, Washington:

The first encouraging word has filled us all with joy. May God save the President.   C. H. GROSVENOR.

H. D. D. TWIGGS TO COL. ROCKWELL.

AUGUSTA, GA., July 3, 1881.

Colonel A. F. Rockwell, Washington:

The people of this city and of Georgia generally profoundly sympathize with the President and with the country in the present calamity. Prayers for his recovery will be offered in the churches to-day.   H. D. D. TWIGGS.

W. H. ROBERTSON TO SECRETARY BLAINE.

ALBANY, July 3.

To the Hon. James G. Blaine, Secretary of State, Washington:

Will you tell me the President's present condition? Reports vary greatly. Reassure him of my deepest sympathy with him in this hour of the nation's peril, and with Mrs. Garfield in the terrible affliction. Prayers more fervent and earnest than ever before for any man, or any cause, will go up to-day from every church and every loyal heart in the land that he may be spared. May a kind Providence grant the petition.

W. H. ROBERTSON.

H. A. BARNUM TO COL. CORBIN.

NEW YORK, July 3.

Colonel H. C. Corbin, Executive Mansion, Washington:

What is the condition of the President at this hour? God grant his preservation to the nation he has served so well and the myriad of friends who love him as a brother.

H. A. BARNUM.

SECRETARY BLAINE TO MR. ROBERTSON.

WASHINGTON, July 3.

The Hon. William H. Robertson, Albany, N. Y.:

We grow more and more encouraged as to the final result, though still most deeply anxious. The President's condition has steadily improved since last night at nine o'clock, and now, at 3 P.M., he is doing as well as his physicians could possibly hope. He has never lost consciousness or courage for a moment, and awaits the issue with more calmness than his surrounding friends.　　JAMES G. BLAINE,
Secretary of State.

GOV. CORNELL TO SECRETARY BLAINE.

ALBANY, July 3.

The Hon. James G. Blaine, Secretary of State, Washington:

This morning's tidings, which were awaited with extreme anxiety, have been received with reverent thankfulness. The improved condition of the President is gratefully accepted as the basis of hope for his early convalescence. Assure the President that the people are thoroughly united in expressions of horror and indignation on account of the wicked crime, as well as in prayerful solicitude for his speedy and complete restoration.　　ALONZO B. CORNELL.

WASHINGTON, July 3.

To the Hon. Alonzo B. Cornell, Governor, etc., Albany, N. Y.:

The President's condition has steadily improved for the past eighteen hours. He is now, at 3 o'clock P.M., doing as well as his physicians could hope. We all feel greatly encouraged, though still profoundly anxious. The President returns his sincere thanks for your warm expressions of sympathy. He bears up wonderfully, and faces death with the calmness of true Christian courage.　　JAMES G. BLAINE,
Secretary of State.

MADRID, July 3, 1881.

To Spanish Minister, Washington:

In the name of the King express to the Government of the United States the profound sorrow that the attempt against the President's life has caused in Spain. His Majesty and his Government fervently hope for the recovery of President Garfield.

LISBON, PORTUGAL, July 3.

Blaine, Secretary, Washington:

Am horrified by the attempt upon the President's life. Await intelligence with intense anxiety.　　MORAN.

JACKSONVILLE, FLA., July 3.

The Hon. James G. Blaine, Secretary of State, Washington:

The citizens of Jacksonville, in common with the entire country, are shocked at the intelligence of the attempted assassination of the President, and desire that you express to Mrs. Garfield their sincere sympathy in this hour of her deep grief, and their hope that the President may be spared to the country, the genius of whose institutions he so grandly illustrates.
MORRIS A. DZEALINSKI,
Mayor of Jacksonville.

COLUMBUS, OHIO, July 3.

The Hon. James G. Blaine, Secretary of State:

The continued favorable reports are gratefully received. I have requested the people of the State to assemble in the churches to-morrow to engage in devotion to Almighty God, and that the celebration of to-morrow shall be conducted in accord with the then physical condition of the President. May God grant him speedy and full recovery is the prayer of all. Please read this despatch to the President. CHARLES FOSTER.

WASHINGTON, July 3, 9.15 P.M.

His Excellency Charles Foster, Governor of Ohio:

The President is deeply touched with the feelings of affection manifested by the people of his native State, as shown by your telegram, just received. His condition is unchanged. No unfavorable symptoms supervened, and his fortitude and cheerfulness are admirable. I trust the pious and devoted example of Ohio may be followed by all the States of the Union to-morrow.

JAMES G. BLAINE,
Secretary of State.

NEW ORLEANS, July 3.

The Hon. James G. Blaine, Secretary of State, Washington:

At a meeting of the Hancock Association of Louisiana, convened by order of the President, at No. 11 Commercial Place, John McEnery called the association to order, and, referring to the recent sad intelligence from Washington of the attempt to assassinate President Garfield, invited the members to manifest their sorrow and sympathy in some appropriate form, whereupon Isaac W. Patton offered the following resolutions:

Be it resolved, That the attempt to assassinate President Garfield has been received and regarded by the members of this association and by their fellow-countrymen as a great calamity to the nation, and arouses in the breasts of all patriotic citizens the profoundest sorrow and sympathy for the President and his family, and grave anxieties for the troubles and turmoil that may result to the Republic from so horrible a crime.

Resolved, That we cherish the most earnest and sincere hope, and unite with all good people in their fervent prayers for the recovery of the President from his great affliction.

These resolutions were unanimously adopted, and were ordered to be telegraphed to the Secretary of State of the United States.   **JOHN McENERY,** *President.*
Robert W. Adams, *Secretary.*

AN ITALIAN SOCIETY TO SECRETARY BLAINE.

Baltimore, July 3.

The Hon. James G. Blaine, Secretary of State, Washington:

Please forward to his Excellency the President of the United States, the profound sympathy of the Italian beneficial society Unione e Fratellanz, of Baltimore, and wishes for his speedy recovery.   **M. VICARI,** *President.*
L. Lazzeni, *Secretary.*

FROM THE PEOPLE OF ROUMANIA.

Bucharest, Roumania, July 8.

His Excellency the Minister of Foreign Affairs, Washington:

The crime at Washington has filled our hearts with horror. In the name of the Government and of the entire people of Roumania I transmit to your Excellency this evidence of the sentiments of grief which the news of the assassination has inspired throughout this country, and I beg you to express these sentiments to the Government and to the family of the illustrious victim.   **I. C. BRATIANO,**
President of the Council of Ministers, and Minister of Foreign Affairs.

MINISTER LOWELL TO SECRETARY BLAINE.

To Blaine, Secretary, Washington:

Messages of inquiry and sympathy have been received from Prince and Princess of Wales, and Duke and Duchess of Teck.

Expressions of interest and sympathy are universal. Calls at my house and the legation are incessant. I have duly forwarded your telegrams to our legations in Europe.

LOWELL, *Minister, London.*

FRANK GOODMAN TO SECRETARY BLAINE.

NASHVILLE, TENN., July 3.

The Hon. James G. Blaine, Secretary of State, Washington:

In behalf of the profession of which President Garfield was an honored member and the Business Educators' Association, I extend to himself and family our profoundest sympathy, hoping for a speedy recovery. FRANK GOODMAN,

Vice-President Business Educators' Association of America.

FROM THE MAYOR OF ST. JOHN.

ST. JOHN, NEW BRUNSWICK, July 3.

The Hon. James G. Blaine, Washington:

The citizens of St. John, New Brunswick, desire to express their deep and heartfelt sympathy with President Garfield and his family in this time of their great affliction. They recognize in the President a great statesman and Christian gentleman, and sincerely trust that in the good providence of the Almighty he may soon be restored to perfect health.

I. JONES, *Mayor.*

MR. HAMLIN TO SECRETARY BLAINE.

BANGOR, ME., July 3.

James G. Blaine, Washington:

Telegrams received. Information of the hopeful condition of the President is a great relief to all, but we are all terribly anxious. Convey my earnest, heartfelt sympathy to the President and family. H. HAMLIN.

FROM THE KING OF SWEDEN.

To the Secretary of State:

SIR: His majesty the King, my august sovereign, has bidden me express the horror with which he has learned of the awful attempt against the life of his Excellency the President of the United States, and the sentiments of sorrowful sympathy which he feels for the whole American people in this hour of their deep affliction, and the sincere prayers which he offers for the speedy recovery of the illustrious invalid, in which the people of the United Kingdoms of Sweden and Norway join.

CLARA MORRIS TO MRS. ROCKWELL.

RIVERDALE, N. Y., July 3.

To Mrs. A. F. Rockwell, Executive Mansion :

For Mrs. Garfield.   At such a time I will not presume to recall myself to Mrs. Garfield by directly addressing her, yet I cannot remain silent.   May I not hope, Madam, that through your courtesy and good judgment the afflicted lady may receive the assurances of my heartfelt sympathy, and earnest prayers for the welfare of her and hers.   Of course, hundreds are at hand to render all great services for the patient, but if I can aid in even the most trivial way, command me I entreat you, and, dear Madam, believe me most respectfully,

CLARA MORRIS.

COLONEL ROCKWELL TO CLARA MORRIS.

EXECUTIVE MANSION, July 4.

Mrs. Clara Morris-Harriott, Riverdale, N. Y.:

Mrs. Garfield wishes me to express to you her grateful appreciation for your kind and heartfelt words.   She feels that the sympathy and prayers of her countrywomen at this time are of measureless value and comfort.   A. T. ROCKWELL.

FROM THE SOCIETY OF THE CINCINNATI.

NEW YORK, July 4.

To Hon. James G. Blaine, Washington, D. C.:

The New York State Society of the Cincinnati have heard with heartfelt sorrow and indignation of the murderous assault upon the President of the United States, and they desire to express to the family of the President their deep sympathy in the

distressing calamity which has so suddenly overwhelmed them
in the deepest grief, and to join their prayers with those of the
whole community that our heavenly Father may bless with success the means used for his recovery, and may continue to our
country and its institutions his care and protection in the severe
trials that may be impending.

Resolved, That a copy of the foregoing, certified by the President and Secretary, be transmitted by telegraph to the Honorable Secretary of State of the United States.

HAMILTON FISH, *President.*

JOHN SCHUYLER, *Secretary.*

REPLY OF SECRETARY BLAINE.

WASHINGTON, D. C.,
EXECUTIVE MANSION, July 4.

*To the Hon. Hamilton Fish, President of the Society of the Cin-
cinnati, N. Y.:*

Accept, on behalf of the President, the sincerest thanks for
the sympathy of your illustrious and patriotic society.

JAMES G. BLAINE,
Secretary of State.

FROM THE ITALIAN CHARGÉ D'AFFAIRES.

NEW YORK, July 2.

To Secretary of State, Washington:

I have just learned with the deepest regret and indignation of
the horrible attempt on the President's life. I sincerely trust
he may recover. CAMPOREALE,
Chargé d'Affaires of Italy.

FROM THE EMPEROR OF JAPAN.

TOKIO, July 4.

To Yoshida, Japanese Minister, Washington:

The despatch announcing an attempt upon the life of the
President has caused here profound sorrow, and you are hereby
instructed to convey, in the name of his Majesty, to the Government of the United States the deepest sympathy and hope that

his recovery will be speedy.   Make immediate and full report
regarding the sad event.   WOO YENO,
Acting Minister for Foreign Affairs.

FROM THE LORD MAYOR OF DUBLIN.

DUBLIN, July 4.

To American Minister, Washington:

Municipal Council, assembled to-day, takes earliest opportunity of expressing great sorrow and regret at dastardly attempt
on life of gallant, distinguished President of United States, and
desires to tender its deep sympathy to the Americans and General Garfield's family.   LORD MAYOR DUBLIN.

MR. PARNELL TO SECRETARY BLAINE.

To Secretary Blaine:

In behalf of Irish members I beg to express our horror at
crime against the Chief Magistrate of American people, and our
earnest prayer that his life may be spared.   PARNELL,
House of Commons.

GOV. COBB TO SECRETARY BLAINE.

MONTGOMERY, ALA., July 2.

To the Hon. James G. Blaine, Secretary of State, Washington:

Profound and universal sympathy here for President.   Telegraph us his condition.   R. W. COBB, *Governor.*

SECRETARY BLAINE TO AMOS TOWNSEND.

To the Hon. Amos Townsend, Cleveland, Ohio:

The President's condition has not materially changed since
morning.   At this hour, 2.30, he is suffering less pain.   He is
entirely calm and courageous.   His mind is clear, and he ac-
cepts whatever fate God may ordain for him with perfect resignation and sublime Christian faith.   We are profoundly anxious
and yet hopeful as to the final result.   JAMES G. BLAINE.

WHITELAW REID TO MRS. GARFIELD.

To Mrs. Garfield:

Love, sympathy, and hope.
WHITELAW REID AND WIFE.

FROM AN EX-CONFEDERATE SOLDIER.

EDENTON, N. C., July 3.

To His Excellency J. A. Garfield :

A blind and wounded ex-Confederate soldier tenders his congratulations on your improved condition. May God raise you to preserve the peace and dignity of the nation.

F. W. BOND.

FROM TWO CATHOLIC BISHOPS.

FORT WAYNE, IND., July 3.

To the President of the United States :

The Catholic Bishops of Peoria and Fort Wayne desire to express their most sincere sympathy and the most earnest wish for your speedy recovery. J. L. SPALDING,

JOSEPH DEVENGER.

FROM THE LADIES OF RICHMOND.

RICHMOND, VA., July 3.

To Mrs. Garfield :

We deeply sympathize with you in your sad affliction. We shall to-day send up many earnest prayers for the speedy recovery of your affectionate husband and our beloved President.

THE LADIES OF RICHMOND.

FROM KING CHARLES OF ROUMANIA.

BUCHAREST, CATROCINI, July 4.

To President Garfield, Washington :

I have learned with the greatest indignation, and deplore most deeply, the horrible attempt against your precious life, and beg you to accept my warmest wishes for your quick recovery.

CHARLES.

M. OUTREY TO MRS. GARFIELD.

PARIS, July 4.

To Madame Garfield, Executive Mansion :

Accept expression of our deepest sympathy. OUTREY.

SECRETARY BLAINE TO AMERICANS IN PARIS.

An important consultation was held this morning, in which Dr. Agnew, of Philadelphia, and Dr. Hamilton, of New York, able and skilful surgeons, were present. The result is not re-assuring, though the conclusion was that recovery is possible. We do not give up hope.   BLAINE,
Secretary.

FROM A DEMOCRATIC CONVENTION.

ZANESVILLE, OHIO, July 4.

In the Democratic Convention of Muskingum County, held here to-day, for appointing delegates to the Democratic State Convention, the unanimous sentiments of the members were expressed in the following resolution offered by Mr. George W. Jewett, son of the Hon. H. J. Jewett, of this city, which were forthwith adopted by the united voices of all present:

Resolved, That, in common with all patriotic citizens, the members of this convention view with horror and indignation the act having for its purpose the taking of the life of our Chief Magistrate, and that we regard such an attempt as the highest and most revolting of crimes;

Resolved, That we extend our heartfelt sympathies to our wounded President and to his gentle wife and family, and prayerfully trust that Providence will save to our country his life, and to his family the kind-hearted man, the brave husband and father, and one the country would learn to know better and to love.   T. F. SPANGLER.

FROM PHILADELPHIA CINCINNATI.

PHILADELPHIA, July 4.

The Hon. J. G. Blaine:

Will you be good enough to communicate to the President the following resolution, unanimously adopted by the State Society of the Cincinnati of Pennsylvania at a meeting held this day:

Resolved, That the present critical condition of President Garfield fills our hearts with the deepest grief and sympathy, and while as a society we utterly condemn the cruel act of the assassin, we offer our fervent prayer to the Almighty Ruler of the universe that the life of our beloved and honored President may be preserved for the best interest of the Republic.

FRANCIS M. CALDWELL,
Secretary.

FROM THE ISRAELITES OF BOSTON.

NEW ERA HALL, July 4, 1881.

The Hon. James G. Blaine, Secretary of State, Washington, D. C.:

The Israelites of Boston, in convention assembled, extend their heartfelt sympathy for President Garfield and their intense indignation at the outrage committed on our honored Executive. Convey our profound sorrow and tenderest sympathy to Mrs. Garfield and family. Our prayers are fervently offered that the President may recover and live to fulfil the promise of his grand career at the helm of our beloved country.

EDWARD S. GOULSTON,
Chairman.

CHARLES MORSE, ⎫
ISRAEL COHN, ⎬ *Committee.*
ISAAC ROSNOSKY, ⎭

CONSUL-GENERAL SMITH TO MR. BLAINE.

MONTREAL, July 4.

To Hon. J. G. Blaine, Secretary of State:

The manifestations of sympathy in this city have been universal. I have just heard that the City Council has adopted a resolution expressive of the deep feeling by all citizens. The late favorable despatches are giving great encouragement.

J. G. SMITH,
Consul-General.

FROM BARTHELEMY ST. HILAIRE.

PARIS, July 3.

To M. de Geofroy, French Minister, Washington:

Be good enough to convey to Mme. Garfield the sentiment of sorrow and sympathy which the President and Government feel. You will express at the same time to the Vice-President

10

of the United States the deep and profound grief which this attempt has caused throughout all France.

BARTHELEMY ST. HILAIRE.

FROM THE FRENCH SECRETARY OF STATE.

PARIS, July 4.

To M. de Geofroy, French Minister, Washington :
Send us frequent news of the President.

LE COMTE DE CHOISEUL,
Under-Secretary of State.

FROM GEORGETOWN COLLEGE.

The President and faculty of Georgetown College congratulate Mrs. Garfield on the improved condition of the President. It is our fervent hope and prayer that the good God who preserved her unto the President may now in turn preserve him unto her and the country.

F. HEALY,
President.

FROM CITIZENS OF DUBLIN.

DUBLIN, July 4.

A great meeting of Dublin citizens under the auspicies of the Land League, celebrating American independence, has unanimously passed resolutions expressing deep sympathy with the President and hope for his speedy recovery, denouncing the outrage and deploring the attack on the chief officer of a free community where the will of the people is the supreme law.

SEXTON, M. P.

FROM PHILADELPHIA'S PEOPLE.

PHILADELPHIA, July 4.

Twenty thousand people present at the exercises of the Bi-Centennial Association of Pennsylvania to-day joined in the solemn expression of a prayerful hope that the encouraging symptoms reported from the bedside of the wounded patriot and statesman may speedily be followed by the assurance of a certain recovery.

E. C. KNIGHT,
President.

CANADIAN SYMPATHY.

MONTREAL, July 4.

This afternoon, just before business was commenced by the Montreal City Council, a motion offered by Alderman Genier and seconded by Alderman George Washington Stephens was carried unanimously: "That the sympathy of the people of Montreal be given to the people of the United States and their condolence extended to the relatives of President Garfield in the terrible calamity that has befallen them." One Alderman regretted that, for once, the trial of the assassin had not been anticipated by Judge Lynch. This fairly represents the feeling among the people of Canada.

QUEBEC, July 4.

In the English Cathedral yesterday prayers were offered for the recovery of President Garfield. Great sympathy is expressed for him and his family, and the hotels and offices of the newspapers and of Consul Wasson are besieged by anxious inquirers for the latest bulletins.

OTTAWA, ONT., July 4.

The excitement still continues here over the attempted assassination of President Garfield, and the latest news is anxiously looked for.

HALIFAX, N. S., July 4.

The reception arranged to take place to-morrow on Her Majesty's steamer Northampton has been postponed until Saturday on account of the critical condition of President Garfield.

VOICES FROM THE PULPIT.

WHAT PROMINENT CLERGYMEN SAID TO THEIR CON-GREGATIONS.

SORROWING AT THE DISCIPLES CHURCH—A SERMON ON THE ASSASSINATION AND ITS CAUSES.

WASHINGTON, July 3.--The plain little wooden Church of the Disciples, on Vermont Avenue, where the Garfield family are accustomed to worship, was thronged at the morning service, despite the heat. No one from the President's household was present. Previous to the arrival of the minister a subdued restlessness pervaded the congregation, and there was much sober comparing of notes and asking of questions in regard to the latest news from the White House. In the absence from town of the Rev. Mr. Power, the pastor, the services were conducted by the Rev. Mr. Harbison, of Cincinnati, who said in the course of his opening prayer:

"And now, O God! in the midst of this deep and dark shadow which has been cast across our land, in the face almost of the death of the President of the nation, we come to thee for strength. Thou alone can support those who are most deeply afflicted, and guide the nation through its imminent peril. We pray to thee for the President. We beseech thee to be very merciful to him. We ask thee, if thou wilt, to save him from death. Oh, may he recover from his wounds. Our hearts yearn for this. We believe that in his great office a mighty work remains to be perfected. We believe that great interests have been confided to his hands. Oh, save him, God. We know not what is best for thee to do; but if it be thy will, oh, for Christ's sake have mercy." (There arose here a subdued chorus of amens from all over the house.) "But if thou wilt take him hence," continued the orator, "as a consequence of this fearful calamity, O God, prepare him for the solemn hour; make him depend upon thee more and more. Bring forth into greater prominence the faith which has characterized his past life, and may the glorious hope of immortality brighten his dying bed." At this moment many were weeping, and sobs were audible from every direction. Mr. Harbison proceeded : " Lord, bless the dear sister, his companion, herself but recently escaped from death. May she be consoled in spirit, and may Providence surround her. Lead her children in the path of righteousness; save them from the sin which is so prevalent in the world, and which is worse than death, and lead them to honor and glory. May there go up from thousands upon thousands of sorrowing homes to-day throughout the land an earnest prayer for the stricken President. Amen."

On arising for the sermon Mr. Harbison said :

" I have here a despatch from brother Power, saying that he will reach Washington at 2 P.M. It has been thought proper that some time to-day we should spend a while together as a church in special prayer-meeting in behalf of the President and his family. Under ordinary circumstances I would order the meeting held immediately after the close of these services; but, in view of the probability of Brother Power's arrival, I suggest that it take place at the close of the evening sermon, a little before 8 o'clock. Let me read you an announcement just received from the White House : 10 A.M.—The President rested quietly and has been greatly refreshed. His improving condition gives additional hope that he will gradually recover. Pulse 114 ; respiration, 18 ; temperature, about normal. Signed Dr. Bliss. I am quite aware," continued the speaker, " that in such a time as this people generally, judging by myself, are not well qualified to think of much else than the deed—the dark and dastardly deed—that has fallen upon us. I suppose that most of you, like myself, were stunned, and have scarcely yet become restored to a normal condition. But though laboring under these difficulties, I will attempt this morning to make some improvement of the sad circumstances surrounding us, and I do not think I can do better, for the glory of God, than to call your attention to the thirty-second verse of the fifteenth chapter of the First Corinthians : ' If, after the manner of men, I have fought the beasts at Ephesus, what advantage is it to me if the dead rise not? Let us eat, drink, and be merry, for to-morrow we die.' I selected this subject before the sad calamity of yes-

terday occurred, and after it occurred I could see no good reason for changing it, for it seems to me that there is ground here
for some practical reflections which we may take to our hearts
now with deeper importance and greater tenderness.   The latter
part of the text emphasizes the event of yesterday.   President
Garfield starts out in the morning joyfully to meet his friends,
expecting to renew old acquaintances, to go back to the old college days, and to mingle with those whom he had not seen in
years, and instantly his life is put in peril and the whole nation is
cast into mourning.   O human life, what a slender thread you
hang by!   Why not get the most pleasure out of it?   Why
should President Garfield continue to hold affiliation with the
people meeting in this little church on Vermont Avenue—people
unpopular, sometimes persecuted, often put to great disadvan-
tages, on account of their belief; people recent in independent organization, but not recent in principles, which are as old as the
Christian religion?   And may it not be that this morning, as he
lies upon his bed of suffering, facing death, he is saying: 'What
is the good?   Why am I identified with a people like this when
there are those who fill their sails with the popular breeze without inconvenience, social or otherwise? In a moment I am strick-
en down, and all this goes for nothing if there is no future, no
resurrection of the dead.' "

The reverend speaker described and contrasted stoicism and
epicureanism in ancient Rome, and continued: "We are passing through a history very similar to that of Rome.   When the
country was founded, the philosophy of stoicism, born of Puri-
tanism, was the belief of the people ; but after the days of simplicity had passed away, there began to be a decadence of the
philosophy.   As wealth increased in a wonderful way, and in-
ventions multiplied for easing life and bringing all the luxuries and
advantages that can be secured in physical surrounding, more and
more the people wanted to believe in materialism, and the grand
old doctrine began to fall into neglect.   It even became unpopular
in some quarters to say that there was a hell for the wicked, until now we find that if a man desires a certain kind of popularity he immediately proclaims himself a materialist.   He is sure
of large audiences and large pay.   It is the most paying invest-
ment a man can make to tell the people that the true Gospel is
the gospel of good living, and to say, 'Let the other world take
care of itself.'   What is the result?   Just exactly as it was in

Rome. The bands of public and private morality are becoming relaxed, and men are beginning to treat human life as of no consideration. Let me read for you from the assassin's letter. He says, ' A human life is of small value.' Yes, if we believe that human life is no more than that of a horse or a dog, it is surely of small value. He goes on : ' Life is a flimsy thing, and it matters little if one goes.' Such are the sentiments which the epicurean philosophy of the present day assumes to weave into a justification for striking down the President of the United States. We have been sowing the wind, and we are reaping the whirlwind. If matters go on as for a few years past, we shall have murders and house-burnings and heart-aches ; we shall have such a depreciated state of society in this country as old Rome saw when her philosophers shunned her gates and sought the retirement of distant villas for the purpose of escaping the existing whirlwinds of passion. Say what you will, that time will come ; it is bound to come. Let me tell you that when pleasure is made the chief god selfishness will be on the throne. Each man will look to securing his own pleasure at the expense of others.

" He who studies the movement of American society cannot fail to see that we are under a reign of selfishness in striking contrast to forty years ago. As one newspaper said this morning, office-seeking, office-hunting, and looking after spoils have become the main object of life. Each man is trying his best to crowd the others out. We are having disgraceful political fights, and we may expect to see these scenes intensified. Money, money, is the craze all over the land ; get money, no matter how, is the popular cry. Why ? Because pleasure is the chief end of man. Such is the tone of American society to-day, and it grieves me to say it. Its apostles are lionized. The men who are stabbing American morals and constitutional government to the vitals are held up as examples to follow and admire. I say to you that the President's assassination is directly chargeable to this philosophy of good living that is pervading the minds of the public to-day, and assassinations will be multiplied unless we call a halt. I predict that in less than twenty-five years, if matters go on as they are going, we will have the Roman arena in this country, and I do not think it improbable that gladiatorial combat will be restored.

" I have thought proper, my dear friends," continued the speaker, " to make these remarks to you to-day to call your attention to the calamity which has occurred, and to the real reason for it. Under the utterances of the assassin we discover the principles of epicurean philosophy. May be that God, in his goodness, intended to awaken the people when he let the head of the nation be stricken. May be he will awaken them. One reason why I had hoped against hope for the President's restoration to health is that I cannot but think he has a great work to perform. Still, it may be that more can be accomplished by his death than by his recovery. I doubt not that a great work was accomplished by the death of Abraham Lincoln. I never doubted that his murder was providential. Even the assassin who struck with such vengeful fury yesterday may have brought good which could not have been secured in any other way. Let us pray, if God wishes, that he will continue the life of James A. Garfield. [Amen.] It is right in any event that our prayers should go up to that end. But if God in his providence thinks it better to take James A. Garfield to himself, we may be content to see him die. It is a hard thing to say, but it may be said. [Sobs.] Whatever the issue, we who follow the Christian philosophy may take consolation to our hearts that God is working out his own ends, and we may trust him. Though the ship of State is now tossing upon the billows, we know that God is at the helm of the universe, and we may depend upon it that the life or death of the head of the nation can only result in calming the ocean and securing to the nation peace and blessing."

The congregation then sang:

"God moves in a mysterious way,
His wonders to perform."

After communion Mr. Harbison announced that the special prayer-meeting would take place at 7.30 o'clock, before the sermon. At the conclusion of the service the congregation lingered to discuss the latest bulletins, and much joy was expressed over the favorable character of the news.

PRAYING FOR THE PRESIDENT.

The little Christian Church on Vermont Avenue was packed to overflowing in the evening. The heat was intense. At 7.30 o'clock the pastor, the Rev. Mr. Power, who had arrived from Cincinnati during the afternoon, said:

The purpose of our congregating together for a few moments to-night before the usual services is not one that I need enlarge upon. It is a matter we can scarcely face. We can say but little except to humble ourselves before God, and leave in the hands of him who has been the dwelling-place for all generations, to work out in his own way our good and the good of the nation, as he has always with all the concern we have brought to him. No words that I can speak can express the depth of feeling of the people all through this country over the sad and appalling intelligence. The assassin said, in harmony with the infidel teaching of the day, that life is but a flimsy dream. Was there ever a falser thought as represented by the case of the noble man he smote? That life is gloriously significant to his family, to his friends, to his Christian brethren, and to the nation over whom he presides. We all feel as if we must bear up before God an earnest prayer that he may be spared. He has borne relations to us that make his life unspeakably precious in our sight. Scarcely one of the brethren who have met him here for years past that does not feel towards him as a personal friend, and I know that the sentiment of the brethren all over the country, in one united voice, goes up to God in his behalf this hour."

The reverend gentleman then delivered an earnest prayer that the life of the President might be spared, and for strength to be given his wife, mother, and children. He was followed by the Rev. Mr. Harbison and several of the deacons in a similar strain. The entire congregation then knelt and prayed together. The scene was very affecting, sobs being audible all over the church. Mr. Harbison then arose and said: " I am free to say, dear brethren, that I have never been at a meeting where I have felt so deeply, we have been so long in the enjoyment of Christian fellowship with President Garfield." After relating several anecdotes of the President's deep religious feeling, the speaker continued :

" I have found nobody in Washington who did not say we esteem, admire, and love the man. A gentleman high in position said to me yesterday, 'I believe him to be as true and pure a man as ever lived.' I was much struck with the reported remark of Secretary Blaine, immediately after the shooting: 'I can't see why any man would kill President Garfield. He would injure no one.' There wasn't a trace of malice in his

10*

composition, and to-night, when we have come to bear him up before the throne of grace, the solemnity deepens as I think of the possibility that his terrible wound may become fatal.   I don't like to think about it, because the people, the nation, the world needs him.   We can ill spare a man of his sort. . . .   When, yesterday afternoon, I saw his wife come up those stairs and enter the room which contained nearly all that was precious to her in life, I asked myself, 'Is it possible that this woman's heart will not break?'   All others were excluded from the room where he lay, while she entered and quietly imprinted the kiss of love upon his lips and exchanged loving words with him.   As I sat there, fearing the result, she emerged, her eyes suffused with tears, and was soon engaged in her work of love and affection. Whether our beloved President lives or dies I believe that God has great ends to serve in the disposal of his servant.   Shortly after receiving the nomination to the Presidency, Gen. Garfield said to me : 'I don't know how this has come about; but one thing is certain, if I am defeated I will not be so greatly disappointed as some of my friends will be.   If I am elected, I will believe there is some purpose in it.   I will wait and see.'   During that campaign I was so deeply impressed with the notion that assassination lay before him that I sat down in my study one day and actually half wrote a letter of warning to him; but then I reflected, 'What am I doing?   What reason can I give?   He will think it a mere whim'—and I tore the letter up.   I don't know to-day why I acted thus, but I had the presentiment and I could not shake it off.   Even should he die I believe that God, who has guided us so long, will still do so.   As Gen. Garfield himself said when Lincoln fell, 'Lincoln is dead, but the nation lives.'   Let us as Christians realize that everything is in the hands of God, and pray for the President and his family.   If the dark pall does at last settle over us and the flags are placed at half-mast, and evidences of mourning are seen all over the land, let us be ready to say, 'Not my will, but thine, O Lord, be done.'"

The Rev. Mr. Power also addressed the assemblage.   He said, among other things :

"In a letter which President Garfield wrote to me after receiving the nomination, he used these words, indicative of the guiding spirit of his life, 'I know not how it may turn out, but I have always tried to meet the duty of every day as it came. I left the rest to God.' He and his wife both seemed to look forward to peculiar trials when he should assume his present position. After the nomination Mrs. Garfield said to me, 'I do not know what responsibilities will come on us, but I feel that God will prepare us to meet them.'"

It was after nine o'clock when the gathering reluctantly broke up.

DR. STORRS'S DISCOURSE.

A Prayer for the President's recovery—Eulogy of Gen. Garfield.

The morning service in the Rev. Dr. Storrs's Church, in Brooklyn, was conducted with special reference to the critical condition of the President. Before beginning the devotional exercises, Dr. Storrs read a despatch he had just received from Washington, dated 10 A.M., saying that the President's state became more hopeful every hour; and that Sir Edward Thornton had just telegraphed the Queen, that there was great hope of ultimate recovery. Dr. Storrs then read a part of the 13th chapter of Hebrews: "Remember them which have the rule over you, who have spoken unto you the word of God; whose faith follow, considering the end of their conversation." In the prayer that followed, he prayed for all who are in danger. "Remember," he asked, "in infinite compassion and love, the President of the United States. Thou knowest how precious is his life in the sight of all this people. Restore him; give him entire recovery if it please Thee. Make him only more sensible of his obligations to Thee. Restore him that he may serve Thee. We thank Thee that our worst fears, thus far, have not been realized. Bring him up, and grant that his life may be illustrious, in holiness and usefulness, for many years to come." The subject of the sermon was "The Insecurity of Human Life." "When yesterday there came tidings," the speaker said, "that the President of the United States had been struck by the bullet of an intending assassin, we were all startled and grieved. He was hurled, instantly, into the very shadow of death. All the circumstances surrounding the shooting were as sadly tragical as could have been conceived by any imagination. Pushed up by his own exertions from the lowest grades of life to posts of honor, he has reached the highest position in the gift of the people. What he has done so far has commended itself to the majority of the people. His term of office, brief as it has been, has been marked by integrity, honor, progress and prosperity. He was going to meet the wife who has also been in the shadow of death. He was going, too, to meet his college friends, and assist in their anniversary exercises. In the midst of a circle of friends, and apparently in the utmost security, he fell by the shot of an assassin. It seems the very irony of fate for the greatest life on the continent to fall at such a moment and by such a hand, after he had gone safely through the shot and shell of battle. It is not merely the individual life that is threatened. His death implies changes in the policy and all the officers of the Government. We cannot tell what. It is a sarcasm on the wisdom that framed our Government that one insane hand should have the opportunity to give such new direction for years to come to the policy of the Administration. All the world is watching that point at Washington. The whole continent pauses in its work and in its pleasure, and it gives us an example, too, of our wonderful advance. Fifty years ago such an event would hardly have been known through the country for weeks and weeks. Now it is the talk of the world. When William of Orange was assassinated, almost exactly 300 years ago, on the 10th of July, 1584, it seemed as if everything must go down. The principles of liberty were not destroyed even when Henry of Navarre was killed, 26 years later, in the streets of Paris. When Lincoln died at the hands of an assassin, 16 years ago, the whole nation turned sick at heart. But that death did not interrupt the principles of liberty, on account of which Lincoln died. "Isn't this Government going to be Mexicanized?" I have frequently heard asked within the last 24 hours. Never while we trust in God. The sea and land will change places sooner, while our principles remain, than our Government can be revolutionized. Two utterances from the President since his injury have touched me very much. One was concerning that brave little woman, his wife. The other was when he said to the doctors, 'Do not be afraid to tell me the worst; you know I am not afraid to die.'" At the conclusion of the sermon, Dr. Storrs read another despatch from Washington announcing that the President was still improving.

THE REV. R. S. MACARTHUR.

An earnest and sympathetic discourse on the attempted assassination of President Garfield was preached yesterday by the

Rev. R. S. MacArthur, pastor of the Calvary Baptist Church, New York. In his prayer, Dr. MacArthur impressively invoked the divine blessing upon this smitten, stricken, and sorrowing nation. "We pray this morning," he said, "as we have never prayed before for the President of these United States. May his noble life be spared, and may the designs of the wicked assassin be frustrated. May the attending doctors be given wis- . dom in their examinations and prescriptions, so that the life of the President will be saved." The text of the discourse was chosen from the nineteenth verse of the first chapter of Second Samuel—"How are the mighty fallen!" Such was the language used by David, said the preacher, in his tender and touching lament over the death of Saul. Each word seems heavy with a sigh and broken with a sob, and although the lapse of ages has intervened since their utterance, many persons will contemplate that stirring exclamation with peculiar significance at this time. A nearer sorrow prevails throughout this broad land. In thousands of families hearts are bleeding and tears are falling, and from thousands of hearthstones prayers are going up for this stricken and afflicted country. Only a few months ago James A. Garfield was inaugurated President of the United States, and no Administration ever opened more auspiciously. The country was at peace and prosperity prevailed everywhere. His friends were legion and his enemies few, although some of the latter were shamefully bitter. General Garfield enjoyed the reputation of being a brave and honorable gentleman, a scholar and a statesman, and the entire country looked upon his opening Administration with confidence and favor. When the President's noble wife was stricken down by serious illness the great heart of the nation throbbed with sincere sympathy for the anxious family, and it was with the deepest regret, too, that the people watched the clouds of political trouble that hung threateningly over the President's head. But recently all these troubles seemed to be passing away. Domestic and political affairs were assuming a more cheerful aspect, and plans were being made by the President and his family for a peaceful and happy summer. The speaker said that since he had known anything of American politics, he had watched with interest the career of General Garfield. The latter was a man of pure and unsullied character, and had been singularly fortunate in his political life. Little did President Garfield imagine on Saturday morning that before night he would be lying on his bed mortally wounded, his soul hovering on the borders of the other world. The suddenness of Saturday's tragedy reveals in its most comprehensive form both the duty and beauty of sympathy. No more kindly feelings have ever been expressed by the American people than those which have been freely manifested towards the Garfield family. And there is good reason for this condition of public feeling. Mr. and Mrs. Garfield are of the people, self-educated and self-made. Not only was General Garfield honored for his great intellectual attainments and broad statesmanship, but Mrs. Garfield also commanded universal admiration for her noble, womanly traits and her superior mental abilities. It is something for the American people to be proud of that their President's wife should be able to converse with many of the representatives of foreign countries in their native language. One of the most significant thoughts suggested by this attempted murder of the President is, said the speaker, the great importance that attaches to the selection of a Vice-President. How remote has been the expectation that General Arthur would ever become President of the United States. During the last few months many persons have felt very much dissatisfied with the conduct of our Vice-President. Those who remembered his honored father have frequently had occasion to wish that the son possessed some of that sterling sense of dignity and honor that characterized the senior Arthur. But Chester A. Arthur was elected Vice-President to do the bidding of one man, and most faithfully has he discharged that obligation. A great many Republicans voted for him under a silent protest, but now should he be called to the Presidential chair we must hope for the best. He will then have a great opportunity to set himself right with the people, and to win their confidence and respect. Should circumstances elevate him to the foremost position in the country, it is to be hoped that he will lay aside all factional feeling, forget all personal prejudices and obligations and be the true representative of the whole people. How little did the shrewdest politicians in Washington and Albany imagine that such a radical change in the political affairs of the nation could occur as that which now threatens us. In the act of the cowardly assassin there appears still another lesson. The man whose wicked deed has plunged a loving family and a great nation into the deepest grief was once a respected and trusted member of society. He stood up in church and made a public avowal of his belief and faith in God. But afterwards yielding to the baser elements of his nature, he began that downward path which has brought him to the murderer's cell. His small vices begat larger ones, and finally he sank into that state of utter moral demoralization which led him to raise his assassin's hand against the first citizen of his country. From the shocking experience of this wretch may be drawn the warning: Beware of the beginning of evil. May God save our young men from sin, for it is obvious now to every mind how the criminal act of one man can plunge a nation into despair. In all of this tribulation, however, none should forget the power and wisdom of the Almighty. God rules supreme, and if His ways at times seem harsh and inscrutable, they are, nevertheless, fraught with some purpose of His own which is destined for our good. As Abraham Lincoln lives to-day in the hearts of an affectionate people, so will James Abram Garfield live, even though he may die. In conclusion, Dr. MacArthur impressively remarked: "We lift our hearts to God to-day, praying that he may stay the hand of wickedness and murder in this great and prosperous land."

REMARKS OF DR. BELLOWS.

A timely, patriotic, and eloquent sermon was delivered yesterday morning by the Rev. W. H. Bellows, D.D., in the Church of All Souls, New York. It was devoted mainly to a review of our political system as organized, operated, and controlled by the "machine." At the conclusion of his remarks upon this topic, in which he condemned the course of the present machine managers as exhibited at Albany, Dr. Bellows referred to the calamity which has just fallen upon the country. "The report that reached us," he said, "seemed too terrible to be credible. So blameless, so free from personal enemies, so growing upon the confidence and respect of the people had our President been, and so calm and tranquil was the country under his benign administration; so little sectional animosity was left in the land and so little divided were the people upon the main policy of the Government, that never did a calamity of this frightful magnitude burst out of a clearer sky! It was as if the beautiful comet in our northern horizon had suddenly swooped down upon the peaceful observers of its course, or the millions that looked wonderingly upon its meteoric splendors, and dashed the earth out of its orbit and heaped the cosmos in ruins. God knows what hopes are centred in the life and energy, the statesmanship and patriotism of our President, the first for many terms who possessed the claims of a trained and experienced legislator, upon the exalted office he filled. It seemed almost a happy accident when party tactics put the right man in the right place, and made a candidate as fit for the office as any in the country the nominee of a triumphant party and at last the President of the nation! And now, in a moment, and by the brutal shot of a disappointed office-seeker, our President lies half dead and in danger of mortal dissolution, while the national heart on the eve of its greatest festival is shocked into a fearful suspense, and waits with alternate hopes and fears upon the hourly bulletins from the bloody chamber where his stalwart frame and manly vigor of constitution struggle uncertainly with the angel of death. There is great alleviation of our sorrow in the fact that thus far no evidence appears of political conspiracy or of sectional or party backing in the frantic act of personal caprice and wayward madness that has laid low our yesterday erect and vigorous chief ruler. If he dies, he dies by the hand of one of his own party and one of his own Western fellow-citizens; an obscure person, without political significance or following, wholly unknown in social or public life. It is painfully true that this madman claims some party reasons for his conduct, and excuses himself by the necessity of putting out of the way an obstacle to the full power of one of the factions in the miserable, and now become fatal, quarrel of the Republican party. There is no reason for thinking he had any prompting or support from those who may benefit by the not improbable vacancy to be created in the Presidential chair. But it is probable, if not certain, that the animosity, the personal abuse, the unseemly and exaggerated tone and character of the quarrel in the party, aggravated by virulence of the press, has suggested the dreadful act of violence that now appalls those who fomented it. It was less inexcusable that sectional bitterness and hate should have bred, while a fearful war between North and South was still going on, the murderous spirit that animated the assassination of Abraham Lincoln! But that a mere quarrel over party spoils should have been able to poison the brain and nerve the arm of a fanatic to slay, not a personal enemy, not his injurer, and not a direct party to the strife, but the beloved and honored President of the nation, in a time of peace and prosperity, when parties have hardly issues enough left open to keep up a decent division, is one of the saddest of warnings whither our disgraceful squabbles within party lines may lead. Is it not a new argument for putting the spoils of office out of party politics when madness, suicide, and murder wait upon its inspiration? Let us hope that the country will come to its senses, and the party in question to its stool of repentance, when it sees what consequences follow on the orgies and accusations and malicious counter cries of factions in Albany and elsewhere. Alas for the day when a second President of the United States welters in the blood of assassination! What unjust, but what injurious, impressions are already left on the European mind by this repetition of the unnatural crime of murdering, not a tyrant, an emperor, a king, but an elective President! How will Russian absolutists rejoice to see the horrors of Nihilistic crimes outdone by the children of a free State, and how will monarchs stiffen and condense the bayonets that guard their thrones when even the mildest and justest rulers over the equal citizens of the most happy and prosperous people cannot move about in their capital without danger to life from assassins? It is dreadful to feel what perverse uses will be made of an accident of frenzied brains to strengthen hateful tyrannies and to insult and disparage true and just principles. Let us swear a solemn oath that the caprices and follies of freemen shall not weaken our faith in liberty, and that the fatal misfortunes that assail our rulers shall not be allowed to recoil on the principles for which they stand. It would be the last counsel of our noble President were he, which God avert, to be called away from us by this atrocious act of violence, to stand faithfully by our American principles, to defend the ship of State, though pilot after pilot were shot down, and to honor and maintain the flag and the freedom of the nation against all assailants and all losses—above all against the malice of foreign depreciators, and, worse than that, against the treachery and domestic distrust and party jealousy and the feebleness of doubts of God's protection for free institutions or of humanity's fitness to receive them.

REV. J. P. NEWMAN'S STRONG LANGUAGE.

The announcement that the Rev. Dr. J. P. Newman was to preach yesterday morning on "The National Calamity" attracted an unusually large congregation to the Central Methodist Episcopal Church, New York. The text was from Proverbs xiv., 24—"Sin is a reproach to any people." Had James A. Garfield, said the preacher, been a Sultan Abdul Aziz, or an Alexander II., spending the people's wealth in riotous living, or populating some Siberia with the flower of our young manhood, his assassination would have found some apologists. But, gentle as a woman, kind as a father, trustful as a brother, his would be the death of kindness itself. General Garfield was our President, and to you and to me he represents the virtue, the civilization, the Christianity, and intelligence of the Republic; and not to us only, but to the world at large. His politics is a matter of no concern to us. Administrating the laws of this great nation, he stood in God's place. His murder is not merely regicide; it is deicide. A blow has been aimed at the very throne of Jehovah itself. Let us search for the causes that have produced this crime. Plainly discernible in the tragedy is the thirst for office, the malignity of partisan strife, the inordinate desire for wealth and luxury, the unworthy estimate of life and its serious responsibilities, and the contempt for religion. In politics, slander has become the chosen weapon, and defamation of character the argument most popular. What can be the influence of this evil? The orations of our leading men—United States senators, Congressmen, State legislators, all politicians—teem with villainous and contemptible onslaught on reputation, which, if uttered in private life, would justly exile their authors forever from decent society. Politics has become but the school for scandal.

Another cause which has led up to this assassination is the universal grasping after office. With all our national brag and bluster we have no civil service. Sixty thousand men are incited to partisan zeal in a Presidential election by the hope of a foreign mission, a consulate, or a clerkship. Faithful and competent men are removed to give place to some favorite or importunate office-seeker. Every official office in the land is on sale. The disgraceful scene recently enacted at Albany results not from a question of fitness for positions of power and trust, but from that other question—who shall wield the patronage of a great State? Men compete for opportunities to lead lives of ease and luxury, and they best secure their desires through politics. Disappointed or opposed, they resort to desperate methods. This political crime I lay at the door of no particular faction. Far from me be the intent of pointing to one faction as the embodiment of the devil, and to another as the personation of the angel Gabriel.

Our much-boasted universal suffrage, our power and our shield, as in our enthusiasm we are wont to term it, is not without its drawbacks, not without its dangers to our nation. I believe in popular suffrage to the full; but in the name of intelligence and virtue and common honesty, not to say decency, I am against the system that places unrestricted power in the hands of the paupers and criminals whom Europe is pouring upon our shores by tens of thousands. [Applause, which the preacher found it impossible to check.] It is a sad fact, but a notorious one, that the ballot has become an article of merchandise. In our last municipal election we honestly elected William Dowd Mayor of New York; but late in the day the influence of money was brought to bear, and the will of the intelligent and moral voters was annulled. Of Mr. Grace I have nothing to say in condemnation. I trust his administration may be pure and successful; he has my heartiest prayers; yet as he was elected, so are men elected in every State and at every election. The republics of Rome and Greece went down only after their free franchise was corrupted; after candidates stalked through the streets offering bribes to supporters and paying gold for votes. The causes which worked out the ruin of those republics is working out likewise the ruin of our own. Let us not be blinded to the truth and the teachings of history.

REV. HENRY WARD BEECHER'S REMARKS.

Mr. Beecher's countenance showed great sadness Sunday morning when he entered the pulpit of Plymouth Church, Brooklyn, and he devoted the entire service to the tragedy at Washington. The church was over-crowded, and many persons turned away from the doors unable to find even standing room within. The services consisted of appropriate music, special prayers by Mr. Beecher and selections of Scripture, with remarks drawn out by the event which was uppermost in every mind. Mr. Beecher was himself affected to tears at times, and handkerchiefs were in use in all parts of the audience. The Te Deum was sung at the opening of the service, and after a brief invocation Mr. Beecher said:—

We are met under circumstances happily most unusual, and it is one of the felicities of the service of our church that we are not tied down to any routine, but are free to follow the leadings of Providence. To-day, even if I could, I would not stand here as a didactic teacher, nor, in the common acceptance of the word, as a preacher. Not that there are not great truths in the word of God adapted to every emergency, but now and then God comes himself, and all men behold his foot-prints and hear his voice. When the providence of God speaks as it does to-day we must take the text from God himself.

Again in so short a time death has been aimed at the chief citizen of this great nation. The assassin's hand in both instances, let us believe, was a hand misguided by a brain more misguided—that of the shadows of insanity the aim has twice been taken, once fatally, and again, let us hope, in the Providence of God without final and fatal result. There were varied emotions preceding the election, but only one voice when it was determined. When President Garfield was called to the head of the Government, he was no longer a candidate, but our President, to every citizen of the United States. Every individual had a right to glory in his ripe usefulness, accumulated wisdom, honest intent, genial and generous disposition and his sanctified ambition, which sought to make, has made and will make him a Christian President over a free Christian people. When the sun rose yesterday there was no shadow across the pathway, full of hope and promise. When it rose to-day the people were in sorrow from ocean to ocean, and, indeed, deep called to deep. And now to-day, on this Sabbath morning, and because it is a Sabbath morning, and on this our communion service, and because it is our communion service, our thoughts are called from usual themes of discourse and dwell upon this calamity. May a great blessing come out of it, let us pray.

Now that the heart of the nation is cool, all men have a generous and just appreciation of the value to the nation of the man who lies on the bed of suffering and peril. I am not surprised at this. When the sound echoed over our whole land of his peril, there was no party, no advocate or adversaries; we were all citizens and not politicians. We are all on one side. If some unmannerly tongue has given utterance to rude and coarse remarks, we must think that it is the hasty utterance of ignorance and not the deliberate of a sane mind. Men shook hands with the pressure of grief at the sad news, and eyes were dim. All men had the same sentiment. All heads were bowed as if in the very presence of the God who dwells in darkness and were awed by his power. It is related by naturalists that in countries where freshets and floods prevail, when animals are driven by the water to take refuge together in the high ground and are hearded by a common terror, they forget their animosities and evil designs and dwell in peace. The rabbit and the fox, the lamb and the wolf, the bear and the deer and the serpent in common peril dwell quietly together and forget opposition. Many not wont to pray silently petitioned God to spare the life of the honored and beloved President.

Mr. Beecher then read the 39th and 41st Psalms. He read with especial feeling this verse: "The Lord will strengthen him upon the bed of languishing; Thou wilt make all his bed in his sickness."

After the reading Mr. Beecher said: "Let us join the millions who are making the space between heaven and earth thick with prayers, besieging the throne of God, that he will have compassion on the nation and spare the life of the President." He then prayed as follows: O Lord, who hast been good to this nation in days gone by; who hast sent wars, famines and pestilences, and withal a growing benefit; who hast rebuked our transgression and washed it away with blood; who made the sun to rise after the night and darkness of war; who then smote the shepherd in the fold, but did not suffer the nation to be destroyed, but restored tranquillity in all its bounds, and again in thy mysterious way hast stretched out thy hand to touch thy beloved, and suffered him to be struck down, and filled the house of light and joy with darkness and trouble—O Lord, wilt thou not stay thy hand? Do thou hold in wisdom and knowledge those who minister to the President. Endue them with divine knowledge. Sustain his strength. Many have been shattered on the battle-field and given over for dead, and yet now live. Enable him to endure the ordeal. Even if through months of suffering, bring him to light. Through a long recovery may thy servant be restored to us. Show the light of thy countenance to him. Thou hast eased him of care, and shut him up in thy pavilion. May no outward obligation trouble him; may his heart rest in thee. May hope in Christ come as the light of the morning to him, and may he be stayed in God in perfect tranquillity. O Lord God! is thy heart hardened? Is thine ear heavy, or thy hand shortened? Thou couldst bring Christ from the dead—canst thou not restore health on the border of the grave? Death is not mightier than thou! Thou who seest the heart, knowest how the poor and needy hope in him, and how the whole people unite in beseeching that the President may not pass from us. May the Holy Ghost fill the house with light and comfort and the balm of consolation. Hear thy servants at thine altars! Strangers are pleading; not strangers in a common grief. Be thou generous, thou who art mighty in mercy; bring hope before the sun goes down. Send from the house of desire, not only the word that he is better, but the hope and joy of restoration. And what shall we promise thee, or what can we give thee? Thou givest all to us; we can give nothing to thee but our gratitude. We will live better and seek to please thee. Regard the desire of millions. O Lord, God of thy servants in ancient days, in wrath remember mercy; restore our sick and establish him in health, and to thy adorable name will be praise forever more.

At the conclusion of the prayer the choir sang "Beyond the smiling and the weeping I shall be soon," and Mr. Beecher said:

The first effect of such an astounding event as this is apt to be confusion and fear. As in an earthquake men lose their trust in the solidity and safety of those things in which their life is built; so when God rends the heavens and a blow is struck at the centre of our affections, we ask, What can happen next? What will the end be? Fortunately for us, in all this we need not look for an unfavorable issue in the providence of God. There is nothing to fear except the evils incident to prosperous times. Such is the nature of free, intelligent government by an educated common people, that the strength of the government is not in itself at all. No official taken away shakes the fabric. There have been times when the ends of the earth seemed to rest on single men. Such was Moses to Israel, Washington to us, Cromwell to England, Cavour to Italy, Bismarck to Germany, Thiers and Gambetta to France. Were they taken, it would seem as if the buttresses were gone and the bridge must go too. These are extreme cases. In our history, when, the war not done, our proudest leader, our distinguished and noble head, now our revered martyr—Lincoln—was taken, it seemed as if all was at an end. But nothing suffered. We have not planted power in any department of government. The power is in the people themselves, and they lend it. If the hand using the power falls, the power is left. The nation stands four square, as the pyramids stand, but not desolate, and not on the bare sand. But around it are as many men as grains of sand around the Egyptian pyramids. Taking the head would not change one great interest. There would be no less ships to sail or building in the stocks; warehouses would be no fewer; wheels in factories would be no less; the hand would work at the anvil the same; and the plough would scour in the soil. Business would flow on with no check; no school, academy, or college would be put out; no church would be closed. The nation is broad, various, strong, and immovable. Until it rots at the sills by its own infidelity and corruption it will stand as unmoved as the mountains. We are spared anxiety from national peril. Other hands would take the reins of government if death should relax the hands now holding. Every department would go on the same, and all interests would be advanced.

But there are lessons for the nation in this. If we review the days of passion and partisan conflict as we now stand by the side of the sufferer, we may learn much. We are likely, in the heat of politics, to destroy all reverence for the Chief Magistrate. No man seeks position without losing reputation, and he is fortunate if character is not lost also. In this moment of sorrow we may see the evil of exaggeration and the injury and wrong of excess. Our father's God is ours. On such an occasion it seems proper to recognize God's great mercy. Our feelings are different than at the time of Lincoln's assassination. Then we were in the dark and troubled period of the war. A storm was in the sky and a tremor in the earth. There was just occasion for apprehension and fear. But it passed; our grief did not, but our fear did. There is no fear to-day. Twice in so few years has God plucked down the head of the Government in widely different conditions. Then, in the war time, the sky was overclouded;

now there is no scud of cloud in the sky. The nation is secure and happy in content and peace. This is the echo of the stroke which took the crowned head in Russia. In that anomalous people, spread abroad, of mixed races, in an inchoate condition, the stroke of death was precipitated on the Czar. It was a spurt of lightning out of the Russian storm-cloud, ever liable to send forth the lances of death. But here we were shut in from violence, with no stroke within or storm without. It was a wandering and wanton shot that struck. It came from no palace, no army, no subterranean depths, but from a lunatic asylum came that arrow of death. In our affliction let our prayers ascend to the God of our fathers not to forget us.

The 80th Psalm, a supplication for mercy, was then read by Mr. Beecher, and he again prayed. He prayed that this nation, which had been lifted up by God and set down in wrath, might have this event overruled to its good. He prayed for all the people in this out-spread land, where all nations are gathered—for the Chinaman, the Japanese, the Indian and the Russian who came to these shores; for all who came from Europe's fertile plains and rugged mountains—that they might agree in this land and this nation might be saved from intestine feuds.

After a hymn had been sung by the congregation, Mr. Beecher again rose and said. It is not fitting that we should go hence before we remember the stricken family of President Garfield in their exquisite suffering. In England noble women are educated for public affairs, and when put in places of honor they demean themselves with peculiar propriety. We are a democratic-republican people, and our women are educated particularly for domesticity and seclusion. It is a matter for congratulation when the President of the nation has reached his high position that he has a wife and household who know how to become their elevated station as if born heirs to titles and courts. If we look at the wives of the Presidents we see almost not a single cloud in the long succession. The succession is not changed. When that model in the family relation, Mrs. Hayes, left the White House it seemed as though an equal to her distinguished worth, as mother, wife and woman that had rejoiced the hearts of the people not could be found. But Mrs. Garfield, while differing much, is worthy to succeed her and need not fear to compare with any of her predecessors. She has just come up from the borders of death only to meet her husband in peril.

Then there is the venerable mother, who should have long preceded her son, who now seems likely to come after him. To-day if there is any woman here with a heart to pray for the stricken family and who remembers the sanctities of the household, let her seek God's blessing on the smitten family.

Mr. Beecher then prayed with deep and earnest feeling for the President's mother and wife and his children. There was scarcely a dry eye among the women in the church when he had ended, and tears found their way to the eyes of many men. In closing the petition he said : " Wilt Thou sustain the wounded man ! And if the way of darkness shall open for him—which must open some time for all feet to tread—wilt God be gracious and enable him to say, ' I fear no evil; Thy rod and thy staff, they comfort me.' May there come to us a voice of triumph from beyond. Lord God of our fathers ! Our God ! Comfort the family, the Government, the nation and the country, and enable all to say earnestly, no matter what the event may be. ' Thy will be done.'"

11

THE EIGHTY DAYS' STRUGGLE FOR LIFE.

REVIEW OF THE CONDITION OF THE PATIENT FROM THE DAY HE
  WAS SHOT TO THE DAY OF HIS DEATH—HIS RELAPSES—DE-
  SCRIPTION OF THE OPERATIONS—THE REMOVAL TO LONG
  BRANCH—HIS LAST DAYS.

President Garfield was shot by Charles J. Guiteau at about twenty minutes past 9 on the morning of Saturday, July 2, in the Baltimore and Potomac Railway station, a few minutes before he was to take the train from Washington to New York, on his way for a trip through New England. The rumor immediately became current that he was dead. This was believed for the moment, and produced the wildest excitement everywhere. It was soon contradicted, however.

At Washington all was confusion and alarm. The wounded man was taken to a room in the station, where he vomited. Drs. Bliss, Reyburn, and several other physicians were hastily summoned, and a preliminary examination of the wound was made. It was found that the ball, which was of 44 calibre, fired from a pistol of the British "bull-dog" pattern, had penetrated the back about four inches to the right of the spinal column, and subsequently it was learned that it had fractured the eleventh rib. Its course was downward and forward. In a few minutes the President was removed to the White House in an ambulance, and at 11.30 a.m. it was officially announced that he had returned to his normal condition, and that his pulse was 63. In the afternoon the reaction took place, and the patient's pulse at 7 p.m. stood at 140. He was reported to be bleeding internally, and it was not deemed best to probe the wound for the ball. On the arrival of Mrs. Garfield from Long Branch, early in the evening, the President became easier, and his pulse fell to 112. It was at this time supposed that the right lobe of the liver had been penetrated, and it was thought that the ball was embedded either in this organ or in the anterior wall of the abdomen. Nausea and vomiting had occurred during the day. In the course of the night the sick man complained of pains in his feet, indicating that a main nerve in his back had been affected by the ball. Few people expected him to live. Sunday was a day of alternating hopes and fears. In the morning he seemed brighter, but in the evening his pulse rose to 120. Peritoneal inflammation was feared. The 10.30 p.m. bulletin was signed by Surgeon-General Barnes and Dr. J. J. Woodward in addition to Drs. Bliss and Reyburn. Monday morning Dr. D. Hayes Agnew, of Philadelphia, and Dr. Frank H. Hamilton, of New York, arrived in Washington, having been summoned at the request of Mrs. Garfield, and approved of the course which had been taken by the attending physicians. In the morning bulletin the tympanites (swelling of the abdomen) was referred to as not having increased. The President vomited slightly during the day. Dr. Agnew, it was reported, stated that the kidneys and stomach were uninjured, but that the liver had been lacerated. Altogether it was a dismal Fourth of July all over the country.

DREAD GIVING PLACE TO HOPE.

On Tuesday a more cheerful feeling prevailed. The President was able to retain food, and the organs of the lower part of the abdomen were found to be uninjured. He did not vomit during Monday night, and the dispatches sent to Drs. Agnew and Hamilton, who had returned home, were encouraging. His pulse varied from 106 to 114. A consultation of medical men was held to consider the question of reducing the temperature in the sick-room, but nothing definite was done until several days later. Wednesday, July 6, the encouraging symptoms were continued. For the first time since the day he was shot the wounded man's pulse fell to below 100, it being 98 at 8.30 a.m., and the first crisis was thought to be passed. He passed a comparatively comfortable day, although the weather was very hot, and asked for substantial food. A simple arrangement to reduce the temperature of the room by the absorption and evaporation of ice-water gave some relief. The next day the patient's face presented a slightly jaundiced appearance; the bulletins were encouraging. On Friday his pulse and temperature were higher than on the day before, a slight fever being caused by the suppuration of the wound. In the morning bulletin it was announced that the wound had begun to discharge healthy pus. The President took more nourishment than usual. Saturday, July 9, the beginning of the second week, was also a hopeful day. The patient was in excellent spirits, and the bulletins were reassuring. On Sunday, July 10, the attending physicians telegraphed to Drs. Hamilton and Agnew that such slight changes as had occurred were for the better. Reference was made from time to time in these dispatches to the consulting surgeons of the morphine and quinine that were administered. The patient's pulse ranged from 102 to 108. The discharge of pus continued to be favorable. On Monday recovery was pronounced probable, and with the exception of the work upon the refrigerating machines the day was uneventful. The next few days showed what was thought to be continued improvement. The fever was less marked, and the patient's appetite was better. On Thursday, July 14, Professors Bell and Taintor arrived at Washington for the purpose of experimenting, in the hope by the aid of electrical instruments of determining the position of the ball in the President's body. On Saturday, July 16, solid food was relished. The patient seemed to be gaining strength daily, and the bulletins were gratifying though monotonous. There were said to be no indications of pyæmia. In view of his apparently steady progress toward convalescence it was decided to issue only a morning and evening bulletin. Solid food was eaten with great relish on Sunday, and the President expressed a desire to take a ride down the river. His pulse during these days was generally below 100, and sometimes down to below 90. The following few days were uneventful. The patient appeared to be improving, his appetite was good, and the wound was regarded as in a healthy condition. Occasionally his pulse would rise higher than usual, but this was said to be due to some minor causes. On Friday some fibres of cloth and a small piece of bone were discharged from the wound with the pus, and the afternoon fever was more marked than usual.

THE PATIENT'S FIRST RELAPSE.

Saturday, July 23, however, three weeks after he was shot, was a day of anxiety. The previous night the patient had been restless, and at 7 a.m. he had a chill which was followed by a fever.   At 11.30 a.m. he had another chill, and at 12.30 p.m. his pulse was 125, temperature 104, and respiration 26.   The wound failed to discharged pus readily, and it was thought that a pus cavity had been formed.   The patient vomited several times during the morning.   Drs. Agnew and Hamilton were hastily summoned, and went to Washington by special train. This was the first serious relapse that the President had had since he recovered from the first effects of the wound, and the feeling of alarm and anxiety was widespread.   The physicians denied that pyæmia had set in.   Other chills followed, and on the following morning Dr. Agnew performed an operation to relieve the pus cavity which had formed a few inches below where the ball entered the President's body.   The cut was about an inch in length and three quarters of an inch in depth, and extended into the original wound.   At night it was found that the pus from the wound was draining through the new opening.   This operation relieved the President, and the fever diminished.   He was free from nausea, and his temperature was lower.   The flow of pus became as free as usual.   The patient bore the operation without flinching.   In the course of this operation it was found that the eleventh rib had suffered a compound fracture.   It was broken in two places and bent inward. Dr. Reyburn was quoted as saying that there were no indications of blood poisoning, and the following day Dr. Bliss expressed the same opinion.   Malaria attacked several of the attendants at the White House, but the President was said to be free from any malarial symptoms.

On Monday, July 25, the patient seemed to be recovering from the effects of his relapse.   The discharge of pus was healthy, and the pulse ranged from 96 to 110.   On the whole it was thought that the new trouble with the wound was only transient.   Tuesday was a day of panics in Washington over wild and absurd rumors as to the President's condition which were not warranted by the facts.   Again he seemed to be on the road to recovery, and fear gave way to a more confident feeling.   At the forenoon dressing a splinter of rib half an inch long was removed from the wound.   Dr. Hamilton, who was not alone in his opinion, expressed the belief that the ball had lodged in the right iliac fossa—that is, in the lower part of the abdomen, on the right side, twelve inches or more from its point of entrance.   Cheering reports continued as to the progress of the patient. His good spirits returned, and his appetite was excellent. On Thursday, July 28, he was moved into an adjoining room while the sick-chamber was thoroughly cleaned. On Friday the symptoms continued favorable, and his ultimate recovery was confidently anticipated. The wound appeared to be in good condition, and the patient rested well and relished his nourishment. Solid food was taken on the following day. His pulse on that day—Saturday, July 30—varied from 92 to 104. On Monday, August 1, the electric induction balance was tried, and the approximate position of the ball was determined. This confirmed the opinion of the surgeons that the ball lay in the front wall of the abdomen, about five inches below and to the right of the navel, and just over the groin. So long as it caused no trouble it was thought best not to attempt to remove it. In the following few days the reports were all encouraging. The President's voice was natural, he took nourishment in the usual quantities, and the febrile symptoms were not such as to cause alarm. His recovery was regarded as only a question of time. It was thought that the ball was becoming encysted. The noon bulletin was again omitted. The patient slept without the aid of morphine.

AN OPERATION PERFORMED.

Nothing of moment occurred until Monday, August 8. The fever on the preceding few days had caused some apprehensions in the minds of the surgeons, and it was thought to be due to some impediment to the flow of pus. The mouth of the original wound had nearly healed, and the incision which was made to relieve the pus sac had become somewhat clogged by the rib. Accordingly the patient was given ether, and a new channel for the outflow of pus was cut by Dr. Agnew below the twelfth rib. It was about three and a half inches deep, and extended into the track of the ball. The operation brought on nausea, and the patient's pulse rose to 118, but soon fell to 100. The flow of pus through the new channel was satisfactory, and the patient was relieved. The next day, Tuesday, the patient's condition was encouraging. Solid food, however, was dispensed with for a time. On Wednesday, the President signed a paper of extradition in the case of an escaped Canadian forger. His fever was less marked than on the day before. Koumiss (fermented mare's milk) and some easily digested

Dont be disturbed by conflicting reports about my condition. It is true I am still weak. and on my back. but I am gaining every day. and need only time and patience to bring me through Give my love to all the relatives & friends & especially to sis Larg Hitty and Mary - Your. loving son - James A Garfield

Mrs Eliza Garfield
Hiram Ohio

solid food were relished. The fever resulting from the operation had abated on Thursday, and the patient's symptoms were very favorable, and he wrote the following letter to his mother, which now has a peculiar and historical interest, as it is the last letter ever written by him :

WASHINGTON, D. C.,
August 11, 1881.

DEAR MOTHER : Don't be disturbed by conflicting reports about my condition. It is true I am still weak and on my back, but I am gaining every day, and need only time and patience to bring me through.

Give my love to all the relatives and friends, especially to to sisters Hetty and Mary.

Your loving son, JAMES A. GARFIELD.

Mrs. ELIZA GARFIELD, Hiram, Ohio.

On the following day, Friday, Dr. Bliss, whose finger became inoculated with pus from the President's wound, was taken sick. The pulse of the President still continued rather higher than was wished, but this was not regarded as alarming. The wound on Saturday was said to be granulating finely, and the improved condition of the patient was noticeable.

TROUBLED WITH DYSPEPSIA.

On Sunday, August 14, the case took a new and unfavorable turn. The President's old enemy, dyspepsia, returned, and he was not able to retain his food as well as for a few days previous. His pulse in the evening was 108. The following day was an anxious one. The patient's stomach rebelled, and caused him to vomit several times. In his weakened condition this was recognized as a serious trouble. He had lost more than fifty pounds during his illness, and it was admitted that if his stomach should refuse to assimilate food the situation would be critical. Secretary Blaine and Secretary Lincoln, who had left Washington, were telegraphed for. The bulletins stated that the patient had not slept well and that his stomach was badly out of order.

In the afternoon the irritability of the President's stomach returned, and he vomited three times. At 6.30 p.m. his pulse was 130, having increased twelve beats since noon. For the

first time since he was wounded, nourishment was administered
by injection. The alarm that spread over the country was increased the next day by the news that the patient had vomited
again several times during the night. His pulse ranged during
the day from 110 to 120. His stomach continued weak, and
nourishment was given by injection. He failed to rally from
the prostration brought on the day before. On Wednesday, a
more hopeful feeling prevailed at the White House. The patient
took small quantities of food in the natural way, and his temperature was lower. His condition on the whole was rather
more encouraging, although, as Secretary Blaine telegraphed
United States Minister Lowell in England, it was extremely
critical. Both Dr. Hamilton and Dr. Agnew were in attendance
during the day.

THE PAROTID GLAND INFLAMED.

On Thursday, August 18, the noon bulletin said that the
President was suffering from inflammation of the right parotid
gland, which is affected when one has the mumps. The symptom was not regarded by the surgeons as serious, and as the
patient retained small quantities of food, the day was regarded
on the whole as one of progress. Some, however, took a more
gloomy view of the case, and in regard to the sentiment outside
the White House it was said : " Almost every one outside the
White House believes that there is a serious vitiation of the
patient's blood, and that this is the cause of the steady decline
in flesh and strength. This vitiation is not thought to amount
to pyæmia, if there is no rapid absorption of virulent matter in
the blood; but it is argued that the blood is in a depraved
condition, and that to this condition is owing all the unfavorable symptoms and the very grave fact, which no one disputes,
that in spite of occasional gains the steady course of the President has been down hill ever since he recovered from the shock
of the wound and made his first rally."

On the following day, Friday, it was announced that the
patient's stomach was resuming its functions. Yet the case
was regarded as critical, owing to the exhausted condition
of the sick man. The parotid gland ceased to give the President pain, and it was hoped that the worst was over. Nourishment was still given by injection, as it was imperative that the
strength of the sick man should be kept up by every possible

means. The parotid swelling was reported in the noon bulletin to be diminishing. The patient's pulse ranged from 100 to 106. Secretary Blaine telegraphed Mr. Lowell that the President was better than he had been for four days. On Saturday, more food was taken by the mouth and less by injection than on the day before. The noon bulletin was delayed, and when it was issued the reason became apparent. The wound, it stated, had been explored to a depth of twelve and a half inches by means of a flexible tube. Before this time the surgeons had been able to examine the wound to a depth of only three or four inches. The deeper penetration was permitted by the separation of a small slough. The wound was said to be in a good condition. The pus was healthy, and Dr. Bliss denied that the President was suffering from pyæmia. His pulse and temperature were a little higher than on the previous day. The only official reference to the parotid swelling was in the morning bulletin, which stated that it was unchanged and was free from pain.

HOPES AGAIN DASHED.

Sunday, August 21, was another bad day, and the hopes of the public were again dashed. During the preceding night the patient had been somewhat restless, and his pulse at 8.30 p.m. was at 106. His mind appeared to be affected by his excessive weakness. In the afternoon he vomited three times, and the process of feeding him by the mouth had again to be suspended temporarily. The vomiting, it was said, was not caused by nausea, but by the accumulation of saliva and phlegm in the patient's throat. The glandular irritation, the supposed cause of the bronchial obstruction, was still troublesome. Salve plasters and poultices seemed to have no effect in reducing the swelling.

The reports that the President's mind was wandering caused the gravest feeling of alarm. This, together with the unusually high fever and the temperature at one time below the normal, made the case a critical one. His coughing deprived him of rest, and he could not regain strength by food administered through the mouth, because he could not retain it. The reports on Monday, the 22d, were slightly more encouraging. In the course of the day about twenty ounces of liquid food were taken naturally and retained. The efforts to scatter the inflam-

11*

mation of the parotid gland were not successful, however, and an operation was talked of. The danger apprehended was from continual waste without an equivalent rebuilding. Slight delirium caused by feebleness and by the long illness was again noticed. Secretary Blaine telegraphed to London that the general condition of the President was serious if not critical. "He is weak, exhausted, and emaciated," said the dispatch, "not weighing over 125 or 130 pounds. His weight when wounded was from 205 to 210 pounds." His failure to gain strength was the cause for alarm. This dispatch caused the gravest feeling of uneasiness everywhere. The surgeons reported the wound to be doing well.

On Tuesday, the 23d, there was a ray of hope, and for a time a better feeling prevailed. Thirty ounces of liquid food were taken naturally and retained, and at one time the patient's pulse was down to 96—the lowest point reached in a fortnight. Fears, however, that the inflamed parotid gland would suppurate occasioned some uneasiness. The temperature and pulse were about the same as on the day before. On the whole the President was thought to be about the same, and the gain, if any, was very slight.

LANCING THE GLANDULAR SWELLING.

On Wednesday, August 24, the parotid swelling became softer than usual, indicating that suppuration had begun. Dr. Hamilton, therefore, took a lancet, and, throwing an antiseptic spray over the swelling without applying anæsthetics in any form, made an incision upward for half an inch and then downward for a like distance into the cheek an inch in front of and a little below the ear. The pulse immediately ran up to 115, but soon fell to 104. Partially hardened pus, in quantity about as large as two peas, was taken out. The President appeared to be relieved by the operation, and it was thought that danger from this source was removed. Late in the evening the arrival of Dr. Agnew from Philadelphia, whence he had been hastily summoned, caused considerable alarm. He was driven to the White House, where the question of the advisability of removing the President was under discussion. The members of the Cabinet were also present. It was decided not to move the patient. Rumors also prevailed that Vice-President Arthur had been summoned to Washington to assume the duties of the Presidency owing to the inability of General Garfield, but these proved to be unfounded.

Thursday, the case assumed a more serious phase. The incision in the glandular swelling did not produce the desired results, and it was still filled with pus confined in cells. The patient's stomach seemed to be doing well, and yet it was seen that he was gradually losing strength, and was hourly becoming less able to throw off the effects of vitiated blood and insufficient nourishment. Of itself the glandular disturbance would not have been a cause for serious alarm, but in the enfeebled condition of the patient it was liable to produce the gravest results. Despite the operation the swelling did not diminish, and the discharge of pus was very slight. This, taken with the fever in the afternoon, caused the deepest feeling of anxiety. The physicians themselves admitted the gravity of the President's condition, but hoped for a favorable turn. Secretary Blaine telegraphed to Mr. Lowell that the patient's mind, at intervals, had been clouded, and that he was losing strength. Friday it was thought that there was only a slight chance of the patient's recovery. The unfavorable symptoms continued. The pulse rose once to 138, and it remained at 136 for some time. The patient on awakening suffered from some mental confusion. The pus from the glandular swelling began to suppurate through the ear, and in the weakened condition of the patient this process, which ordinarily would be regarded as an encouraging sign, was looked upon as an additional cause for alarm. That the patient's blood was poisoned Dr. Bliss admitted. The wound, he said, looked badly. The sides were flabby, and the pus was thin, watery, and unhealthy. The only hope left was based upon the President's stomach. Should this fail him the end would only be a question of hours. In the noon bulletin the surgeons stated frankly for the first time that his condition was critical.

NEAR DEATH'S DOOR.

Saturday, August 27, was another day of terrible suspense and anxiety. It was popularly supposed that the death of the President was only a question of a day or two, or perhaps a few hours. The bulletins held out little hope. In the morning and at noon the President's pulse was 120. His temperature was about a degree higher at noon than at 8.30 a.m. He was feebler than on the day before. The only encouraging symptom was his ability to take and retain liquid food naturally. No change was observed in the parotid swelling or in the wound. In the afternoon, however, the conditions were somewhat more encouraging. His mind was clearer, and his pulse fell to 106. In the evening he asked for milk toast, which was given to him. A better feeling prevailed, and this was increased on Sunday, when the patient seemed to have emerged from the valley of the shadow of death. His pulse was less frequent, and no trouble was experienced with the stomach. His pulse fell to 100, and respiration and temperature were normal. Another incision was made in the parotid swelling to facilitate the escape of pus. The wound looked better than it had on the day before.

There is not much to be said about the week that followed. Little change was noticed in the condition of the patient. He seemed to hold his own from day to day, but made little if any perceptible progress toward recovery. It was regarded as an encouraging sign, however, that he did not grow worse, and the despondency of the preceding week gave way to hope for his ultimate recovery. The bulletins were monotonous, and the statement was made day after day that the condition of the patient did not differ materially from what it was at the same hour on the preceding day. Some of the symptoms were encouraging. The glandular swelling decreased in size, and the patient's pulse was at times as low as 90 and 95. He slept fairly well at night. Wednesday evening, August 31, his pulse ranged from 108 to 116, and caused some uneasiness, but the next day the fever subsided somewhat, and there was thought to be a slight improvement in his condition. Solid food was taken in considerable quantities with relish.

The sultriness of the weather the last of the week reopened the question of the President's removal from the White House. The air in Washington is full of malaria in September, and it was decided by the Cabinet and the surgeons that his removal was imperative. The President himself expressed a preference for Long Branch, inasmuch as it was inexpedient to undertake a journey to Mentor, and this was finally determined upon on Saturday, September 3. His condition was comfortable, and it was thought that there would be less risk in taking the journey

than in remaining in Washington. Late Saturday evening there
was a slight disturbance of the patient's stomach, and he vomited
twice in the night. The vomiting was caused by phlegm in the
throat, it was thought, and was unaccompanied by serious results. His pulse was somewhat higher on Sunday than on Saturday. The prospect of going to Long Branch seemed to make
the patient slightly restless and nervous. The parotid swelling
continued to improve, and the condition of the wound remained
about the same.

REMOVED TO LONG BRANCH.

Nothing of special importance occurred until Wednesday,
September 7, when the President was safely removed to Long
Branch by rail. Elaborate preparations had been made for the
journey. Shortly before 6 a.m. the patient was carried down-
stairs and placed in an Adams Express wagon, in which he was
driven from the White House to the special train which had been
fitted up for his reception. His pulse before he left the White
House was 118, temperature 99.8, respiration 18. The car in
which he was placed had been carefully fitted up with a spring
bed, by which the motion of the car was reduced to a minimum.
The road to Long Branch, by way of Philadelphia, Monmouth
Junction, and Sea Girt, was cleared of all trains, and the journey
was made rapidly and without accident. Crowds of people were
present at many of the stations, but they kept perfectly quiet.
Up to Philadelphia the President seemed to enjoy the ride, but
from Philadelphia to Sea Girt he was restless and seemed to be
exhausted by the journey. The salt air which blew through the
car on its journey from Sea Girt to Long Branch revived him
somewhat. The train reached Elberon at a few minutes past 1
o'clock, and the President was immediately removed to the room
which had been prepared for him in the cottage of Mr. C. G.
Francklyn. At 6.30 p.m. his pulse was found to be 124, temperature 101.6, respiration 18. The increased pulse was said to
be due to the excitement and fatigue incidental to the journey.
In the evening the fever was less marked.

On the following day, despite the intense heat that prevailed
at Long Branch, the President expressed himself as "feeling
better," and the physicians were hopeful of speedy progress
toward health. At the President's own desire, Drs. Barnes,

Reyburn, and Woodward withdrew from the corps of attending surgeons, after signing the official bulletins of that day, the President believing that a smaller number of attendants could manage the case as well as the number at first engaged upon it.

Slight but positive improvement, with few fluctuations, was made by the President, until Sunday, the 11th, when some anxiety was caused by the announcement of a rise in pulse, temperature, and respiration, and a distressing cough revealed the presence of some lung trouble, supposed to be the formation of a pus cavity in the right lobe, from which pus was discharged into his throat.   At the same time there was a marked improvement in the condition of the parotid gland, some of the affected portion sloughing away, to the relief of the patient, and on Monday there was a change for the better, the lung trouble partially subsiding, the gland and wound making good progress in healing, and the stomach continuing to perform its functions well.   The favorable symptoms continued on the following day, when the President was placed for the first time in a reclining chair, and spent half an hour there without bad results.   The lung trouble apparently grew less, and the patient no longer felt the continual sense of fatigue of which he had formerly complained: On Wednesday, the 15th, he was again placed in the reclining chair, and partook, among other things, of some fruit, with evident relish.   Less progress was perceptible, however, than on the previous day, and it became apparent that he was suffering from an abscess in the lower part of the right lung, the result of septic infection of the blood.   Thursday there was no change in his condition.   He took food in variety, though his appetite was not strong.   His determination to get well wavered a little at times, and he once expressed fear that bringing him to the seaside would be of no avail after all.

Public anxiety increased greatly on Friday, September 16th, as the President coughed a great deal ; the sputa was purulent ; the wound was not healthy in appearance, and the discharge from it was thin and watery.   At times his respiration was 22. He was again afflicted with bed-sores, and although his stomach acted well, and he ate more food than usual, he was evidently growing weaker.

Respiration

THE BEGINNING OF THE END.

Half an hour before noon on Saturday, September 17th, a severe chill set in, lasting for fully half an hour. Slight evidences of a chill had been discovered the preceding night, but the physicians had been able to keep it under control. The attack of the chills was followed later by profuse perspiration and high fever. Toward night the patient felt slightly relieved. In the evening of the following day, Sunday, a chill lasting for fifteen minutes excited the gravest apprehensions among the President's attendants. The patient suffered severely from its effects. Though the patient felt relieved a few hours later, the physicians were of the opinion that the situation was very critical.

HIS LAST DAY.

Monday, September 19, opened ominously. A chill lasting about fifteen minutes occurred at 8.30 a.m. It was followed by a considerable febrile rise and sweating. The bulletin issued at 12.30 p.m. stated that the sufferer's general condition remained unchanged ; his temperature at that time being 98.2, pulse 104, respiration 20. Ever since the first chill had seized the patient he had been sinking slowly and gradually. Immediately after the issue of the second bulletin dispatches were sent by Secretary MacVeagh to Secretaries Blaine and Lincoln to hasten their return to Elberon. A dispatch was also sent to Vice-President Arthur. Everybody seemed to be convinced that the crisis was at hand. The evening bulletin gave scarcely any encouragement. As the evening passed the patient seemed to grow weaker and weaker, and at 10.35 p.m., after a struggle for life lasting seventy-nine days, death relieved the sufferer.

PULSE, TEMPERATURE, AND RESPIRATION.

The following table shows the fluctuations in the President's pulse, temperature, and respiration from day to day up to the time of his death. The figures are taken from the morning, noon, and early evening bulletins :

DATE.	PULSE.			TEMPERATURE.			RESPIRATION.		
	A.M.	M.	P.M.	A.M.	M.	P.M.	A.M.	M.	P.M.
July 3......	....	....	120	....	....	100	..	..	20
July 4......	108	110	126	99.4	100	101.9	19	24	24
July 5......	114	110	106	100.5	101	100.9	24	24	24
July 6......	98	100	104	98.9	99.7	100.6	23	23	23
July 7......	94	100	106	99.1	100.8	100.2	23	23	23
July 8......	96	108	108	99.2	101.4	101.3	23	24	24
July 9......	100	104	108	99.4	101.2	101.9	24	22	24
July 10......	106	102	108	100	100.5	101.9	23	22	24
July 11......	98	106	108	99.2	99.8	102.8	22	24	24
July 12......	96	100	104	99.6	100.8	102.4	22	24	24
July 13......	90	94	100	98.5	100.6	101.6	20	22	24
July 14......	90	94	98	99.8	98.5	101	22	22	23
July 15......	90	94	98	98.5	98.5	100.4	18	18	20
July 16......	90	94	98	98.5	98.4	100.2	18	18	19
July 17......	90	94	98	98.4	98.5	100.2	18	18	20
July 18......	88	98	102	98.4	98.5	100.7	18	18	21
July 19......	90	92	96	98.5	98.5	99.8	18	19	19
July 20......	86	88	98	98.4	98.4	99.6	18	18	19
July 21......	88	92	96	98.4	95.4	99.9	18	19	19
July 22......	88	98	98	98.4	98.4	100.2	17	18	19
July 23......	92	125	118	97.4	104	101.7	19	26	25
July 24......	98	118	104	98.4	99.8	99.2	18	24	23
July 25......	96	104	110	98.4	98.4	101.8	18	20	24
July 26......	102	106	104	98.4	98.4	100.7	18	19	22
July 27......	94	90	95	98.4	98.4	98.5	18	18	20
July 28......	92	94	104	98.4	98.5	100.5	18	18	20
July 29......	92	98	98	98.4	98.4	100	18	19	20
July 30......	92	98	104	98.5	98.5	100	18	20	20
July 31......	94	100	104	98.4	98.5	90	18	19	20
Aug. 1.....	94	100	104	98.4	98.4	99.5	18	19	20
Aug. 2.....	94	99	104	98.4	88.4	100	18	19	20
Aug. 3.....	96	100	102	98.4	98.4	99.4	18	19	19
Aug. 4. ...	90	96	102	98.4	98.4	100.2	18	18	19
Aug. 5.....	88	98	102	98.4	98.4	100.4	18	18	19
Aug. 6.....	92	100	102	98.4	98.5	101.8	18	19	19
Aug. 7.....	96	104	104	98.7	100	101.2	18	20	20
Aug. 8.....	94	104	108	98.4	100.2	101.9	18	20	19
Aug. 9.....	98	104	106	99.8	99.7	101.9	19	19	19
Aug. 10.....	104	110	108	98.5	98.6	101	19	19	19
Aug. 11.....	100	102	108	98.6	98.6	101.2	19	19	19
Aug. 12.....	100	100	108	98.6	99.3	101.2	19	19	19
Aug. 13.....	104	102	104	100.8	99.2	100.7	19	18	19
Aug. 14.....	100	96	108	99.8	99.3	100.8	18	18	19
Aug. 15.....	108	118	130	100.2	99	99.6	20	19	22
Aug. 16.....	110	114	120	98.6	98.3	98.9	18	18	19

DATE.	PULSE.			TEMPERATURE.			RESPIRATION.		
	A.M.	M.	P.M.	A.M.	M.	P.M.	A.M.	M.	P.M.
Aug. 17....	110	112	112	98.3	98.7	98.8	18	18	18
Aug. 18....	104	108	108	98.8	98.4	100	17	18	18
Aug. 19....	100	106	106	98.4	98.8	100	17	17	18
Aug. 20....	98	107	110	98.4	98.4	100.4	18	18	19
Aug. 21....	106	108	108	98.8	99.4	99.2	18	18	18
Aug. 22....	104	104	110	98.4	98.4	100.1	18	18	19
Aug. 23....	100	104	104	98.4	98.9	99.2	18	18	19
Aug. 24....	100	104	108	98.5	99.2	100.7	17	17	19
Aug. 25....	106	112	112	98.5	99.2	99.8	18	19	19
Aug. 26....	108	118	116	99.1	100	99.9	17	18	18
Aug. 27....	120	120	114	98.4	99.6	98.9	22	22	22
Aug. 28....	100	104	110	93.4	99.5	99.7	17	18	20
Aug. 29....	100	106	110	98.5	98.6	100.5	17	18	18
Aug. 30....	102	116	109	98.5	98.9	99.5	18	18	18
Aug. 31 ...	100	95	109	98.4	98.4	98.6	18	17	18
Sept. 1....	100	108	108	98.4	98.6	99.4	17	18	18
Sept. 2....	100	108	104	98.4	98.7	99.2	17	18	18
Sept. 3....	104	104	102	98.6	98.4	99.6	18	18	18
Sept. 4....	108	106	110	98.4	98.4	99	18	18	18
Sept. 5....	102	114	108	99.5	99.5	99.8	18	18	18

On Tuesday, September 6, the President was removed by rail to the Francklyn cottage, Elberon, Long Branch, N. J. In the early morning, before leaving Washington, his pulse was 118; during the journey it fell to 110, and even lower; and at 6.30 p.m., when the only official bulletin for the day was issued, and the President had been in his new quarters several hours, his pulse was 124, temperature 101.6, and respiration 18. The record of the bulletins thereafter is as follows:

DATE	PULSE			TEMPERATURE			RESPIRATION		
Sept. 7....	106	114	108	98.4	98.4	101	18	18	18
Sept. 8....	104	94	100	98.7	98.4	99.1	18	17	18
Sept. 9....	100	100	100	98.5	98.4	98.8	17	17	18
Sept. 10....	100	100	100	99.4	98.5	98.7	18	18	18
Sept. 11....	104	110	110	98.8	100	106	19	20	20
Sept. 12....	100	106	100	98.4	99.2	98.6	18	20	18
Sept. 13....	100	100	100	99.4	98 8	98.4	20	20	20
Sept. 14....	100	104	112	98.4	98.8	99.2	19	20	21
Sept. 15....	100	102	104	98.4	98.9	99.2	20	21	21
Sept. 16....	104	116	104	98.6	99.8	98.6	21	21	22
Sept. 17....	108	120	102	99.8	102	98	21	24	18
Sept. 18....	102	116	102	98	100	98.4	18	20	20
Sept. 19....	106	104	102	98.8	98.2	98.4	22	20	18

DEATH OF THE PRESIDENT.

HIS LAST MOMENTS.

A SUDDEN AND UNEXPECTED END—THE ANNOUNCEMENT A SUR-
PRISE — THE CABINET SUMMONED AND VICE-PRESIDENT
ARTHUR INFORMED.

THE END.

A wasp flew out upon our fairest son,
And stung him to the quick with poisoned shaft,
The while he chatted carelessly and laughed,
And knew not of the fateful mischief done.
And so this life, amid our love begun,
Envenomed by the insect's hellish craft,
Was drunk by Death in one long feverish draught,
And he was lost—our precious, priceless one!
O mystery of blind, remorseless fate!
O cruel end of a most causeless hate!
That life so mean should murder life so great!
What is there left to us who think and feel,
Who have no remedy and no appeal,
But damn the wasp and crush him under heel?

                                        J. G. HOLLAND.

LONG BRANCH, Sept. 19.—The President of the United States
died to-night unexpectedly at 10.35 o'clock. Between 9 and
10 o'clock almost all the correspondents who had been closely
watching the case left the Elberon and went to the West End to
finish their dispatches and place them upon the wires there.
The information that the President was sinking fast was sent to
the West End Hotel at 10.45. At once the correspondents
and others hastened to Elberon. When they reached that spot
no particulars could be learned. At first Warren Young had
brought the news across the lawn to the hotel. At 11.05 Attorney-General MacVeagh appeared in the hotel, took posses-

sion of the Western Union wire in the name of the government and sent to Vice-President Arthur a dispatch informing him in the briefest manner that the President was dead, and saying that he would at once consult the other members of the Cabinet. The members of the Cabinet were at once summoned. In a few minutes, having started from the West End before the reception of the summons, they were at Elberon, and, arm in arm, they walked across the lawn in the darkness to the cottage, where the dead President lay.

Judge-Advocate-General Swaim, who was with the President the night of his death, gives the following description of great interest of the President's last moments of life: "It was my night to watch with the President. I had been with him a good deal of the time from 3 o'clock in the afternoon. A few minutes before 10 o'clock I left Colonel Rockwell, with whom I had been talking for some minutes, in the lower hall and proceeded upstairs to the President's room. On entering I found Mrs. Garfield sitting by his bedside. There were no other persons in the room. I said to her, 'How is everything going?' She replied, 'He is sleeping nicely.' I then said, 'I think you had better go to bed and rest.' I asked her what had been prescribed for him to take during the night. She replied that she did not know; that she had given him milk punch at 8 o'clock. I then said, 'If you will wait a moment I will go into the doctor's room and see what is to be given during the night.' She then said, 'There is beef tea downstairs. Daniel knows where to get it.' I then went into the doctor's room. I found Dr. Bliss there, and asked him what was to be given during the night. He answered, 'I think I had better fix up a list, and will bring it in to you pretty soon.' I then went back into the surgeon's room, and had some little conversation with Mrs. Garfield. She felt of the President's hand and laid her hand on his forehead, and said, 'He seems to be in a good condition,' and passed out of the room. I immediately felt his hands, feet, and knees. I thought that his knees seemed a little cool and got a flannel cloth, heated it at the fire, and laid it over his limbs. I also heated another cloth and laid it over his right hand, and then sat down in a chair beside his bed. I was hardly seated when Dr. Boynton came in and felt the President's pulse. I asked him how it seemed to him. He replied, 'It is not as strong as it was this afternoon, but very good.' I said, 'He seems to be doing well.' 'Yes,' he answered and passed out. He was not in the room more than two minutes.

"Shortly after this the President awoke. As he turned his head on awakening I arose and took hold of his hand. I was on the left-hand side of the bed as he lay. I remarked, 'You have had a nice comfortable sleep.'

"He then said, 'Oh, Swaim, this terrible pain!' placing his right hand on his breast, about over the region of the heart. I asked him if I could do anything for him. He said, 'Some water.' I went to the other side of the room and poured about an ounce and a half of Poland water into a glass and gave it to him to drink. He took the glass in his hand, I raising his head as usual, and drank the water very naturally. I then handed the glass to the colored man Daniel, who came in during the time I was getting the water. Afterward I took a napkin and wiped his forehead, as he usually perspired on awaking. He then said, 'Oh, Swaim, this terrible pain! press your hand on it.' I laid my hand on his chest. He then threw both hands up to the side and about on a line with his head, and exclaimed, 'Oh, Swaim! can't you stop this?' And again, 'Oh, Swaim!'

"I then saw him looking at me with a staring expression. I asked him if he was suffering much pain. Receiving no answer, I repeated the question, with like result. I then concluded that he was either dying or was having a severe spasm, and called to Daniel, who was at the door, to tell Dr. Bliss and Mrs. Garfield to come immediately, and glanced at the small clock hanging on the chandelier nearly over the foot of his bed and saw that it was ten minutes past 10 o'clock. Dr. Bliss came in within two or three minutes. I told Daniel to bring the light. A lighted candle habitually sat behind a screen near the door. When the light shone full on the President's face I saw that he was dying. When Dr. Bliss came in a moment after I said, 'Doctor, have you any stimulants? he seems to be dying.' He took hold of the President's wrist, as if feeling for his pulse, and said, 'Yes, he is dying.' I then said to Daniel, 'Run and arouse the house.' At that moment Colonel Rockwell came in, when Dr. Bliss said, 'Let us rub his limbs,' which we did. In a very few moments Mrs. Garfield came in and said, 'What does this mean?' and a moment after exclaimed, 'Oh! why am I made to suffer this cruel wrong?' At 10.30 o'clock the sacrifice was completed. He breathed his last calmly and peacefully.

"At the final moment the following persons were present: Mrs. Garfield and Miss Mollie Garfield, Drs. Bliss, Agnew, and Boynton, General Swaim, Colonel and Mrs. Rockwell, J. Stanley Brown, C. O. Rockwell, and Daniel Spriggs."

Dr. Boynton gives the following account of the death-scene:

Just before 10 o'clock, as the cottage was closing, he went up to the President's room, and upon feeling the President's pulse noticed it was weaker. Without awakening the President he called the attention of General Swaim to the fact, and then, thinking a change was impending, he went over to the hotel to send some dispatch. He was almost immediately summoned. Upon going over in haste and entering the room he saw clearly that the President was dying. Most of the family had arrived in the room; all the surgeons were found in time except Dr. Hamilton. Scarcely a word was spoken by any one, as it was clear to all at a glance that the President was dying. As those summoned came in they silently took their places about the bed. Colonel Rockwell stood at the head, General Swaim first to the left, next Mrs. Garfield, who gently held her hand on the President's face and breast. Next stood Mrs. Rockwell. Dr. Boynton stood to the right of the President's head, next Dr. Agnew, and next to him Dr. Bliss. Private Secretary Brown stood a little in the rear and to the left of Mrs. Garfield. "Dan," the colored man, was a little way from the foot of the bed. Miss Mollie Garfield was near the door.

All stood silently in these positions watching the dying man. Once or twice there were low whispers among the surgeons. Dr. Agnew held the pulse, and Dr. Boynton listened for the heart, but could hear no sound. The only treatment attempted was to give a hypodermic injection to allay pain. The President lay perfectly still after he first called for General Swaim and told him of the pain over his heart. He simply gasped slowly and at intervals, and thus watched he passed quietly away in about twenty minutes. Not a muscle moved except in the gasping, and there was no quiver or expression to tell of pain. At death, the eyes rested half closed, as if in partial sleep. Mrs. Garfield was strongly affected, but said nothing, and did not break down. After death she left the room quietly, but returned in about half an hour and sat by the bed, scarcely speaking until about 2 o'clock. At that hour Dr. Boynton urged her to retire, which she did.

One present in the room at the time of the death says Mrs. Garfield bore herself with surprising fortitude. Her Christian courage did not forsake her for a moment. She remained a short time after the death was apparent to all, then withdrew quietly to her own room. Miss Mollie Garfield was overcome from the moment of the sudden summons to go to her father's bedside, and gave full vent to her grief in spite of every effort at self-control. To most there, as to all outside, the sudden and unforeseen news came more as a bewildering shock than as an event which could be measured or realized. Hours after men walked and talked of it as of a matter scarcely tangible.

Secretary Windom, Secretary Kirkwood, and Postmaster-General James had just returned to their rooms and retired. They spent the time after their arrival at the Francklyn Cottage in discussing the preparations for the obsequies and kindred affairs, but took no formal action except in regard to telegraphing the Vice-President. Secretary Windom said that he had been trying to convince himself, and had almost succeeded, that there was still a chance for recovery, when he was suddenly requested by Mr. Jameson to open his door and the startling announcement was made that the President was dead.

"I had been depressed all day," said Postmaster-General James, "and could not get rid of the idea that the end was near, yet I think it shocked us all more than it would have done had death resulted soon after the shooting."

"I was in bed," said Secretary Kirkwood, "and the summons came like a thunder-clap out of the clear sky. I have had little hope of his recovery for several days, but this was a surprise."

"I believe he was ready for death," said Mr. James; "no man was better prepared."

"Yes," added Secretary Windom, "he was not afraid of it. He has discussed the matter during the last two or three days with his attendants, and his words have shown that he was considering the sad probability very calmly. Yes, he was ready on the very day he was shot, when he expected to die. He said to Mrs. Windom, 'That is all right, all right.'"

No words can describe the grief which the tone and subdued manner of the speakers betrayed. Hands were clasped at parting as if in this common sorrow they fain would sustain each other.

ELBERON COTTAGE, WHERE THE PRESIDENT DIED, WITH TEMPORARY TRACK LAID TO THE DOOR OF THE COTTAGE.

The suddenness with which the news of the death came can hardly be realized by one not at Elberon. The cottage was closed at 10 o'clock for the night. The two doorkeepers, Ricker and Atchison, had strolled down to the beach for a short walk before going to bed. Suddenly Ricker said to Atchison that the house was all lighted up. They both started up, and at the cottage door met Private Secretary Brown, who told them that the President was very low, and asked them to call the surgeons and the Attorney-General and other members of the Cabinet. Dr. Boynton was talking in the hotel office at the time. He hastily ran toward the cottage, and in a moment or two returned and announced that the President was rapidly sinking, and again he returned to the death-chamber. Attorney-General MacVeagh was in bed, but he was up and dressed in two or three minutes. A carriage was hastily dispatched for the other members of the Cabinet at the West End, but they did not arrive till some minutes after the sad event had occurred. The first news of the death of the President which reached the outside of the cottage was carried by Warren Young, one of the White House clerks. He carried in his hand some dispatches which had been indited to relatives of the President. He was asked about the condition of the President, and replied, " All is over."

HOW THE PRESIDENT'S MOTHER BORE THE NEWS.

At six o'clock on Tuesday morning the sad news was received by telegram at a place called Solon, near Mentor, where the President's mother was stopping with a married daughter named Mrs. Larabee. The dispatch was placed in the hands of the daughter. Her mother was sleeping calmly, and the old lady did not awake until 8 o'clock. At that time Mrs. Larabee passed her door with a heavy heart, and found her dressed and engaged in reading the Bible. It was thought best not to break the news until Mrs. Garfield had eaten breakfast. Oddly enough the old lady did not insist upon hearing the news until the meal was finished. Then, taking the fatal telegram from the shelf, she was about to read, but Miss Ellen took it from her trembling hands.

"Grandma," she said, "would you be surprised to hear bad news this morning?"

"Why, I don't know," said the old lady.

" Well, I should not," said Mrs. Larabee; " I have been fearing and expecting all the morning."

"Grandma," said Ellen, " there is sad news."

" Is he dead ?" asked the old lady tremulously.

" He is."

The quick tears started in the sensitive eyes. There was a violent paroxysm of grief. No expression of frenzy told of the anguish within.

" Is it true ?" she asked with quivering lips. " Then the Lord help me, for if he is dead what shall I do ?"

She was rendered weak and a little nervous by the announcement, and was obliged once or twice to repair to her room, where in solitude she might begin to comprehend the awful truth; but she was not content to remain there, and soon returned to the sitting-room.

About half-past 9 o'clock Mrs. Garfield was found sitting in a rocking-chair waiting for news. The morning paper she read with eagerness. " It cannot be that James is dead," she muttered. " I cannot understand it. I have no further wish to live, and I cannot live if it is so." Although her general health is good at present, many fear that her words are prophetic, and Mrs. Larabee dares not hope otherwise herself. But feeling keenly as she does her great affliction, never once has she hinted at a lack of faith in the Supreme One that all is not intended for the best.

" It is providential," she said. " I can firmly believe that God knows best, and I must not murmur."

The writer visited the aged mother of the dead President at her humble home near Solon. It is an unpretentious little home, provided by the kindness of the dead President, for it is no sin to remind the American people, who mourn the loss of this great-hearted and great-brained ruler, that all his kindred are poor. Not one is above daily toil, and, except for the promotions of the past few years, it is doubtful whether even he would have been. It does not seem to be any part of the Garfield family training or inclination to be money-getters. The little house is built upon the ground, being only a story and a half high. Two lines of great apple-trees guard the walk from the gate through the hedge up to the parlor door. To-day the little room seemed hung in mourning by the looks of all who were about it. A few cut flowers which grew in the garden near by were in a glass dish upon the table, and to the right upon another little table sitting against the wall large and excellent photographs of Garfield and Arthur sat side by side. On the opposite wall hung an engraving of Garfield as a boy, soldier, and President. In this room sat General Garfield's aged mother and Mrs. Larabee, her daughter, as well as Mrs. Larabee's youngest daughter. The aged mother seemed much depressed with her great sorrow, but bore up bravely.

"I am starting upon my eighty-first year to-day," said she, "and it may be my last. This is a terrible sorrow, a fearful affliction for me to bear, but doubtless God knew best when to take him. He was the best son a mother ever had—so good, kind, generous, and brave. If he had to die, why didn't God take him without all the terrible suffering he endured? I suppose I ought to think that it is for the best, and yet I cannot. He had, I know, fulfilled the full measure of his ambition. He had reached the highest place in the regard of his countrymen."

"Did you ever see such an uprising?" she said eagerly. "That ought to break the fall for me, but it doesn't seem to. I want my boy. It seems so hard, too, that we could not have been with him in his dying hours. There are his sisters, who played with him in his childhood, and who loved him as I did. It seems so hard that he should die away from us."

As if gathering hope for the future, the courageous and loving mother, long past the allotted time of man or woman in years, added, "I cannot last long, and the other world will be brighter for his presence." Referring to the place of his burial she said: "It is proper that he should be buried in Cleveland. It is the capital of the county in which he was born and of the section where he grew into prominence. Mentor had been his home but a short time, although he had intended it should be the balance of his life. Most of his years have been spent at Solon and Orange, and it seems best that his final resting-place should be near the places that he loved best."

The brave old lady often trembled with emotion while talking thus pathetically of her distinguished son. He seemed to fill her whole heart, and she never tired, she said, even in her affliction, of seeing people who knew him and would talk to her about him. "It is wonderful," said she, "how I live upon thoughts of him. I ride a little every day to get the fresh air

12

and look at the fields and places he loved so well. I am so glad you have been over to the old homestead. He loved every foot of it. He and his brother built the frame house for me near the well where the pole has been erected. It was rude carpentering, indeed, but they both took their first lessons in it, and I always loved the old home. It was burned after we left it. I am very glad you saw Henry Boynton. He and James were such ardent friends. He knows all about his early life and struggles. The whole people are helping me to bear this terrible affliction. I am getting the kindest and most affectionate letters and telegrams from all sections of the country."

It is really surprising to see how the hearts of the people, especially in the West, have turned from mourning over the dead to giving sympathy to the living. A whole bundle of letters and telegrams lay in the President's mother's lap, breathing in tenderest terms the most hearty sympathy for her in her bereavement. From the presence of the mother to the village graveyard I passed, as soon as a walk of half a mile would bring me there, and within a few feet of the main gate for foot travellers I saw the grave of the President's father. He had his body disinterred some years since from its resting-place upon the farm at Orange and brought to this little village churchyard almost under the shadow of the Disciples' church. A plain marble slab marks the spot where his remains lie. It bears the inscription, " Abram Garfield. Died May 3, 1833, aged 33." A cloud of creeping myrtle covers the ground and a Norway pine stands guard over the grave. In the other end of the town is the little church of the Disciples, steepleless and decaying, where General Garfield used to preach.

ELBERON, Sept. 20.—The sun's face wore a deep coppery tint as he looked up over the waters this morning, and threw his earliest rays upon the closed shutters of the cottage of death. The wind, which for a week had been coming from seaward and at times blew a gale, came now from the west and was hushed to a gentle zephyr. The billows which for days had lashed the sands in anger now murmured softly of that eternity of which they were the fittest symbol. The sky was cloudless, but a mellow haze hung over the ocean, obliterating the horizon line and blending sea and sky in one. A single craft, miles distant, floating as it seemed upon nothing, like a soul just parted from time, was making its slow way with all sails set to catch the breeze toward the north.

At the cottage the quiet of death prevailed. At a little distance, on all sides, armed sentinels with fixed bayonets paced their beats in silence, guardians as it seemed of that border line between now and hereafter, beyond which the living might never pass. The flag, which since the arrival of the President at Elberon has been floating from a pole thrust out of an upper window of the cottage, was draped with black, but beyond this no outward sign of mourning was apparent. The first comers were the journalists, but in their demeanor the customary eagerness of competition was not apparent. Fifty million people would before night read the truths they had come to gather, but their subject of inquiry was death and mourning, and decorous propriety befitting the occasion was always to be respected.

By half-past seven a dozen people had gathered in groups upon the porches of the hotel. Doctors Bliss, Hamilton, and Agnew were in consultation at that portion of the hotel nearest the cottage where lay the remains of the man who had been for eleven weeks the object of their solicitude and skill. They talked of the events of the night just past, and of the nights and days which had preceded it. They talked of the coming autopsy, and agreed that it should be postponed until the arrival in the afternoon of their Washington associates in the medical councils upon the case.

Dr. Bliss said in regard to the immediate cause of the President's death that he believed it resulted from the coagulation of blood, which the heart in its enfeebled condition was unable to force off. General Swaim, he said, had evidently not at first fully appreciated the imminence of the crisis, but had called Dr. Bliss immediately. "I stepped in at once," said the Doctor, "and as a ray of light fell across the invalid's face I said, 'My God! he is dying. Send for Mrs. Garfield.' It was virtually a painless death. He suffered at first, but unconsciousness came, and with that his sufferings were at an end."

At half-past ten Secretaries Windom, Kirkwood, and Hunt, and Postmaster-General James arrived at Elberon, and were invited at once to the Attorney-General's cottage, situated about as far to the northeast of the hotel as the Francklyn cottage in which the dead President lay is to the southeast. There they remained during the forenoon discussing the details of the events which had just transpired, in which they were all so deeply interested. A half-hour later General Grant, with his son and a friend, drove up, and the ex-President spent an hour in gathering information of the last hours of President Garfield.

Meanwhile the undertaker and his assistants had arrived and were preparing the body of the President for embalmment and burial. The body showed the loss of flesh to a degree painful to look upon. Only the face preserved anything like the appearance when in health. The beard in a measure contributed to this, serving to conceal the hollowness of the cheeks. The body was laid upon rubber cloths placed upon the floor to await the autopsy, which lasted about three and a half hours. One of the gentlemen present makes the following statement in regard to it:

The ball was not found until the various parts of the abdomen were explored and cut asunder. The ball in its course broke the eleventh rib, fractured the spinal column, but did not touch the spinal cord. It lodged two and a half or three inches directly to the left of the spinal column in the mesentery. The channel which has hitherto been supposed to be the track of the ball proved to be a pus cavity formed by the burrowing of the pus downward.

The catheter which was always used by the surgeons is believed to have bent upon itself, deceiving the surgeons in regard to the real depth of the wound. There was a large abscess between the liver and the gall-duct, which according to the same authority was metastatic. This abscess was not connected with the track of the wound or the channel formed by burrowing. On each of the kidneys was a small abscess. The lungs, especially the right one, were badly diseased. A large amount of pus flowed freely from the bronchial tubes, while by cutting into the tubes a considerable amount of pus was discovered in little metastatic abscesses; there was purulent infiltration of both lungs. This pus was healthy. There were no abscesses in the liver itself, but those in the kidneys were metastatic or pyæmic. There were adhesions of the lungs to the chest-wall at the upper part of each lung, showing a previous pleurisy; whether it antedated the shooting the examination did not show. The intestines were very adherent one to another, showing the existence of former peritonitis. The abscess in the right kidney was not opened. The rigors from which the President has been suffering for a few days were probably caused by the abscesses between the liver and the gall-duct.

The following official bulletin was prepared by the surgeons who were in attendance upon the late President:

By previous arrangement a post-mortem examination of the body of President Garfield was made this afternoon in the presence and with the assistance of Drs. Hamilton, Agnew, Bliss, Barnes, Woodward, Reyburn, Andrew H. Smith, of Elberon, and Acting Assistant-Surgeon D. S. Lamb, of the Army Medical Museum of Washington. The operation was performed by Dr. Lamb. It was found that the ball, after fracturing the right eleventh rib, had passed through the spinal column in front of the spinal cord, fracturing the body of the first lumbar vertebra, driven a number of small fragments of bone into the adjacent soft parts, and lodging below the pancreas, about two inches and a half to the left of the spine, and behind the peritoneum, where it had become completely encysted.

The immediate cause of death was secondary hemorrhage from one of the mesenteric arteries adjoining the track of the ball, the blood rupturing the peritoneum, and nearly a pint escaping into the abdominal cavity. This hemorrhage is believed to have been the cause of the severe pain in the lower part of the chest complained of just before death. An abscess cavity, six inches by four in dimensions, was found in the vicinity of the gall bladder, between the liver and the transverse colon, which were strongly adherent. It did not involve the substance of the liver, and no communication was found between it and the wound.

A long suppurating channel extended from the external wound, between the loin muscles and the right kidney, almost to the right groin. This channel, now known to be due to the burrowing of pus from the wound, was supposed during life to have been the track of the ball.

On an examination of the organs of the chest evidences of severe bronchitis were found on both sides, with bronchopneumonia of the lower portions of the right lung, and, though to a much less extent, of the left. The lungs contained no abscesses, and the heart no clots. The liver was enlarged and fatty, but not from abscesses. Nor were any found in any other organ except the left kidney, which contained near its surface a small abscess about one third of an inch in diameter.

In reviewing the history of the case in connection with the autopsy, it is quite evident that the different suppurating surfaces, and especially the fractured, spongy tissue of the vertebræ, furnish a sufficient explanation of the septic condition which existed.

D. W. BLISS,   FRANK H. HAMILTON,
J. K. BARNES,   D. HAYES AGNEW,
J. J. WOODWARD,   ANDREW H. SMITH,
ROBERT REYBURN,   D. S. LAMB.

THE FINAL SCENE AT ELBERON—RELIGIOUS SERVICES IN THE COTTAGE—DEPARTURE OF THE CORTEGE FOR WASHINGTON.

The slow, solemn tolling of a church bell the next morning was the only sound that broke the hush that had fallen upon Elberon when the heart of the chief stopped beating. There was no military ceremony, no dirge save that of the breakers hard by, no pomp, no display of any kind, and the monosyllabic clanging of the bell seemed like a mournful repetition of the one word, "Dead." All was as plain as befitted the character of the man and the office he had held.

Early in the twilight the military guard was doubled around the cottage where lay all that was mortal of the late President. A notice had been issued the night before that the people would be admitted to see the body at an early hour, and the notice not only brought hundreds from the immediate vicinity, but many from considerable distances. The lawn around the cottage was thronged as early as 7 o'clock, and by half-past 8 there were probably three thousand persons standing looking at the cottage door and waiting for the moment when they could enter. At half-past 8 the word was given, and from the crowd which had been kept at a distance to the steps of the house a line was formed between sentries.

VIEWING THE PRESIDENT'S REMAINS.

One by one the people entered and passed into the room on the southwest corner on the ground floor. In the centre of the room stood the coffin in which the body had been placed. The casket was a perfectly plain one, covered with black cloth, the only ornaments being the heavy silver bars that run along the sides and the silver plate having the following inscription:

JAMES ABRAM GARFIELD;
Born November 19, 1831.
Died President of the United States, September 19, 1881.

The face of the President was exposed by the turning down of the upper part of the coffin-lid. It was terribly changed from its appearance before his illness, so much so that very many who had known him in life said in hushed tones, " I would not recognize him." Not only was the emaciation appalling, but the lines drawn by suffering were graven in his face until it was haggard beyond description. It is said that he had fallen away almost two fifths of his usual weight, and it was easy to believe this from the appearance of the face. No sign was visible of the affection of the parotid gland, the beard being so arranged as to cover the scar. There was some discoloration noticeable on the face, but this was not altogether the mark of death. A plaster cast of his face had been taken, and the oil applied to the skin had slightly stained it. His left hand lay across his breast in a position that was said to be habitual with him in life. His right hand lay down at his side. He was dressed in the suit of clothes which he wore when he was inaugurated as President last March. The clothes had fitted him then, and not all the art of the undertaker could make them look to-day as if they had been made for him.

RELIGIOUS SERVICES.

There was a conspicuous absence of floral adorning. A " V " was formed of two palm branches placed upon the coffin. It was the emblem as well as the initial of the victory he had achieved. For only an hour were the people admitted to view the body. At half-past 9 o'clock Chief Justice Waite, Secretary and Mrs. Blaine, Secretary and Mrs. Windom, Secretary and Mrs. Hunt, Postmaster-General and Mrs. James, Secretaries Lincoln and Kirkwood, and Attorney-General MacVeagh arrived at the Francklyn cottage, and the doors were closed. In addition to the Cabinet officers and their wives there were present only the members of the family and attendants and a few personal friends, numbering in all not more than fifty individuals when the religious services began. At Mrs. Garfield's request the Rev. Mr. Young, the pastor of the Presbyterian church of Long Branch, conducted these services. He had been requested by Colonel Rockwell, on account of the brevity of the time at command, to occupy no more than five minutes. He read the following passages from the book of Revelation and the Epistles to the Corinthians:

" ' Blessed are the dead who die in the Lord. Yea, saith the Spirit, that they may rest from their labors; and their works do follow them. We know that if our earthly house of this tabernacle were dissolved, we have a building of God, a house not made with hands, eternal in the heavens. Therefore we are always confident, knowing that while we are at home in the body we are absent from the Lord. We are confident, I say, and willing rather to be absent from the body and to be present with the Lord. For to me to live is Christ, and to die is gain. I am in a strait betwixt two, having a desire to depart and to be with Christ, which is far better; there the wicked cease from troubling, and the weary are at rest. And there shall be no more death, neither sorrow, nor crying, neither shall there be any more pain. And there shall be no night there; and they need no candle, neither light of the sun; for the Lord God giveth them light: and they shall reign for ever and ever. Behold, I show you a mystery; we shall not all sleep, but we shall all be changed, in a moment, in the twinkling of an eye, at the last trump. For this corruptible must put on incorruption, and this mortal must put on immortality. So when this corruptible shall have put on incorruption, and this mortal shall have put on immortality, then shall be brought to pass the saying that is written, Death is swallowed up in victory. O death, where is thy sting? O grave, where is thy victory? The sting of death is sin; and the strength of sin is the law. But thanks be to God, who giveth us the victory through our Lord Jesus Christ.' Let us pray."

After reading these passages he offered the following prayer:

" O Thou who walked through the grave of Bethany, that open grave of the brother in Bethany! O Thou who hadst compassion on the widow of Nain as she bore her beloved dead! O Thou who art the same yesterday, to-day, and forever, in whom is no variableness nor shadow of turning, have mercy upon us at this hour, when our souls have nowhere else to fly! But we fly to Thee. Thou knowest these sorrows that we bow under. O thou God of the widow, help this stricken heart before Thee. Help these children and those that are not here. Be their father. Help her in the distant State who watched over him in childhood. Help this nation that is to-day bleeding and bowed before Thee. Oh! sanctify this heavy chastisement to its good. Help those associated with him in the government. O Lord, grant from the darkness of this night of sorrow there may arise a better day for the glory of God and the good of man. We thank Thee for the record of the life that is closed for its heroic devotion to principle. We thank Thee, O Thou Lord, that he was Thy servant, that he preached Thee, Thy noble life and example, and that we can say of him now, "Blessed are the dead who die in the Lord, their works do follow them." Now, Lord, go with this sorrowing company in this last sad journey. Go, bear them up and strengthen them. O God, bring us all at last to the morning that has no shadow, the home that has no tears, the land that has no death, for Christ's sake. Amen."

All had been made ready for the departure, which occurred immediately after the religious services. The special train which was to convey the remains with their escort to Washington had been backed up on the track that was laid so short a time ago to bring the President to the seashore. It was composed of an engine, a baggage car, the funeral car, the private car of President Roberts, of the Pennsylvania Railroad, and a car for the attendants. After all the luggage had been put on board, the coffin was carried by the undertaker's assistants into the funeral car. This had been draped in mourning and lined on the side and on the ceiling with black cloth. Near the ceiling a line of festooned flags had been made and the chandeliers were draped with serge. The coffin was placed in the centre of the car on a low platform that had been prepared, and the twelve soldiers who composed the guard of honor took their places around it. Mrs. Garfield, heavily veiled, was escorted to her car, into which went also Harry Garfield, Miss Mollie Garfield, Colonel Swaim, Colonel and Mrs. Rockwell, Miss Lulu Rockwell, Dr. Boynton, and Mr. C. O. Rockwell. In the next coach were the members of the Cabinet and their wives, and in the next were Private Secretary J. Stanley Brown, Colonel H. C. Corbin, Executive Clerk Warren S. Young, Mr. John Jameson, Mr. J. R. Van Wormer, Mr. Ridgely Hunt, the son of Secretary Hunt; Mr. C. F. James, the son of the Postmaster-General; Secretary Lincoln's private secretary, Mr. Jay Stone, and the personal attendants upon the President and Mrs. Garfield.

PRESIDENT ARTHUR AND GENERAL GRANT.

The crowd of people on the lawn had been gently pushed back by the soldiers after the house was closed, but all stood waiting to see the train start. The tolling of the church bell was still the only sound, but at exactly 10 o'clock the engineer rang his bell once and the train started very slowly. In a little less than ten minutes it stopped within a quarter of a mile of the Elberon station, where it met the special train that had brought President Arthur and ex-President Grant from New York. Here another guard of soldiers had been stationed to keep back the crowd that had gathered there, and General Arthur and General Grant stepped across from one train to the other and entered the car where the members of the Cabinet sat. As the funeral train started again it was noticed that the new President was talking earnestly with Mr. Blaine.

In less than one hour it could hardly have been told that such scenes had been around the cottage. The great crowd melted away in silence. No one at all remained excepting the permanent residents, the hotel people, and the servants. The cottage had been locked at once upon the exit of the funeral party. The keys were given to Mr. Jones, at the hotel, with Mr. Francklyn's peremptory order that no one should be admitted excepting his own servants. The smooth lawn that is the pride of the place has been trampled and disfigured in the last two weeks, and little paths are worn here and there by the footprints of the sentries and messengers. The excitement and the crowds have robbed the place of the elegant neatness which was its characteristic, and which it will take time and great pains to restore.

THE JOURNEY TO WASHINGTON—RECEPTION OF THE REMAINS AT THE NATIONAL CAPITAL.

It was precisely five minutes to 10 o'clock when the funeral train started from in front of the Francklyn cottage at Elberon. Five minutes later it had traversed the line of track which two weeks ago had been laid down by the Jersey Central Railroad to convey the President to the cottage door. Thence, when General Arthur had come aboard from his own special train, accompanied by General Grant, it moved slowly to the south. It passed Elberon station proper at 10.12, and at 10.16 passed through Ocean Grove and Asbury Park. There were gathered at this place eight or ten thousand people. The men stood with uncovered heads, and there was no demonstration. The bells tolled as the train went by.

PROGRESS OF THE TRAIN.

No stop was made until the train reached Sea Girt, at 10.30. There it only drew up to leave the tracks of the New Jersey Central road and turn to the westward over the line of the Pennsylvania Company. Sea Girt was passed at 10.30, Farmingdale at 10.37, Freehold at 10.56. Monmouth Junction, forty-six miles from Elberon, was passed at 11.26. There the train entered upon the tracks of the direct line of the Pennsylvania Railroad between New York and Philadelphia. At all the places mentioned great crowds had gathered, and the same observance of the requests sent out to the people was noted. The only demonstration of any kind was the ringing of bells and the presence in silence of the people.

STREWING THE TRACK WITH FLOWERS.

At Princeton, the students of the college, two miles back over the bluff, had come down to see the train pass by. They brought with them great baskets of cut roses and flowers, and these they spread over the tracks of the railroad. It was strewn for several hundred yards with blossoms, and they were able to pass some flowers into the train as it slacked up to receive them. Between Princeton and Monmouth Junction the train took water from the trough between the tracks without stopping. The run from there to Lamokin, fourteen miles to the northward, was made without incident.

Trenton, sixty-one miles from Elberon, was passed at 11.49, Norrisville at 11.52, Tullytown at midday, and Bristol at 12.05. About a thousand people gathered at Bristol. As the train passed there was good order, and the crowd was very quiet. Cornwall was passed at sixteen minutes after 12; Holmesburg Junction at twenty-two minutes after 12; Frankford, twenty-nine minutes after 12 ; and the train slowly drew into Philadelphia at forty-four minutes after 12. Instead of going to the depot it was switched to the left just at the Callow-hill Street bridge, and pursued its course rapidly along the Union Railroad that leads to Gray's Ferry, which is the junction of the Philadelphia, Wilmington and Baltimore line.

AT PHILADELPHIA.

Great crowds gathered all along the four or five miles of the Pennsylvania Railway running through Philadelphia, and stood in solemn silence awaiting the passage of the train. The crowd was not made up of ordinary idle spectators. It was composed of people all bearing the signs of sympathetic grief in their countenances, who in their subdued manner and ready compliance with police orders gave some token of the deep feeling that existed. At sixteen minutes to 1 o'clock the funeral train appeared in sight of the West Philadelphia station at the upper end of the depot, and as it rapidly approached the tunnel the faint tolling of the State House bell was borne on the air. As the solemn tones were heard and the train came nearer the officers reverently raised their hats, an example which was followed by the male spectators. The usually noisy street became quiet, not a train was in motion in the railroad yard, and the street cars halted while the sorrowful cortege passed through the tunnel. The only sound to be heard was the muffled tolling of many bells.

AT GRAY'S FERRY.

A crowd not quite so large as that in the neighborhood of the Pennsylvania Railroad depot was assembled about the Gray's Ferry station, where the train was to stop. Some three hundred people were stationed on the wagon bridge over the railroad and scattered for a hundred yards along the track. Sixty police officers were placed along the platform to keep the crowd from pressing forward. The heavily draped funeral train drew slowly up and stopped at the station. The officers raised their hats and the crowd became stilled. Senator Jones, of Nevada, who had arrived at this point on the limited express a few moments before, took his place in the car containing the Cabinet and the train moved on.

TIME FROM ELBERON.

In stopping at Philadelphia the train had been one hour and fifty-two minutes from Elberon. When, two weeks ago, the President had journeyed to Long Branch the same distance was covered in one hour and thirty-seven minutes. The train left Gray's Ferry at seven minutes to 1, passed Paschall four minutes later, and was at Chester at eight minutes after 1. At Lamokin the train was stopped for water and coal, and once more was on its way.

AT WILMINGTON.

At Wilmington many thousands of people had gathered, blocking the depot. The train moved slowly through, the engine bell being rung as it went, as if in unison with the tone of the bells of the church spires of the city. Elkton was passed at three minutes after 2 o'clock. At fifteen minutes past 3 the train pulled into the Charles Street station at Baltimore. The usual crowd was there in respectful and sad silence. Only a brief stop was made here, the engineer was changed, and the train was once more on its way.

The run—forty miles—was made in an hour and six minutes to Washington. There was no incident of any sort. The people stood at the depots, the church bells tolled, and the flags at half-mast waved their mammoth folds. In Baltimore the crowd was perhaps greater than at any other point along the line.

ON THE ADVANCE TRAIN.

On the train that came in advance of the funeral train was the car of the general manager of the Pennsylvania Railroad, Frank Thompson. There rode with him to Philadelphia Drs. Barnes, Woodward, and Lamb, Mr. George W. Childs and Mrs. Childs. After that the gentlemen went upon the limited train, and the car itself was detached at the West Philadelphia station. Among the passengers on the limited train were George Bliss, District-Attorney Rollins, and Senators Kellogg and Jones. The latter, however, as stated, dropped off the limited express at Gray's Ferry and continued his journey by boarding the funeral train when it drew up at that station.

RECEPTION OF THE REMAINS.

About noon the crowd began to assemble in the vicinity of the Baltimore and Potomac depot, and by 4 o'clock there were at least twenty-five thousand people, including the military and court officials, surrounding the depot. The military, which began to arrive at 3 o'clock, formed on Sixth Street, fronting the depot, the right resting at the corner of Pennsylvania Avenue. A few minutes before 4 o'clock the officers of the army and navy, in full-dress uniform, headed by General Sherman and staff, proceeded to the platform of the car-shed, drew up in line, and stood ready to receive the train when it arrived. There were present General W. T. Sherman, Adjutant-General Drum, who superintended the forming of the military; Generals Mc-Keever, Ruggles, Sacket, Baird, Meigs, Holabird, Sawtell, Card, and Hazen; Paymaster-General Brown, Colonels Curtis, Nickerson, Goodfellow, Barr, Chandler, Moore, McClure, and Febiger; Surgeons Crane, Swart, and Shufelt; General MacFeely, Commissary-General of Subsistence; Colonel Gilman, General Parke, Colonels Elliott, Farquhar, and Adams, and a number of captains and first and second lieutenants.

The navy was represented by Rear-Admiral Nichols, Commodores Earl, English, and Wells; Commander Picard, Surgeon-General Wales, Paymaster-General Cutter, Chief Engineer Shock, Naval Constructor Easby, Judge-Advocate Remey, Colonel McCawley, commandant of marines ; Captains De Kraft, Fillebrown, Howison, and all the naval officers in the city. Besides these there were on the platform Commissioners Dent, Morgan, and Twining ; District-Attorney Corkhill, Assistant Secretary of State Hitt, Marshal Henry, Second Assistant Postmaster-General Elmer, a number of other prominent officials, and a few newspaper correspondents.

WAITING THE ARRIVAL.

The depot, both inside and out, was heavily draped with black muslin, and the hundreds that assembled within its walls spoke in whispers and seemed to realize the sad situation. Outside the crowd was as orderly and quiet as could be, and they stood for several hours without causing the police on duty any annoyance. Ropes were stretched along the curbing to prevent the vast multitudes from crowding into the streets. At 4 p.m.

the limited express train from New York came puffing into the depot, and many mistook it for the Presidential train. This train was shortly afterward backed out, and everything was put in readiness for the arrival of the remains of President Garfield and his grief-stricken family.

THE ARRIVAL.

At exactly twenty-eight minutes to 5 o'clock the train bearing the lifeless body of the late President glided slowly and solemnly into the depot. As Mrs. Garfield, dressed in deep mourning, appeared at the door every head inside the depot was uncovered. She leaned upon the arm of Secretary Blaine and her elder son, Harry. Behind her came Miss Mollie Garfield, accompanied by General Swaim and Miss Rockwell. Mrs. Garfield and her daughter, accompanied by Mrs. James and Mrs. Mac-Veagh, were driven immediately to the residence of the Attorney-General. After they had departed the rest of the mourners left the car and proceeded to the pavement, when Undertaker William Spear provided them with carriages. The first carriage contained ex-President Grant, Senator Jones, and General Beale. Following the ex-President's carriage came President Arthur, accompanied by Secretaries Blaine and Windom and Chief Justice Waite. Next came Secretaries Lincoln, Hunt, and Kirkwood, and Postmaster-General James, followed by Attorney-General MacVeagh, Dr. Boynton, General Swaim, and Colonel Rockwell. The last carriage contained Private Secretary Brown, Colonel Corbin, C. O. Rockwell, and Warren Young.

THE CASKET.

After they had been placed in carriages and assigned a position in the line of procession the coffin was brought out, borne upon the shoulders of ten sturdy soldiers of Company D, First United States Artillery, commanded by Second Lieutenant Thomas C. Patterson, and was placed in the hearse, which was drawn by six gray horses, their harness being draped with crape. As the body-bearers emerged from the depot every head in the vicinity was again uncovered and remained so until the remains were placed in the hearse and the procession moved away from the depot. The United States Marine Band, stationed opposite the entrance, meanwhile played the beautiful air known as "Nearer, my God, to Thee," in such an impressive and solemn strain as to cause tears to flow from the eyes of the thousand of witnesses to this touching spectacle.

PROCESSION TO THE CAPITOL.

Everything being in readiness, General Ayers in command, the solemn procession proceeded to the Capitol in the following order :

Donch's Band,
Company A, Washington Light Infantry, Colonel W. G. Moore.
Union Veteran Corps, Captain S. E. Thomason.
Pistorio's Band.
National Rifles, Colonel J. O. P. Burnside.
Washington Light Guard, Lieutenant F. S. Hodson.
Capitol City Guards (colored), Captain T. S. Kelley.
Full Marine Band and Drum Corps.
Four companies United States Marines, Colonel C. G. McCawley.
Second Artillery Band.
Five companies of Second Artillery, four foot and one light battery.
General Ayres.
Washington and Columbia Commanderies Knights Templar.

The first carriage contained W. S. Spear, the undertaker; then came the hearse, with the body bearers walking close alongside. The officers of the army on the right and the navy on the left formed a guard of honor, after which came the President, Cabinet, and distinguished mourners.

ALONG THE ROUTE.

The sidewalks, windows and housetops along the entire route of the funeral procession were crowded with spectators, who remained with uncovered heads until the entire cortege had passed. A more solemn sight was never witnessed in Washington. There was not the slightest indication of confusion or demonstration, and not a sound broke the stillness which prevailed, except occasionally a smothered sob inspired by the mournful dirges of the bands and the sad, sorrowful surroundings. The route of the funeral procession was up Sixth Street to Pennsylvania Avenue, thence to the Capitol by way of the south wing, thence to the east front, where the military were drawn up in line, the right resting on the Senate side and the left resting upon the House side. As the funeral cortege approached the steps leading to the rotunda, directly opposite Greenough's statue of Washington, the order was given to present arms, and the Marine Band at the same time again played "Nearer, my God, to Thee." Almost the entire assemblage, which at this time was estimated at over thirty thousand, was moved to tears.

LINES FORMED.

Just before the cortege approached the following distinguished gentlemen formed themselves into two lines at the foot of the east staircase, that the sad procession might pass into the building between the lines. They were: Associate Justices Matthews and Harlan, ex-Justice Strong, Senators Davis of West Virginia, Ingalls of Kansas, Garland of Arkansas, Kellogg of Louisiana, Representatives Townsend of Ohio, Wilson of West Virginia, Shelley of Alabama, Thomas of Illinois, J. Randolph Tucker of Virginia, Urner of Maryland, Phillips of Kansas, and also Sergeant-at-Arms R. J. Bright of the Senate, Sergeant-at-Arms of the House J. G. Thompson, Clerk of the House George M. Adams, Doorkeeper of the House C. W. Fields, Architect of the Capitol Edward Clark, Official Reporter of the Senate Dennis Murphy, W. S. Roose and others.

ENTERING THE CAPITOL.

As the cortege slowly moved up the grand marble stairway leading to the bronzed door entrance of the rotunda, it was the most pathetic and saddening scene that those present had ever looked upon. Very few dry eyes were in the multitude, and a sea of sorrowing faces looked upon the sight with suppressed emotion.

Immediately following the coffin was President Arthur and Secretary Blaine, arm in arm, and then the following in the order named, two abreast: Secretary Windom and Chief-Justice Waite, Generals Grant and Beale, Secretaries Lincoln and Hunt, Secretary Kirkwood and Postmaster-General James, Attorney-General MacVeagh, Colonel Rockwell and General Swaim, Colonel Corbin and Private Secretary Brown, Dr. Boynton and William S. Roose, Warren S. Young and Marshal Henry, District-Attorney Corkhill and A. A. Adee, Charles A. Benedict and S. W. Rogers, George W. Tinsdale and Major Twining.

Then came the District of Columbia Commissioners. Bringing up the rear were the army and naval officers, who had previously formed lines up the steps, the army officers on the right and naval officers on the left. The coffin was slowly placed upon the catafalque, with the feet of the corpse pointing to the east.

LOOKING AT THE DEAD.

All those present then passed in single file upon the left side of the catafalque, stopping a moment to take a final view of the features of the dead President. The lid of the casket when lifted exposed to view the face and nearly all the upper portion of the body.

CLOSE OF THE CEREMONIES.

As the funeral attendants and others viewed the remains they passed out of the rotunda through the door by which they entered. None lingered beyond a few moments by the coffin. A few minutes after the dignitaries passed out the military moved off by way of the north carriage-ways of the Capitol grounds, and when a few squares had been traversed up Pennsylvania Avenue the procession dispersed. The carriage visitors drove to their respective domiciles with no ceremony or regularity. The crowd was not long in departing, and the first ceremonies attending the lying in state of the corpse were readily performed.

GUARD OF HONOR.

At 3 o'clock in the afternoon the surviving comrades of the Army of the Cumberland, all of whom were personal friends of the late President, marched into the rotunda, headed by General T. T. Crittenden.

WASHINGTON IN MOURNING HABILIMENTS.

The city looked sad in its black decorations and the whole community seems drowned in sorrow. Pennsylvania Avenue, from the eastern branch to Georgetown Heights, a distance of five miles, presented an unbroken line of mourning. A noteworthy feature was that no one house on either side of this great distance was without its display of black cloth. Pictures of General Garfield bordered in mourning were hung out at many places. In fact the entire District of Columbia was draped in mourning. Thousands and thousands of yards of the sombre material were visible at every turn, and banners, flags, street cars, vehicles, awnings, and signs were trimmed with black cambric. A more universal display of grief has not perhaps been seen in the history of any city or town of the world. Little or no business was transacted either of a public or local nature, and the public buildings were closed.

THE CAPITOL BUILDING.

The Capitol building was plainly and unostentatiously decorated in black. Large streamers were flowing from its massive proportions on the east and west fronts, and at the north and south wings the pillars were wrapped and festooned, and the exterior of the dome was encircled at proper altitudes with the material of the day. The grand circular colonnade surrounding the first circuit of the dome was heavily draped, although it appeared insignificant when viewed from the plateau so far beneath it. Upon the interior the decorations were of a more extensive character, although, of course, nothing but black figured in the display. The Senate Chamber was closed, and no attempt made to decorate it. The House of Representatives was elaborately draped. The desks and chairs had been piled upon either. side the aisle leading from the corridor to the Speaker's desk. The paintings on the walls were hung in drapery, and large black streamers reached from the seats in the gallery, falling in arches over the doors leading from the lobby and hat rooms into the floor of the House. Officials of the House had this done upon their own responsibility. However, the House and Senate wings were practically shut off from the rotunda by temporary partitions, covered with black cloth, placed across the north and south doors of the rotunda.

THE ROTUNDA.

The great point of interest was the rotunda, where the body of the late President was lying in state. It is circular in shape, is 100 feet in diameter, and has a stone flagging pavement. There are four Revolutionary and four historical oil paintings, covering the wall a few feet above the floor. They are about twelve by twenty-eight feet in size, and were covered at the top with black cloth, the ends hanging down about five feet below the frames. At all the lower corners rosettes were attached with graceful streamers floating from them. Black bands and festoons covered the inside of the dome at each of the projecting circuits. The four doors were capped and girdled in folds of crape. The east door, through which the cortege passed, was more elaborately festooned than any other point.

THE CATAFALQUE.

In the centre of the rotunda was placed the catafalque, which was about three feet above the floor. It is the same one that held the casket incasing the remains of President Lincoln, and had been stowed away in the crypt of the Capitol for the past sixteen years. It consists of a platform about a foot high, twelve feet long, and six feet wide. Upon this is another platform two feet high, three feet wide, and nine feet long. The lower platform was covered with perfectly black Brussels carpet. The sides and ends of the upper platform are covered with heavy black corded silk. Around the upper edge is silk fringe and tassels three inches long. Over this and midway between the top of the catafalque and the bottom platform are two silver mouldings running around the sides and ends. The top, upon which rested the coffin, was covered with black cloth. In viewing the remains one steps upon the lower platform, which elevated the viewer just high enough to get a complete view of the face of the President. The grand allegorical fresco, by Brumidid, in the crest of the dome, hung over the catafalque 200 feet above, like a picture in the clouds.

MEETING OF CABINET MEMBERS.

All the members of the Cabinet met at the residence of Secretary Blaine, and the conference, which was held with closed doors, continued fully an hour. Secretary Windom was the first to leave, and was followed a few minutes later by Attorney-General MacVeagh and Postmaster-General James. The latter was asked as to the nature of the meeting, but the Attorney-General, interrupting, said:

"We must decline to say anything now. We have too much business to consider. Our meeting at Mr. Blaine's was simply of a sociable nature, and that is all we can tell you about the matter." It was said upon good authority, however, that among the topics discussed by the Cabinet was the wording of certain dispatches addressed to the Governor of Ohio and the Mayor of

Cleveland relative to the funeral ceremonies over the dead President.

CROWDS OF PEOPLE REVERENTLY PASS GARFIELD'S BIER.

REMARKABLE ASSEMBLAGE FILING THROUGH THE ROTUNDA OF THE CAPITOL—RICH AND POOR PAYING A LAST TRIBUTE OF RESPECT—THE COFFIN CLOSED AT NIGHTFALL OWING TO DECOMPOSITION.

WASHINGTON, Sept. 22.—The scene at the Capitol to-day was in many respects the most remarkable that has ever been witnessed in the United States. All day long the Capitol and its grounds were crowded with all classes of people, drawn together by the profound feeling prevailing in reference to the death of the late President. The most remarkable feature of the scene was the mixed character of the multitude of people that constantly poured through the vast rotunda to gaze upon the shrunken and emaciated features of the late Chief Magistrate, and the quiet and orderly manner in which this multitude conducted themselves. The East Park, beyond the line of people formed for admission to the Capitol, was filled with vehicles of every description, from the handsome barouche of the wealthy city denizen to the rough market cart of the poor colored farmers of Virginia and Maryland, who in many cases brought their entire families to gaze upon the face of the dead President, and whose horses and mules wore harness composed for the most part of odd leather straps taken from sets of harness long ago cast aside as worthless and held together by pieces of rope and twine. In very many cases the harness was composed almost entirely of ropes. The sorry-looking vehicles of these people and their still more sorry-looking animals stood beside handsome carriages and richly caparisoned horses. For once there was a universal feeling prevailing in the public mind and the thoughts of all classes ran in the same direction. The ragged and toil-stained farm-hands from Virginia and Maryland and the colored laborers of Washington stood side by side with the representatives of wealth and fashion, patiently waiting for hours beneath the sultry September sun for the privilege of gazing for a minute on the face of the dead President.

All through Wednesday night and to-day this heterogeneous mass moved slowly, but with funereal solemnity and regularity, through the Capitol. A double line of people extended down the broad stone steps leading to the east entrance of the building, and, after winding like a huge serpent about the open space in front of the Capitol, stretched southward across the boundary of the park until its rear end was invisible from the bronze doors through which its advance guard was constantly disappearing without visibly reducing its dimensions. Notwithstanding the mixed character of the multitude and the numbers that composed it, there was no disorder or confusion. A few policemen were present to preserve order outside the building, but their services were not required, except to direct people to the end of the line.

In the rotunda, where the body of President Garfield is lying in state, there is at present no representative of the civil or military power, the guard being composed exclusively of resident members of the old Army of the Cumberland, of which Gen. Garfield was a conspicuous member, and who experienced no difficulty whatever in controlling the obedient masses that constantly passed during the day. The people moved up to the east door and were admitted to the rotunda in ranks of two, and passing on either side of the casket in the same order, moved to the west door, through which the exit was made to the West Park. In this way an average of about 100 persons per minute have passed through the rotunda to-day, and yet there was not an unseemly act committed nor a loud word spoken. This extraordinary reverence for the dead President is the best possible evidence of the depth of the popular feeling, and a striking illustration of the patriotic and law-abiding character of the American people.

The face of the dead President has undergone a slight change since it was first exposed yesterday. The work of decomposition is making rapid progress, and in order to hide the decay as much as possible the glass was removed to-day from the coffin and the face carefully powdered. Nothing of interest beyond this occurred during the day in connection with the lying in state, except a visit to the rotunda from ex-Presidents Grant and Hayes, after having witnessed the swearing in of President Arthur by the Chief-Justice. The two ex-Presidents moved quietly and sadly to the side of the coffin, and taking a place in the line of visitors gazed for a minute on the face of their successor, and then, arm in arm, silently retraced their steps to the Senate wing of the Capitol. Very few people recognized the two ex-Presidents, and their visit was so brief and unexpected that their presence at the side of the coffin was not noticed by more than five or six persons to whom they were both personally known.

It was discovered to-night that the body of the late President was decomposing so rapidly that it was determined to close the coffin, and it is probable that it will not be again opened. The face, which was partially discolored when the body arrived here, has now become overspread with a livid hue, adding to its ghastliness and making the sight too horrible for public exposure. In addition to this marked and terrible change in the face there is emitted from the casket a perceptibly unpleasant odor, showing that the body is not in condition for further public inspection. In view of this changed condition it is doubtful whether the family will consent to have the coffin again opened. The fact that it is closed has had no effect whatever upon those who desire to pass through the rotunda, and the crowd to-night is almost as great as at any time during the day. Mrs. Blaine and Mrs. Windom were the first to call attention to the condition of the body. These two ladies visited the Capitol this evening, and on looking at the face of the dead President requested those in charge to close the coffin, remarking that they were convinced Mrs. Garfield would be shocked if she were made acquainted with its terrible condition. As none of those in charge had authority to close the coffin, the exposure continued until the members of the Cabinet could be communicated with, when an order was given to cover the face against further exhibition.

Several beautiful floral contributions of novel design were deposited, near the head of the coffin, during the day. First, there is a wreath of natural ivy lying flat upon the stone floor. Beyond this is a broken column, about three feet high, surmounted by a white dove. Next to this is a representation of "The Gates Ajar." The gates and bars are composed of ferns fastened on wire previously shaped to represent a double gate, one side of the gate being partly open. The posts from which the gates are swung are composed of white rosebuds, planted in beds of yellow and white flowers, and surmounted by globes of immortelles. This beautiful offering was contributed by members of the Vermont Avenue Christian Church, and was universally admired by the passing crowd. The gates are large enough for a person to walk through if opened to their full extent. Next to this floral triumph was a crown of white flowers with a delicate fern entwined about the crest, and beyond this stood a broken column, surmounted by a white dove in the attitude of alighting. Next there was a large pillow of white roses with the words " Our Martyr President," worked in immortelles. This floral display terminates as it begins, with a wreath of ivy laid flat on the stone floor. The ferns, which are so abundant in the making of these artistic designs, are of the species which were used at the death of Senator Sumner. Then they were seen in this country for the first time. In addition to the floral contributions above described, there was received to-day from her Majesty Queen Victoria, through Mr. Victor Drummond, Chargé d'Affaires of the British Legation at Washington, a handsome wreath, which now rests upon the casket. This wreath was laid on the casket by Mr. Drummond at the command of Queen Victoria, cabled to-day. A card attached to the wreath reads as follows : " Queen Victoria, to the memory of the late President Garfield. An expression of her sorrow and sympathy with Mrs. Garfield and the American Nation. Sept. 22, 1881."

The body will lie in state until noon to-morrow, when the public will be excluded from the Capitol in order that the arrangements may be made for the funeral services, which are to be held at 3 o'clock under the direction of the Rev. F. D. Power, Pastor of the Christian Church in this city, of which President Garfield was a member. Mr. Power will conduct the services at the special request of Mrs. Garfield. At the conclusion of the religious services, which will occupy about one hour, the body will be removed to the Pennsylvania Railroad depot, and taken by special train direct to Cleveland. Six members of the Christian Church have been selected by Mrs. Garfield to carry the body from the rotunda to the hearse, and from the hearse to the funeral car at the depot. These six gentlemen are A. K. Ingle, William S. Roose, H. C. Stier, W. W. Dungan, Benjamin Summy, and D. F. Moore. The Philharmonic Society will render appropriate music during the religious services at the rotunda, consisting of the following selections : " To Thee, O Lord, I yield my spirit," from the oratorio of "Saint Paul," and the familiar hymns, "Jesus, lover of my soul," and "Asleep in Jesus, blessed sleep." The body will be escorted to the depot in about the same order in which it was brought to the Capitol.

On arriving at the depot the body will be placed in a car attached to the funeral train, which will consist of three of the most elegant of the Pullman Car Company's coaches and a funeral car, all elaborately decorated. The funeral car proper will be opened at the side, admitting a view of the coffin as the train passes along. The other three cars will be occupied by Mrs. Garfield and members of the family and personal friends, together with the members of the Cabinet, the physicians who were in attendance upon the President, ex-Presidents Grant and Hayes, and the committees appointed by the Senate and House. Another train will immediately follow the funeral train, upon which will be the Senators, members of Congress, Justices of the Supreme Court, and other distinguished persons who have been invited to attend the funeral. On Saturday morning the trains will be met at the Ohio State line by Gov. Foster and his staff.

A meeting of the members of the House of Representatives was held on Tuesday afternoon, September 20, and a committee, consisting of Messrs. Randall, Kasson and Townsend, was appointed by the chair to meet a similar committee appointed by the Senate, to determine what action should be taken in the premises. On their return to the chamber the committee reported that it had been agreed that a committee of eight members should be appointed by each House to escort the body to Cleveland; that a special train should be chartered to convey the other senators and members to that place, and that ex-Presidents Grant and Hayes should be invited to accompany them. On motion of Mr. Randall a similar invitation was extended to ex-Speaker Banks, and then the report of the committee was agreed to. It was further determined that the members of the House should meet in the hall of the House to-morrow at 2 o'clock and attend the funeral ceremonies in a body. There will be a space in the rotunda set apart for their accommodation, and the Sergeant-at-Arms was instructed to furnish each member with symbols of mourning. By the action of the meeting Mr. Tucker, of Virginia, was appointed Chairman of the Escorting Committee, the other members of which will be Messrs. Kasson of Iowa, Randall of Pennsylvania, Hiscock of

13

New York, Wilson of West Virginia, Thomas of Illinois, Townsend of Ohio, and Shelley of Alabama.

A meeting of the members of the Senate was held in the Vice-President's room, Senator Anthony presiding. The following senators were present: Messrs. Anthony, Hale, Dawes, Edmunds, Morrill, Saulsbury, Bayard, Kellogg, Davis, of West Virginia, Camden, Sherman, McMillan, Garland, Pugh, Morgan, Jones, of Nevada, Blair, Mitchell, and also ex-Senator Hamlin. The Committee of Conference reported that, on conferring with the House Committee, it was deemed best to charter a special train for the use of the senators and members and such guests as they should desire to invite, which report was accepted, and the Sergeant-at-Arms was instructed to make the necessary arrangements. It was decided to postpone the adoption of resolutions upon the death of President Garfield until the meeting of the Senate in regular session. The Chairman then announced the following as a committee on the part of the Senate to accompany the body: Senators Anthony, Sherman, Bayard, Ingalls, Pugh, Blair, Camden, and Morgan. The meeting then adjourned.

LAST HONORS AT THE CAPITAL.

FUNERAL SERVICES IN THE ROTUNDA OF THE CAPITOL—SCRIPTURAL PASSAGES AND PRAYERS—VISIT OF THE STRICKEN WIDOW—STARTING OF THE FUNERAL TRAIN.

WASHINGTON, Sept. 23.—It has been a day of universal mourning. Had the late President died as plain Congressman Garfield, with no tragic or pathetic concomitants to the sad event, it might have been said of him that no man in this community would have left so many personal friends to mourn his departure. From the highest in official and social life to the coachman who drove him out or the servant at his table, all who had ever come in contact with him formed something near akin to affection for him; and he was so essentially a man of the people, always so approachable, that none were repelled. Hence his personal friends numbered thousands. Therefore to-day, when his remains were to be taken away to their distant resting-place, each individual in the vast crowds which witnessed the departure felt that in some sense he had a right to call himself a mourner.

Six short months ago the man made his exit through the east doors of the rotunda of the Capitol on the occasion of his inauguration as President of the United States. Then 20,000 people greeted him with enthusiastic cheers, bands played their loudest, and great cannon boomed their deepest thunder. To-day his dust was brought through the same doors, borne by the loving hands of his Christian fellows in the Church, surrounded as then, by all that was notable and eminent in official life, and witnessed again by 20,000. But now there was funereal silence. In all the vast assemblage no voice was raised. Bared heads were bowed in silent grief. There was no crowding or rushing. Slowly the mourning cortege made its careful way down the granite steps. Tenderly the casket containing his mortal remains was lifted into place. The draped flags and drums, the measured cadences of the funeral march or the plaintive melody of a hymn of promise, the slow and orderly wheeling into line of march, made the contrast with the event to which all minds reverted more startling than words can find power to depict. The day was clear and warm. Although it had become known that the casket had been closed and would not again be opened for the public, great crowds assembled early to see the outside of the coffin which contained his body. For hours they filed slowly in and gazed upon the casket and the flowers. The guards of honor stood like statues in their places near the coffin.

MRS. GARFIELD'S SAD VISIT.

At 11 o'clock the doors of the rotunda, and a few moments later those of the other parts of the Capitol, were closed to all. Guards were placed at intervals in the corridors of the building, and while all who desired were thereafter permitted to go out, none were allowed to enter. There was surprise and some fault-finding at first; but when it was said that the occasion for these precautions was the last visit of the widow to her dead, all were content to let it be as she desired, in quiet and privacy.

At twenty minutes past 11 two closed carriages drove up to the east lower entrance of the Senate wing, and the occupants alighted and passed up the private stairway to the Vice-President's room. All the corridors and passage-ways upon the main floor of the Senate wing were quickly barred to all comers, and instructions were given by Sergeant-at-Arms Bright, of the Senate, to the employees and Capitol police on duty to keep themselves completely hidden in the recesses of the doors and windows while Mrs. Garfield passed through to the rotunda. The rotunda itself was entirely cleared, the guard of honor retiring from view for the time being. In a few minutes the little procession emerged from the Vice-President's room, and passing around through the east corridor, proceeded in the following order through the silent and desolated main passage-way of the building: Sergeant-at-Arms Bright leading; then followed Mrs. Garfield, leaning upon the arm of General Swaim, Harry Garfield, Mollie Garfield and Miss Rockwell, Colonel and Mrs. Rockwell, and Attorney-General MacVeagh and Mrs. Swaim. Not a sound was heard save the soft pattering of feet upon the marble floor as the little company, robed in the sombre garments of deepest mourning, passed silently on.

At the threshold her companions stopped, and when she entered alone the doors were closed. Beyond that threshold, rank nor power, curiosity, nor even imagination, might venture to intrude. The lid of the casket had been removed, and for twenty minutes the widow remained by all that was earthly of her honored dead. She came out closely veiled, and bearing a few flowers taken from the offerings of affection which had been placed upon the casket, and, taking the arm of General Swaim, departed as silently as she came. It was fitting that she who had given up so much that the public might have its own brief opportunity to pay its tribute of affection, should for one moment reclaim it to herself, and that no eye should dare to witness nor ear dare to hear, the sobbings of that widowed heart.

THE RELIGIOUS SERVICES.

At 12 o'clock the doors were reopened, but only for the admission of those who had tickets, or who by their official positions were entitled to enter for the purpose of taking part in the last ceremonies of respect to the dead President. Circles of chairs, sufficient to seat perhaps three thousand, had been placed in a position on all sides, leaving aisles to each of the four entrances to the rotunda. For an hour only the members of the Army of the Cumberland, the guards of honor and a few who had duties in connection with the preparations for the ceremonies were present. Then a few ticket-holders came in and took the seats reserved for them. Great crowds surrounded the doors, but remained for the most part in silence. Gradually the throng increased, now a diplomat with his attendants in glittering court-dresses and now a society or a committee in regalias and plumes in sober black making their appearance, and in turn taking their places. Conversations were carried on in subdued tones or in whispers.

A few moments before 2 o'clock the Beauseart Commandery of Knights Templar from Baltimore filed in and deposited a handsome floral tribute to the dead President. A few minutes later a number of the members of the Diplomatic Corps entered and took the seats assigned to them in the rear of the sofas placed for the accommodation of the Supreme Court, the members of which soon after entered headed by Chief-Justice Waite. At 2.40 Colonel Rockwell, Dr. Boynton, Private Secretary Brown, Messrs. Judd, Pruden, Warren Young, Hindley and Duke, Mr. and Mrs. Bolney, Colonel and Mrs. Corbin, Mrs. Pruden, Mr. and Mrs. Montgomery, and Mrs. Dean, representing the household of the late President, entered and took the seats reserved for them. The members of the House filed in through the south door, preceded by the officers of that body and by ex-Speakers Randall and Banks. They were followed by the senators, Senator Anthony leading, who entered by the north door. At 3 o'clock the Cabinet and distinguished guests entered in the following order: President Arthur, and Secretary Blaine, ex-Presidents Grant and Hayes, Secretary and Mrs. Windom, Secretary and Mrs. Lincoln, Secretary and Mrs. Hunt, Attorney-General and Mrs. MacVeagh, Secretary Kirkwood, and Postmaster-General James, and Generals Drum and Beale. The vast assembly rose as of one accord to honor the new President, and when they had regained their seats the ceremonies were opened with the hymn, " Asleep in Jesus," beautifully rendered by the volunteer choir.

PASSAGES OF SCRIPTURE READ.

The Rev. Dr. Rankin then ascended the raised platform at the head of the catafalque and read in a clear, distinct voice the following Scriptural selections:

The Lord reigneth. The floods have lifted up their voice. The Lord on high is mightier than the voice of many waters. Clouds and darkness are round about him; righteousness and judgment are the habitation of his throne. By him kings reign and princes decree justice. He changeth the times and the seasons. He removeth kings and setteth up kings.

For there is no power but of God. The powers that be are ordained of God. Whosoever, therefore, resisteth the power, resisteth the ordinance of God; and they that resist shall receive to themselves damnation. Cease ye from man whose breath is in his nostrils; for wherein is he to be accounted of? For behold the Lord, the Lord of hosts, doth take away from Jerusalem and from Judah the mighty man, the man of war, the honorable man, and the counsellor and the eloquent orator.

There is no man that hath power over the spirit to retain the spirit; neither hath he power in the day of death; and there is no discharge in that war. There shall he be at rest with kings and counsellors of the earth, which built desolate places for themselves. The clods of the valley shall be sweet unto him; and every man shall draw after him as there are innumerable before him. There the wicked cease from troubling, and there the weary be at rest.

Then answered Jesus unto them: Verily, verily, I say unto you, He that heareth my Word and believeth on Him that sent me, hath everlasting life and shall not come into condemnation; but hath passed from death unto life. To him that overcometh will I grant to sit with me on my throne; even as I also overcame, and sit down with my Father in his throne. Blessed are they that do his commandments that they may have right to the tree of life, and may enter in through the gates into the city. And they shall see his face, and his name shall be in their foreheads.

And he went a little further, and fell on his face and prayed, saying: O my Father, if it be possible let this cup pass from me. Nevertheless, not as I will, but as thou wilt.

It became Him for whom are all things, and by whom are all things in bringing many sons to glory, to make the Captain of their Salvation perfect through suffering. The disciple is not above his master nor the servant above his lord. It is enough for the disciple that he be as his master and the servant as his lord.

Let not your hearts be troubled ; ye believe in God, believe also in me.   I will not leave you comfortless ; I will come to you.   Leave the fatherless children ; I will preserve them alive. And let thy widow trust in me.

And it came to pass, when they came to Bethlehem, that all the city was moved about them.   And they said, Is this Naomi? and she said unto them, Call me not Naomi, call me Mara ; for the Lord hath dealt very bitterly with me.   I went out full, and the Lord hath brought me home again empty.

For a small moment have I forsaken thee ; but with great mercies will I gather thee.   I hid my face from thee for a moment, but with everlasting kindness will I have mercy on thee, saith the Lord, thy Redeemer.

And Jacob died and was gathered unto his people.   And Joseph went up to bury his father.   And there went up with them both chariots and horsemen ; and it was a very great company.   And when the inhabitants of the land saw the mourning, they said, This is a grievous warning to thee.   And they did unto him according as he had commanded them.   For they carried him into the land of Canaan and buried him in the cave of the field of Machpelah which Abraham bought for a possession of a burying-place.

And I heard a voice from heaven saying unto me, Write, Blessed are the dead which die in the Lord from henceforth. Yea, saith the Spirit, that they may rest from their labors, and their works do follow them.

I would not have you to be ignorant concerning them which are asleep, that ye sorrow not even as others which have no hope. For if we believe that Jesus died and rose again, even so them also that sleep in Jesus will God bring with him.   Wherefore, comfort one another with these words.   Faithful is he that calleth you, who also will do it.

The Lord gave, the Lord hath taken away.   Blessed be the name of the Lord.

DR. ERRETT'S PRAYER.

The Rev. Dr. Isaac Errett then offered prayer.   He spoke in a clear but low tone of voice, and with much evidence of deep feeling, but many of his utterances were lost.   He said :

Our beloved President is dead.   Raised by the voice of the people to the Chief Magistracy of this great nation, he was stricken down by a murderous hand—cut off in his glorious promise, and all the high hopes and expectations connected with his administration of public affairs sunk into disappointment and nothingness. O Lord, as we stand in the presence of this fearful calamity, may our hearts be exceedingly humbled before Thee, and as we are short-sighted, we pray that Thy hand may be reached down, and we may be taken through this darkness out into the light; and enable us to realize that even in thickest darkness Thou dost not forget to be merciful. And while we deeply feel beyond what we can say in words, the bitterness of this affliction we cannot forget.

O Lord, how much we have to be thankful for. We desire to praise Thee that though the President is dead the nation lives, that though our Chief Magistrate is thus cruelly and violently taken away from us the Government moves on in the peaceful performance of all its functions, that there is no jar in its machinery, and that the blessings of a good Government are still continued to us in all the land. For this we praise Thee, and we humbly pray that the President who sits near to our departed President may be filled with all love of righteousness and truth, and be prepared in everything by the blessing of God for the faithful performance of his responsible duties. May he be able to guide the affairs of this nation with discretion, may party animosity and strife and sectional division be overcome by means of this sacrifice, so that, one people in a deeper sense than we have ever been, there may come blessings out of this terrible affliction.

The reverend gentleman then in conclusion paid an eloquent and touching tribute to Mrs. Garfield, referring to the noble and Christian spirit which she had exhibited in the hour of sorrow and tribulation, and exhorting her to look to God in the days of her affliction. He invoked the divine blessing on the fatherless children: that the sons should, under the benediction of God, grow up to a noble manhood, and that the bereaved daughter might rise into a true, a glorious womanhood, and live to be the comfort of her widowed mother. He appealed to God to have pity on the dear old mother over the mountains waiting for the dead body of her darling son, now that she was old and gray-haired.

As the closing words of the prayer died away, the Rev. F. D. Powers, of the Vermont Avenue Christian Church, of which President Garfield was a member, delivered a feeling address. He spoke in a clear voice, and was distinctly heard in every portion of the hall.

The cloud so long pending over the nation has at last burst upon our heads. We sit half crushed amid the ruin it has brought. A million million prayers and hopes and tears, as far as human wisdom sees, were vain. Our loved one has passed from us. But there is relief. We look away from the body. We forget, for a time, the things that are seen. We remember with joy his faith in the Son of God, whose Gospel he sometimes himself preached, and which he always truly loved. And we see light and blue sky through the cloud structure, and beauty instead of ruin; glory, honor, immortality, spiritual and eternal life in the place of decay and death. The chief glory of this man, as we think of him now, was his discipleship in the school of Christ. His attainments as scholar and statesman will be the theme of our orators and historians, and they must be worthy men to speak his praise worthily. But it is as a Christian that we love to think of him now. It was this which made his life to man an invaluable boon, his death to us an unspeakable loss, his eternity to himself an inheritance incorruptible, undefiled, and that fadeth not away.

He was no sectarian. His religion was as broad as the religion of Christ. He was a simple Christian bound by no sectarian ties, and wholly in fellowship with all pure spirits. He was a Christologist rather than a theologist. He had great reverence for the family and relations. His example as son, husband, and father is a glory to this nation. He had a most kindly nature. His power over human hearts was deep and strong. He won men to him. He had no enemies. The hand that struck him was not the hand of his enemy, but the enemy of the position, the enemy of the country, the enemy of God. He sought to do right, manward and Godward.

He was a grander man than we know. He wrought even in his pain a better work for the nation than we can now estimate. He fell at the height of his achievements not from any fault of his, but we may in some sense reverently apply to him the

13*

words spoken of his dear Lord, " He was wounded for our trans-
gressions, he was bruised for our iniquities, the chastisement of
our peace was upon him."   As the nations remember the Mace-
donian as Alexander the Great and the Grecian as Aristides
the Just, may not the son of America be known as Garfield the
Good ?

Our President rests; he had joy in the glory of work, and he
loved to talk of the leisure that did not come to him.   Now he
has it.   This is the day, precious because of the service it rendered.   He is a freed spirit; absent from the body he is present with the Lord.   On the heights whence came his help he
finds repose.   What rest has been his for these four days?   The
brave spirit which cried in his body, " I am tired," is where the
wicked cease from troubling and the weary are at rest.   The
patient soul which groaned under the burden of the suffering
flesh " Oh, this pain," is now in a world without pain.   Spring
comes, the flowers bloom, the buds put forth, the birds sing.
Autumn rolls round, the birds have long since hushed their
voices, the flowers faded and fallen away; the forest foliage
assumes a sickly, dying hue, so earthly things pass away and
what is true remains with God.

The pageant moves, the splendor of arms and the banners
glitter in the sunlight, the music of instruments and of oratory
swells upon the air.   The cheers and praises of men resound.
But the spring and summer pass by, and the autumn sees a
nation of sad eyes and heavy hearts, and what is true remains
of God.   " The eternal God is our refuge, and underneath are
the everlasting arms."

THE REV. MR. BUTLER'S PRAYER.

At the conclusion of Dr. Power's address, the Rev. J. G.
Butler offered prayer as follows :

Our Father, we bow before thee with bleeding hearts.   Thy
judgments are unsearchable and Thy ways past finding out.   We
rejoice in the light that comes from Thy throne in this hour of
darkness, and adore Thee as our Covenant God, the God of our
now sainted President, and the Sovereign among earth's rulers.
There is forgiveness with Thee, and we come with penitent
hearts in the name that is above every name.   We thank God
for the life of His servant around whose remains the nation's
host gathers in sorrow, for his patriotism and purity, for his

courage and patience, for his faith and piety—the faith that was first in his now heart-stricken mother. The Lord deal very tenderly with her and preserve her unto everlasting life. God be praised for the blending of hearts at the mercy-seat asking the life of our President Father, not as we will, but as Thou wilt. Thy wisdom and love are infinite and unerring. Sanctify this faith-trial to the nation to the glory of Thy name. Thou compassionate Saviour, we commend to thee very tenderly her whose faith and courage made Thy servant strong in his days of weakness. We thank Thee for the gathering of helpful sympathy around her in this her darkest hour. Thou wilt keep and bless her and the fatherless ones entrusted to her training. Oh, that they may walk in the faith of their father and of their mother and of their grandmother. Keep them all from accident upon their journey, bearing this sacred dust to its last resting-place. Help us to look beyond the home of the soul, where the child shall find its mother and the mother the child, and where they die no more. God be praised for the institutions of freedom and religion, the rich heritage of our fathers, which survive the death of rulers and of people. Make us worthy of Thee. Give us the wisdom and courage needed to protect and perpetuate, thus making us more and more a pattern among the nations. Endow with wisdom and grace Thy servant upon whom the great responsibilities of administration have so suddenly come. Bless his Cabinet, coming from their anxious and loving ministries of sorrow in the chamber of suffering and death. Oh, that all our rulers may ever rule in Thy fear, and that our land may be noted for righteousness and peace—the spirit of justice and equity animating those who make and execute the law, that all the people may enjoy peace and prosperity. Make us worthy subjects of the coming kingdom of our Lord and Saviour Jesus Christ, to whom with Thee, O Father, with the ever-blessed Spirit be dominion and power and glory, world without end. Amen.

Immediately after the close of the services the floral decorations were all removed (Mrs. Garfield having requested that they be sent to her home at Mentor) except the beautiful wreath, the gift of Queen Victoria, which had been placed upon the head of the coffin when the lid was closed, and which remained there when the coffin was borne to the hearse, and will lie upon it till the remains are buried; this touching tribute of Queen Victoria greatly moved Mrs. Garfield, as only a woman can feel a woman's sympathy at the time of her greatest earthly sorrow.

The street scenes were only repetitions of what was seen here on Wednesday, when the body was received from Elberon. The pavements, windows, and roofs of houses all along the route of the march from the Capitol to Sixth Street were crowded and fairly packed with people. For hours before the time for the arrival of the body at the depot, the streets for several squares were blocked so that all travel was stopped except the passage of the street cars. Inside the depot the arrangements were complete and even sumptuous.

THE START FOR CLEVELAND.

The funeral train was divided into two sections of some six or seven Pullman palace-cars each, and all the afternoon the gentlemen in charge of the different organizations of the cortege were engaged in bringing in supplies of all kinds. The large size of the party, consisting of the Cabinet, Army and Navy officers, Senators and Representatives, and the impossibility of securing such supplies on the road, made it necessary to have it done beforehand. Mr. Wormley, the famous restaurateur, was asked to attend to this part of the programme. The hearse reached the depot at 4.20, at which moment the Marine Band played a solemn air. The Army and Navy officers marched out to the gateway, and stood in two lines with heads uncovered, while the artillery sergeants bore the coffin on to the platform and thence into the car, as they had taken it out on Wednesday. The Cabinet followed slowly and at intervals, the crowds on the outside preventing the prompt arrival of their carriages. The pall-bearers were followed closely by the Army and Navy officers and White House employees. Then came General Grant and Mr. Hayes, arm in arm. Directly after came the President, holding to the arm of Mr. Blaine, and with Attorney-General MacVeagh on the other side. Then came Secretary and Mrs. Lincoln, Secretary and Mrs. Windom, Secretary and Mrs. Hunt, Secretary and Mrs. James, and the others in irregular order. Mr. Blaine and General Beale returned in a few moments escorting the President and General Grant back to their carriage.

The remainder of the party came in promiscuously, and were assigned to their places in the cars as rapidly; and a few minutes after 5 o'clock the funeral train passed out of the depot, followed at a short interval by the Congressional train.

As the crowds turned sorrowfully homeward, there was a realization of the fact that Washington City, and the whole country as well, has taken leave forever of a great man—one who for twenty years has filled a large space in the national esteem.

THE LAST SAD JOURNEY.

THE RAILROAD LINED WITH PEOPLE ALL THE WAY FROM WASHINGTON—FLOWERS STREWED ON THE TRACKS.

CLEVELAND, OHIO, September 24.—The funeral train of six coaches bearing the body of President Garfield left the Baltimore and Potomac station in Washington at 5.15 o'clock yesterday, passing out of the city amid the tolling of bells and in the presence of many thousand silent people. The first coach was the Pennsylvania Railroad president's private car—No. 120 —reserved for Mrs. Garfield and her family. Miss Mollie Garfield, the only daughter of the dead President, crept into her mother's arms as the train moved slowly away from the capital, and in her efforts to soothe the little one's grief the President's widow became brave and calm. Fresh flowers were scattered before the train, and there were few dry eyes in the groups surrounding Mrs. Garfield at this tender exhibition of the people's grief and sympathy. Mrs. Mason and Mrs. Reed, cousins of Mrs. Garfield, remained with her. The Rev. Isaac Errett, of Cincinnati, who will preach the funeral sermon at Cleveland; the Rev. Mr. Powers, of the Christian Church at Washington; General Swaim, Colonel Rockwell and wife, Marshal Henry, Private Secretary Brown, Dr. Hawkes, the tutor of the Garfield boys; Miss Rockwell and Harry Garfield, the late President's eldest boy, were the occupants of the other private car. The members of the Cabinet, with their wives, occupied the second coach, the Pullman hotel car Marlborough. All looked sadly out at the crowd, and but few words were exchanged. The third car, the Lindell, bore the officers of the army and navy. In the fourth was the coffin of the dead President, and with it a guard of honor, among whom was Major Clapp, a comrade of

General Garfield ir the Forty-second Ohio Volunteers, and one of the witnesses of the late President's marriage. The guard of honor was composed of Lieut. E. W. Weaver, of the Second Artillery; Sergeant-major Salter, and eleven non-commissioned officers and privates. The fifth coach contained the Congressional committee.

Baltimore was reached in one hour and thirty minutes. A very large assemblage was at the Charles Street depot. Cut flowers were thrown into the coaches as they passed slowly through the outskirts of the city. The line of cars moved slowly through the crowd that surrounded the Charles Street station, and passed out on the track of the Northern Central Railroad. The locomotive divided the great assemblage of people into two compact masses on either side of the train. This gathering of men and women and children of every condition of life looked on in reverential silence. Col. Rockwell, who had been leaning his head on his hand looking out of the window, suddenly straightened up and said in a low tone to those around him: "This is a far different scene from what I witnessed here on Monday morning, the 28th day of February. We were going the other way then, and right about there in the car the man who lies dead yonder stood in the full strength of manly age. He had just returned from the platform, where he had been bowing to the crowd who came here to welcome him on his way to the White House. It was a cold day, and his face was flushed with pleasure and excitement. He made every one happy about him in his old-time way. His ambition was satisfied, his friends and his family were about him, and the future seemed very bright. The crowd outside was howling itself hoarse for him. What a splendid type of American manhood he was. Look at the contrast now. In there he lies, a poor mass of clay, and the crowd that shouted for him six months ago stands there weeping for him to-day."

The speed of the train was increased after leaving Baltimore. York, the largest town on the line, was reached at 8.20. Night fell, with lowering clouds, and the darkness was almost impenetrable. A large crowd of people, notwithstanding, met the train at this point. Rough-visaged miners lifted their little children up so that they might see the coffin of the dead President as the body was borne slowly away to its last resting-place. The funeral train did not stop after leaving Baltimore until Yorkhaven, a small coaling station, was reached, twelve miles below Harrisburg, on the Susquehanna. The journey of 120 miles, from Washington to the State capital of Pennsylvania, was almost without incident. Wherever a village or a house was to be seen there were sad faces turned sorrowfully towards the black-clad train bearing the dead President from the capital of the nation to the grave. With tolling bells the train rolled through the larger villages, passing between lines of factories and dwellings hung with black. There had been from early morning a total suspension of business in every place along the line.

At a late hour Col. Rockwell and Gen. Swaim, Dr. Boynton and the Rev. Mr. Power left Mrs. Garfield's car for the night. In the Army coach Generals Sherman, Sheridan, and Hancock were joined by several members of the Cabinet and ex-President Hayes. Supper was prepared in the hotel car after leaving Bridgeport, opposite Harrisburg. Bonfires were lighted in the little mountain hamlets, and the bells were tolled as the train passed on. The whole population of neighboring villages assembled along the railroad. The train did not cross the Susquehanna to Harrisburg, but continued by the Northern Central track up the right bank of the river, and in seven miles reached Marysville, in the gap of the Blue Ridge. The train was timed to arrive at 9.36 in the evening, and it came three minutes later. The church bells rang at intervals of every half-minute, and in the town hall of the village a meeting was being held at which the sorrow and grief of the people at the President's death was expressed. Engine No. 91, belonging to the Middle Division of the Pennsylvania Railroad, was here attached to the train, and it was placed in charge of Superintendent H. Carter, T. H. Ely, superintendent of machinery; John B. Rood, foreman; Mr. Wells, the local train-master; and W. D. Cramer. These officers were to conduct the train over the mountains to Altoona. The greatest care was taken in perfecting the local railway arrangements, a pilot-engine proceeding fifteen miles in advance of the funeral train to see that the track was clear. At Marysville a delay of seven minutes was made. The Congressional train followed twenty minutes later, and was placed in charge of new railroad officers for the rest of the long and sad journey over the mountains to the lake.

The Congressional train arrived at Marysville, Penn., at 10.15

last night, and Don Cameron's private car was then attached to it. The car contained but three persons, Senators Don Cameron and Logan and ex-Senator Chaffee. At Marysville the second train was thirty minutes behind the funeral train. To show how well the road was guarded on the occasion of this lamentable journey it may be stated, on the authority of an official of the Pennsylvania Railroad Company, that every switch between Baltimore and Pittsburg was manned, and men to watch the track were placed at every half mile on the route, and reported to the conductor of the train by lantern signals at every half-mile station designated by the officials. The train left Altoona on time at 1.40 this morning, and passed Johnstown at 3.15 a.m. About 3000 people had congregated at the depot, standing uncovered and silent. The bells of all the churches, school-houses, and engine companies were tolled. Derry station was reached at about 4.30 o'clock. Hundreds had gathered here, and the same scenes were enacted when the train entered the Union depot at Pittsburg at 5.40 this morning. Fully 5000 people had assembled at the depot, and in the streets through which the train was to pass. No demonstration was made, save the tolling of all the bells throughout the city and the firing of minute guns by the Knapp Battery. A committee of fifty citizens was on hand, and, like the crowd, stood with their heads bowed and uncovered. The scene was very solemn and impressive, and will not soon be forgotten by those who participated. During the fourteen minutes' stop at Pittsburg, while the train was been shifted to the Cleveland and Pittsburg Railroad tracks, no one ventured to speak a word above a whisper, and the funeral party kept themselves out of sight. The train drew out of the depot at 5.45, and slowly crossed the bridge to Allegheny City, where a car containing the Cleveland committee was attached. More people even than in Pittsburg lined the tracks through Allegheny City and the parks along the line of the railroad. Where it passed through the West Park the tracks were covered with plants in full bloom and beautiful and expensive floral tributes. The train steamed out of Allegheny City at 6.20, amid the tolling of bells, but there were no other demonstrations.

The second, or Congressional, train left Altoona at 2.15 a.m., drawn by two locomotives. There were several hundred people in the depot, many of whom were ladies. The train reached

Derry, Penn., at 4.45 a.m., when it stopped for water. Many people of both sexes were in waiting along the track at that unusual hour to see the train pass. At Derry it was 30 minutes behind the first train. After daylight people could be seen in bunches of 10 or 15 at many different points along the line of the road. The nearer to Pittsburg the train approached the more frequent became the crowds, and all the small stations were filled with men, women, and children. The train arrived at Pittsburg at 6.17 a.m., where breakfast was taken. The funeral train had left Pittsburg 20 minutes earlier. It had stopped for about 15 minutes, but breakfast was not partaken of. The Congressional train left Pittsburg at 7.05. For a long distance out of the city people were to be seen in groups on either side of the track. The local committee from Cleveland arrived at Pittsburg last night in a special car appropriately draped, which was attached to the train, making ten cars in all, and all were draped with the exception of that occupied by Don Cameron and his party.

At Sewickley a stop of five minutes was made in order that the funeral train might get 30 minutes in advance, it having been decided to keep the two trains that distance apart. The train arrived at Rochester at 7.43 o'clock. A large number of people were gathered at the depot, and Post No. 183 of the Grand Army of the Republic was drawn up in line to receive the train. As the Congressional train moved out of Rochester the members of the Grand Army were ordered by the commanding officer to raise their hands in salute, in which position they remained until the last car had passed. As usual, in passing all of the towns, men, women, and children of all classes were gathered on either side of the track, while at the depot several hundred were congregated. Congressman Hanna, chairman of the Cleveland local committee, passed through the train with Sergeant-at-Arms Thompson, and was introduced by him to the gentlemen with whom he was not acquainted. Mr. Hanna was accompanied by a gentleman from Cleveland who had charge of the arrangements for quartering the guests in this city. Those who desired it have been invited to take up their abode at private residences, many citizens of Cleveland having extended that courtesy. For those who prefer them hotel accommodations have been provided.

The drapery on the first car caught fire this morning while

the train was in motion, but was extinguished before much damage had been done. A post of the Grand Army of the Republic was drawn up in front of the depot at East Liverpool, Ohio, which was reached at 7.58, when the train passed in the order of salute. A band of music was in attendance and played a funeral dirge. A beautiful arch was erected over the main street, tastefully decorated. The fire department was also drawn up in line, and about 1000 people were congregated at the station and along the track. The Congressional train here caught up with the funeral train, which was delayed because of a request of Mrs. Garfield that the coach in which she was should be placed in the rear of the train. The ladies did not sleep well last night because of the heat and being too close to the engine. The funeral train made another stop at Wellesville Junction, about three miles from Wellesville, to take in water. The car shops of the company are situated here, and the employees, with their wives and children, were assembled in a body to witness the passing of the train. Across the front of one of the largest shops was stretched a wide piece of canvas, on which was painted in prominent letters, " We Mourn our Dead President." The people stood quietly by when the train stopped, scarcely any of them moving until it again started. At Wellesville proper there was a large crowd, and as the funeral train stopped for some time, the assemblage had an opportunity to partially gratify their curiosity. Ex-President Hayes, Secretaries Blaine and Lincoln, and Postmaster-General James sat at open windows facing the people, and many men shook hands with the distinguished gentlemen, and as the train moved out of the depot followed it with their eyes as long as it was possible to do so. Some of the women took their little children up to the car windows to have them shake hands with the inmates. In one instance Postmaster-General James took a little child up and kissed it.

At one of the stations passed a large number of the male portion of the crowd were in a kneeling position as the train rolled by.

One reason for Mrs. Garfield's requesting that her car be placed at the rear of the train was that she desired to be out of · reach of the crowd on arriving at Cleveland. Whenever the train has made a stop the curtains of Mrs. Garfield's car have been drawn down. The manifestations of sympathy for the dead President were most marked along the entire route. The houses from a mansion to a log cabin were draped in mourning at all points. At Salineville, Ohio, there was quite a gathering of all classes of people. Coal-miners, with their lamps on their hats and clothes covered with dirt, just as they had rushed from the mines, were mingled with well-dressed men and women. A number of coal-mine boys, with lamps on their hats, were drawn up in martial line in front of the depot.

At 10 o'clock this morning lunch under the supervision of Wormley, of Washington, was served to those on the second section of the train. A few miles west of Salineville there is a heavy grade, and the engine was unable to take the train up it. Another engine was sent for to assist, and the train was delayed 25 minutes awaiting its arrival. At Summitville, Ohio, there was a large gathering to view the passing of the trains. The main streets were filled with occupied vehicles and the depot was crowded with people. The same scenes were repeated at Bayard, Ohio, and other stations along the route. From the number of carriages at each place it would seem that the people had come to town from all the surrounding country.

Alliance, Ohio, was the next point at which the Congressional train stopped. The crowd here was immense, and manifestations of grief were recognizable on every hand. There were about 3000 people present when the funeral train passed. While the Congressional train was standing in the Alliance station quite a number of people gathered around Senator Don Cameron's car and requested the privilege of shaking hands with that gentleman and Senator Logan. The wishes of only a few of them, however, were granted. At Atwater, the next station west of Alliance, quite a crowd was gathered at the station. The train stopped for water at Ravenna at 11.31. Here a large number of people were assembled. The buildings were draped in mourning, and there was a general manifestation of sorrow. This was the last stop which the train made before reaching its destination.

At 1.30 this afternoon the train bearing the remains of the murdered President arrived here on schedule time, and 20 minutes later the Congressional train rolled into the depot. The mournful journey had been made without accident of any kind, and the pageant had been witnessed by more sorrowing citizens than ever before looked upon a funeral train in this country.

THE MURDERED PRESIDENT'S BODY RESTING IN THE CITY OF HIS
OLD FRIENDS—THE PROCESSION DOWN EUCLID AVENUE—
PLACING THE BODY ON THE CATAFALQUE IN THE PUBLIC
SQUARE—ELABORATE FLORAL OFFERINGS AND DECORATIONS.

All that remains on earth of James A. Garfield now lies in the
heart of this city, which he loved so well.   It has been a sad
day in Cleveland.   Upon the streets which have so often felt
his step, the people walked with mournful faces, for under the
dark canopy on their public square lay the body of him who
was the flower of the manhood of their State, whom they had
given to their country, and who had yielded up his life in their
country's service while holding the highest office which the
Republic could bestow upon him.   All classes and all ages are
bowed in sorrow, for in health he was very near to all, and
his sufferings had brought him close to the heart of every
family.   The dark train, which passed like a dreadful shadow
over the country, bright with the light of a September sun,
found men and women kneeling or standing, with uncovered
heads and tearful eyes, along the way in the State where the
struggles of his youth and the achievements of his manhood
were equally well known.   It is a great blow to the people of
North-eastern Ohio and this city.   It is not the hearty, cheerful,
robust man with his hand extended to every one, who comes
back to the scenes of his youth and the people whom he so long
represented and so warmly loved ; it is the voiceless clay, soon
to be hidden in the darkness of the tomb.

As the funeral train sped on its way from the East over the
mountains to the shore of Lake Erie its passage was noted and
announced here from every station, so that the time of its arrival was well known to those who were awaiting it.   It was
said that the train would reach the Euclid Avenue station at
1.15 o'clock.   For several hours before that time the people of
the city and the surrounding country had been gathering around
the station and on the broad sidewalks which lie between it and
the Public Square.   The work of displaying the symbols of
mourning upon private dwellings and public buildings had been
finished, but at 1 o'clock workmen were still engaged in completing the pavilion which shields the catafalque and the arches
which have been erected on each side of the central square.   At
1.20 those who were standing upon the platform of the Euclid

Avenue station saw the black engine and its line of shrouded cars approaching, and at 1.21 the funeral train rolled in, while the engineer slowly tolled his bell. So heavy was the funeral drapery that very little of the ordinary exterior of the engine, tender, or cars could be seen. Black flags hung from the pilot, and the sides of the tender were completely hidden by the folds which had been placed over them. Here and there on the passenger cars the drapery had been slightly disturbed by the wind which had blown upon the swiftly moving train, but nearly all of the folds remained intact.

For a moment after the train had stopped the silence was unbroken and no one appeared at the doors or windows. Then the relatives and friends and members of the escort stepped down upon the platform. The arrangements were not of so formal a character as at Long Branch and Washington. Among the first who appeared was Marshal Henry, the late President's trusted friend, whose big heart and warm sympathy are not concealed by a sturdy exterior. He had come at last with the body of his friend to those friends in Ohio, between whom and the suffering President he had been a link of communication. Next appeared the General of the Army in full uniform, and he was followed by a long line of the prominent officers of the Army and Navy who were to take their places in the escort. These distinguished men and some of the attendants of the White House, with the members of the Cleveland committee, gathered in little groups upon the platform and consulted in low tones. Near Gen. Sherman stood Gen. Winfield S. Hancock, with tearful eyes. He had come to bear his part in paying respect to his late commander, whom he had opposed in vain upon the field of politics. His eyes were not fixed upon the group around him, and he seemed to be thinking of the awful event which had taken from life the man who had reached the position which he also had striven to attain. In a few minutes the officers formed in two lines, between which passed the stricken relatives and friends and the members of the late President's Cabinet. There were Dr. Boynton, the untiring nurse and faithful friend ; Gen. Swaim and Col. Rockwell, who had loved the President with the love of brothers ; Col. Corbin, with the orphaned daughter of the President leaning upon him, and then the noble widow, with her son, and the Secretary of State, careworn and sorrowful. Mrs. Garfield was at once taken to the house of a friend, and she did not appear in the procession. These were followed by ex-President Hayes, Chief-Justice Waite, Secretary Windom, Gov. Foster, the Rev. F. D. Power, pastor of the little church on Vermont Avenue, in Washington, with which the late President had been connected, and the Rev. Isaac Errett; Postmaster-General James and Mrs. James, Secretary Lincoln, Attorney-General MacVeagh and Mrs. MacVeagh, Secretary Hunt, J. Stanley Brown, the late President's private secretary, and Warren S. Young; Dr. Hawkes, the tutor of the late President's sons; Associate Justices Strong and Matthews, of the Supreme Court, and others who had served the late President during his illness, or who were members of the official escort.

As soon as these living occupants of the train had departed, the soldiers of the Second Artillery, to whom had been assigned the duty of bearing the coffin to the hearse, came forward to remove the body from the car. Their white helmets and blue and red uniforms were in strong contrast with the dark garments of the relatives and friends. The coffin was gently moved from its resting-place, passed through the door of the car, and placed upon the shoulders of the artillerymen, who bore it along the platform and through the lines to the street, where the hearse was guarded by the veterans of Gen. Garfield's old regiment, the Forty-second Ohio Volunteers, who bore the clothing of civil life. The commanderies of Knights Templar and the Cleveland Grays and other organizations were awaiting the movements of the procession. The hearse was a plain but costly one, furnished by local undertakers, and drawn by four handsome black horses, which were covered with black robes fringed with silver. The body of the hearse was enveloped in crape. A colored man led each horse. These colored men had performed the same duty at the obsequies of President Lincoln.

Several members of Congress had come directly to this city to join the procession, and these appeared on the platform before the arrival of the second section of the funeral train, which carried the remainder of the Congressional delegation. The funeral train arrived at 1.21, the casket was placed in the hearse at 1.31, and the doors of the hearse were closed at 1.34. The Congressional train soon arrived, and its occupants formed in line upon the platform. Among those who had come were

Senators Sherman, Bayard, Ingalls, Pugh, Anthony, Camden, Blair, Morgan, Garland, Edmunds, Beck, Kellogg, Jonas, Jones of Florida, Jones of Nevada, Groome, Logan, Hawley, Cameron of Pennsylvania, Senator-elect Miller and ex-Senator Chaffee, ex-Speaker Randall, Representatives J. R. Tucker, Hiscock, Kasson, Amos Townsend, Wilson, and McCook, and ex-Representative Starin. Gov. Jewell, of Connecticut; Sergeant-at-Arms Bright, of the House, and Commissioner Loring were also in the line. Senator Pendleton had awaited the coming of the train at the station.

Great crowds had gathered around the depot. The tops of the neighboring houses were covered with men and women, and an old baggage-car was so covered with human beings that the wood-work could not be seen. Down the avenue as far as the eye could reach the lines of sorrowing people extended. The Congressional train moved away from the station while the procession was forming. The cars, like those of the funeral train, were heavily draped in mourning. The people crowded into the center of the street, but were restrained by the members of a local military company. In the open space in front of the depot stood a photographer aranging his camera. Near at hand were the delegates from Columbia Commandery, No. 2, Knights Templar, of Washington, and the members of Oriental and Holywood Commanderies, of this city.

The scene on Euclid Avenue was grand, impressive, and affecting. There are few thoroughfares in the world which rival this in beauty. The broad roadway runs for miles between rows of stately dwellings, which are surrounded by spacious grounds and shaded by numerous trees from the station to the public square. The sidewalks and broad porches were filled with people. The display of symbols of mourning and grief upon the house-fronts was remarkable. Some of the larger mansions were almost hidden in folds of black. The pillars of porticos were covered with black and white. Large portraits of the murdered President were frequently exhibited. Huge anchors of black and white had been placed in the windows. Flags at half-mast with wide black borders floated from many a lofty staff. In some of these exhibitions rare taste was shown. The avenue, like the business streets, had put on mourning garments, and in the outskirts of the city, where the poor live in humble dwellings, the display was universal.

The mournful journey to the catafalque was begun. In advance were three platoons of policemen, each line stretching from one curbstone to the other. These were followed by Col. John M. Wilson, United States Army, and staff, who rode in front of the Cleveland Grays' band, whose drums were muffled and whose bright instruments were bound with crape. A fine body of mounted men, the First City Troop, rode slowly behind the band and preceded the carriages which contained the local Committee of Arrangements. These were followed by Gov. Foster, of Ohio, and his staff. Next in order marched delegates representing Columbia Commandery, No. 2, Knight's Templar, of Washington. Directly in the rear of these was the body of the President, drawn by black horses, which were held by colored grooms by means of silver cords. The body was guarded by the United States artillerymen who had borne it from the railway car. Following the body were eight drummers whose drums were muffled and covered with crape. The outer guards consisted of long lines of Knights Templar from local commanderies. These were followed by the Cleveland Grays, a company wearing gray uniforms and huge shakos of bearskin. Their marching was superb. Then came the sorrowful handful of veterans from Gen. Garfield's old regiment, the Forty-second Ohio Volunteers, in citizen's clothing. There were forty-six of these men, and they carried their torn and bloodstained battle-flags closely furled and bound with crape. A long line of carriages then appeared, bearing the members of the Cabinet, the officers of the Army and Navy, the Governors of States, Senators, Representatives in Congress, and other distinguished visitors. In one carriage were Gen. Sherman, Admiral Nichols, and Gen. Sheridan. As the horses walked slowly past, other well-known faces were seen—those of Secretary Windom, Gen. Swaim, Secretary Hunt, Postmaster-General James, Attorney-General MacVeagh, Secretary Blaine, Secretary Lincoln, Speaker Randall, Gov. Jewell, in a carriage by himself; in another carriage, Senator Edmunds, Senator Garland, Senator Beck, and Sergeant-at-Arms Bright; in another, Senators Groome, Jonas, and Pendleton; in another, Senators Kellogg, McMillan, Hawley, and Miller, and in another, Col. Corbin and other near friends of the family.

The procession moved slowly to the measures of a mournful dirge. At 3 o'clock the vanguard reached the black arch which spanned the entrance of the public square. The road-ways around the square were blocked with people, but there were very few within the enclosure. Unfortunately, the arch had not been completed, and some of the woodwork was not yet covered with cloth, nor had the pavilion over the catafalque itself been finished. Men had been busily engaged upon it all the morning, and the derricks were still by its side. The pavilion is an imposing structure. The floor upon which the cata-falque rests is 5½ feet above the ground, and is approached over an inclined plane from the east and the west. The pavilion is square, and the arched openings face the four points of the compass. At the apex of the roof is a large gilded globe. The arched openings at the sides are 24 feet wide and 30 feet long. The floor is 45 feet square. The columns at the angles of the pavilion are graced by minarets of festooned flags, and from each corner hangs a large black banner. Draped field-pieces are placed a short distance from each corner. The façades are or-namented with beautiful floral emblems. The floral offerings displayed within the pavilion are rare, and some of them deserve description. A large cross of begonias and ivy, with arms of ferns and begonias, bears a heart made of rosebuds. Beneath is an anchor of white balsams. A large Bible of white balsams lies open, its pages studded with rosebuds, carnations, and tube-roses. Part of a beautiful altar piece consists of an open book of pink and white balsams and tuberoses, with pale yellow buds on the pages. A cross of white balsams, white asters, white roses, and carnations towers above it. A lyre of balsams and rosebuds lies against a green column, over which birds hover. Another piece represents a dreary stubble-field, brown and bare, bearing one garnered sheaf, at the foot of which lies a sickle of balsams and rosebuds and tuberoses, and the word "Gathered" in purple immortelles. There is a beautiful floral picture of "The Gates Ajar." A monument of white balsams and tube-roses has its base banded with pink, and upon the apex is a dove with folded wings. There are many massive emblems made of rare flowers. A lighthouse of balsams, tuberoses, begonias, and geranium leaves, with a broad base of fern leaves and begonias, bears a shield on which in purple immortelles are the words: "Garfield—a Beacon to Posterity." In another structure the States are represented by columns of ivy or smilax, with the name of each in white immortelles, while over all is an arch

14

which bears the words, "Columbia mourns her son." Another example of artistic skill represents a ship dismantled and wrecked, with her sails and ropes torn. She is beating upon rocks, and flowers and leaves are floating away on the waves. A list of these offerings would be almost endless. Two carloads of them were sent from Cincinnati.

When the police reached the archway at the entrance of the public square, the space within the pavilion was guarded by soldiers, who mournfully paced to and fro. The breeze from the lake fitfully shook the great black banners which hung from the corners of the pavilion. As the head of the procession entered the public square, the bell of the First Presbyterian Church, near at hand, began to toll. The band, continuing the dirge, filed in and stood at one side of the space between the arch and the pavilion. The Templars followed them, and formed in lines extending on each side of the way from the arch to the catafalque. The delegates from Columbia Commandery entered the pavilion. The remaining Templars guarded the space over which the body must pass. Marshal Henry and the local committee came up the inclined plane, and the grooms led the black horses into the public square. The Templars presented their swords. The band began the mournful strains of Pleyel's Hymn, playing softly and tenderly. Gov. Foster and his staff took places in the pavilion, and then the eight artillerymen took the coffin from the hearse and bore it slowly up the inclined plane to the catafalque, upon which they placed it. The clay which had been James A. Garfield was lying in the city of his dearest friends. It had almost reached its last resting-place.

The scene was one to be remembered. There was a deep solemnity about every action and every whispered word. The eye, glancing down between the lines of Templars and through the archway, saw the troops quietly wheeling and preparing to depart. So still was it in the presence of the great multitude which surrounded the square that the rustling of the plants which adorned the pavilion as the breeze swept by them was plainly heard. The coffin having been deposited in its place, the hearse was taken away. The Templars wheeled before the pavilion and prepared to depart. Twelve privates of the Cleveland Grays marched to the front of the pavilion and then, three at a time, went up and took their places as guards around the catafalque. They were directed by Adjutant-General Smith to allow no one to enter the pavilion. The remainder of the company departed, and the Templars followed them, leaving four of their number to act as guard. Three minutes afterwards the war-worn veterans of the Forty-second Ohio Volunteers marched up to the entrance of the pavilion, and passed out of the square by a gate at the right. The ceremony was over.

The structure and the whole square was illuminated by electric lights. Upon one side of the pavilion a long fire-ladder extends to the roof to aid the workmen. The gilded pillars of the catafalque have been draped with crape. Upon the coffin lay the palm leaves and the wreath sent by Queen Victoria, which have not been removed since the body was placed in the Capitol. At the head of the coffin laid a scroll bearing the following words:

> "Life's race well run,
> Life's work well done,
> Life's crown well won,
> Now comes rest."

THE MARTYR LAID AT REST.

LAST SAD RITES OVER PRESIDENT GARFIELD'S BODY — A GREAT ASSEMBLAGE GATHERS TO DO HIM HONOR—THE SCENE IN THE PAVILION—ELOQUENT WORDS FROM THE REV. DRS. ERRETT AND JONES—THE FUNERAL PAGEANT—THE PATH TO THE VAULT CARPETED WITH FLOWERS—PUTTING AWAY THE DEAD CHIEF FOREVER.

CLEVELAND, Sept. 26.—The last honors have been paid to the clay which once held the soul of James Abram Garfield, and the last page of the pathetic record which began on the 2d of July has been turned, and the body of the murdered President now lies in that beautiful cemetery which he had chosen for his last resting-place. Brought to them from the sea through ranks of sorrowing people, the relatives, neighbors, and friends have to-day seen it laid away in the house of silence in the city of the dead. They have known that the whole civilized world was mourning with them over the coffin of one whose birth-place was a log cabin in the wilderness. They have seen his body followed to the tomb by a mighty procession, in which the plain people and the poor laborer walked with the greatest statesmen and soldiers of the Republic. They sent him forth, they have received him again. He will greet them no more, but the memory of his greatness and his goodness will forever be the most precious possession of his State and of the honest people among whom he was born and by whose side he grew until his name was known wherever intelligence and integrity are honored and freedom is prized.

Throughout the night the stream of mourners never ceased to pass the coffin, which lay in state at the centre of the public square. Beyond the gates there was some conversation in the line, but when the mourners had passed under the arch on which the onward steps of the late President's life were so simply and plainly symbolized, all these sounds were hushed, and nothing could be heard except the steady shuffle of feet upon the pathways. The electric lights shone down upon the bared heads of these sorrowing friends and the sleeping soldiers stretched upon the grass. The night passed and dawn came, but still the people passed on by the coffin. The special trains in the morning brought thousands more who sought places in the line. But as the time for the beginning of the funeral ceremonies drew near it became necessary to close the gates, and at 9.10 o'clock the stream was checked. It is estimated that about two hundred thousand persons have passed the coffin since it has lain in Cleveland.

At a little before 10 o'clock the preparations for the ceremonies upon the public square began. South of the pavilion and catafalque a large number of seats had been placed for the guard of honor, the justices of the Supreme Court, the governors of States, the members of the United States Senate and House of Representatives, the officers of the army and navy, members of the Army of the Cumberland, the classmates of the late President, the mayors of cities, members of boards of aldermen and councilmen, and the representatives of the press. In the rear of these seats were the singers who were to supply the music. Near the justices and governors was a little place reserved for the clergymen who were to conduct the services. The sun's rays were oppressively hot, and while those entitled to seats were taking their places the funeral car which was to bear the body to the cemetery was drawn into the square from the east by twelve black horses, harnessed four abreast. Each horse was covered by a black robe, fringed with gold, and the six grooms, who performed a similar duty when the body of President Lincoln was in Cleveland, were in attendance, holding the horses by black cords. The platform of the car was eight feet wide and sixteen feet long, and the height of the structure was twenty feet. The sombre canopy was supported by six columns, draped in black broadcloth and garlands of immortelles. Festoons of black broadcloth, with wreaths of white immortelles, were suspended from the cornice. At the four corners were standards supporting flags furled and draped in crape, and at the four corners of the cornices of the canopy were black and white plumes. Other plumes were at each corner of the lantern which rose above the canopy, and before this lantern were an urn and wreaths of white immortelles. Between the pillars could be seen the raised platform on which the body was to be placed. The spirited horses taxed the strength of the grooms to the utmost as they strove to guide them.

Although the reserved seats were not filled, the streets around the public square were blocked with great masses of people. Beyond them could be heard the sound of marching men who were wheeling into the long line of the procession. The Marine Band of Washington came in through the west gate and marched around the pavilion to the east gate on their way to their places. Following them were Knights Templar. Upon the grass at the left of the catafalque were the cameras of two enterprising photographers. At 10 o'clock the chosen members of the Cleveland Grays and the four Templars were still guarding the body. A few of the reserved seats were occupied. Near their chairs were Chief Justice Waite, Associate Justice Matthews, and Associate Justice Strong, shielded from the burning sun by umbrellas. Upon the table lay a large Bible, to be used by the clergymen. A few minutes later General W. T. Sherman came to his seat with Adjutant-General Rogers, General Sheridan, Admiral Stanley, General Hancock, Commodore English, Quartermaster-General Meigs, Surgeon-General Wales, of the navy, Adjutant.-General Drum, Chief Paymaster Lodker, Colonel Tourtellotte, and Colonel Ward. They were followed by Senators Baldwin, Kellogg, Logan, Don Cameron, Jonas, Conger, Miller, Pendleton, Beck, Edmunds, Garland, Blair, Pugh, Ingalls, Anthony, Morgan, Bayard, Sherman, Camden, Jones of Florida, McMillan, Sawyer, Hawley, Harrison, and Saunders, and ex-Senator McDonald. Each Senator wore a broad white sash or regalia on which was a rosette of black and white. The sun beat down on them unmercifully and the heat was hard to endure. The space from the catafalque to the funeral car was guarded for the first time by rows of weatherbeaten marines from the Michigan, which was lying in the harbor. The number of persons on the funeral pavilion rapidly increased after 10 o'clock. Among those who came was ex-President Hayes, who could be seen talking with ex-Secretary Evarts. While the distinguished persons to whom seats had been assigned were taking their places, carriages were seen coming into the public square. The first carriage was drawn by two beautiful white horses. The door was opened, and a young man with a mournful face alighted and then assisted to the ground a lady clad in deep black. These were the President's widow and his son Harry. With them was one of the President's little boys. Another figure, bent with age and leaning on the arms of two of the late President's devoted friends, slowly ascended the inclined plane and took a seat on the north side, not far from the coffin. This was the late President's mother, who saw him assume his high position in Washington, and whom he tenderly kissed on that day after he had taken the oath at the east front of the Capitol. Other carriages came, bearing other relatives of the dead President and the members of his Cabinet. These took their places in the pavilion. Mrs. Blaine stood for some time by the side of the catafalque shielding from the sun the venerable head of the late President's mother, which was lying on the coffin which held the body of her son. The aged lady wept quietly, and prayed. There were many tearful eyes in the pavilion. A long line of Representatives took their places in the rear of the Senators. Among these were ex-Speaker Randall, ex-Speaker Banks, and Messrs. Hiscock, Starin, Hubbell, Townsend, Newberry, McKinly, McCook, and Chalmers of Mississippi. Each of the Representatives wore a broad white sash. Soon afterward Governor Cornell, of New York, and his staff came and took their seats. The other governors present were Bigelow, of Connecticut; Foster, of Ohio; Ludlow, of New Jersey; Hoyt, of Pennsylvania; Cullom, of Illinois; Gear, of Iowa; Porter, of Indiana; Blackburn, of Kentucky; Smith, of Wisconsin; Jackson, of West Virginia; Pitkin, of Colorado; Jerome, of Michigan; Hawkins, of Tennessee; and Jarvis, of North Carolina.

For some time the carriages continued to pass before the pavilion, until nearly all the space in it was occupied by the relatives and near friends of the departed hero.

THE SERVICES IN THE PAVILION.

Then the clergymen took the seats reserved for them. Around a small table sat the Rev. Isaac Errett, of the Church of the Disciples; the Right Rev. Bishop Bedell, of the Protestant Episcopal Church; the Rev. Dr. Houghton, of the Methodist Church; the Rev. Jabez Hall, of the Church of the Disciples, and the Rev. Dr. Charles S. Pomeroy, of the Presbyterian Church. The programme was as follows:

GARFIELD OBSEQUIES.

Sept. 26, 1881, Cleveland.

Services at Pavilion.

The Hon. J. P. Robison, presiding.
Singing by the Cleveland Vocal Society.
Reading of Scriptures by the Right Rev. Bishop G. T. Bedell.
Prayer by a representative of the Methodist Episcopal Conference in session in Painesville.
Singing by the Cleveland Vocal Society.
Address by the Rev. I. Errett, of Cincinnati.
Hymn to be read by the Rev. Jabez Hall, of the Euclid Avenue Christian Church, and sung by the Cleveland
Vocal Society.
Prayer and Benediction by the Rev. Charles S. Pomeroy.

Services at Lake View Cemetery.

Remarks by the Rev. J. H. Jones, Chaplain of the Forty-second Regiment.
Singing by the Cleveland German vocal societies.
President Garfield's favorite ode.
Prayer and Benediction by President B. A. Hinsdale.

At 10.40 o'clock the relatives and friends and distinguished persons in the reserved seats were in their places, and Dr. Robison arose and said, " The exercises will be opened now by singing by the Vocal Society of Cleveland." When the singing was ended Bishop Bedell read the first and second verses of the fourteenth chapter of Job, the first four verses of the 90th Psalm, a large portion of the fifteenth chapter of First Corinthians, and the 13th verse of the fourteenth chapter of Revelations. These passages were read clearly and impressively. The prayer which followed was offered by the Rev. Ross M. Houghton, over whose head another clergyman held an umbrella.

" O God, our Father, we bow before Thee with the weight of a great sorrow upon our hearts. Our beloved President is dead, and all our hopes which depended on his wisdom and his integrity for their fulfilment are blighted. Just why Thou hast suffered this sore trial to come upon us we cannot tell, for as Thou hast not informed us of the secrets of Thy government, Thy thoughts are not our thoughts, Thy ways are not our ways. We bow in humble submission to Thy will, and we pray for divine help that we may not, for one moment even, doubt Thy wisdom or love. May the dark clouds that hang over us burst in blessing on our heads. O God, we acknowledge our sins and implore Thy mercy; we rest in Thy love, and we trust Thee to do for us all that is wisest and all that is best. We pray, O God, that this great disappointment and this great grief may be for the nation's good and Thine own everlasting glory. We rejoice in the light from Thy throne, which already begins to dispel our darkness, and we believe that although the earnest prayer of this nation for the recovery of our President has not been granted, still Thou might not fail in Thine infinite mercy and in Thine infinite love, through his death, to bring to us blessings more available. O God, we thank Thee for the noble, grand character of our departed President, which stood out so prominent before the nation and before the world; and we pray that the righteousness which he loved and which he exemplified may prevail in all the land. Amid all changes, Thou only art the abiding One. The world and the things of the world are passing away, but in the possession of Thy love we are safe and secure. Hide us there, O God, till all earth's calamities be over and past. Regard in mercy, we pray Thee, the aged mother, the devoted wife, and orphan children of our departed ruler, as their hearts are overwhelmed. O compassionate Saviour, draw them to Thyself; may they rest upon Thy bosom; may they find peace and hope and joy in the fulfilment of Thy precious promises. May the mantle of the noble father fall upon those worthy sons, and may every member of this stricken family be able to say through the inspiration of love and submission, 'Father, Thy will, not mine, be done!' Grant, O God! that this calamity, this great affliction, may draw this family and this suffering nation to a nearer relationship and a more loving fellowship with Thee, and amid the mysteries of seemingly conflicting dispensations, grant that we may look forward by faith to the day when we shall hear Thy voice say, 'Said I not unto them, If thou wouldst believe thou shouldst see and live'? Let also Thy blessings, rich and full, rest upon Thy servant who has been called upon to fulfill the grave responsibilities of Chief Magistrate of the nation so suddenly and unexpectedly. Bless his Cabinet. Bless all who are associated with him in the affairs of this Government. May they be men after Thine own heart. May we be, and continue to be, despite our calamities, a prosperous and happy people. Prepare us with Thy divine help and divine blessing for the further duties of this solemn hour, and grant to us when we lay aside all that is mortal and all that remains of our beloved brother in the silent grave, it may be with the blessed hope of the resurrection from the dead where we shall be forever with the Lord. Guide us by Thy counsel; afterwards receive us to Thine excellent glory. We ask it through Christ the Lord. Amen."

During this prayer the fire-alarm sounded. The Ashtabula Light Artillery had begun to fire minute guns in Lake View Park, and from this time on the reports were plainly heard on the square.

THE REV. DR. ERRETT'S ADDRESS.

The address made by the Rev. Isaac Errett did not depend for effect upon the graces of oratory or the beauties of rhetoric. It was a plain and earnest review of the life and work of the late President, an appeal to the living to profit by the lessons of his death, and a prayer that the stricken family might find comfort in communion with God. His text was as follows:

" And the archers shot at King Josiah, and the King said to his servants, Have me away, for I am sore wounded."

" His servants, therefore, took him out of that chariot and put him in the second chariot that he had, and they brought him to Jerusalem, and he died and was buried in one of the sepulchres of his fathers, and all Judah and Jerusalem mourned for Josiah.

14*

" And Jeremiah lamented for Josiah, and all the singing men and the singing women spake of Josiah in their lamentations, and made them an ordinance in Israel, and, behold, they are written in the Lamentations.

" Now the rest of the acts of Josiah and his goodness according to that which was written in the law of the Lord.

" And his deeds first and last, behold, they are written in the Book of the Kings of Israel and of Judah.

" For behold, the Lord, the Lord of Hosts, doth take away from Jerusalem and from Judah the stay and the staff; the whole stay of bread and the whole stay of water; the mighty man and the man of war, and the prophet, and the ancient, the captain of fifty, and the honorable man, and the counsellor, and the cunning artificer, and the eloquent orator.

" The voice said, 'Cry,' and he said, ' What shall I cry?' All flesh is grass, and all the goodliness thereof is as the flower of the field. The grass withereth, the flower fadeth, because the Spirit of the Lord bloweth upon it. Surely the people is grass, the grass withereth, the flower fadeth, but the word of our God shall stand forever."

Dr. Errett spoke as follows:

" This is a time for mourning that has no parallel in the history of the world. Death is constantly occurring every day and every hour, and almost every moment some life expires and somewhere there are broken hearts and desolate homes; but we have learned to accept the unavoidable, and we pause a moment and drop a tear and away again to the excitements and ambitions of life and forget it all. Sometimes a life is called for that plunges a large community in mourning, and sometimes whole nations mourn the loss of a good king, or a wise statesman, or an eminent sage, or a great philosopher, or a philanthropist, or a martyr who has laid his life upon the altar of truth and won for himself an envious immortality among the sons of men. But there was never a mourning in all the world like unto this mourning. I am not speaking extravagantly when I say this, for I am told it is the result of calculations carefully made from such data as are in possession that certainly not less than 300,000,000 of the human race share in the sadness and the lamentations and sorrow and mourning that belong to this occasion here to-day. It is a chill shadow of a fearful calamity that has extended itself into every home in all this land, and into every heart, and that has projected itself over vast seas and oceans into distant lands, and awakened the sincerest and profoundest sympathy with us in the hearts of the good people of the nations, and among all people. It is worth while, my friends, to pause a moment and to ask why this is. It is, doubtless, attributable in part to the wondrous triumphs of science and art within the present century, by means of which time and space have been so far conquered that nations, once far distant and necessarily alienated from each other, are brought into close communication, and the various ties of commerce and of social interests and of religious interests bring them into contact of fellowship that could not have been known in former times. It is likewise, unquestionably, partly due to the fact that this nation of ours has grown to such wondrous might and power before the whole earth, and which is, in fact, the hope of the world in all that relates to the highest civilization—that sympathy with this nation and respect for this great power leads to these offerings of condolence and expressions of sympathy and grief from the various nations of the earth, and because they have learned to respect and recognize that the nation is stricken in the fatal blow that has taken away our President from us. And yet this will by no means account for this marvellous and world-wide sympathy of which we are speaking. Yet it cannot be attributed to mere intellectual greatness, for there have been, and there are, other great men; and, acknowledging all that the most enthusiastic heart could claim for our beloved leader, it is but fair to say that there have been more eminent educators, there have been greater soldiers, there have been more skilful and experienced and powerful legislators and leaders of mighty parties and political forces. There is no one department in which he has more eminence where the world may not point to others who attained higher and more intellectual greatness. It might not be considered more righteously here than in many other cases; yet perhaps it is rare in the history of nations that any one man has combined so much of excellence in all those various departments, and who as an educator and a lawyer and a legislator and a soldier and a party chieftain and ruler has done so well, so thoroughly well, in all departments, and brought out such successful results as to inspire confidence and command respect and approval in every path of life in which he has walked and in every department of public activity which he has occupied. Yet I think when we come to a proper estimate of his character and seek after the secret of this world-wide sympathy and affection, we shall find it rather in the richness and integrity of his moral nature, and in that sincerity, and in that transparent honesty, in that truthfulness, that lay the basis for everything of greatness to which we do honor to-day.

"I may state here what perhaps is not generally known as an illustration of this. When James A. Garfield was yet a mere lad, in this county a series of religious meetings were held in one of the towns of Cuyahoga County by a minister by no means attractive as an orator, possessing none of the graces of an orator, and marked only by entire sincerity, by good reasoning powers, and by earnestness in seeking to win souls from sin to righteousness. The lad Garfield attended these meetings for many nights, and after listening to the sermons night after night, he went one day to the minister and said to him: 'Sir, I have been listening to your preaching night after night, and I am fully persuaded that if these things you say are true it is the duty and the highest interest of every man of respectability, and especially of every young man, to accept that religion and seek to be a man. But, really, I don't know whether this thing is true or not. I can't say that I disbelieve it, but I dare not say that I fully and honestly believe it. If I were sure that it was true I would most gladly give it my heart and my life.' So, after a long talk, the minister preached that night on the text, 'What is truth?' and proceeded to show that, notwithstanding all the various and conflicting theories and opinions in ethical science, and notwithstanding all the various and conflicting opinions in the world, there was one assured and eternal alliance for every human soul in Jesus Christ; that every soul was safe with Jesus Christ; that He never would mislead; that any young man giving Him his hand and heart and walking in His pathway would not go astray; and that, whatever might be the solution of ten thousand insoluble mysteries, at the end of all things the man who loved Jesus Christ and walked after the footsteps of Jesus, and realized in spirit and life the pure morals and the sweet piety, was safe, if safety there were in the universe of God; safe, whatever else were safe; safe, whatever else might prove unworthy and perish forever. And he seized upon it after due reflection, and came forward and gave his hand to the minister in pledge of his acceptance of the guidance of Christ for his life, and turned his back upon the sins of the world forever. The boy is father to the man, and that pure honesty and integrity, and that fearless spirit to inquire, and that brave surrender of all the charms of sin to convictions of duty and right, went with him from that boyhood throughout his life, and crowned him with the honors that were so cheerfully awarded to him from all hearts over this vast land. There was another thing—he passed all the conditions of virtuous life between the log cabin in Cuyahoga and the White House, and in that wonderfully rich and varied experience, moving up from higher to higher, he has touched every heart in all this land at some point or other, and he became the representative of all hearts and lives in this land; not only the teacher but the representative of all virtues, for he knew their wants and he knew their condition, and he established legitimately the ties of brotherhood with every man with whom he came in contact. I take it that this vow, lying at the basis of his character, this rock on which his whole life rested, followed up by the perpetual and enduring industry that marked his whole career, made him at once the honest and the capable man who invited and received in every act of his life the confidence and trust and love of all who learned to know him.

"There is yet one other thing that I ought to mention here. There was such an admirable harmony of all his powers; there was such a beautiful adjustment of the physical, intellectual, and moral in his being; there was such an equitable distribution of the physical, intellectual, and moral forces, that his nature looked out every way to get at sympathy with everything, and found about equal delight in all pursuits and all studies, so that he became, through his industry and honest ambition, really encyclopædic. There was scarcely any single chord that you could touch to which he would not respond in a way that made you know that his hand had swept it skilfully long ago, and there was no topic you could bring before him, there was no object you could present to him, that you did not wonder at the richness and fullness of information somehow gathered; for his eyes were always open, and his heart was always open, and his brain was ever busy and equally interested in everything—the minute and the vast, the high and the low, in all classes and creeds of men. He thus gathered up that immense store and

that immense variety of the most valuable and practical knowledge that made him a man, not in one department, but all
around, everywhere in his whole beautiful and symmetrical life
and character.

" But, my friends, the solemnity of this occasion forbids any
further investigation in that line, any further details of a very
remarkable life, for with these details you are familiar, or, if
not, they will come before you through various channels hereafter.   It is my duty in the presence of the dead, and in view
of all the solemnities that rest upon us, now in a solemn burial
service, to call your attention to the great lesson taught you,
and by which we ought to become wiser, purer, and better men.
And I want to say, therefore, first of all, that there comes a voice
from the dead to this entire nation, and not only to the people,
but to those in places of trust, to our legislators and our governors and our military men and our leaders of parties, and all
classes and creeds in the Union.   The great lesson to which I
desire to call your attention can be expressed in a few words.
James A. Garfield went through his whole public life without
surrendering for a single moment his Christian integrity, his
moral integrity, or his love for the spiritual.   Coming into the
exciting conflicts of political life with a nature as capable as any
of feeling the force of every temptation, with temptations to unholy ambition, with unlawful prizes within his reach, with every
inducement to surrender all his religious faith and be known
merely as a successful man of the world, from first to last he has
manfully adhered to his religious convictions and found the
more praise, and gathers in his death all the pure inspiration of
the hope of everlasting life.   I am very well aware of a feeling
among political men, greatly shared in all over the land by those
who engage in political life, that a man cannot afford to be a
politician and a Christian; that he must necessarily forego his
obligations to God and be absorbed in the different measures of
policy that may be necessary to enable him to achieve the desired result.   Now, my friends, I call attention to this grand
life as teaching a lesson altogether invaluable just at this point.
I want you to look at that man.   I want you to think of him
when, in his early manhood, he was so openly committed to
Christ and the principles of the Christian religion that he was
frequently found among a people who allow a large liberty, occupying a pulpit.   You are within a few miles of the spot where

the great congregations gathered, when he was yet almost a boy, just emerging into manhood, week after week, and hung upon the words that fell from his lips with wonder, admiration, and enthusiasm. It was when he was known to be occupying this position that he was invited to become a candidate for the Ohio State Senate. It was with the full knowledge of all that belonged to him, in his Christian faith and his efforts to live a Christian life, that this was tendered him; and, without any resort to any dishonorable means, he was elected, and began his legislative career. When the country called to arms, when the Union was in danger and his great heart leaped with enthusiasm and was filled with holiest desire and ambition to render some service to his country, it required no surrender of the dignity or nobleness of his Christian life to secure to him the honors that fell upon him so thick and fast, and the successes that followed each other so rapidly as to make him the wonder of the world, though he entered upon that career wholly unacquainted with military life, and could only win his way by the honesty of his purpose and the diligence and faithfulness with which he seized upon every opportunity to accomplish the work before him. Follow him from that time until he was called from the service in the field and the people of his district sent him to Congress, their hearts gathering about him without any effort on his part. They kept him there as long as he would stay, and they would have kept him there yet if he had said so. He remained there until, by the voice of the people of this State, he was made Senator, when there were other bright and strong and grand names—men who were entitled to recognition and reward, and altogether worthy in every way to bear senatorial honors. Yet there were such currents of admiration and sympathy and trust and love coming in and centring from all parts of the State that the action of the Legislature at Columbus was but the echo of the popular voice when, by acclamation, they gave him that place, and every other candidate gracefully retired. And then again, when he went to Chicago to serve the interest of another, when, as I knew, his own ambition was fully satisfied, and he had received that on which his heart was set, and looked with more than gladness to a path in life for which he thought his entire education and culture had prepared him. When wearied out with every effort to command a majority for any candidate, the hearts of that great convention turned on every side to James A. Garfield. In spite of himself and against every feeling, wish, and prayer of his own heart, this honor was crowded upon him, and the nation responded with holy enthusiasm from one end of the land to the other, and in the same honorable way he was elected to the chief magistracy under circumstances which, however great the bitterness of party conflict, caused all parties not only to acquiesce, but to feel proud in the consciousness that we had a chief magistrate of whom they need not be ashamed before the world, and unto whom they could safely confide the destinies of this mighty nation. Now, gentlemen, let me say to you all, those of you occupying great places of trust who are here to-day, and the mass of those who are called upon to discharge the responsibilities of citizenship year by year, the most invaluable lesson that we learn from the life of our beloved departed President is, that not only is it not incompatible with success, but it is the surest means of success, to consecrate heart and life to that which is true and right, and above all question of mere policy, wedding the soul to truth and right and the God of truth and righteousness in holy wedlock never to be dissolved. I feel just at this point that we need this lesson.

"This great, wondrous land of ours, this mighty nation in its marvellous upward career, with its ever-increasing power, opening its arms to receive from all lands people of all languages, all religions, and all conditions, and hoping in the warm embrace of political brotherhood to blend them with us, to melt them into a common mass, needs this lesson of virtue, so that when melted and run over again in a new type of manhood it will incorporate all the various nations of the earth in one grand brotherhood, presenting before the nations of the world a spectacle of freedom and strength and prosperity and power beyond anything before known. Let me say the permanency of the work and its continual enlargement must depend on our maintaining virtue as well as intelligence, and making dominant in all the land those principles of pure morality that Jesus Christ has taught us. Just as we cling to that we are safe, and just as we forget and depart from that we proceed toward disaster and ruin. And when we see what has been accomplished in a mighty life like this we have an instance of the power of truth and right which spreads from heart to heart, and from life to life, and from State to State, and finally from nation to nation,

until, these pure principles reigning everywhere, God shall real
ize His great purpose, so long ago expressed to us in the words
of prophecy, that the kingdoms of this world are become the
kingdoms of our God and of his Christ, so that over the dead
body of James A. Garfield may all the people join hands and
swear by the Eternal God that they will dismiss all unworthy
purposes and love and worship the true and the right, and in
the inspiration of the grand principles that Jesus Christ taught
seek to realize the grand ends to which His word of truth and
right continually point us.

"I cannot prolong my remarks to any great extent. There are
two or three things that I must say, however, before I close.
There is a voice to the Church in this death that I cannot pause
now to speak of particularly. There is a tenderer and more
awful voice that speaks to the members of the family; to that
sacred circle within which his really true life and character were
better developed and more perfectly known than anywhere else.
What words can tell the weight of anguish that rests upon the
hearts of those who so dearly loved him and shared with him
the sweet sanctities of his home; the pure life, the gentleness,
the kindness, and the manliness that pervaded all his actions and
made his home a charming one for its inmates and for all who
shared in its hospitalities? It is of all things the saddest and
most grievous now that those bound to him by the tenderest ties
of the home circle are called to yield him to the grave; to hear
that voice of love no more; to behold that manly form no
longer moving in the sweet circle of home; to receive no more
the benediction from the loving hand of the father that rested
upon the heads of his children and commanded the blessings of
God upon them; the dear old mother who realizes here to-day
that her fourscore years are after all but labor and sorrow, to
whom we owe, back of all I have spoken of, the education and
training that made him what he was, and who has been led
from that humble home in the wilderness side by side with him
in all his elevation, and assured him the triumph and the glory
that came to him, step by step, as he mounted up from high to
higher, to receive the highest honors that the land could bestow upon him; left behind him, lingering on the shore, while
he has passed over to the other side; what words can express
the sympathy that is due to her, or the consolation that can
strengthen her heart and give her courage to bear this bitter be

reavement ? And the wife, who began with him in her young womanhood, and has bravely kept step with him, right along through all his wondrous career, and who has been not only his wife but his friend and his counsellor through all their succession of prosperities and this increase of influence and power, and who, when the day of calamity came, was there, his ministering angel, his prophetess, and his priestess, when the circumstances were such as to forbid ministrations from other hands, speaking to him the words of cheer which sustained him through that long fearful struggle for life, and watching over him when his dying vision rested on her beloved form, and sought from her eyes an answering gaze that should speak when words could not be spoken, of a love that has never died, and that now must be immortal. And the children, who have grown up to an age when they can remember all that belonged to him, left fatherless in a world like this, yet surrounded with a nation's sympathy and with a world's affection, and able to treasure in their hearts the grand lessons of his noble and wondrous life, may be assured that the eyes of the nation are upon them, and that the hearts of the people go out after them. While there is much to support and encourage, it is still a sad thing, and calls for our deepest sympathy, that they have lost such a father and are left to make their way through this rough world without his guiding hand or his wise counsels. But that which makes this terrible to them now is just that which, as the years go by, will make very sweet and bright and joyous memories to fill the coming years. By the very loss which they deplore, and by all the loving actions that bound them in blessed sympathy in the home circle, they will live over again ten thousand times all the sweet life of the past, and though dead he will still live with them, and though his tongue be dumb in the grave it will speak anew to them ten thousand beautiful lessons of love and righteousness and truth. May God, in His infinite mercy, fold them in His arms and bless them as they need in this hour of thick darkness, and bear them safely through what remains of the troubles and sorrows of their earthly pilgrimage unto the everlasting home where there shall be no more death nor crying, neither shall there be any more pain, for the former things shall have forever passed away. We commit you, beloved friends, to the arms and the care of the everlasting Father, who has promised to be the God of the widow and the Father of the fatherless in His holy habitation, and whose sweet promise goes with us through all the dark and stormy paths of life—'I will never leave thee nor forsake thee.'

" I have discharged now the solemn covenant and trust reposed in me many years ago, in harmony with a friendship that has never known a cloud, a confidence that has never trembled, and a love that has never changed. Farewell, my friend and brother, thou hast fought a good fight; thou hast finished thy course; thou hast kept thy faith; henceforth there is laid up for thee a crown of righteousness which the Lord, the righteous Judge, will give to thee in that day; and not unto thee alone, but unto all them who love his appearing."

Dr. Errett was listened to with close and earnest attention. He spoke for forty minutes, and when he closed a hush for a moment hung over the vast audience.

The Rev. Jabez Hall then read General Garfield's favorite hymn, which was beautifully sung by the Vocal Society:

> Ho, reapers of life's harvest,
> Why stand with rusted blade
> Until the night draws round the
> And day begins to fade?
> Why stand ye idle, waiting
> For reapers more to come?
> The golden morn is passing,
> Why sit ye idle, dumb?
>
> Thrust in your sharpened sickle
> And gather in the grain;
> The night is fast approaching
> And soon will come again.
> The Master calls for reapers,
> And shall he call in vain?
> Shall sheaves lie there, ungathered
> And waste upon the plain?
>
> Mount up the heights of wisdom
> And crush each error low.
> Keep back no words of knowledge
> That human hearts should know.
> Be faithful to thy mission
> In service of thy Lord,
> And then a golden chaplet
> Shall be thy just reward.

DR. POMEROY'S PRAYER.

The Rev. Dr. Pomeroy then closed the ceremonies with the following prayer:

"Eternal and ever-blessed God, thou alone art great. Clouds and darkness are round about thee. Righteousness and judgment are the habitation of thy throne. The eyes of all the world are upon us to-day as solemnly we prepare to lay away the remains of our beloved chieftain in the tomb. The hearts of fifty millions are throbbing with our hearts as we pass through these solemn obsequies. And yet, O God, more impressive to us than all is the fact that, though we are poor and needy, the great God thinketh upon us. We thank thee, gracious Father, that we sorrow not to-day as those who are without hope, for we know that since Jesus died and rose again even so them, also, who sleep in Jesus will God bring with him. We thank thee, Father, for the very existence of such a man as him we mourn to-day. We thank thee that thou didst give him to our love, and we do bless thee, above all, that thou hast now bestowed upon him the greatest promotion of his advancing life, even a seat at thy right hand in the glory of thy heavenly throne. Abide with us, gracious God; let thy gracious blessing rest upon these whose sorrow must be so much more intimate and intense than ours; upon this mother and this widow and the fatherless children, whom we commit in all confidence to thy divine and gracious care. O God! O God! be our shield. We thank thee for what thou hast done for thy people through these hours of darkness that have come out in light through thy blessing in the hope we entertain for him and for ourselves. We bless thee that thou hast crushed out skepticism under the power of this sorrow; that thou hast led the people to press toward the throne of heavenly grace in supplication, and that thou art ready still further to bless us and the nation whose God is the Lord. Now abide with us our Father; abide with us even as a people, and at last take us all; and as this great flood of humanity pours over the brink of death into the gulf of eternity, grant that we may, like him for whom we grieve to-day, be received into everlasting habitation, to be forever with the Lord, and all the praise shall be thine, through Jesus Christ, our Saviour. Amen.

"And now, the grace of our Lord Jesus Christ, the love of

God, our Father, and the communion of the Holy Spirit, be and remain with you all. Amen."

THE MARCH TO LAKE VIEW CEMETERY.

The long column had formed in Superior Street and Euclid Avenue, and now the body was to be taken from the catafalque and placed in the funeral car. The people who had been admitted to the square formed on both sides of the passage from the catafalque to the gate, and the Marine Band played tenderly " Nearer, my God, to Thee," while the artillerymen approached the coffin. Reaching the foot of the inclined plane, they halted. Near the head of the coffin was a sorrowful group of the late President's dearest friends. There were Gen. Swaim, Col. Rockwell and Secretary Brown. These men have grown old since that fatal 2d of July. Especially true is this of Col. Rockwell. Near them was Mrs. Rockwell, weeping, and Capt. Henry and William S. Roose, of Washington, a gentleman who, in company with the undertakers, has had charge of the body. In the rear of this group were the near relatives, who were soon to appear. The artillerymen walked slowly up the inclined plane, and stood at the head of the catafalque. The clergymen followed them. The coffin was lifted and placed on the shoulders of the artillerymen, who bore it very slowly to the funeral car, and placed it upon the support prepared for it there. While they were passing the Marine Band played " In the Sweet By-and-By." Following the body and the undertakers came Daniel Spriggs, the late President's faithful colored servant. The carriages for the mourners were brought to the foot of the inclined plane. Col. Rockwell and Harry Garfield, supporting Mrs. Garfield, and accompanied by one of the younger boys, then came from the pavilion. Then came the President's aged mother, slowly walking with her grandson James and Col. Corbin. The President's daughter, Mollie, weeping, came with her mother's father. There were many others, including Dr. Boynton, who has been deeply affected by the sufferings and death of the President; Mrs. Rockwell, who had found it very difficult to endure this last scene. As the relatives left the pavilion the familiar faces of ex-President and Mrs. Hayes were seen there; with them was their daughter Lucy. By the side of the ex-President stood his former Secretary of State. Leaning against one of the gilded pillars of the catafalque was Secretary

Blaine. In the foreground, Gen. Swaim, Col. Rockwell, and Secretary Brown remained—a group of the nearest friends of the dead. Then the members of the Cabinet, with their wives, came down to their carriages. First came Mr. and Mrs. Blaine, then Mr. and Mrs. Windom, Mr. and Mrs. Hunt, Mr. and Mrs. Lincoln, Mr. and Mrs. James, Mr. and Mrs. MacVeagh, and Mr. Kirkwood. The trio of devoted friends and the ex-President were the last who left the spot where the President's body had lain.

The grand procession passed out Superior Street and Euclid Avenue to the entrance of the cemetery. The sidewalks of the beautiful avenue were crowded with people, many of whom had come to the city from places many miles away. The citizens distributed 20,000 sandwiches and 20,000 gallons of ice water to the civil and military visitors. The crowds along the avenue were so large that in some places they occupied the private lawns. Barrels of water were placed at short intervals along the way for the use of all. The entire line was patrolled by soldiers of the Ohio National Guard. When the head of the column reached the black arch which had been erected over the entrance of the cemetery, the ranks were opened and the body of the dead President, borne upon the funeral car, passed in between the long ranks of soldiers and civilians. The head of the column reached the gate a few minutes before 2 o'clock. Upon the piers of the arch were these inscriptions:

> "Lay him to sleep whom we have learned to trust."
> "Lay him to sleep whom we have learned to love."
> "Come to rest."

AT THE GATES OF THE VAULT.

From the gate to the public vault in which the body was to be temporarily deposited the way was guarded by soldiers. Very few persons had been allowed to come into the cemetery, and those who had come, together with part of the Fourteenth Regiment of the Ohio National Guard, of Columbus, Col. George D. Freeman, and the Curry Cadets, of Marysville, Capt. W. M. Leggett, were gathered at or near the vault. In front of the vault, a narrow roadway passes between two divisions of the lake. To the right rises the beautiful knoll on which the President's body was placed, and where the grand monument for which dollar subscriptions are now being taken will be erected.

In front of the entrance of the vault was a black pall about 40 feet long and 20 feet wide. The ground under the pall had been covered with evergreen sprigs until it seemed to wear a green carpet. Upon the evergreens the lady school-teachers of Cleveland had scattered roses, geraniums, and immortelles in rich profusion. The flowers were more plentiful just at the entrance of the vault. The vault's iron gates were standing open, and the bars were almost hidden by smilax. The dark interior had been beautified by rare flowers and vines. There could be seen a great lyre of flowers, sent by the Brazilian Legation at Washington; a cross and crown, given by the Bolivian Legation; and a beautiful wreath, the gift of the ladies of Dubuque, Iowa. The people around the vault awaited in silence the arrival of the procession. Just opposite the vault was the ever-present camera of the photographer. An artist was sketching the vault for an illustrated paper. The minute-guns were distinctly heard.

At 2.15 o'clock the dark clouds which had been gathering in a threatening manner for some time let fall a shower which drove the people to the shelter of the evergreens. The wind arose and shook the great black pall, and twisted the young trees on the edge of the lake. A piece of tarpaulin was hastily thrown over the trestles which the undertakers had brought to aid them in taking the body from the car. Men crawled under this improvised tent. The water gathered in the folds of the pall and threatened to break it down. A soldier walked under it and thrust his bayonet through the cloth. An officer climbed a little ladder and cut holes in the pall with his sword. The water then poured down upon the beautiful carpet of evergreens and flowers. Ten minutes later the rain almost ceased to fall, but in a short time the drops came down again. From that time onward the rain continued, although the clouds frequently seemed to be breaking away. The spectators who had no umbrellas crouched under the branches of the trees.

At 3 o'clock the members of the German singing societies marched along the roadway and took places by the side of the vault. Ten minutes later Gov. Foster and his staff appeared in front of the vault in a drizzling rain. At 3.30 the Marine Band, of Washington, marched by playing the Garfield funeral march, and took a station beyond the vault on the left. Three minutes later came three horsemen—Chief Marshal Barnett, and Gen. Meyer and Major Goodspeed, of his staff. They were at once followed by the First City Troop of Cleveland, a fine body of men, excellently mounted, and clad in uniforms of black and yellow. Marching behind them were the commanderies of Knights Templar, the members of which formed a single rank facing the vault, while the troopers continued the line to the left.

No sound was heard as the funeral car drew near. Its wheels passed noiselessly over the earth. The grooms were finding it difficult to restrain the twelve black horses. The artillerymen still marched by the side of the car. Colored men held the canopy by cords running down from the corners of the cornice. The immortelles around the pillars had been soaked through and through with rain, and the old colors, furled and draped, were dripping. The palms of victory had slipped from the top of the coffin to the floor of the car, but the wreath sent by Queen Victoria was yet in its place. A great piece of tarpaulin was at once laid upon the carpet of evergreens and flowers, and an inclined plane was placed at the rear of the car. While the artillerymen were getting ready to lift the body from the car, the white horses of Mrs. Garfield's carriage walked up to a spot just in front of the door of the vault. The window of the carriage was lowered. Upon the back seat were President Garfield's wife and mother. The venerable lady's sad face appeared for a moment and was then withdrawn. Then the President's widow drew back her veil and looked out upon the beautiful carpet of flowers. Upon the box, beside the driver, sat Daniel Spriggs, the faithful colored servant of the dead man. Dr. Robison walked to the door of the carriage and spoke to those who were within. Then Harry Garfield and James Garfield opened the door and stepped out. Daniel stepped down from the driver's seat and stood by the rear wheel of the carriage, his hat in his hand, and his head bowed in grief. The clergymen and some others came under the pall before the door of the vault and awaited the removal of the body. The artillerymen marched the length of the tarpaulin, countermarched, walked up the inclined plane, and stood on the car beside the coffin. It was lifted, carried out of the car, and then placed on their shoulders. Slowly they bore it down and then over the evergreen carpet and under the pall to the door of the vault. The mother and the widow of the late President watched this mournful journey from their carriage. The artillerymen bore the body into the vault and placed it on the supports prepared for it there. It had reached the house of silence. As it passed between the iron gates the President's mother looked fixedly at it and then drew down her veil. The President's widow covered her face with her hands and wept. The Marine Band, stationed near at hand, played "Nearer, My God, to Thee." As the beautiful strains were heard the venerable lady whose son had been placed in the vault looked out and her face was radiant. Gen. Swaim and Col. Rockwell went down to the carriage and spoke to her.

THE REV. MR. JONES'S ADDRESS.

Dr. Robison then announced that some remarks would be made by the Rev. J. H. Jones, who went out to the war with Gen. Garfield. The former Chaplain of the Forty-Second Ohio Volunteers stood under the pall and spoke as follows:

"Our illustrious friend has completed his journey—a journey we must all make, and that in the near future. Yet when I see the grand surroundings of this occasion I am led to inquire, Was this man the son of the emperor, of the king that wore the crown? For in the history of this great country there has been nothing like this seen by the people, and, perhaps, in no other country. Yet I thought, perhaps, speaking after the manner of men, that he was a prince, and this was offered in a manner after royalty. He was not, my friends. It is not an offering of a king. It is not as we are taught, an offering to earthly kings and emperors, though he was born a prince and a freeman, the great Commoner of the United States. Only a few miles from where we stand less than 50 years ago he was born, in the primeval forests of this State and this County, and all he asks of you now is a peaceful grave in the bosom of the land that gave him birth. I cannot speak to you of his wonderful life and works. Time forbids and history will take care of that, and your children's children will read of this with emotion when we have passed away from this earth. But let me say that when I was permitted, with these honorable men, to go to Pittsburg, as one of a committee to receive his mortal remains, I saw from that city to Cleveland hundreds and thousands of people, many of them in tears. Then I asked myself the meaning of all this, for I saw the working men come out of the rolling mills, with dust and smoke all over their faces, their heads uncovered and tears rolling down their brawny cheeks, and with

15

bated breath.   I asked, What is the meaning of all this? because it casts down a working man?   He was a working man himself, for he has been a worker from his birth almost.   He has fought his way through life at every step, and the working man he took by the hand.   There were sympathy and brotherhood between them.   In the small cottages, as well as in the splendid mansions, there are drapings on the shutters, and it may have been the only veil a poor woman had, as with tears in her eyes she saw us pass.   I asked why; what interest has this poor woman in this man?   She had read that he was born in a cabin, and that when he got old enough to work in the beech woods he helped to support his widowed mother.   Then I saw the processions and the colleges pouring out; the local professions and the civic societies and the military all concentrated here.   And he has touched them all in his passage thus far through life, and you feel that he is a brother.   He is, therefore, a brother to you in all these regards.   But when a man dies his work usually follows him.

"When we sent Gen. Garfield to the Capitol at Washington he weighed 210 pounds.   He had a soul that loved his race; a splendid intellect that almost bent the largest form to bear it.   You bring him back to us a mere handful of some 80 pounds, mostly of bones, in that casket.   Now I ask, Why is this?   I do not stop to talk about the man that did the deed.   'Vengeance is mine, saith the Lord, I will repay.'   He sees the terrors of a scaffold before him probably, and the eternal disgrace which falls to the murderer and assassin, and he is going down to the judgment of God amid the frowns of the world.   But where is James A. Garfield whom we lent to you seven months ago?   Many of you were there at the time of his inauguration and witnessed the grand pageant which passed in front of the Capitol, and the grandest that was ever had in the nation was held on that occasion.   And now comes this unwelcome but splendid exhibition, that will be read of all over the world with regret.   For Secretary Blaine, in a business-like manner, made out that there were 300,000,000 people of the world mourning the death of President Garfield, and offering up sympathy.   Where is he?   Here is all that is left of him—the grand, bright and brilliant man.   Now that soul that loved, that mind that thought, and has impressed itself upon the world, must come back, for if thoughts live will that precious thought cease?   In reason he speaks and in example lives. His thoughts and mighty deeds still flourish in structure. We shall get him back, fellow-citizens. In conversation with one nearest and dearest to him, she said when she thought of his relations as a husband, a son, and a statesman, having reached the highest pinnacle to which man can be elevated by the free suffrage of our 50,000,000 of people, there was no promotion left for her beloved but for God to call him higher. He has received that promotion. He believed in the immortality, not only of the soul but of the body, and that the grave will give up the dead. He must live, and, my friends, that was the hope that sustained him. It was with him in the war, and the enemy never saw his back; they never looked upon his back; he was fortunate in every contest in being on the victorious side. But the grandest fight he ever made he made in the last 80 days of his existence, fought, not because he himself personally expected to live, but the doctors told him to hope. He loved his wife and children, and he hoped. 'I am not afraid to die, but I will try,' said he, 'to live.' And then he was not conquered except by simple exhaustion. It seems to me that no good man by the name of Abraham can be a President of the United States and can be long absent from Abraham's bosom, for both of them have been called, and early, to the Paradise of God, and their spirits look down upon us to-day. He is in the society of Washington and Lincoln and the immortal hosts of patriots that stood for their country.

"Let me say in conclusion: There was a man in ancient Bible history that killed more in his death than he did in his life, and I believe that to be true with James A. Garfield. I doubt whether there is a page that equals this in sympathy and love, and not only in this country, but all over the world. Have you ever read anything like this? You brethren here of the South I greet you to-day; and you brethren of the North, East, and West, come; let us lay all our bitterness in the coffin of the dear man. Let him carry it with him to the grave in silence. Till the angels disturb the slumbers of the dead, let us love each other more and our country better. May God bless you and the dear family, and as they constitute a great family on earth, I hope they will constitute a great family in the kingdom of God, where I hope to meet you all in the end. Amen."

THE HOUSE OF SILENCE.

At his left, near a group of correspondents, stood Secretary Blaine. Upon the other side of the speaker were ex-President Hayes and ex-Secretary Evarts. Near them stood the faithful Dr. Boynton and the three friends—Swaim, Rockwell, and Brown. As soon as the chaplain had ceased to speak the German societies sang Horace's famous ode, "Integer Vitæ." Daniel Spriggs remained by the carriage with folded hands and downcast eyes. His kind master had gone forever from his sight.

After all who had assisted in the ceremonies had been formally thanked by Dr. Robison, and the representative of the relatives, the exercises were brought to an end by a short prayer offered by President Hinsdale. Immediately afterward the people walked up to the evergreen carpet and picked up buds and sprigs and bits of immortelles to treasure up as mementoes of the day and the mournful event. Secretary Blaine, the Rev. Mr. Errett, and others went to the carriage in which were the President's wife and mother. The artillerymen came forth from the vault. Their duty had been performed. The carriages, the people, and the troops moved away and returned to the city. The noblest son of the nation had been laid at rest.

A DAY OF MOURNING IN EUROPE.

SYMBOLS OF GRIEF DISPLAYED AND MEMORIAL SERVICES HELD IN MANY PLACES.

LONDON, Sept. 26.—In London to-day the signs of mourning are general and spontaneous, and all agree that there was never such a general wearing of mourning for a foreigner. Even many of the carters and draymen have their whips decorated with crape, and in what are usually the busiest thoroughfares, such as the Strand, Fleet Street, and Cheapside, many of the shops and all the daily newspaper offices are partially closed. Many shops display large portraits of President Garfield in their windows. The hotels display flags at half-mast and have their blinds lowered. The latter indication of mourning is also visible at all the royal palaces, at the Mansion House, at a number of private residences throughout the metropolis, and at the political and private clubs. A majority of the church bells are tolling, and in many of them midday services are held. When the guard was relieved at St. James's Palace the band, under the direction of Godfrey, played a dead march and other music of a similar character. There was a great crowd present. In the business portion of the West End of London, particularly in Regent Street and Oxford Street, there is hardly a shop not showing some sign of mourning.

There was another remarkable demonstration at Dr. Parker's City Temple, which was crowded to overflowing, there being hundreds outside unable to gain admittance. The pulpit was draped with crape and the Stars and Stripes blended, and with a magnificent white wreath. The service was begun with the anthem, "Sleep thy last sleep," followed by the dead march, "So be thou faithful unto death." Prayer was offered by the Rev. Newman Hall, the burden of which was "Thy will be done." The solo "I know that my Redeemer liveth" was then sung by Miss Beebe. Dr. Parker took as his text—"As in Adam all died." He said the funeral is attended by the whole civilized world. It is impossible to recall an instance where deeper sympathy has been displayed by one nation for another. President Garfield's greatness in life was concealed by modesty, but is now seen by every one. He sketched General Garfield's career, showing its wonderful vicissitudes. He had handled the world bravely. The throne which knew him best was that he has left in the hearts of the people. As the next name to that of the Queen, that of Queen Lucretia Garfield stands in all English hearts. Death won a poor victory compared with hers. She behaved with a heroism which would thrill the world. At the suggestion of Dr. Parker a message expressing admiration and the deepest sympathy was cabled to Mrs. Garfield, all the audience simultaneously rising as a sign of assent. The service concluded with a solo by Antoinette Sterling, and the hymn "Nearer, my God, to Thee."

The Manchester *Guardian* appears to-day with a deep mourning border. At various towns in England to-day—some even, as Portsmouth, having no particular connection with America— the municipal authorities have requested the inhabitants to show their respect for the late President Garfield by closing some of their shutters, more particularly during the funeral. In London a number of offices connected with America are draped in black.

All the omnibus drivers are ordered by the Omnibus Company
to have crape on their whips. All the flags on the River Thames
are at half-mast, as are also those on many of the halls of the
city companies. The officers of the Direct United States Cable
Company and Anglo-American Telegraph Company on Throg-
morton Street were conspicuous by their display of the American
flag hoisted at half-mast and covered with crape.

At the afternoon service at Westminster Abbey to-day the
prayers of the congregation were requested for the widow and
family of President Garfield. Canons Cheadle, Duckworth, and
Farrar assisted at the service.

The Rev. Dr. Hermann Adler, in his sermon at the Bayswater
Synagogue, paid a tribute to the memory of President Garfield.

The *Pall Mall Gazette* this evening says: " To-day when
England and America stand as mourners beside one grave we
may venture to hope that the bitter memories and dividing animosities engendered by the Revolutionary war are finally passed
away," and suggests that England and America shall endeavor to
arrange some kind of an informal union for the prevention of
internecine strife. " If a European concert, despite almost
insurmountable difficulties, is recognized as a political necessity,
why should there not be an Anglo-American concert wide enough
to include in one fatherland all English-speaking men."

A Berlin correspondent says: " Dr. von Schloezer, the German Envoy Extraordinary and Minister Plenipotentiary to the
United States, takes with him to Washington autograph letters
of the Emperor William and Prince Bismarck, expressing their
heartfelt condolence with the widow of the late President.

Accounts of mourning manifestations in honor of the late
President come from Northampton, Oxford, and every part of
the kingdom, and even from remote towns of Ireland and Scotland. A constant stream of addresses of condolence from nearly
every provincial borough and from political societies of every
shade of opinion continues to arrive at the American Legation.

Memorial services were held in the Church of St. Martin-in-
the-Field this evening. Long before their commencement the
approaches to the church were crowded with English and
American mourners of both sexes. The building was soon
crowded and not an available inch of room was left. The services opened with the hymn, " O God, our help in ages past,"
and later on the hymn " Nearer, my God, to Thee" was sung

many weeping at the melancholy application of the simple words. Mr. Lowell, the American Minister, was present. The Archbishop of Canterbury officiated and delivered an address. He said: " This is a mournful day, even here, although at so great a distance. Had the solemn scene of the funeral obsequies taken place in some neighboring cemetery, I doubt whether the effect would have been more deeply felt. A feeling of consternation, not merely dismay, prevailed throughout this community when the news was flashed across the Atlantic that the loved President of a great people had been smitten by a mysterious blow. In our alarm we thought there must be existing in the world some vile combination working in the dark against the progress of civilization. Afterward we learned that the deed originated in vulgar avarice, or ambition thwarted by the determination of an upright chief." The Archbishop then sketched General Garfield's life from labor to college, from college to camp, and from camp to the Presidency, which, he said, was the life of an honest, straightforward, and vigorous lover of his country, opening up a picture of manhood such as we are little acquainted with in this country. Civilization has lost no common man in Gen. Garfield. Thank God, England and America are not disunited, but may be brought to better understand and love each other by our union in the common sorrow.

LIVERPOOL, Sept. 26.—The Mayor of Liverpool and the principal officers of the city attended in state the special funeral services in memory of the late President at the pro-cathedral, which was filled with leading citizens. Business was generally suspended and the bells tolled.

LEAMINGTON, Sept. 26.—At a special meeting, the Town Council has passed a vote of sympathy with the widow of President Garfield.

PORTSMOUTH, Sept. 26.—Muffled peals were rung from the parish church. All the foreign consulates have lowered flags, and similar honors were paid by the port and the garrison. The blinds of most of the private residences are drawn.

WINDSOR, Sept. 26.—The American flag is hoisted at half-mast on the Town Hall. Many of the shops are partially closed. The bells at the Castle and the parish church tolled for an hour.

GLASGOW, Sept. 26.—The flags are at half-mast and the bells were tolled for an hour. The principal markets have closed for the afternoon.

Manchester, Sept. 26.—Business is to a great extent suspended. There was a funeral service in the cathedral.

Cairo, Egypt, Sept. 26.—Public funeral services were held at the American mission chapel here at 9 o'clock this morning. All the Ministers and Consuls and a number of Europeans were present.

Bradford, Sept. 26.—A most impressive meeting of our townsmen was held at the Exchange here, the Mayor presiding. A resolution of condolence and sympathy for the death of the President was passed, the immense crowd standing meanwhile motionless and uncovered.

Paris, Sept. 26.—President Grévy and the diplomatic body were represented at the service in memory of President Garfield at the chapel in the Rue de Berri.

A service was held to-day at the Protestant chapel in the Rue St. Honoré. The church was draped in black. Mr. Morton, the United States Minister, received the diplomatic body. The whole American colony was present, together with M. Say, President of the Senate; M. Barthélemy St. Hilaire, Minister of Foreign Affairs; Gen. Farre, Minister of War; M. Tirard, Minister of Agriculture and Commerce, and M. Cochery, Minister of Posts and Telegraphs. Gen. Pittié, represented President Grévy, and Admiral Peyron represented the Minister of Marine. M. Vernes, President of the Paris Consistory; the Rev. M. Recollin, and Bishop Dudley delivered eloquent addresses recalling Gen. Garfield's intelligence and honesty and the deep sorrow which has fallen on the widow and mother. The speakers laid strong emphasis on the ties uniting the two republics, and referred to the departure at the present moment of the French delegation for Yorktown. M. Recollin conjured Americans to terminate all party divisions, so that there should be no longer a North and a South, but one people.

Madrid, Sept. 26.—The American Society has adopted a resolution expressing profound regret at the death of President Garfield.

PULPIT WREATHS.

SERMONS BY PROMINENT CLERGYMEN ON THE DEATH OF THE PRESIDENT.

A SIGN TO THE PEOPLE—THE BITTER MEDICINE OF GRIEF FOR THE HEALING OF THE NATION'S SICKNESS—DR. DIX ON THE ABSORBING TOPIC OF THE DAY.

The Rev. Morgan Dix, of Trinity Church, New York, preached from the text Ezekiel xxiv. 19—"And the people said unto me, Wilt thou not tell us what these things are to us?" It was the office of the prophets of the old time, said the preacher, to declare to the people the meaning of the dispensations of Almighty God. Under inspiration they had the key to the mysteries by which man is compassed about, and knew how to explain what otherwise might have gone unnoticed or unsolved. And special signs were given—things that surprised and startled and fixed the attention, things which evidently meant something—and the observers were wont to gather about the prophet or seer and listen to his statement of the purpose of God veiled under the sign. The entire cast of the public thought was religious. Men looked for symbols and wonders and strange acts; they knew that all is of God and can be traced up to God; they knew not, in each instance, how; they wished to know, and asked to be told, and thus in the strange events and noted experiences of the year they learned God's will, God's purposes, his mercies and his judgments. It was a rare, a blessed life, to feel God near them, to hear his voice, to read the very meaning of his acts; it lifted those who had that privilege high above the rest, and made them a peculiar people among all nations of the earth. And what of us and of the world in our own day? Are we, then, so far off from God that no message comes to us direct from him? that no

15*

signs are given? that we have no interpreter? Not at all, surely
not. Through the Gospel and the Son of God we are brought
nearer unto him, nearer than ever. As the apostle saith, "The
law made nothing perfect, but the bringing in of a better hope
did, whereby we draw nigh to God." Be it far from the
thought of any Christian man to admit that God's voice is not as
distinct, that God's meaning is not as plain, now as in the days
long past. He made the world, he governs it. To use the
comfortable words of our collect, "His never failing providence
ordered all things in heaven and earth." Whatever cometh has
a meaning. The events of the hour and the day are not the
result of chance; they are like voices to man from another
realm; we must be able, we are able, to discover what they are
to us. The prophetic office has not failed; it still exists and is
executed among us. That office consisted mainly in teaching
man the will of God; the forecasting of the future, the
announcement of things to come, was a secondary and extraordinary function; the steady daily work of the prophet was to
teach in God's name. And that prophetic office continues in
full force; it is the great office of the Church of Christ; it is
the duty laid on the ministry of that Church to interpret, to
explain, to clear up the dubious, to make the crooked plain, to
bring dark things to light, to draw forth the deep moral from
transitory phenomena, and so to enforce it on intellect and conscience that when the signs are passed away the things signified
may abide with us, making us better men. And this is the
difference between the censure and criticism of the mere human
observer and the solemn judgments of the Church. On the one
hand it is the surface only which is swept by the keen eye; on
the other hand it is the depth that is sounded to that point at
which the upper agitation ceases. The popular record con-
tains what is seen, what catches the eye, what gives material to
the artist for his pictures, what absorbs and moves the imagination and the sympathies which exist alike in all. But the
Church in her prophetic office tells us more—what things are to
us, what lessons they bring of righteousness, temperance and
judgment to come; and so she makes men thoughtful, and
sends them, full of it, to their knees in silent adoration of the
Everlasting God, and sets them thinking what they can do to
keep the salutary impressions from passing away and leaving
them, as before, indifferent, careless, irreligious.

A SIGN FROM GOD.

Dear brethren, a sign is now before us, great, mighty, portentous. It has been before our eyes week after week, growing ever more alarming, filling the land with astonishment, hearts with dread, eyes with weeping for the things that have come on the land. This is, if ever such was since the world began, a sign from God—a sign to the nation, a sign to other nations, a sign to every one by himself, and to each house and family apart. And, as by an irresistible instinct, men have hastened to render that sign still more fearfully impressive by the lavish paraphernalia of death and his dark abode. The city has been turned into one vast house of mourning. One cannot walk about, one cannot look forth from his window, one cannot move a step without beholding what reminds him of the sombre terrors of the grave. I know nothing more striking, nothing more edifying, than this common movement of all sorts and conditions of men—of the evil and the good, of the godly and the ungodly, of the careless and profane as well as the devout believer, of persons of all estates and conditions, of all professions, of all minds and wills, unnumbered, yet unanimous—hastening to put into some visible expression the confession, the admission that the glory of man is as the flower of grass; that human life is but a vapor which appeareth for a little time, and then vanisheth away. Have ye weighed this sufficiently? Have ye thought how astounding, how overwhelming is the sound of this universal voice, crying as one, " Dust we are and unto dust shall we return "? If the voice of the people be indeed the voice of God, then it is not so much the people whom we hear to-day as God Almighty speaking to us through them—repeating the old lessons so soon forgotten, condemning human pride, pouring contempt on human glory, asserting the omnipotence of death, and reminding each living soul that the time is short, that there is neither wisdom, nor device, nor knowledge, nor power in the deep furrow of the tomb. This sign is now before us; displayed more distinctly than those in the heavens, wherein we have been looking, recently, upon the pale trains of comets wheeling their mysterious course through space; this sign is standing in full sight from every quarter of the land. The question may be asked, What is it to us? " Wilt thou not tell us what these things are to us?" So said the people to their

prophet of old.   And may ye reverently ask of those who speak
to you in the name of God, the ministers of that great Christian
body which has and keeps the truth.   And if ye ask it, let them
answer, as they should, not by delivering their own opinions, not
by setting forth their views as men, and so, like other men,
entitled to form judgments on passing events, which judgments
may be right or wrong, but by declaring things out of the living
oracles—old truths, first principles, weighty matters of law.   It
is to this task that I would address myself, remembering whose
minister I am—to the question about the inmost meaning of
the sign, its purport as verily and indeed showed to us by God
through the strange and striking act of man.   This is the province of the Church—her sole province.   The journals of the
day have given the public all the information that could be
gathered by the utmost industry and ingenuity.   They have
told the story from the beginning to the moment we have
reached; they hsve set before us, so plainly that nothing could
be plainer, the horrid crime, the long suffering, the household
and domestic details, the professional treatment, they have
written the biography of the dead, and fully told his life; they
have followed the unrolling of the awful drama, and have
related every minutest incident of its process.   The sign, in its
outward aspect, could not have been more perfectly portrayed,
more scientifically recorded in the register of the history of this
eventful year.   All this is as it should be, but with these things
the Church has naught to do.   Hers it is not to repeat nor to
amplify, nor to tell over again what has been well told, but to
go down far below to reach something deeper, to read the
meaning of these things in that innermost place where God and
man meet at length, and where we must be still, and bow the
head, and listen while he speaks.   After the wind, and the
earthquake, and the fire, comes the still, small voice.   It is the
utterance of the Spirit addressing the soul of man.   And if he,
whom the nation mourns to-day, could speak to his people and
his countrymen, he would no doubt bid us rather think what
these things are to us, than go on dwelling exclusively on the
violence and misery inflicted on his now lifeless body and on
the bereavement of the nation from whom their head has thus
atrociously been taken away.

INTERPRETATION OF THE SIGN.

The sign tells us of the utter vanity of human things. Shadows are we, and vapor; and, if this life be all, then no more. It is awful to think of one being lifted up head over 40,000,000 or 50,000,000 of men honored, exalted, trusted in, hailed with loud and general cries of joy, and then instantly struck into darkness and dust. It is awful to think that a man should by patience, industry, talents, virtues, by the very labor of the hands and sweat of the brow, work up to such a place modestly and honestly and religiously withal, only to be levelled at one blow at the instant in which he stood at the summit of honor and power. It is awful to think of a man watched all those years by eyes of love, prayed for, upborne by devoted affection, followed to his triumph by simple, tender hearts, and turning to them with entire attachment to show that his happiness was mainly in seeing them happy, and then cast head-long in the very midst of that affrighted little flock bleeding, agonized, dying. "Vanity of vanities!" It is, in all history, among the most pathetic pictures we ever saw or ever shall see. Who, after this, dare glory in wisdom, might, strength; in love, in honor, in the sweetness of these transient hours? Who that remembers that sign can helping saying with dread, "I myself also am but a man!" The utter hollowness and emptiness, the almost derisory vanity, of our mortal condition. Think first of that. The sign tells us of the brutality, the madness, of human nature. Ah! yes; glorify it as they will, this human nature, of which so much is expected, to which so much is ascribed, what is it at length but brutal, hateful, horrible ? If the murdered man be a sign of the vanity of our estate his assassin is a sign of the depravity of our condition. Man has in him still the cunning, the ferocity, the cold, pitiless temper of the worst order of the brutes. And this attests the need of a redemption for him; a cleansing, a conversion to God. It shows that such a work of moral repair is beyond all human power; it demands a God to transform the devil into the angel. It ought to make us shudder when we think of our own sin, which is in its essence and quality the same as that of the trembling wretch who now lies awaiting his doom. It ought to make us laugh to scorn and drive away the fools who deny the sinfulness of sin, and talk against the penitential and disciplinary doctrine and system of our Christian religion. The sign, more-over, is an instance of that horrible crime, the defiling of a land with blood. It has always been so considered. Human blood, shed lawlessly and when it ought not to be shed, defileth the land in which it is spilled. It calls for expiation ; it bids men rise up, and, as well as they can, cleanse it away. And since Almighty God is Lord over all the people, when he suffers such defilement to occur it is a sign of judgment. Wicked things are done among us; pride, luxury, extravagance increase, with blasphemy of God's holy name, desecration of his day, neglect of his worship, reversing of his laws, abandonment of Christian principle, falsifying of standards of right and wrong; selfish-ness, drunkenness, infidelity, fornication, systematic child mur-der before birth, dissolute manners, divorces. " Shall I not visit for these things, saith the Lord ?" He does visit; and we see the innocent blood shed and the land defiled thereby. This bids to deep repentance, amendment of morals, return to God ; to putting away the sin by righteousness and washing out the stain by pleading the precious blood of Christ in expiation of the deep, dark sins with which society is poisoned, and by which, if unchecked, it shall in time be broken up.

GOD'S SOVEREIGNTY DECLARED.

The sign declares to us the sovereignty of God by subjecting us to his righteous judgments. There is no escape from the teaching of religion or moral government of the deed unless in the notion that things here come by an iron fate or by mere chance, or else that we will have no opinion about them, but let things go as they list and give ourselves no thought to them. But this is an hour in which the people are in no mood for such trifling. They do not believe that the death of the President was the result of chance, nor yet that it came of a rigid, inflex-ible fatalistic order, without will or purpose or moral method ; nor are they saying, " Oh, never mind how things in this world are so long as we remain secure." There are great searchings of heart; there is a great, purposeful, solemn thought awake every-where. What meets it save the old truth of the moral govern-ment of God? He it is who orders or permits whatever occurs on earth, in heaven, in hell, above, below, around us. And we are powerless without him. We shall not be able to avert the like or worse calamities unless he help, and his help must be sought through the searching of his judgments and strict conformity to his will. It may be that there are those who do not feel in all this that God is chastening, afflicting, punishing, visiting. That is the acme and practical outcome of atheism. If that were the general feeling, or even a widespread feeling, well might one despair and ask to be taken away; for nothing can be conceived so hopeless as the state of that man or that people who could deny that God visits for sin at the very instant in which his blows are descending on the guilty and his judgments are in the land.

Yet once more—the sign is a sign full of light, sweetness and glory. It shows how God can turn evil to good, the gloom of death into the brightness of day. Is not this altogether wonderful? Perhaps no more atrocious act was ever perpetrated than that of this assassination. And yet we see what it has led to. How it has drawn us together, softened our hearts, revived our faith in goodness and virtue. What an ideal of patience, resignation to God's will, faith in him, fortitude, have we now set up among us! Who is not the better for it all? What unforeseen results have flowed from that? Are we not all, for a time, like brethren beloved, children of one house, united heart to heart and hand to hand. If there be nothing more horrible than the dire act itself, surely there is nothing sweeter than the wide sympathy, the unification of such multitudes of people, not here only, but through the civilized world, drawn to each other by pity, by tenderness, by reverence for simple, virtuous, homely ways, and by a deep religion which undoubtedly lies at the inmost depths, even in hearts where we hardly suspected its existence.

STRENGTH OF THE ETERNAL PROMISES.

The sign tells us much besides, too much to declare at once. But last of all, it assures us of the strength of the eternal promises. Not here are the crown, the reward, the peace. They shall be beyond these fading scenes. This life cannot be all; set in the midst of so many and great dangers, so full of care and sorrow, and in an instant cut off. Surely this is not all; surely there must be more to come; and here the promise of the Gospel meets us, bidding us set our hopes on things above, and showing to faith and love the inheritance incorruptible and undefiled and that fadeth not away.

I come back to the question of the text—" What are these things to us?" O brethren, let us rather ask, What are they not to us? Certainly the Lord is among this people, though some know it not; it is his own voice that we hear. These things, not regarded in the religious light, were but a nine-days' wonder, impressing us for a time, then forgotten; and, apart from the clear shining of the lamp of God upon them, they were but like fitful gleamings which early die away into darkness and night. But it shall not be so. This time of mingled light and shadow, this day not dark nor light, neither day nor night, shall be forever remembered, and for many, many years influential in our borders. It was the time of God's visitations, when it pleased him, by bitter medicine of grief, to heal our sickness, to restore a moral tone to the people, to revive old faiths, to set old truths full in view, to give us a view of the next world, to humble the pride of man, to bring him low at the steps of the great throne, to lead him to give glory and honor to the King of Kings and Lord of Lords. I have told you something of what all this is to you. And let me add affectionately a bidding to prayer. To-morrow is the day when the dust shall return to dust again. Keep it thoughtfully, calmly. Profane it not by the pursuits of ordinary life. Humble yourselves under the mighty hand of God, and let this be the double burden of our petitions, that Almighty God will sanctify the common affliction to the whole nation, and that, by his holy inspiration, he will bring it home, for repentance, amendment of life, and stirring up of faith and zeal to every man in the lesser round of his own uncertain and dangerous life.

GARFIELD'S VICTORY IN DEATH.

HIS BENEFICENT POLICY STRONGER NOW THAN THOUGH HE HAD SERVED HIS FULL TERM.

Thousands were unable to get into the Brooklyn Tabernacle. The auditorium was hung with black. Dr. Talmage took his text from Judges xvi. 30—" So the dead which he slew at his death were more than they which he slew in his life." It sometimes occurs, said Dr. Talmage, that after an industrious and useful and eminent life, in the closing hour a man will achieve more good than in all the years that preceded. My text has a very graphic illustration in the overshadowing event of this hour. President Garfield during his active life was the enemy of sin, the enemy of sectionalism, the enemy of everything small-hearted and depraved and impure, and he gave many a crushing blow against these moral and political Philistines; but in his dying hours he made the grandest achievement. The eleven weeks of his dying were mightier than the half century of his living. My object this morning is for inspiration and comfort to show that our President's expiration has done more good than a prolonged administration possibly could have accomplished. Had he died one month before he was shot down by the assassin he would not have had his administration fairly launched. Had he died six months from now by that time his advanced policy of reform would have destroyed the friendship of many of his followers. Had he died many years from now he would have been out of office and in the decline of life. There was no time in the last fifty years when his deathbed could have been so effective, and there could have been no time in the fifty years to come when his deathbed could have been so overwhelmingly impressive. We talk a great deal about the faith of the Christian and the courage of the Christian and the hope of the Christian, but all the sermons preached in the past twenty years on that subject put together would not be so impressive as the magnificent demeanor of our dying Chief Magistrate.

NORTH AND SOUTH UNITED.

President Garfield's death more than a prolonged administration has consummated good feeling between the North and the South. It is not shaking hands over a bloody chasm according to the rhetoric of campaign documents, but it is shaking hands across and over a palpitating heart large enough to take in both sections. He in his dying moment took the hand of the North and the hand of the South and joined them, and with a pathos that can never be forgotten practically said, "Be brothers." Ah, my friends, he has done in his death what he could not have done in all his life. Where are the flags at half-mast to-day? At New Orleans and Boston, at Chicago and Charleston. The bulletins of his health were as anxiously watched on the south side of Mason and Dixon's line as on the north side.

Ever and anon we thought we had our old difficulties settled and our old grudges adjusted, but the quarrel broke out in some new place. It seems now that the requiem of to-day must forever drown out all sectional prejudices. After what we have seen during the last eleven weeks the people of the South must be welcomed in all our Northern homes as we of the North would be welcome in all the Southern homes. If at any future time some one should want to kindle anew the fires of hatred he would find but little fuel and no sulphurous match. South Carolina and Massachusetts, stand up and be married. Alabama and New York, stand up and join hands in betrothal. Georgia and Ohio, stand up while I pronounce you one. "And whom God hath joined together let not man put asunder." No living man could have accomplished this.

Dr. Talmage went on to say that President Garfield's death accomplished more than his life in setting forth the truth that when our time comes to go the most energetic and skilful opposition cannot hinder the event, and then demanded, "Who knows but that God may make this national trouble the purification of all the people?"

MRS. GARFIELD'S LAST HOUR IN THE WHITE HOUSE.

Poor Mrs. Garfield! I never read anything more pathetic in my life than what I saw in the newspapers on Friday, when they said she had gone to the White House to gather up the private property of the family to have it taken to her home in Ohio. Can you imagine any greater torture than for her to go through those rooms in the White House associated with her husband's kindness and her husband's anxieties and her husband's sufferings? You see she had with her womanly arms fought on his side all the way up the steep of life. She had helped him in severe economics when they were very poor, and with her own needle she had clothed her household and with her own hands she had made them bread. In the dark days when slanderous assault frowned upon him she never forsook him. They had fought the battle of life and gained the day, and they were seated side by side at the tip-top to enjoy the victory. Then the blow came. What a reversal of fortune! From what midnoon to what midnight! Some say it will kill her. I do not believe it. The same God who has helped her on until now will help her through. The mighty God who protected James A. Garfield at Chickamauga and in the fiery hell of many battles will, when these members of the broken family circle come together next week in their little home at Mentor, protect and comfort the wife, the children and the aged mother. I invoke the grace of high Heaven· on those seven broken hearts.

Ascend, thou disenthralled spirit! Ascend and take thy place among those who have come up out of great tribulation and had their robes washed and made white in the blood of the Lamb! This Samson of political power, this giant of moral strength, had in other days, like the man of the text, slain the lion of wrathful opposition and had carried off the gates of wrong from their rusty hinges; but the peroration of his life was mightier than all that preceded. " And so the dead which he slew at his death were more than they which he slew in his life."

While I try to comfort you to-day there is a lesson that comes sounding from the tramp of the Senatorial pall-bearers and rolling out from the roaring wheels of the draped rail train flying westward and coming up from the open grave that awaits our dead President. " Put not your trust in princes nor in the son of man in whom there is no help. His breath goeth forth ; in that very day his thoughts perish. Happy is he that hath the God of Jacob for his help." Fare thee well, departed chieftain ! Fare thee well !

As Dr. Talmage retired from the verge of the platform Professor Morgan played " The Dead March in Saul," and the vast assemblage, every man and woman of whom was attired in plain black, slowly separated.

SUBMISSION TO GOD'S WILL.

LESSONS FROM THE DEATH OF PRESIDENT GARFIELD—SERVICES IN THE CHURCH WHERE PRESIDENT ARTHUR WORSHIPS.

The entrance to the Church of the Heavenly Rest, on Fifth Avenue, New York, the church where President Arthur attends, was handsomely draped. A portière of black broadcloth was looped up against the granite columns of the portico, and above it an American flag, covered with crape, reached out into the street. Within the edifice the altar was overhung with a semi-transparent black cloth, through which a white cross and the word "Jesus" on a violet altar cloth were barely visible. The pastor, Rev. Dr. Howland, was assisted by the Rev. Dr. Morgan, an English clergyman. Dr. Howland announced that there would be a ceremonial service in the church to-day at two o'clock, that being the hour assigned by the Bishop of the diocese as the likely time when the remains of the late President will be given back to earth. Dr. Howland was suffering from the effects of a severe cold, but expressed a hope that he would be able to say a few words upon Garfield's life, character and death to-day. The hymn "God bless our native land" preceded the sermon, which was delivered by Rev. Dr. Morgan. His text was "Our Father which art in Heaven: Thy will be done."

In all lands where the Bible was known, the preacher thought that the words "Our Father which art in Heaven" were better known and oftener spoken than any other contained in the holy book. It was the tenderest phrase known to the Christian heart. In the midst of the bereavement which afflicted the American people so deeply, in the memory of the cruel crime which cost them the life of their well-loved President, he as a stranger among them could understand how hard it must be for many Americans to say to their Heavenly Father, "Thy will be done." It did seem like a needless crime, it did seem as if the life of the victim might have been spared, but it seemed so to minds which cannot understand the Divine purpose, cannot see the end of the Divine intention. The speaker desired to make it easier, if he could, for his hearers to speak these words of submission. He compared the Father in Heaven to the best of earthly parents, and said that while the latter often erred in their treatment of children it must be remembered that the former could not err. God always knew what was best for his children. There was perhaps no relationship on earth so strong and lasting as the relationship of parent to child. He did not refer to those parents, of whom the world had far too many, who care not whether their children's footsteps tended towards heaven or towards hell; but he spoke of the conduct of the best of earthly parents, the most prayerful, the most devoted. It was impossible for earthly parents to know to a certainty the talents and dispositions of their children, and hence it was impossible for them always to decide what was best for their children, earnestly and unselfishly as they might desire to do so.

HUMAN FALLIBILITY.

How often it was that a parent, guided by the best of intentions, thrust his child into a business for which he was utterly unsuited, refusing to allow him to choose an occupation wherein he would become the most useful and the most happy. How often it was that a parent, looking only to what he believed to be the child's best good, led him into a matrimonial alliance which could not be a happy one. Such were some of the mistakes of earthly parents despite all their love for their children and their desire to secure their happiness. But the heavenly Parent knows all about his children—knew every heart-beat and every word that passed their lips as well as the words that were unspoken. He knew how many talents he had given to each and how each disposition turned. He never made mistakes. He mixed up the bitter and the sweet of every life so that it should yield the greatest glory to him and develop best for its own eternal good. Could the mother forget her child? Yes, even that might be; but God was ever mindful of his children. God had refused to prolong the life of the beloved President of the United States; he had refused it deliberately and because it was best to refuse it. Let Christians be sure of that. Let them know that God was always right. Let them kneel before the body of the dead President was yet consigned to the tomb; let them kneel now and say, "Our Father which art in Heaven, the blow is a heavy one; the providence is dark; but thou knowest best; we can trust thee when we cannot understand thee."

SPRINGS OF CONSOLATION.

HARD TO LEAVE THIS BEAUTIFUL WORLD — GARFIELD'S SOLDIERLY BEARING—SERMON BY THE REV. DR. COLLYER.

"Every valley shall be exalted and every mountain and hill shall be made low. And the crooked shall be made straight and the rough places plain. And all flesh shall see it together for the mouth of the Lord hath spoken it" (Isaiah xl. 4 and 5) was the text selected yesterday by Dr. Collyer in the Church of the Messiah. Applying it to the death of President Garfield he said : We can meet no more as we met last Sunday with some little gleam of hope. That which we greatly feared has come, and human hope is slain with the human life. And while we must all find deeper springs of consolation than this, that there is no more sorrow or crying for our dear friend, who seems to have died in every home, and to be mourned for as their very own by every family, and while we are sure to find such consolation in God's good time, I confess it is hard for any of us to do this just now, because while we must submit to the inevitable doom which has fallen on the nation we are not re-signed to it. Nor was he resigned to it who is dead, and to my mind it is of all things natural and right that we should stand in this attitude, not towards heaven, God forbid, but toward the evil powers that have taken his life. When death comes in what we have to call the course of nature, and strong men fall in the midst of their days, we have to be quiet, usually, and to say it was God's will. But the first impulse, and the last, I trust, in such a sorrow as this, is to say, with such light as we have to guide and help us, it cannot be God's will any more than it is ours that we should lose our President in this infernal way, and the stroke did not come from Heaven, but from hell, to all human seeming; so why should we give up to it and try to be resigned, and say that, in some way we cannot yet under-stand, it will be all right, when this that crushes the nation's heart and has torn the life out of the noblest man among us, and outraged the most sacred covenant we can make, and brought the banner of the nation down to half mast, and set fifty millions of men, women and children weeping by one grave, and cast a great, black blot against the whole glory of the Republic—how can this bring resignation? I have said hun-dreds of times that the sun never shone on a nation so gentle and so ready to look for the silver lining in the blackest clouds as this of ours, and to forget and forgive. But instead of the deep heart out of which all this springs it would reveal a heart shallow and worthless beyond measure, and only eager to be having its good time again if we were not full of rebellion and wrath against this cruel stroke, and bound to search for the reasons which lie beyond the evil spirit incarnate in the man who struck the blow.

LOVING THE WORLD.

It is a consolation to me that we are not resigned then, and do not mean to be, but stand ready to turn on the very pulpits in which men would teach us already that God was in it all and to say, " How do you know that? Where is your authority!" We would fain believe that God will bring good out of this great, sad evil, but it is the evil we have to front and fight, and to make that seem good to us would it not paralyze the very nerve of our frames? The mind of our dead President was one with ours. He wanted to the very last to live, and said so, and scanned the poor, thin face for some sign that it might be so, and was no more resigned to go than we were to have him go, and felt as we do that, so far as we can understand the divine love which encircles all our lives, it was not God's will that he should perish. Now, nothing he has done seems more beautiful to me than the grand, soldierly resolution to hold on to his life and have the whole worth of it for his own sake and for ours. Life was dear to him. He loved the world. It was a beautiful world. When he had taken the great, solemn oath standing before all the people, the first thing he did was to turn to his old mother and his wife and kissed them, sealing in that grand, simple way the oath he had taken to serve us well. In some men that would have been the merest clap-trap ; in James Garfield it was the fine flower of his whole manhood. They take the sacrament when they are crowned in the great old lands; that was his sacrament, and the noble old mother blessed her son, and the sweet, true wife her husband, and the children's hearts beat quick and proud for their father, and surely since the world was made we have seen nothing more sacred than this in which the old home life flashed out for an instant in that new beatitude. And so the home and the home treasures were what the good President fought for through the weakness and the pain. How could he submit if there was any help on earth or in heaven? He saw the fear in the face that had challenged him once out of all the world, and heard it in the voice to which his heart answered, and heard it in the sobs of the children, and then the instinct of a true man who has all these treasures to guard rose towering like some great angel over the threat of dissolution. I love to think of this splendid soldierly bearing as he lies there dead, and while it is all the harder for

us to lose such a man there is still another little spring of consolation that he suffers no longer, who suffered so much.
Something had been surely lost had he been resigned and submissive and said, " It is the will of God, and so I suppose it is
all right."

HIS TRUE CHARACTER SHOWN BY DEATH.

SERMON BY REV. DR. CHAPMAN AT ST. PAUL'S METHODIST EPIS-
COPAL CHURCH.

" Lessons of the Event" was the subject of the morning discourse in St. Paul's Methodist Episcopal Church, at Fourth Av.
and Twenty-second St. Dr. Chapman, the pastor, preached.
The church was draped, and from the pulpit was suspended a
large portrait of President Garfield.

We are gathered, said the preacher, under the shadow of a
great sorrow, and a greater crime. Our hearts are sad, and our
eyes are filled with tears, not merely that a good and wise man,
a great statesman, and the Chief Magistrate of our nation, is
dead, but also that he was killed by the bullet of an assassin.
It would be a pleasant way to spend the hour in eulogizing the
name of James A. Garfield. The claims of his public life will
need volumes to contain them; but it is perfectly proper in the
house of God and on the Lord's Day to note the effect of this
crime upon the country which we love.

That assassination is to be the tool of political reformers in
the future there is no reason to believe, nor that the crime was
planned or known to any one but the depraved fanatic who
struck the blow; but it is doing no one injustice to say that
history teaches that a person who starts or aids a crime by
slander and calumny must share the blame with him who does
the deed. I have no objections to parties in politics—they are
a necessary factor in a republican form of government; but I
do protest in emphatic terms against one party blackening the
character of its opposing candidate in the effort to elect its own
man. Political campaigns, if rightly conducted, are educational
in their effect, but not if scandal forms the chief argument.
The bullet of an unprincipled, disappointed office-seeker has
subdued all opposition and disarmed all criticism, and the whole
world mourns to-day. Would to God it had not been left for

such a cause to teach us the true character of James A. Garfield! If this spirit of sympathy shall teach us to have more charity for those in authority, our beloved President will not have died in vain. One lesson taught us is that a public officer is elected not to dispense Federal patronage in return for votes, but to fulfil the duties of his office. There is nothing that should make every true American honor the memory of Garfield so much as the fact that he himself was President and not another; and Lord help his successor to follow in his footsteps, and not to be led by any advisers. By birth, education, moral character and ability, our President was a peer among men. Political intrigue did not advance him through the successive steps from the log hut to the White House, but pluck and worth. His life furnishes an example worthy the study of every young man who seeks an example to follow, and is worthy the study of every man of riper years who would learn how to conduct his public life in the best way. His domestic life was grand. The chief corner-stone of all our institutions is the Christian home. Blessed be God for such a mother and such a wife as we have seen this summer. His religious life was also beautiful, and in the years to come there will be three great names in the history of our country, Washington, Lincoln and Garfield.

WHAT THE PEOPLE MUST LEARN.

THE REV. HENRY WARD BEECHER AT PLYMOUTH CONGREGATIONAL CHURCH.

There were three or four hundred persons in front of Plymouth Church before 10 o'clock, and when the Rev. Henry Ward Beecher ascended the pulpit three quarters of an hour later there was not a seat to be had in the church. All the aisles were filled, and the crowd extended out into the street as far as the force of his voice could be heard, while three or four hundred went away when they found that there was no chance of obtaining admittance. The church was trimmed simply but tastefully. The pillars of the organ were entwined with white crape, while from the top of the organ were suspended graceful folds of black and white. Pieces of black and white crape, extending around the building, were attached to the cornice and also to the railing of the gallery. To the right of Mr. Beecher was a handsome bank of flowers, and at his left was a bunch of pampas grass. Mr. Beecher said in the course of his announcements for the week that during the last summer for the first time in thirty years he had been able to remain in comfort at home. He trusted that in the future he should be able to begin preaching on September 15 instead of October 1. His text was Psalms ciii. 15–17, and cii. 24–27.

How short, said Mr. Beecher, is human life at the longest. We spend years in gathering knowledge, and die just as we get ready to use it. We learn how to live only to pass on. Yet we are not allowed to live even the short life allotted to man. A full life is accounted fourscore years, yet the average one is not more than twoscore. The babe grows up to maturity, but the web is broken and man stumbles on the threshold of his usefulness. Moralists and poets have filled the world with sad strains at the shortness of life, and to-day we stand before a strange manifestation of Providence. Why is it that the good man dies, apparently in the beginning of his usefulness? Why is it that the hero to whom we pinned our faith has passed away? We had gone through the war victoriously, and had lived through reconstruction; we had fought the fight against greenback money and won; we had just entered on the skirts of our promised land, when our leader, our Joshua, was stricken down. He was a man who united the best elements of his fellow-countrymen; he was firm yet gentle, and in him the lion and the lamb seemed to lie down together; he was not an empty partisan, but he looked at all questions with a calm and unbiassed mind; he had a love for learning, and he had acquired it by hard and incessant labor; he had been bred upon hardship and poverty, and he had lived by the sweat of his brow; moreover he had been a preacher of righteousness. With almost the first sound of the trumpet he had gone forth to defend his country, and he earned a name as one of her leading generals. Later he entered the highest councils of the nation, and from that time on his name was found connected with every advanced measure.

At length the Republic called Garfield to its highest office, because he was the very man for the place. Call the names of all the men honorable and useful in the courts, the army, and the navy, or in mercantile life—was there any one of them more needed than he was? Four months only he presided over the nation, but his administration gave splendid promises of usefulness. But that bright vision has vanished. "Garfield has been shot!" flashed along the telegraph wires, and the whole world wept with his family. The drama is now ended. For weeks he lay fighting for his life. There were no more laurels to put on his brow and God took him. After twenty years the train bore him westward. He who entered Washington four months before amid the clanging of bells and the joyous shouting of the people was borne away in silence. Such a funeral march as that was never seen. Along its route men forgot to sleep, and watched its passage at all times of the night with bowed heads and in silence. "Blessed are the dead that die in the Lord." For them there are no more burdens or sorrows. Around the burial-place of this man let mothers gather with their children, to teach them to be brave and to be honest.

But let us turn to the sublime God from these human measurements. What is time to him? Man's life is like the bubble on the sea, which rises to the surface and gleams brightly in the sun, but only to burst. God measures all events by eternity, so that which may seem to us to be confusion is a benefit in his eyes. And so some benefit may arise to us from this disaster. Sometimes a single act may outweigh the rest of a man's life. So from Garfield's death we may gain something, although not in an exactly similar way. Washington is revered for his life, but how much more elevated his memory would have been if he had met with a tragic death for his country. Wise and gentle as our Saviour's life was, his death was of much more importance. Although we hoped to reap so much from Garfield's life, we may reap even more from his death. The North and South have felt for the first time the healing balm of mutual sympathy and grief. The wounds left by the war, and not yet healed over, will be mollified. There has been no division in the nation's sorrow, and its whole heart has beaten together. Charleston has felt the loss as bitterly as Philadelphia, and New Orleans has been as sincere in her grief as New York. Nor have party lines divided this sympathy.

But still more striking than the unity of the nation in its grief has been the unity of mankind. When Lincoln was shot, the world was shocked rather than grieved. England had not yet learned wisdom, while the hands of France were still red with the blood of Mexico. But now no nation has been so obscure that it has not expressed its sorrow. From Russia and Turkey on the east to Japan on the west there has been a common sorrow. I think that never before has the heart-blood of the world been so stirred. But if this is the first time, may it not be the last!

This sympathy had also a moral comfort. Were there ever before so many prayers offered up? The Mussulman, the Catholic, the Protestant, all prayed to God as they knew him, and in their own formality. But did God refuse to answer them, and is prayer a fiction? In the lower sphere God gave no answer, but in the higher one he did. Is there no other answer of prayer save in continuance of life? Could we not be more fortified and strengthened by President Garfield's death than by his life? Is this not a more sublime answer to our prayers? We see people dying everywhere; but except in the case of near relations or friends we scarcely feel that death is an affliction. But why should Garfield not die? Because we looked upon him as a tree from which we should gather only good fruit? But is it not better to have its branches raised higher so that it will benefit the whole world?

There are some lessons, continued Mr. Beecher, to be drawn from President Garfield's death, and there is one which I wish particularly ambitious young men should profit by. Our Government may be compared to a stately mansion which many are desirous of entering. Some walk boldly up to its front entrance and go in; but others seek to enter by the back way, from which all the refuse comes. By the nature of our Constitution we are obliged to send men to our legislative bodies, and sometimes the ones selected are not the most suitable persons. But we cannot bear to have the public ideal destroyed and the opinion prevail that he who would enter politics must give up his honor, and advance by ignoble means. And when we behold a man struggling honorably for a political career and equipping himself as a statesman, it is an example that honor and integrity are not incompatible with political advancement, and that man's life will be an example as Washington's has been.

In the simplicity of our habits there has been no need of protection around our Presidents. And it is still true that public opinion, with us, is better than the guard of any European monarch. There is no sense here of wrongs inflicted upon generation after generation to stir men up to madness against their rulers. Our laws are of our own making and can be changed. Then only a short time must pass before we are freed from the most hateful ruler. Yet our legislation is incomplete. I would not have a guard if I were the President, for I had rather take the bullet than be protected from my fellow-citizens. But an attempt on the life of a man whom we have elected as our leader, and upon whom we all rely, should be treason, and its punishment should be death. [Applause.] But let this be done by law. No man has any more right to assassinate Guiteau than he had to assassinate President Garfield. Let us stand for the administration of justice. When the Rebellion ceased neither bullet, sword nor halter slew one man, and the moderation of our people impressed the whole world. And if Guiteau should die unlawfully there would be a spot upon our escutcheon. I have been angry with the miscreant, but I have obeyed the command of the Lord not to let the sun go down on my anger. Indignation has had its day; now let law have its day. I have a right to speak thus of Guiteau. He once was with us, but not of us. He sat in this sanctuary among the worshippers. Robert Burns expressed a faint hope in one of his poems that the devil might yet be turned around the corner and be saved. Let us hope that Guiteau's life will not be ended suddenly by that wanton sentiment into which you have blown a breath.

But what shall we say of that sorrowful group, Garfield's family; of the mother, whose son preceded her, and of the wife who has shared her husband's elevation? Love needs the presence of the loved one, and chastened though she is, there is no one that needs our prayers more than she. May the blessing of God, enriched by the tears of a whole people, rest upon his children, and may his sons follow in his footsteps.

————

WORDS OF COMFORT AND WARNING.

THE REV. DR. BELLOWS AT ALL SOULS' UNITARIAN CHURCH.

At All Souls' Church the Rev. Dr. Bellows took for his text Isaiah lix. 7 and 8. Points from his sermon are as follows:

We are assembled about the still open grave of our dead President. To-morrow while our watch is still kept, it will be closed, in the presence of a nation on its knees, and with benedictions in its mouth and tears in its eyes. Distant nations are near to us to-day and to-morrow, and great cathedrals and synagogues and even mosques will send up prayers to the One God and Father, that our loss, recognized as a bereavement for humanity itself, may be sanctified and consoled. It is an experience unique in its majesty, its world-wide recognition, its flawless beauty and tragic pathos. Already the tender suggestions of the text are realized. A few days ago we were overwhelmed, as if by the shadow of God's wrath; to-day, we already feel the holy light in the thunderous cloud and the soft mercy that drops in tears from its awful frown.

What passion of sorrow remains unknown to the nation's anguished and foreboding heart? We have wept ourselves dry; we have prayed and pleaded until our lips have wearied themselves and almost God. To him has been accorded the extraordinary privilege of hearing his own eulogy, of witnessing beforehand the grief attending his own loss! He has handled the wreaths that now lie upon his coffin, and felt with his sensitive instinct the love that was already pouring into his grave! O happy, fortunate man, to know the grief and affection that waited not his death to speak out the fullest tribute that could follow it! Say not he died too soon! When such a beautiful consummation has been possible—unequalled in the history of humanity!

The long suspense for the more hopeful and less informed is over. The only sure thing we have known for weeks about the President's case was that he was alive. No public prudence, no political policy, no medical etiquette, no professional caution could disguise that fact. When the history of his case is fully known, as it soon must be, we shall learn how much of the encouragement and hopefulness that have existed on the official bulletin was real, and not merely scientific and professional. I doubt not his responsible physicians have fully performed their duty, and have given the President the absolute benefit of the one chance in a hundred, which he was brave enough to accept. We may perhaps learn something of value when we know not only the truth, which we may safely say has never been violated, but the whole truth, which as safely we may say, either that it has not been deemed prudent to reveal it, or, as it now appears, was not surmised by the skill that watched his bedside. I hope it will come home to the common heart that nothing is so prudent and wise as the whole truth, and that in desperate illness, false hopes and roseate reports are not useful and safe. It has seemed strange that the country has caught its most trustworthy bulletins of the President's illness from the daily messages of the Secretary of State to our British Minister, and that it was deemed wise to deal with foreign courts and all Europe with a frankness not due to the simplicity of the American people themselves. As to the storm likely to burst around the heads of the President's physicians, I wish to record my deep conviction that they have applied the most laborious pains and the utmost skill to his recovery, and the assuaging of his pains and weakness.

It is pleasant to see what testimonies are coming in to the magnanimity, courage, prudence of our new President. There seems to be a profound resolve not to judge him in advance, and to give him the benefit of every doubt. The new President has the temptations of all his past, to put the administration President Garfield began off its track, to switch into the old Custom House groove and into the old spoils system plan. I can even believe that hitherto he has thought that to be true statesmanship, and is sincere in regarding the hoped-for policy of Civil Service Reform as wild and childish in its weak innocence. Well, if that is to prove his policy—if he has learned nothing to change his old and long-known opinions—then let him be warned that he has troubles before him too serious to be hastily invoked. The American people are in no mood to go back into a low, factious and partisan policy. They have awakened to the beauty of justice, reason, candor and common sense. They will not, at least not now, submit to the party whip and the usages of the old caucus system, where a few in an inner ring outwitted the general wish. General Arthur has a noble opportunity. He has had, too, a most gracious, if suffering, period for reflection. He can if he will, by fidelity to the spirit and policy with which the late Administration has been exalted, go on without a break and get the love and honor of the whole people by proving himself the people's President, and not the President of a party, much less of a faction. If he falls as low as that, or does not at once rise far above it, he will be the least honored among the little-honored predecessors who have risen to the high office by the death of its chosen occupant. God knows with sincerity and heartiness we pray that he may be wise and prudent, and that the mantle of his predecessor may fall upon him. If he wishes to lose all the greatness now thrust upon him, he has only to take advantage of his position, to undo all his predecessor has done, and to leave undone all he contemplated and has left ready to be finished.

But he will not so disappoint his generous and trustful friends. There was a King Arthur, with his knights, celebrated in English song, who is the centre of all that is inspiring, beautiful and sacred in the early legends, and the later poetry of our motherland. That name may again become glorious. It has a great and almost unequalled opportunity; but it must not be coupled and surrounded with the knights who have hitherto rolled the honor of the Empire State in the dust. Alas, the Empire State has for generations been chiefly governed from the tail and not from the head; and the one peril, when a citizen of New York is President, is that the malignant influence of Albany and city partisan politics (always hateful) should throw its lurid shade over the whole policy and tone of the country. Let one Arthur redeem the Empire State to honor and justice and a wide patriotism, and he shall receive the lustre and share the splendor of that ancient Arthur, King of British and Welsh Celts, and not the slave of the modern Celts, who have so long ruled the City and State of New York.

ENDEARED TO THE PEOPLE AS A BROTHER.

THE REV. DR. J. H. RYLANCE AT ST. MARK'S PROTESTANT EPISCOPAL CHURCH.

St. Mark's Protestant Episcopal Church was well filled yesterday morning. The pulpit was appropriately decorated with flowers. The Rev. Dr. J. H. Rylance and the Rev. Mr. Morgan conducted the services. Dr. Rylance's sermon on the dead President was entitled " A Grievous Mourning." The preacher said in part:

To the utmost circumference of this vast country and among all the civilized people of the earth there is grievous mourning over the death of one of our fellow-citizens. Such a spectacle of woe has seldom been witnessed in the history of the world. Many will recall the horror of April, 1865, but the sorrow over the taking off of Lincoln was less widespread than now. Men gather round the form of President Garfield because he represented the cause of reunion and political amity, to which he had devoted himself throughout a brilliant public career. Hence lamentations reach us from every part of the land. Old animosities are brushed away. More brilliant pageants have been seen at funerals of kings and emperors, but this event comes home very closely to the bosoms of the American people. The general grief springs partly from the heroic history of the man. He was a genuine son of the soil, he was early inured to labor, and he never prostituted his power to partisan ends. Had God's hand smote him invisibly, or had he fallen on the field of battle, our grief would be deep, but submissive; but such a taking off by a cowardly assassin without provocation adds desperation to our sorrow. It is to be hoped, for the sake of human nature, that it will be found to be the work of a madman; but woe to him if it shall be shown to have been the work of malignant malice.

The President's Christian resignation, his love of mother, wife and children, his murmured words, "The people, the people— my trust," have endeared him to us as a brother. When the perturbations of feeling have died down the abiding verdict on the President's career will be that it will be lasting in its influence, and this opinion will be without qualification. He was a lover of peace, but not at the expense of what he believed to be true. He belonged to a party from conviction, but was never a partisan. He was a statesman of large experience and solid acquirements.

How proud we should be that American civilization could produce such a man, and that universal suffrage could place him on the seat occupied by Washington, Jefferson and Lincoln! And yet how sad that it was to be undone by the deadly shot of an assassin! Yet it was not wholly undone. Such a life is a precious seed, sure to bring forth abundant fruit. He, being dead, yet speaketh, and will continue to speak to unborn generations. Not a schoolboy who reads the history of his life but will be a better man for it. While the American people put the seal of approval on such a man we need have no fears of the doings of demagogues.

16*

We owe President Arthur our prayers. In minor matters he may err, but in the main things we may hope for his success. Of all men, he must feel how dearly the people loved their fallen chief. Let him follow in the footprints left for his guidance, and a like love may also be his. He must dismiss worthless men who feed at the public expense, and appoint men of moral worth in their places. Character must be the prime requisite for those who seek to serve the nation.

CONSOLATIONS OF THE HOUR.

THE REV. DR. W. M. TAYLOR AT THE BROADWAY TABERNACLE, NEW YORK.

At the Broadway Tabernacle yesterday the pulpit was heavily draped in deep mourning and the pulpit furniture was covered with black cloth. The organ behind the pulpit was hung with the same material, and the entire railing of the gallery was covered with graceful festoons of black. A large congregation was present, nearly every seat in the body of the church and the gallery being taken. The Rev. Dr. Taylor, the pastor, preached on the death of the President. The text was from Numbers xx. 28: "And Moses stripped Aaron of his garments, and put them upon Eleazar, his son; and Aaron died there in the top of the mount." He spoke, in part, as follows:

That is an old history that is here described, but in some of its features it has been repeated in our own country in the life of our beloved President. Of him it can be truly said that he ascended the mountain—attaining the highest office in the gift of the people. With his history the people are familiar, from the time he was a boy in his humble home to the night the tolling of bells announced that he was dead. We saw in him the most complete representative of the best elements of the nation. Alas! alas! he reached the summit like Aaron. During his illness the people were admitted to his bedchamber; each of us had our hands upon his pulse. In many a song for years to come will reference be made to his heroic suffering and courageous sayings. In this publicity we find much consolation. It elevated into full view a noble example. From the first he was a man who was led by conscience; from the day he would not take a right of way for

his boat by stratagem on the canal until the day of the Conven
tion that nominated him.   He was a Christian, and he was not
ashamed of his religion.   He said little, but it was more a matter of principle than emotion.   He was always more ambitious
for excellence than for position.   The Presidency came to him
unsought, the people calling him to office because of what they
saw he could do for them.   So in the elevation of such a man
we find consolation, and are thankful that such a career has been
brought so prominently before the public eye.   In his devotion
to his wife and mother and children we find an example ; and
in the wife, too, whose place is second only to that of her husband—if indeed it be second—in the hearts of the people.

We find another consolation in the unification of the people.
For the first time in many years there is no sectionalism in our
broad land ; all are bowed and weeping over the bier of Garfield.
It looks as if the feud of years was being healed by his blood. I
think too the feeling will sweep away the abuses that make public offices the rewards of party selfishness.   Even if the assassin
be insane, office-seeking shaped his conduct ; and if he prove to
be responsible, may nothing prevent his suffering the extreme
penalty of the law !   There has been a growing tendency to put
to death this nefarious system.   Woe to the man who attempts
to prevent its death.   Over the bier of Garfield let the people
pledge themselves that he did not die in vain, and determine to
slay the system, for if it is not slain it may bring the assassination of the nation.

The other nations of the world have also sat with us around
the sick-bed.   Thus have we been brought together in a bond
of universal brotherhood.   Sympathy has come alike from palace and cottage, and the Queen of England has performed her
queenliest acts in sending her messages of consolation.

We must also sympathize with the present Chief Magistrate,
who under such sorrowful circumstances has been placed in a
trying position.   He has before him the noblest opportunity if
he only improve it.   He has made mistakes, but they may serve
as beacon-lights to guide him aright.   Let us give him our confidence, so that it can never be said that the people failed him
in the hour of his extremity.

Another thought is that God is with us.   Never have such
earnest prayers been offered as in the past few weeks.   Are they
not tokens of God's being with us ?   God lives.   We have no

doubts or misgivings about him who is to be laid away. Great is the contrast between the gloom of our loss and the gladness of his gain.

LAMENTED AS A MAN, NOT A POLITICIAN.

THE REV. DR. VINCENT AT THE CHURCH OF THE COVENANT.

The Rev. Dr. Vincent preached yesterday morning in the Church of the Covenant, at Park Avenue and Thirty-fifth Street, from Psalm lxv. 5 : "By terrible things in righteousness wilt thou answer us, O God of our salvation ; who art the confidence of all the ends of the earth, and of them that are afar off upon the sea." The pulpit was heavily wound with black, and there were signs of mourning upon the organ. Dr. Vincent said:

An intelligent pagan reading these words would be strangely bewildered. How can terror and salvation flow from the same God ? It is a question that not paganism nor philosophy nor science can answer, and its solution can be found nowhere but in the Word of God. No announcement is needed of the event which suggests these thoughts. The blow has fallen upon the nation. Our President is dead, and we can only say "Thy will be done." God is addressed by the Psalmist as a hearer of prayer. One of the most startling features of the calamity that overshadows the land to-day is its relation to prayer. President Garfield went into office with a more universal prayer attending him than any other President ever did. It was known that he had difficulties and corruption to contend against, and the cry of the nation arose like incense to the Throne of Grace invoking the blessing of the Lord upon him. Few who prayed so earnestly looked to see an assassin's bullet for an answer to their prayers.

Some of us heard the sad news of the crime far away among the hills. Then began the daily anxiety underlying all pleasure and all business, like the monotonous moan of the ocean. All through these long weeks what a tidal wave of unceasing prayer has been ascending to Heaven for the life of the President. To-day we have the answer—the terrible answer. There is something awfully impressive in this tremendous denial of a nation's prayer. What shall we say ? What can any one say ? We can only say that the God who does all things well has refused us an answer because the answer could not have been right. It is better that

God's will should have been done than that a nation's prayer should be answered. Go back to the agony of Gethsemane, where our Saviour prayed, " Let this cup pass from me, if it be possible; yet not my will, but Thine, be done." If we have thought that our prayers were to be answered by the bending of God's will to ours, we deserve no answer ; but if we have prayed always with the thought uppermost, " Thy will be done," then our prayers are truly answered.

The nation cried for the freedom of the slaves from their bondage. The prayer was answered, but by terrible things, of which the dying thunders still fill the air. But the answer has come, and the slaves are free. God's righteousness, with all its terrors, leads to salvation, and a great chastisement like this means a tremendous purpose of salvation if the nation will accept the lesson. This affliction we may assign to the series of disciplinary providences.

Every good man is meant to be a warning and an inspiration to his fellows. Such a gift of God was our late President. One lesson sealed by his death is the lesson of character, and it is the more impressive in this instance because he was the direct out-growth of our national life. It is not a politician but a man that we lament. It is needful sometimes that one man should die for the people. Let us pray that this lesson of sorrow may never be lost.

FINDING HOPE IN IMMORTALITY.

THE REV. DR. CRAWFORD AT ST. LUKE'S METHODIST EPISCOPAL CHURCH.

The Rev. Dr. Crawford preached yesterday morning at St. Luke's Methodist Episcopal Church on " Lessons from the Death of President Garfield." His text was Psalm xxxix. 5 : " Verily every man at his best state is altogether vanity."

We have, the speaker said, all been accustomed, I suppose, to think of our late President as an uncommon man. I do not know of any one of whom this description, " man in his best state," is more true. It is not yet time to give President Gar-field his place in history, but his name is associated with those of great men. Washington, Jefferson, Lincoln and Garfield will go down to history together. His early struggles placed him in sympathy with the people, and that sympathy he never lost. He never broke the connections that bound him to the friends of his poverty and early life. He was a most cultured man. It is said that Secretary Evarts on returning from Europe brought gifts for all his friends, selected according to their varied tastes. For President Garfield he brought a beautiful edition of the works of a Greek poet. You look back at the fifty years of his life, and they seem like years spent in making a President. When he went to the National Convention no preparation for his nomination had been made. His choice seemed like the choice of David among his brethren. One was taken before the High Priest and then another, but none was chosen until the God-appointed David came forth.

President Garfield was singularly happy in his family relations. When he went to school his future wife was a schoolmate with him; when he taught school she was his pupil. Finally they were married, and what a family life has theirs been. I think this country is in need of nothing so much as examples of true family life. I am appalled when I see men whose family life is such as no man can bear to speak of receiving the honors of the country. About six months ago James A. Garfield and his wife started from their country home. He was to be the most prominent man in the country, and she the most prominent woman. Now they go back to the same home. She is a sorrowing widow with a memory of untold pains and suffering, and he a wasting corpse, whom even the eyes of man cannot look upon. "Verily man in his best state is altogether vanity." But can such a man die? When the body lies in the grave, is that all? How I rejoice to think that President Garfield still lives. The thought of a glorious immortality will help us in our grief. We must remember that God still reigns, and that his providence overlooks the affairs of men. Was God with James A. Garfield in his early poverty? You say yes. Was God with him in college and on the battle-field, when the bullets flew fast about him? You say yes. But was he not also with him even on that fated second of July?

OUR BEST PRESIDENTS MURDERED.

THE COURAGE OF THE VICTIM, THE COWARDICE OF THE ASSASSIN
—SERMON BY THE REV. DR. R. S. STORRS.

The Rev. Richard S. Storrs, D.D., pastor of the Church of the Pilgrims, Brooklyn, preached in the morning upon the lessons to be drawn from the life and death of the deceased President. The church inside and out was draped with mourning emblems. "We are often impressed," said Dr. Storrs, "by the fact that in our intense experiences we cease to take distinct account of the progress of time. We do not count by the successions of day and night, by the series of weeks following each other, but we reckon our progress by the experiences one after another to fill our souls. Perhaps we are as impressively reminded of this to-day as we have ever been in time past. Looking back to-day twelve weeks ago, when the tidings of the assault upon the President had just reached us, it seems sometimes as if it were but yesterday—it seems again as if many months had passed since that event was so sadly made memorable. But we know the successions of the experiences through the interval we have been passing. It seems as if all the wisdom of our fathers; all the wisdom of modern counsel; all the wisdom and counsel of the nation itself in its elective action were at the mercy of one insignificant and deadly spirit. The end has come, and now the nation drapes itself in mourning, not merely in the churches where great assemblages congregate, but on every house hangs the insignia of grief. The national flag clings to its staff, heavy with crape and wet with tears. The civilized world pauses on its ways of pleasure to join in the sad ceremonies. To-day I ask you to hear the voice of God in the lessons which he brings to us through this sad and strange and unexpected dispensation of his providence. Men sometimes say that the cause of Providence is not in it at all. It was mere human mortals. It was the insanity of a mind disordered. But God's providence controls the wills of men. That which has been intended even in defiance to him is made to bow and bend and submit itself before the incoming of his slain. Garfield was perfectly accustomed to the responsibilities and strain of public life; he had gone through the deadly storm of bullets on the battle-field; he had been more than once prostrated with sickness, and then rallied. It seemed certainly that his life was safe for the four years to come. The nation did not feel it necessary to wall him around with any peculiar force. But God has taught us this lesson to the nation again and again. It is a fact to be observed that every President who has died in his office has been one upon whom the heart of the nation was peculiarly resting with confidence in his wisdom. Harrison, Taylor, Lincoln—all died at a crisis. We are not drawn to that wretched assassin in jail, because we hear he shrinks in fear; that he is continually in apprehension of violence; that he moans and groans in this apprehension. I do not know that our hearts rather rejoice that so much punishment at any rate has come upon him. Where are the infidel harangues to-day? Where is the doctrine of the divine right of assassination to-day, which has been so eloquently asked in this country? I see holier purity, the white banners of a better civilization marching on to the end of the history of the people.

MEMORIAL SERVICES OF THE G. A. R.

The memorial meeting under the auspices of the various Grand Army Posts of Kings County, New York, was attended by over 5000 people. It was a display of popular feeling in every respect worthy of the cause, and was characterized by a degree of earnestness and sincerity which could not well be mistaken. The immense edifice was crowded soon after the doors were thrown open—crowded to an insufferable extent. Not only was every seat occupied, but the aisles were blocked, and movement in any direction was out of the question. More people were turned away than the building could possibly have accommodated, and those within paid dearly for the privilege. It was intensely hot, and circumstances were rendered so much the more unpleasant by the surroundings that two women fainted, while there was complaint of suffering endured on every hand. The meeting, however, was eminently successful. There were present no less than a thousand veterans of the war, who occupied front seats, and who marched to the Temple in the order specified on the printed programmes, the gathering point being on the corner of Willoughby and Classon Avenues.

The veterans marched down Willoughby Avenue to the Clermont Avenue Temple to the notes of muffled drums and quietly took the places assigned them. The Grand Army badge which they wore was draped in crape, and black silk rosettes were on their arms. General E. B. Fowler was in command, the posts participating being as follows: Harry Lee Post, 21 ; Devins Post, 148; Barbara Freitchie Post, 11; Rankin Post, 10 ; Thatford Post, 3 ; J. H. Perry Post, 89 ; Mallery Post, 84 ; Mansfield Post, 35 ; Winchester Post, 197 ; Hamilton Post, 152 ; Duport Post, 187 ; Ford Post, 161 ; Kerswill Post, 149 ; Frank Head Post, 16 ; T. S. Dakin Post, 206 ; German Metternich Post, 122 ; W. L. Garrison Post, 207 ; the Hancock Legion and the Fourteenth Regiment Veterans.

The interior of the building gave evidence of the national grief. Festoons of serge swung gracefully from column to column, entwined the arches, and overshadowed the big organ in the rear.   On the platform were the members of Dr. Fulton's choir, who supplied the singing, and a few invited guests. Major-General Henry W. Slocum presided, and by his side sat Rev. Mr. Beecher, whose entrance into the building, despite the fact that it is devoted to religious purposes, was greeted by tremendous applause. The only speakers were General Slocum and Mr. Beecher, the services being concluded by 10 o'clock. Barbara Freitchie Post, No. 11, carried a life size picture of Garfield as he appeared in uniform, underneath which were the words, " We mourn the loss of our comrade."   This picture was placed by the side of the speaker's stand, overlooking the draped empty chair, which signified the death of an army comrade.   Shortly after 8 o'clock Dr. George S. Little called the meeting to order, and after stating its object, nominated General Slocum for chairman. The nomination was unanimously confirmed, and on stepping to the front of the platform General Slocum spoke as follows:

SPEECH OF GENERAL SLOCUM.

LADIES AND GENTLEMEN AND MEMBERS OF THE GRAND ARMY OF THE REPUBLIC—As has been stated to you, you have assembled here to give expression to your feelings and views of the assassination of our comrade, who was President of the United States.   It seems to me to be exceedingly appropriate for you, who as soldiers served with him during the war, and who, during the last ten or twelve years, have been comrades with him in the Grand Army of the Republic, to meet for a purpose like this, and yet I know full well that not one among you meets to mourn his loss simply as a soldier or simply as a comrade. You mourn his death as a loss to our country of one of the greatest and wisest rulers that the people have ever chosen. [Applause.] There is not one of you, I will presume to say, who has not re-cognized him as a great-hearted and large-brained and generous man. You mourn for him as one who has set an example in all the relations of life, such as but few of our public men in this country have ever done. While we are assembled here, in every city, in every village, in every hamlet in this land, from North to South and from East to West, people are congregated for a similar purpose, and yet of all the millions who are to-day mourning the loss of Garfield, how few there are who have ever enjoyed any personal acquaintance with him; how few there are in this land who have ever had the opportunity of tak-ing him by the hand and receiving that cordial, earnest grasp which ever made the man who received it a life-long friend. Not one in ten thousand people ever saw the countenance of Garfield. I shall never forget my first interview with him. After the repulse at Chickamauga our Government was forced to send troops from the Army of the Potomac to the West. We found the Army of the Cumberland with its supplies cut off, its soldiers on half rations, its animals dying by hundreds. At the earliest opportunity I saw General Garfield who was then chief of staff. He had entered the army eighteen months before without the slightest military training—never having had any connection with a military organization, yet by his zeal and by his good sense he had risen to be chief of staff of the Army of the Cumberland. Notwithstanding all the depressing circum-stances by which that army was surrounded Garfield was most cheerful, and, as I ever met him afterward, full of courage, full of pluck. I found, on mingling with the officers and men, that there was not one word spoken except in praise of him as a soldier. [Applause.] He had been in the service but one year and a half, and had raised himself to that high place and had obtained his promotion as major-general by the common con-sent and approbation of every one of his associates. You mili-tary men know that there are quite as many jealousies in military life as in civil life, and when a man gets to a high place with the common consent of all around him, you can always rest assured that he deserves it, and Garfield got that.

AS GENERAL SLOCUM KNEW HIM IN CONGRESS

I next met General Garfield in the House of Representatives, having been sent there myself from this district. As I say, I met him there and soon learned to admire him just as much as a statesman as I admired him as a soldier. Garfield was an earnest, honest, thorough-going Republican—I was a Democrat. Notwithstanding the fact that he was an honest, thorough-going partisan, there was never in all his career the slightest vindictiveness, and this i say with great pleasure. He was as kind towards the people of the South as to his neighbor—kind and conciliatory. Look at his Congressional career and you will find no hatred of the Southern people. While I was in Congress with him both the great political parties gave evidence of being infected with a heresy in regard to financial matters which in my judgment would have brought dishonor and disgrace on our country. Notwithstanding the fact that both parties seemed to be sated with this heresy, Garfield never lowered his colors; not one word that he uttered could be construed as antagonistic to the best interests of the government. And I honor him for this as much as for any other act in his life. We are all disposed to look upon this event as a great calamity. It is in some respects a great calamity, and yet all these great calamities have their compensations, and I suppose this will have. This sad event will call to the minds of the rising generation more forcibly than ever the career of General Garfield. His career, his whole life will be known in every household; it will serve as a beacon light to all, pointing out the way to honor and to fame. I trust, too, it will have another effect. We have been troubled in this country within the last twenty years by a class of men known as communists—men who want some change or law which will give a poor man a chance. Read the life of James A. Garfield. Read the life of Abraham Lincoln. Read the lives of these two men, I say, and then tell me does any poor man want a more beneficent government than that furnished right here in the United States? It has had another effect. It has buried all sectional animosities. I believe that every fair-minded man will agree with me when I say that the death of

Garfield has been as sincerely lamented in the South as in the North. This event covers the grave of all sectional animosity in this country. It should have, and I think it will have, a still broader effect. All nations on earth have evinced their sympathy with the American people, and with the family of our late President, and particularly has this been the case with regard to England and her noble queen, who sent messages which touched the hearts of all sincere Americans. It may have the effect of bringing great nations to recognize the propriety of settling their differences by arbitration instead of at the cannon's mouth. It certainly ought to be the effect so far as England and America are concerned, where so much kindly feeling has been exhibited. There is no class of men in the world that can better appreciate having differences between countries settled by arbitration than the class now before me. You are soldiers, and I ask you all to lift up your voices in favor of settling all differences between foreign nations as men ought to settle them in a quiet and peaceable way. I am afraid I have taken up too much of your time, but I could not avoid saying what I have said.

An anthem was chanted by the choir, prayer was offered by Rev. Dr. Thompson of Williamsburg, and a chant, "Rest, Garfield, Rest!" was sung by a quartet club. Then followed the memorial service as prescribed by the Grand Army of the Republic, Commander Squires conducting it. "I know that my Redeemer liveth" was sung, and then General Slocum introduced Rev. Mr. Beecher as the speaker of the evening.

HENRY WARD BEECHER'S SPEECH.

MR. CHAIRMAN, LADIES AND GENTLEMEN—After services so impressive and at so late an hour, and under circumstances in which you suffer so much inconvenience by heat and crowding, I shall not prolong my remarks to any considerable length. We are living at a period which will be considered in days to come an epoch. Few are aware of how great is the phenomena of which you are spectators and in which you are actors. For the first time in the history of the human family there has been an uprising of the whole world, civilized and uncivilized, on account of the death of one man. It never happened before. It is itself not only new—it is the sign of a new dispensation, the herald of a brighter day. The world at last knows that all mankind are of one blood, one lineage, one hope, and we have the realization at last of the spirit of the Lord Jesus in which we are all brethren, throughout the civilized and the uncivilized world. During that terrible battle of the couch through which Garfield passed (and he has been as brave against death as on the battle-field he was in the midst of death), during all those long and weary days the eyes of the whole world have been upon him, and the voice of prayer has gone up. If I could stand at the gate of heaven and describe the number and fervency of the prayers, assuredly your hearts would spring up with wonder and gratitude. Not alone they that believe as we believe, but those that believe at all in Providence and Divinity. The Pope in Rome, the Archbishop in England, the simple Quaker, the most enthusiastic Methodist, as well as the more stately worshippers of ritual—everywhere, crowned and uncrowned have been represented by their cries and tears at the throne of divine mercy for weeks and for months. Did ever such a spectacle occur before? What has started them so? Was this a man of such genius that his light shone as the rising of the sun? Garfield was a man of great intellectual force, but not a man of illuminating genius. Was it because he was an Alexander or a Napoleon, an overmastering general? He was an able general, but not in any such sense as to attract the attention of the civilized world. What has been the reason for this universal sympathy? Partly because he represents the peculiar economy of this nation, and partly because he represents the highest elements in man's universal consideration of human nature. Do you know that ninety nine men out of every hundred in this world have no business here—if you consider the estimate of their superiors. The mass of mankind are worthless in the estimate of genius and of philosophy. What are men good for? To make armies, to be used as bricks with which to build houses. The world over mankind have been accustomed to be trodden under foot. They have been taught by their rulers that resignation and submission and contentment and humble sphere was most becoming —been taught to sink their individuality and take a back seat; whereas, the true spirit of the gospel goes to show that each man is himself an empire, and that every empire is strong in proportion as the individual citizen is strong and free to act.

INDIVIDUAL MANHOOD.

America represents more clearly the true gospel aspect of individual life than any other country. Men are beginning to find out even in the most remote corners of the world that there is one land where every individual is counted as one, as a unit, the real value of which no language can compass or describe. The hand of the Lord that made me and you, that gave you and me something of himself, has imparted to us something of his own ascendency, and we shall live when the sun has forgot to burn, and when the whole universe has gone to ruin. The poorest man, black or white, red or yellow, has that in him which is immeasurably greater than the most sublime grandeur or the noblest genius that ever blossomed under the sun. This is the doctrine of America, and it was in its belief that our fathers came here. Although it was not phrased in this way, the real battle of the Reformation was for the right of a man to be a man. Our fathers came here partly for commerce, but more largely to develop institutions that would recognize individual manhood, and all our laws and customs springing from New England and sweeping westward over prairie and across mountain have this supreme tendency. Our fathers brought with them the idea of the dignity, and the union, and the grandeur of the State being in proportion to the power and the liberty and the strength of the individual. If there has ever been a man in our nation that represented precisely these views, it was James A. Garfield. He was not born in luxury, and no silken-clad nurse took him from his sighing mother to cry in purple. He was born at the bottom—just enough to eat and drink, and nothing more. Not enough money for an education in the pocket of his father. The poorest boy that attends our common schools in this city is just a thousandfold greater and better off than Garfield when he was Jim Garfield, the little boy trotting barefoot around the Ohio village. But he was his own school-house. He was ashamed of ignorance, and when other men slept and snored he found a gold mine, from the veins of which he brought precious treasure. As he grew up he knew almost every phase of the lowest experiences; he knew full well what it was to see power and greatness above him. He didn't run to the corner grocery store and cry out "Communism;" he didn't

lie lazy all his days and then cry out that the State was bound
to help him; he didn't squander in pleasures all the money that
he earned, and then cry out for a reorganization of society. He
was a man who learned and practised all the virtues in quietude and simplicity with self-confidence until he became a
teacher himself. Then called from that task he became a
preacher of righteousness.

AS TEACHER AND PREACHER.

Both as teacher and preacher his heart was towards his kind.
His business was to enrich others and not himself. When the
war broke out he gave himself to his country. He went into
the field, and withheld himself from no hardships. He knew
what the war meant and what he meant—emancipation and
liberty. Because of what he and men like him have done, you
gentlemen of a dusky color who are sitting here to-night are
recognized as the equals of those around you. People did not
think much of America twenty-five years ago. They have
changed their minds since. I had occasion to say one time, regarding a case in Kansas, that a rifle was better than the Bible,
and I tell you still that in the eyes of the whole world moral
suasion is often better issued from the battle-field than anywhere else. When we marshalled armies such as dwarfed those
of Europe, and conquered the desperate and skilful men that
were opposed to us; when our citizens, on disbanding, returned
to the civic occupations of life without a murmur, I aver that
no officer and no man that carried a musket has from that day
to this conspired against the liberty, the law, or the institutions
of the land. When these people were tempted by the devil of
repudiation, they said, "Get thee behind me," and even politicians took the hint. When afterwards a meaner devil attempted to juggle with the currency of the country the common
people saw through it and made the currency honest, so that a
man might pay a bill and not blush. Now, this spectacle has
gone abroad and men have come into a new realization of what
national life is. If there can be fifty millions of men free in
every respect, and each man a part of God's universe; if these
men can wage war, pay their bills without grumbling, suffer
taxation, maintain peace, go back to their occupations after, not
in the least shattered in spirit, and live happily—if this great
nation can thus exemplify what liberty means, then every poor

man in every quarter of the globe will look to us and say,
" That is the home of the poor man, the home of true manhood, and the home for me." They come from Ireland and
England and Scotland, they pass over from Greece and Turkey
and Russia and China, from all quarters of the globe—all seeking themselves in seeking us. The tidings of what this land
really is have gone abroad to all the poor throughout the world.
Now, Mr. Garfield, as the advocate of such men and such principles, stood before the world as the advocate of the rights of
the common people, and when he was struck down every poor
man on the face of the globe felt that " our hero has been
slain." This it is that has given such universality of interest to
this proceeding. How came it that the aristocrats abroad and
the Queen of England poured out the treasure of her all-enrich-
ing heart? Because Mr. Garfield was not merely a representative man and a noble man according to the highest and most
elevated acceptation of the term, but he was a good man, and
all of his impulses were towards kindness and love.

THE COMMON HUMANITY OF MAN.

He shone because he could not help himself. He represented
the common humanity of man carried to its highest excellence,
because the spiritual man fully developed itself in him. Garfield subdued the inferior powers of his nature. The things
best known of him were those things which coupled him in the
highest and best way with the welfare of his fellow-man. It is
the admiration of the world that Christianity has gone so far
that all men begin to feel that there is nothing on the face of
the earth so noble, beautiful, and attractive as a full-grown,
right-minded, loving soul of a strong man. No picture, no
sculpture, nothing anywhere, after all, is so attractive to men as
a man of God, and therefore a man of the common people. It
is all these things that have given to Garfield the universal interest of the whole human family. Let me say a word beyond
this: Has the world lost him? When the farmer goes into the
field and scatters the seed, does he lose it? Will not every
single kernel die that it may bring forth one hundred-fold?
Garfield never could have been so influential in Washington as
he is now. Having laid down his life for a principle,
that principle has had atonements. The laying down of
his life is the resurrection of his faith and power throughout the

whole world. His influence will come down again as the dew or the rain upon the grass. Is there nothing more than eulogy that we can do for him? Yes. Carry out the work that he began. The might of this nation is increasing, the wealth is becoming gigantic, the government holds a power which is waxing with every generation, the struggle for ascendency is becoming greater, and our danger in the future lies in putting too much power into the hands of ambitious men. Garfield went to Washington with pledges and with a disposition to see that a civil service system should be established by which the corruptions which had sullied politics should be purged out. You must complete that work. I believe that Mr. Arthur will undertake to do it. If he should undertake to purge our government of its corruption in these respects, he will at the end of his term be scarcely second to the man he succeeds. If Mr. Arthur should go away from this purpose he will be as a broken bucket at the cistern and will draw no water.

Mr. Beecher went on to refer to Guiteau, saying that he was not among those who could refuse to pray for him. He referred to the mother, the wife, and family of the deceased President, and concluded by saying that he hoped God would bless the household in order that there might be another generation of Garfields.

The benediction was then bestowed and the gathering dispersed.

MEMORIAL SERVICES AT THE BROOKLYN TABERNACLE.

The memorial service at the Tabernacle was a great demonstration. At half-past 6 o'clock upward of 2000 people were in front of the building, patiently awaiting the opening of the doors. The crowd rapidly increased, so rapidly that the building was opened earlier than had been contemplated, and at 7 o'clock it was literally packed to the outer doors. Pews and aisles were jammed, and even the preacher's platform was invaded. It was estimated that there were between six and seven thousand people crowded into the vast auditorium. The heat was intense. The church was appropriately decorated. A picture of the late President, flanked by flags draped in mourn-

17

ing, was placed on the front of the organ, directly over the pastor's chair. Mr. George W. Morgan, the organist, and Mr. Peter Ali, the celebrated cornetist, furnished the instrumental music, which was of the finest description. They played at intervals during the evening. Their rendering of "Inflammatus" and "Cujus Animam," from Rossini's "Stabat Mater," was especially brilliant. Mr. Morgan never played better, and Mr. Ali surpassed all his previous efforts.

Upon the platform were Rev. Dr. Talmage, who conducted the services, Supreme Court Judge Edgar M. Cullen, Corporation Counsel William C. DeWitt, U. S. District Attorney Tenney, Congressmen William E. Robinson and J. Hyatt Smith, Bernard Peters, Senator William H. Murtha, Henry Hartcau, and others. At 8 o'clock the meeting was opened by Dr. Talmage, who explained that Mayor Howell, who was to have presided, had gone to attend the funeral at Cleveland. He said that those who would address the meeting that evening would have the widest liberty to say whatever their sympathies or patriotism might suggest. Dr. Roche led in prayer, and the great congregation then united in singing the grand old hymn, "Nearer, my God, to thee," with overwhelming effect. At the close, Dr. Talmage introduced as the first speaker, Judge Joseph Neilson, of the City Court, who was received with applause.

SPEECH OF JUDGE NEILSON.

MR. CHAIRMAN, LADIES AND GENTLEMEN—I have no hope whatever of being able to say anything appropriate to this solemn occasion. Others may find words of consolation, teach us to be resigned to the dispensation which has fallen upon us. And yet, we have some lessons taught us of present and perhaps of future value. Since the news of the assassination reached us we have had a changeful life. The first whisper of that event came over us like a cold storm. That storm continued for weeks—now and then the clouds breaking, a rift letting in a gleam of sunshine, and then the pall settling black and dark as ever. But from out that tempest we have come, and, by our representatives to-day, we have laid the President in his last earthly home, and death has put upon his brow the coronation seal. How much he loved life we all know. There was the grand office in which we had placed him, placed him honestly and honorably—the Presidency of the United States. He had a charge to keep, doubtless meant to keep it. There were friends very near and very dear to him; there was his family, some of them yet so young that they needed his hand to train and lead them. So he clung to life strongly during all those weeks. Well, now, we have this consolation, we did for him what we could. So with us, I believe, from all the information I have, that they called in the best (I make no invidious comparisons), I mean among the best of the medical and surgical profession to attend him. There is just one other thought, with your permission. They speak of monuments here, and, to our grateful surprise, they speak of monuments beyond the seas. That is well; commends our people to others, and others to us. Still, I have thought, and think still that if, after the President was smitten and before he died, he could have had a full, realizing sense of the sympathetic heart of the American people in respect to him, could have seen that all parties and all classes of people everywhere throughout the length and breadth of the land, from sea to sea, united in their wish that he might recover, united in detestation of the crime—and if, moreover, beyond all that, he could have had a prophetic view of what should occur after his death—if he could have seen that the great cities of the land would be represented at his funeral, that everywhere demonstrations of attachment, respect, affection and regret would be met with, I think he would have said, "Give me this! all this, rather than piles of granite mountain high!"

Mr. Morgan played the "Dead March in Saul," the congregation, at the request of Dr. Talmage, rising and remaining standing during the performance, as the people did in St. Paul's, London. Dr. Talmage introduced Mr. Tenney as a personal friend of the late President and as a man whose eloquence had mightily moved the people of this and other States. Mr. Tenney was warmly received.

SPEECH OF A. W. TENNEY.

My Fellow Citizens—We have assembled here to-night as citizens of a great city, and of a great republic, to place a tribute of affection and regard upon the newly-made grave of our loved and martyred President. The circumstances that have called us together are inexpressibly sad as they are peculiarly thrilling. Assassination has again entered the executive chamber of this

nation and done its worst.   A life, measured by what it has accomplished, without a parallel, a career without a rival, a record
without a stain, a courage in the face of death that has challenged
and won the admiration of the world, a patience in long suffering almost akin to divinity itself, has at last received the crown
of martyrdom.   To-day, under an early autumnal sky, within
the limits of the fairest city of all the West, by the shore of the
blue waters of Lake Erie, in sight of the very spot where stood
the log cabin in which he was born, within an hour's ride of the
house and the farm he loved so well, this mighty people with
bowed heads and bleeding hearts have laid to rest one of the
grandest men of our race.   Child of no fortune, heir to no
throne, and yet at the age of 49 years and 10 months he dies
the most loved and honored man within the circuit of the sun.
Born in poverty, matured in want, educated to the hardest kind
of hard work, and yet, with his own right hand he breaks the
invidious bars of birth

> And ascends Fame's ladder so high
> That from the round at the top he stepped to the skies.

But America mourns not alone the death of her illustrious son.
Nations are in tears; the world is in mourning because Garfield
is dead.   Not because he was President of this Republic, but
because he was, in the fullest meaning of that word, a man.
England, by order of the Queen, puts on court mourning because of the death of the President of the United States—
an imperial honor which she has never before conferred
upon any dead, either at home or abroad, except those of royal
blood.   More than this, even Victoria, Queen of the British
Isles and queen of women, steps from the royal throne she so
greatly adorns to that higher and loftier station held and occupied by every loving Christian woman, and across three thousand
miles of sea she cables again and again her love and sympathy
not only to this nation, but to that other queenly woman—to
that stricken wife and mother, who by her devotion, her fortitude and her love takes her place by the side of her martyred
husband in the affectionate regard of the entire human family.
God bless Queen Victoria for the love and sympathy she has
shown this nation and the nation's widow during those days of
anguish and of tears!   Turning from the mournful present we
face the coming dawn of the near future.   Garfield is dead, but
the government by the people and for the people still lives.

Men may say, and some do so, that because two Presidents have been assassinated within sixteen years, America is fast becoming like Russia, Mexico and Central America. No, no, my countrymen; the perpetuity of the American Republic depends not upon the lives of Presidents or Senates. It lives in the hearts and patriotism of the people, and it will die and cease to be only when they shall prove themselves recreant to their trust and forgetful of their duty. We want no more assassination of Presidents, and as one thing to prevent this we want no coquetting with the technicalities of the law in behalf of the assassin we now have on hand. But we want for him the judgment of the law, like the wrath of Almighty God, to be swift, certain and sure. Though clouds and darkness are around and about us, there is no occasion for despondency. The helm of state is in safe hands, and I counsel you, my countrymen, to be of good cheer. I know President Arthur, and I know him to be an honest, patriotic man, a man who thoroughly believes in the great principles that underly our American Government. A man of great experience, of broad and liberal views, of transcendent executive ability, of great caution and mature judgment, and who, having the courage of his own convictions, will dare to do right. He is right at heart, and I firmly believe and so prophesy, that he will prove himself a worthy successor of President Garfield.

Hon. William E. Robinson was the next speaker. After the applause with which he was greeted had subsided, he said:

SPEECH OF HON. WILLIAM E. ROBINSON.

The first time I saw James A. Garfield was in Wall Street, at the vast meeting of our citizens which stood aghast in front of the Custom House, in April, 1865, the day after the assassination of Abraham Lincoln. Simeon Draper, Edwards Pierrepont, Moses H. Grinnell, General Butler and others had made speeches. I sat on the platform, near the presiding officer, Mr. Draper, and remember the protest which General Garfield entered against the country becoming a nation of assassins. How little he then thought that the very next one to fall as Lincoln fell should be himself! I don't remember that he used the language blazing to-night in letters of fire on the columns of our City Hall, "God reigns, and the government at Washington still lives!" The next time I saw him was when I met him in Congress. We were both at Willard's and I saw him every day. One day he asked me to give him the history of my life, as he had understood that I had fought my own way from boyhood. He had a desire to become acquainted with James T. Brady, and I enjoyed their hearty greeting of each other in Mr. Brady's room. Mr. Garfield had strong religious feelings. He had early joined the body known as Christians or Disciples of Christ or Reformed Baptists, or perhaps more generally Campbellites. The Disciples were scattered over Western Pennsylvania, Virginia, Kentucky, Ohio and Indiana, and in some of the large cities, and now number themselves by the hundred thousand. It might be mentioned that the founder of this sect, of which Mr. Garfield was the most illustrious disciple, was a native of the same village in which President Arthur's father was born. I have heard a great many things from this platform and pulpit which I like, and nothing has pleased me more than the honest growl from its distinguished pastor, on Friday evening last, against the patronizing palaver of tyrants. I would not repel the sympathy of a Magdalen or a monarch, for it is a sign of vast progress when the proudest among the despots of the earth write letters of sympathy to the noble wife of one who earned his living on a tow-path. But

"Timeo Danaos et dona ferentes."

I value more the sympathy of the poor and the honest condolence of labor. I prefer the widow's mite to the more ostentatious contributions of wealth and fashion. This calamity has given us higher hopes and broader views of our destiny. How grand was the character of our beloved President. How noble the elements displayed in the heroic conduct of his wife, and how consoling to all Americans are the hopes and assurances of the stability of our institutions. There are many heroic American boys now toiling on the tow-path of life, who will yet sustain the high character of American manhood as developed in James A. Garfield, and thousands of our American girls, now at our public schools, who if subjected to similar trials will develop similar traits of heroic American womanhood as illustrated by his wife. We have buried our dead, and in his grave I trust we have buried our sectional hatreds and political follies. The South and the North grasp loving hands over his closing grave. Conspicuous by his auspicious presence, the grand soldier of Gettysburg pays his proper homage to him who won his laurels on the bloody field of Chickamauga. I am here to fling a modest flower as his funeral is passing. I stand in this vast tabernacle, in my own district, which gave eight thousand Democratic majority, to deplore, and thus fitly represent my constituents in deploring, the loss of a Republican President. Had he lived his administration should have had my support in all that an honest Democrat could do to make the country happy and prosperous under it, and I think I represent truly the Democrats, as well as the patriotic masses of the Republican party who reside in this district, when I say that to his successor I shall give similar support. I was among the five million American voters who cast our votes for the unsuccessful candidate, but General Garfield was and General Arthur is the constitutional President of a great and united people, whose representatives should make no factious opposition to an honest administration, trying to serve the best interests of a common people.

SPEECH OF WILLIAM C. DE WITT.

There is no need, ladies and gentlemen, for my voice to swell the general anthem of sorrow or of praise over the death of the President. It is time to turn our eyes to brighter things. The funeral rites are ended. The chief whose death has nearly broken the nation's heart now lies buried in the bosom of his own beloved Ohio. The obsequies have been adequate. The mourners comprise the whole American people, and the sombre tokens of bereavement mark every household in the land. Poetry and oratory have exhausted themselves in pathos and eulogy. Garfield sleeps to-night under a wide canopy of showering and shining stars. Memory's urn is full and the historic cemetery at Cleveland will hereafter breathe forever of the fragrance of the flowers of every State and of every clime. Night closes in upon the scene, and the offices of mourning and of sorrow are discharged. It would be a sad commentary upon an intelligent people if they exhausted themselves in ebullitions of feeling alone upon the event. The hour has arrived to consider the lessons taught by the terrible calamity and the immediate and the exigent needs of our country and the future. So far as I say anything, let me reason with you upon the practical aspects of this sad occasion, and let me take up the liberty which your distinguished pastor extended when he said this was a platform for free speech.

GUITEAU'S DOOM.

There is an individual question that may be disposed of in a few words, which I think still requires comment. We feel a shock of unutterable shame and resentment at the thought that such a fiend in human shape as Guiteau could be born of woman. I cannot conceive what purpose his being has in the economy of the universe, unless it is to confound the theory of Darwin about the "survival of the fittest," and to operate as a knock-down argument against the proposition of Mr. Ingersoll, that infinite justice does not require an eternal hell. This thing answers those two purposes. Guiteau is undoubtedly, in a metaphysical sense, a lunatic—a raving, ranting, infernal lunatic. But our people hesitate to believe this, because they think it follows that, being a lunatic in a general sense, he will not be liable to the punishment of death. As I have been introduced as the lawyer of this occasion, permit me to inform you that such is not the law. The grand old English common law, the finest and richest heritage which we have received from our ancestors, prevails in Washington, and it requires only this measure of sanity in order to hold a man guilty of crime: If Guiteau knew that what he did was wrong, that it was murder and punishable by death, he fills the measure, and is responsible for his act. Now if all men who were not entirely sane were irresponsible in the criminal law, there would be more liberty and license than any peaceable citizen would like. None of us are entirely sane, I fear. There is a streak of unsoundness in everybody, and there is a terribly broad track of lunacy in this miserable wretch; but he knew what he did was wrong, that the shot he fired entailed homicide, and that the punishment established for the crime was death. Hence, the American people need have no apprehension that leaving him to the law he will be convicted and hung. The gallows will receive new infamy from his death, and his character, as I have already intimated, will add great strength to the old orthodox notion of eternal punishment which has prevailed in the church in whose edifice I have the honor now to stand. But there is a wider field than any individual question thrust upon us now.

THE PAST TWENTY YEARS.

Our country needs reformation. That is evident. As I had occasion to say the other night, the past twenty years have been thronged with most unnatural and startling events. I make no comment upon them, but they seem like the features of a hideous dream. We had five years of war, not ordinary war against a foreign enemy, but home-made war—the hand of brother bathed in brother's blood; fratricidal war carrying to their long homes a million and more than a million of our people. Within these past twenty years we have witnessed corruption and dishonor pervading all branches of the public service—local crime seated in local office—State corruption running riot in the State Legislature, and even the government at Washington victimized by hordes of dishonest employees. Within twenty years we have had one President impeached and tried for high crimes and misdemeanors—another holding office for four years under a title which was, to say the least, far from satisfactory even to his own supporters, and now two Presidents—as I said before, I make no comments upon these facts; I wish only that the American people may reason, may look at the truth and look at these facts, and see what are the lessons of the hour—I say we have had two Presidents who have fallen at the hand of the assassin. If these events had occurred among a passionate and thoughtless people, they would not be so remarkable. Look at them dispassionately, as the historian will look upon them a hundred years hence. The singularity of them is that they have occurred among an intelligent and a prosperous people. A poor man will be excused for being seen in a poor coat, but why should the rich go about like tramps? Why should the American people, great, intelligent, wealthy, powerful, have thrown out in the progress of their events these stupendous happenings? It is not the fault, as I have said, of the masses; it is not the fault of our civil law, for the wisest civil law on earth prevails in this country; it is not the fault of our government, for the government, as has been said here to-night, framed by Washington and his compeers, constitutes the finest fabric of human government that ever blessed the earth. What is it, my friends? I think I know, and if you will allow me, without any manifestation of criticism, I will undertake to tell you with that frankness which I try to employ whenever I am addressing my fellow-men:

17*

THE MONSTER EVIL.

The party warfares, the manner of administering political parties, is the monster evil of the times. What have we? The Democrat clings to his party because of some faith in the principles of Jefferson and the revolution of '98, some devotion to community independence and State rights—things that are as inopportune as the fashions of the Knickerbockers. The Republican adheres with boundless enthusiasm to his party, because it was the party of emancipation, the party which, he claims, carried the country triumphantly through the war—things great, as I am glad to see my applauding friends regard them, yet things of the past. Neither party represents the living and agitating issues of the hour. If you have any views upon the questions of protective tariff or free trade—which party represents them? It may be that in the glittering symbols of a party platform something is presented, but the adherents of each party are actually divided almost in half upon that issue. If you have distinctive views upon the question of civil service reform or upon the great or growing questions arising from the universal concentration of wealth in the hands of the few, the upgrowing of large corporations and their influence upon the administration of government—if you have strong convictions on either one of these questions—neither party gives full expression to your views. I would just as soon think of sending a young man to do his courting among the inmates of the Old Ladies' Home as to send any patriot with strong views on any of the live issues of the times to either of the present political parties for a proper exposition of his sentiments. Now, it was never the design that a party should last so long upon dead issues. The sovereignty of this country rests with the people. The crown is in the hands of the masses, and the theory of the fathers was that our government was to represent the voice of the people; but now the voice of the people must go and pipe itself, instead of through the cornet of some new and present party, through some old revolutionary and broken horn. If a man be up for office, it is not how well he can serve. The idea of a man running for local office in any city of the country being selected with reference to the particular views he has in respect to the resolutions of '98, State rights, emancipation, or some other national issue! They have no more to do with local government than his views about the obliquity of the ecliptic, or the moons of the planet Jupiter. Not a bit. Nor have his views on these national questions any more to do with the candidate for State office, and so I say it is we have here a form of popular expression in the shape of party which does not give vent to the sentiment and the spirit of the masses—which quarrels forever over dead issues, and hence by bearing down upon the one point makes a lunacy among the masses instead of a government of the people. And it was this perpetual agitation, it has been this perpetual agitation which has led largely to the events to which I have alluded.

A NOVEL PROPOSITION.

In the liberty that was extended to me, let me say, for one, I believe the wisest and the greatest and the most heroic thing that President Arthur could do would be to imitate the example of General Washington, in whose Cabinet sat the State rights Jefferson and the Federalist Hamilton, and select the new Cabinet indifferently from the leading men of each political party, and range his administration upon all the living issues of the times, and then at its close take upon it the fair verdict of the people at the polls. I understand that the hide-bound partisan and politician would carp and rave at such an act; but I believe the American people would rise to a full appreciation of so novel and grand a piece of statesmanship. Now, my friends, these are the ideas that I think meet for the occasion. 1 hope there will be no more wrangling for Federal patronage, such as has its blossom in this poisonous thing that is to die. I hope there will be no more abusive quarrelling between parties after there has been such a manifestation of common sympathy and common patriotism. I trust the American people will come up to a new and a better time. We want a new dispensation and another day, and as we journey up out of the shadows of this hard and painful gloom—out of the valley of this most unusual night, let us press on to the mountain tops. Lo! the morning dawns, and there shall be for our country a new heaven and a new earth.

LIFE OF JAMES A. GARFIELD.

HIS ANCESTORS AND BIRTHPLACE.

ON both his father's and his mother's side General Garfield comes of a long line of New England ancestry. The first of the American Garfields was Edward, who came from Chester, England, to Massachusetts Bay as early as 1630, settled at Watertown, and died June 14, 1672, age ninety-seven. One of the family, Abraham Garfield, a great-uncle of General Garfield, was in the fight at Concord Bridge, and was one of the signers of the affidavits sent to the Continental Congress at Philadelphia to prove that the British were the aggressors in that affair, and fired twice before the patriots replied. After the Revolutionary War several members of the family left Massachusetts and settled in Central New York. General Garfield's father, Abram Garfield, was born there in 1799. He lived there till his eighteenth year, when he went to Newburg, Ohio, and soon after settled near Zanesville. He was a tall, robust young fellow, of very much the same type as his famous son, but a handsomer man, according to the verdict of his wife. He had a sunny, genial temper, like most men of great physical strength, was a great favorite with his associates, and was a natural leader and master of the rude characters with whom he was thrown in his forest-clearing work and his later labors in building the Ohio Canal. His education was confined to a few terms in the Worcester district school, and the only two specimens of his writing extant show that it was not thorough enough to give him much knowledge of the science of orthography. He was fond of reading, but the hard life of a poor man in a new country gave him little time to read books, if he had had the money to buy them. The weekly newspapers and a few volumes borrowed from neighbors formed his intellectual diet.

On the 3d of February, 1820, Abram Garfield and Eliza Ballou were married in the village of Zanesville by a justice of the peace named Richard H. Hogan. The bridegroom lacked nine months of being twenty-one years of age, and the bride was only eighteen. Eliza Ballou's father was a cousin of Hosea Ballou, the founder of Universalism in this country. Eliza was born in 1801. The Ballous are of Huguenot origin, and are directly descended from Maturin Ballou, who fled from France on the revocation of the Edict of Nantes, and with other French Protestants joined Roger Williams's colony in Rhode Island, the only American colony founded on the basis of full religious liberty. The gift of eloquence was undoubtedly derived by General Garfield from the Ballous, who were a race of preachers.

The newly-wedded pair went to Newburg, Cuyahoga County, Ohio—now a part of the city of Cleveland—and began life in a small log house on a new farm of eighty acres. In January, 1821, their first child, Mehitabel, was born. In October, 1822, Thomas was born, and Mary in October, 1824. In 1826 the family removed to New Philadelphia, Tuscarawas County, where the father had a contract to construct three miles of canal. In 1827 the fourth child, James B., was born. This was the only one of the children that the parents lost. He died in 1830, after the family returned to the lake country. In January, 1830, Abram went to Orange Township, Cuyahoga County, where lived Amos Boynton, his half-brother—the son of his mother by her second husband—and bought eighty acres of land at $2 an acre. The country was nearly all wild, and the new farm had to be carved out of the forest. Boynton purchased at the same time a tract of the same size adjoining, and the two families lived together for a few weeks in a log house built by the joint labors of the men. Soon a second cabin was reared across the road. The dwelling of the Garfields was built after the standard pattern of the houses of poor Ohio farmers in that day. Its walls were of logs, its roof was of shingles split with an axe, and its floor of rude thick planking split out of tree-trunks with a wedge and maul. It had only a single room, at one end of which was the big cavernous chimney, where the cooking was done, and at the other a bed. The younger children slept in a trundle-bed, which was pushed under the bedstead of their parents in the daytime to get it out of the way, for there was no room to spare; the older ones climbed a ladder to the loft under the steep roof. In this house James A. Garfield was born, November 19, 1831.

The father worked hard early and late to clear his land and

plant and gather his crops.   No man in all the region around
could wield an axe like him.   Fenced fields soon took the place
of the forest; an orchard was planted, a barn built, and the
family was full of hope for the future when death removed its
strong support.   One day in May, 1833, a fire broke out in the
woods, and Abram Garfield, after heating his blood and exert-
ing his strength to keep the flames from his fences and fields,
sat down to rest where a cold wind blew, and was seized with a
violent sore throat.   A country doctor put a blister on his neck,
which seemed only to hasten his death.   Just before he died,
pointing to his children, he said to his wife, " Eliza, I have
planted four saplings in these woods.   I leave them to your
care."   He was buried in a corner of a wheat-field on his farm.
James, the baby, was eighteen months old at the time.

HIS BOYHOOD.

The childhood of James A. Garfield was passed in almost
complete isolation from social influences save those which proceeded from the home of his mother and that of his uncle
Boynton.   The farms of the Garfields and Boyntons were partially separated from the settled country around by a large tract
of forest on one side and a deep rocky ravine on another.   For
many years after Abram Garfield and his half-brother Boynton
built their log cabins the nearest house was seven miles distant,
and when the country became well settled the rugged character
of the surface around their farms kept neighbors at a distance
too great for the children of the two families to find associates
among them, save at the district school.   The district school-
house stood upon a corner of the Garfield farm, and it was there,
when nearly four years old, that James conned his " Noah
Webster's Spelling Book," and learned his "a-b ab's."

James was put to farm work as soon as he was big enough to
be of any use.   The family was very poor, and the mother
often worked in the fields with the boys.   She spun the yarn
and wove the cloth for the children's clothes and her own,
sewed for the neighbors, knit stockings, cooked the simple
meals for the household in the big fireplace, over which hung
an iron crane for the pot-hooks, helped plant and hoe the corn
and gather the hay crop, and even assisted the oldest boy to
clear and fence land.   In the midst of this toilsome life the
brave little woman found time to instil into the minds of her

children the religious and moral maxims of her New England ancestry. Every day she read four chapters of the Bible—a practice she keeps up to this time, and has never interrupted for a single day save when lying upon a sick-bed. The children lived in an atmosphere of religious thought and discussion. Uncle Boynton, who was a second father to the Garfield family, flavored all his talk with Bible quotations. He carried a Testament in his pocket wherever he went, and would sit on his plough-beam at the end of a furrow to take it out and read a chapter. It was a time of religious ferment in Northern Ohio. New sects filled the air with their doctrinal cries. The Disciples, a sect founded by the preaching of Alexander Campbell, an eloquent and devout man of Scotch descent, who ranged over Kentucky, Ohio, Virginia and Pennsylvania, from his home at Bethany in the "Pan Handle," had made great progress. They assailed all creeds as made by men, and declared the Bible to be the only rule of life. Attacking all the older denominations, they were vigorously attacked in turn. James's mind was filled at an early day with the controversies this new sect excited. The guests at his mother's house were mostly travelling preachers, and the talk of the neighborhood, when not about the crops and farm labors, was usually on religious topics.

At the district school James was known as a fighting boy. He found that the larger boys were disposed to insult and abuse a little fellow who had no father or big brother to protect him, and he resented such imposition with all the force of a sensitive nature backed by a hot temper, great physical courage, and a strength unusual for his age. His big brother Thomas had finished his schooling and was much away from home, working by the day or month to earn money for the support of the family. Many stories are told in Orange of the pluck shown by the future major-general in his encounters with the rough country lads in defence of his boyish rights and honor. They say he never began a fight and never cherished malice, but when enraged by taunts or insults would attack boys of twice his size with the fury and tenacity of a bull-dog. A few years after the death of his father the house was enlarged in a curious fashion. The log school-house was abandoned for a new frame building, and the old structure was bought by Thomas Garfield for a trifle, and he and James, with the help of the Boynton boys, pulled it down and put it up again on a site a few steps in the rear of the Garfield dwelling. Thus the family had two rooms and were tolerably comfortable, as far as household accommodations were concerned. In these two log buildings they lived until James was fourteen, when the boys built a small frame house for their mother. It was painted red and had three rooms below and two under the roof.

James often got employment in the haying and harvesting season from the farmers of Orange. When he was sixteen he walked ten miles, to Aurora, in company with a boy older than himself, looking for work. They offered their services to a farmer who had a good deal of hay to cut. " What wages do you expect ?" asked the man. " Man's wages—a dollar a day," replied young Garfield. The farmer thought they were not old enough to earn full wages. " Then let us mow that field by the acre," said the young man. The farmer agreed ; the customary price per acre was 50 cents. By 4 o'clock in the afternoon the hay was down and the boys earned a dollar apiece. Then the farmer engaged them for a fortnight. James's first wages were earned from a merchant who had an ashery where he leached ashes and made black salts, which were shipped by lake and canal to New York. He got $9 a month and his board, and stuck to the business for two months, at the end of which his hair below his cap was bleached and colored by the fumes until it assumed a lively red hue. Afterward he went to Newburg, where an uncle lived, who had a piece of oak-timbered land to clear on the edge of Independence township. James agreed to chop 100 cords of wood at 50 cents a cord. He boarded with one of his sisters, who was married and lived near by. He was a good chopper, and easily cut two cords a day.

The view of Lake Erie and the passing sails stirred afresh in him the ambition to be a sailor, which almost every sturdy farmer's boy feels who reads tales of sea-fights and adventures in the quiet monotony of his inland home. He resolved to ship on one of the lake craft, and with this purpose he walked to Cleveland and boarded a schooner lying at the wharf, and told the captain he wanted to hire out as a sailor. The captain, a brutal, drunken fellow, was amazed at the impudence of the green country lad, and answered him with a torrent of profanity. Escaping as quickly as he could from the vessel, the lad walked up the river along the docks. Soon he heard himself called by name from the deck of a canal boat, and, turning around, recognized a cousin, Amos Letcher, who told him he commanded the craft, and proposed to engage him to drive horses on the tow-path. The would-be sailor thought that here was a chance to learn something of navigation in a humble way, preparatory to renewing his application for service on the lakes. He accepted the offer and the wages of "ten dollars a month and found," and next day the boat started for Pittsburg with a cargo of copper ore. It was called the Evening Star, was open amidships, and had a cabin at the bow for the horses and one at the stern for the men. On the return trip the Evening Star stopped at Brier Hill on the Mahoning River, and loaded with coal at the mines of David Tod, afterward Governor of Ohio, and a warm friend of Garfield the major-general and member of Congress. The boating episode in Garfield's life lasted through the season of 1848. After the first trip to Pittsburg the boat went back and forth between Cleveland and Brier Hill with cargoes of coal and iron.

Late in the fall the young driver, who had risen to the post of steersman, was seized with a violent attack of ague, which kept him at home all winter and in bed most of the time. All his summer's earnings went for doctor's bills and medicines. When he recovered, his mother, who had never approved of his canal adventure, dissuaded him from carrying out his project of shipping on the lakes. To master one passion she stimulated another—that of study. She brought to her help the district school-teacher, an excellent, thoughtful man named Samuel D. Bates, who fired the boy's mind with a desire for a good education, and doubtless changed the course of his life. He went to the Geauga Academy, at Chester, a village a few miles distant, and began a new career.

He repulsed all efforts to persuade him to join the church, and when pressed hard stayed away from meetings for several Sundays. Apparently he wanted full freedom to reach conclusions about religion by his own mental processes. It was not until he was eighteen and had been two terms at the Chester school that he joined his uncle's congregation. He was baptized in March, 1850, in a little stream putting into the Chagrin River. His conversion was accomplished by a quiet sweet-tempered man, who held a series of meetings in the school-house near the Garfield homestead, and told in the plainest and most straightforward manner the story of the Gospel. A previous perusal of Pollok's "Course of Time" had made a deep impression upon him and turned his thoughts to religious subjects.

FIGHT FOR AN EDUCATION.

The country schoolmaster who helped Mrs. Garfield dissuade her son from going as a sailor on the lakes in the spring of 1849 was a student at Geauga Academy, a Free Will Baptist institution in the village of Chester, ten miles away from the home of the Garfields in Orange. The argument which finally turned the robust lad from his cherished plan of adventure was advanced by his mother, and was that, if he fitted himself for teaching by a few terms in school, he could teach winters and sail summers, and thus have employment the year round. In the month of March, with $17 in his pocket, got together by his mother and his brother Thomas, James went to Chester with his cousins, William and Henry Boynton. The boys took a stock of provisions along, and rented a room with two beds and a cook-stove in an old, unpainted house, where lived a poor widow woman, who undertook to prepare their meals and do their washing for an absurdly small sum. The academy was a two-story building, and the school, with about a hundred pupils of both sexes, drawn from the farming country around Chester, was in a flourishing condition. It had a library of perhaps one hundred and fifty volumes—more books than young Garfield had ever seen before. A venerable gentleman named Daniel Branch was principal of the school, and his wife was his chief assistant. At the end of the term of twelve weeks he went home to Orange, helped his brother build a barn for their mother, and then worked for day wages at haying and harvesting. With the money he earned he paid off some arrears of doctors' bills left from his long illness. When he returned to Chester in the fall he had one silver sixpence in his pocket. Going to church next day he dropped the sixpence in the contribution-box.

He had made an arrangement with Homan Woodworth, a carpenter in the village, to live at his house and have lodging, board, washing, fuel and light for $1.06 a week, and this sum he expected to earn by helping the carpenter on Saturdays and at odd hours on school days. The carpenter was building a two-story house, and James's first work was to get out siding at 2 cents a board. The first Saturday he planed fifty-one boards, and so earned $1.02, the most money he had ever got for a day's work. That term he paid his way, bought a few books, and returned home with $8 in his pocket. He now thought himself competent to teach a country school, but in two days' tramping through Cuyahoga County failed to find employment. Some schools had already engaged teachers, and where there was still a vacancy the trustees thought him too young. He returned home completely discouraged and greatly humiliated by the rebuffs he had met with. He made a resolution that he would never again ask for a position of any sort, and the resolution was kept, for every public place he has since had has come to him unsought.

Next morning, while still in the depths of despondency, he heard a man call to his mother from the road, "Widow Gaffield" (a local corruption of the name Garfield), "where's your boy Jim? I wonder if he wouldn't like to teach our school at the Ledge." James went out and found a neighbor from a district a mile away, where the school had been broken up for two winters by the rowdyism of the big boys. He said he would like to try the school, but before deciding must consult his uncle, Amos Boynton. That evening there was a family council. Uncle Amos pondered over the matter, and finally said, "You go and try it. You will go into that school as the boy, 'Jim Gaffield;' see that you come out as Mr. Garfield, the school-master." The young man mastered the school, after a hard tussle in the school-room with the bully of the district, who resented a flogging and tried to brain the teacher with a billet of wood. His wages were $12 a month and board, and he "boarded around" in the families of the pupils.

He had $48 in the spring—more money than had ever been in his possession before. Before returning to Chester he joined the Disciples' Church, and his religious experience together with his new interest in teaching, caused him to abandon his boyhood ambition of becoming a sailor. During his third term at the academy he and his cousin Henry boarded themselves. At the end of six weeks the boys found their expenses for food had been just 31 cents per week apiece. Henry thought they were living too poorly for good health, and they agreed to increase their outlay to 50 cents a week apiece. James had up to this time looked upon a college course as wholly beyond his reach, but he met a college graduate who told him he was mistaken in supposing that only the sons of rich parents were able to take such a course. A poor boy could get through, he said, but it would take a long time and very hard work. The usual time was four years in preparatory studies and four in the regular college course. James thought that by working part of the time to earn money he could get through in twelve years. He then resolved to bend all his energies to the one purpose of getting a college education.

From this resolution he never swerved a hair's-breadth. Until it was accomplished it was the one overmastering idea of his life. The tenacity and single-heartedness with which he clung to it and the sacrifices he made to realize it unquestionably exerted a powerful influence in moulding and solidifying his character. He began to study Latin, philosophy and botany. When the spring term ended he went home again and worked through the summer at haying and carpentering. Next fall he was back at Chester for a fourth term, and in the winter he got a village school to teach in Warrensville, at $16 a month and board.

Returning to Orange in the summer, he decided to go on with his education at a new school just established by the Disciples at Hiram, Portage County, a petty cross-roads village, twelve miles from a town and a railroad. His religious feeling naturally called him to the young institution of his own denomination. In August, 1851, he arrived at Hiram, and found a plain brick building standing in the midst of a corn-field, with perhaps a dozen farm-houses near enough for boarding places for the students. He lived in a room with four other pupils, studied harder than ever, having now his college project fully anchored in his mind, got through his six books of Cæsar that term, and made good progress in Greek. In the winter he again taught school at Warrensville, and earned $18 a month. Next spring he was back at Hiram and during the summer vacation he helped build a house in the village, planing all the siding and shingling the roof.

At the beginning of his second year at Hiram, Garfield was made a tutor in place of one of the teachers who fell ill, and thenceforward he taught and studied at the same time, working tremendously to fit himself for college. His future wife recited to him two years in Greek, and when he went to college she went to teach in the Cleveland schools, and to wait patiently the realization of their hopes. When he went to Hiram he had studied Latin only six weeks and had just begun Greek, and was therefore just in a condition to fairly begin the four years' preparatory course ordinarily taken by students before entering college in the freshman class. Yet in three years' time he fitted himself to enter the junior class, two years further along, and at the same time earned his own living, thus crowding six years' study into three, and teaching for his support at the same time. To accomplish this, he shut the whole world out from his mind save that little portion of it within the range of his studies, knowing nothing of politics or the news of the day, reading no light literature, and engaging in no social recreations that took his time from his books.

In the spring of 1854 he wrote to the presidents of Yale, Brown and Williams, telling what books he had studied, and asked what class he could enter if he passed a satisfactory examination in them. All three wrote that he could enter the junior year. President Hopkins, of Williams, added this sentence to the business part of his letter, " If you come here, we shall do what we can for you." This seemed like a kindly hand held out, and it decided him to go to Williams. He had been urged to go to the Disciples' College in Bethany, Virginia, founded by Alexander Campbell, but with a wisdom hardly to be expected in a country lad devotedly attached to the sect represented by the Bethany school, he sought the wider culture and broader opportunities of a New England college.

LIFE AT COLLEGE.

When Garfield reached Williams College, in June, 1854, he had about $300 which he had saved while teaching in the Hiram school. With this money he hoped to manage to get through a year. A few weeks remained of the closing school year, and he attended the recitations of the sophomore class in order to get familiar with the methods of the professors before testing his ability to pass the examinations for the junior year. The examination for entering the junior class was passed without trouble. Although self-taught, his knowledge of the books prescribed was thorough. A long summer vacation followed his examination, and this time he employed in the college library, the first large collection of books he had ever seen. His absorption in the double work of teaching and fitting himself for college had hitherto left him little time for general reading, and the library opened a new world of profit and delight. He had never read a line of Shakespeare, save a few extracts in the school reading-books. From the whole range of fiction he had voluntarily shut himself off at eighteen, when he joined the Church, having serious views of the business of life, and imbibing the notion, then almost universal among religious people in the country districts of the West, that novel-reading was a waste of time, and therefore a sinful, worldly sort of intellectual amusement. When turned loose in the college library, with weeks of leisure to range at will over its shelves, he began with Shakespeare, which he read through from cover to cover. Then he went to English history and poetry. Of the poets Tennyson pleased him best, which is not to be wondered at, for the influence of the laureate was then at its height.

Garfield studied Latin and Greek, and took up German as an elective study. One year at college completed his classical studies, on which he was far advanced before he came to Williams. German he carried on successfully until he could read Goethe and Schiller readily, and acquired considerable fluency in the conversational use of the language. He entered with zeal into the literary work of the school, joined the Philologian Society, was a vigorous debater, and in his last year was one of the editors of *The Williams Quarterly*, a college periodical of a high order of merit.

At the end of the fall term of 1854 came a winter vacation of two months, which Garfield employed in teaching a writing-school at North Pownal, Vermont. He wrote a bold, handsome, legible hand, not at all like that in vogue nowadays in the systems taught in the commercial colleges, but a hand that was strongly individual, and was the envy of the boys and girls who tried to imitate it in his Vermont class. It is said that a year or two before Garfield taught his writing-class in the North Pownal school-house, Chester A. Arthur taught the district school in the same building.

At the end of the college year, in June, Garfield went back

to Ohio and visited his mother, who was then living with a
daughter in Solon. His money was exhausted, and he had to
adopt one of two plans, either to borrow enough to take him
through to graduation at the end of the next year, or to go to
teaching in order to earn the money, and thus break the con-
tinuity of his college course. He then hit upon the plan of
insuring his life, and assigning the policy as security for a loan.
His brother Thomas undertook to furnish the funds in instal-
ments, but becoming embarrassed was not able to do so, and a
neighbor, Dr. Robinson, assumed the obligation. Garfield gave
his notes for the loan, and regarded the transaction as on a fair
business basis, knowing that if he lived he would repay the
money, and that if he died his creditor would be secure.

His second winter vacation Garfield spent in Poestenkill, New
York, a country neighborhood about six miles from Troy, where
a Disciple minister from Ohio, named Streeter, was preaching,
and where he soon organized a writing-school to employ his
time and bring him in a little money. Occasionally Garfield
preached in his friend's church. During a visit to Troy he
became acquainted with the teachers and directors of the public
schools of that city, and was one day surprised by the offer of a
position in them at a salary far beyond his expectations of what
he could earn after his graduation and return to Ohio. It was
the turning-point in his life. If he accepted he could soon pay
his debts, marry the girl to whom he was engaged, and live a life
of comfort in an attractive Eastern city ; but he could not finish
his college course, and he would have to sever the ties with his
friends in Ohio and with the struggling school at Hiram, to
which he was deeply attached. Had he taken the position his
whole subsequent career would no doubt have been different.

During his last term at Williams he made his first political
speech—an address before a meeting gathered in one of the
class-rooms to support the nomination of John C. Fremont.
Although he had passed his majority nearly four years before,
he had never voted. The old parties did not interest him ; he
believed them both corrupted with the sin of slavery ; but when
a new party arose to combat the designs of the slave power it
enlisted his earnest sympathies. His mind was free from all
bias concerning the parties and statesmen of the past, and he
could equally admire Clay or Jackson, Webster or Benton. He
is the first man nominated for the Presidency whose political

convictions and activities began with the birth of the Republican party.   He was graduated August, 1856, with a class honor established by President Hopkins and highly esteemed in the college—that of metaphysics—reading an essay on "The Seen and the Unseen."

TEACHER AND PREACHER.

Before Garfield graduated at Williams College the trustees of the Hiram Eclectic Institute elected him teacher of ancient languages, and the post was ready for him as soon as he got back to Ohio.   It was not a professorship, because the institution was not a college, and did not become one until 1869, long after his connection with it ceased.   A year later, when only twenty-six years old, he was placed at the head of the school with the title of Chairman of the Board of Instruction, the Board waiting another year before conferring upon him the full honors of the Principalship.   He continued to hold the position of Principal until he went into the army in 1861.   He was nominal Principal two years longer, the Board hoping he would return and manage the school after the war ended.   When he went to Congress he was made Advising Principal and Lecturer, and his name was borne upon the catalogues in this capacity until 1864.

Before he went to college, Garfield had begun to preach a little in the country churches around Hiram, and when he returned he began to fill the pulpit in the Disciples' Church in Hiram with considerable regularity.   In his denomination no ordination is required to become a minister.   Any brother having the ability to discourse on religious topics to a congregation is welcomed to the pulpit.   His fame as a lay preacher extended throughout the counties of Portage, Summit, Trumbull and Geauga, and he was often invited to preach in the towns of that region.

One of his former pupils says of his peculiarities as a teacher :

" No matter how old the pupils were, Garfield always called us by our first names, and kept himself on the most familiar terms with all.   He played with us freely, scuffled with us sometimes, talked with us in walking to and fro, and we treated him out of the class-room just about as we did one another.   Yet he was a most strict disciplinarian, and enforced the rules like a martinet.   He combined an affectionate and confiding manner with respect for order in a most successful manner.   If he wanted

MRS. JAMES A. GARFIELD.

to speak to a pupil, either for reproof or approbation, he would generally manage to get one arm around him and draw him close up to him. He had a peculiar way of shaking hands, too, giving a twist to your arm and drawing you right up to him. This sympathetic manner has helped him to advancement. When I was janitor he used sometimes to stop me and ask my opinion about this and that, as if seriously advising with me. I can see that my opinion could not have been of any value, and that he probably asked me partly to increase my self-respect and partly to show me that he felt an interest in me. I certainly was his friend all the firmer for it."

ENTRANCE INTO POLITICS.

He cast his first vote in 1856 for John C. Fremont, his own political career thus beginning with the first national campaign of the Republican party. Before leaving Williams College he made a speech to the students on the question of slavery in the Territories, and during the fall, after he returned to Hiram, he spoke in the Disciples Church, in reply to Alphonso Hart, of Ravenna ,who had delivered a Democratic address there a few nights before. Then a joint debate was arranged at Garretsville, between Hart and Garfield which attracted a good deal of local attention and is well remembered to this day by the older farmers of Portage County. This debate launched Garfield as a political speaker. His reputation as a stump orator widened steadily from that debate until it embraced first the State of Ohio and then the nation.

A year after he took charge of the Hiram school Garfield married Lucretia Rudolph, his fellow-student and pupil in former years, to whom he had engaged himself before he went to Williams College. Their love had stood the test of time and absence, and now that he had made his place in the world and felt that he could support a family, there was nothing to hinder its consummation. The marriage took place at the house of the bride's parents, November 11, 1858.

His labors upon the stump, beginning in 1856, with perhaps a score of speeches for Fremont and Dayton in country school-houses and town-halls in the region around Hiram, were extended in 1857 and 1858 over a wider area of territory, and in 1859 he began to speak at county mass-meetings. His first appearance at a big meeting was at Akron, where his name was

18

put upon the bills below that of Salmon P. Chase. There the young teacher met for the first time the great anti-slavery leader whom he had honored and admired from his boyhood, and a friendship sprang up between the two which endured until Chase's death.

In January, 1860, he went to Columbus, and took his seat in the State Senate. The campaign of 1860 made him widely known throughout the State. He found time to read law assiduously while he was in the Legislature. In 1858 he made up his mind that his future career should be at the bar. He therefore entered his name as a law student in the office of Williamson and Riddle, in Cleveland, and got from Mr. Riddle a list of books to be studied. In 1861 he applied to the Supreme Court in Columbus for admission to the bar, was examined by a committee composed of Thomas M. Key, a distinguished lawyer of Cincinnati, and Robert Harrison, afterwards a member of the Supreme Court Commission, and admitted. His intention was to open an office in Cleveland, but the breaking out of the war changed his plans.

HIS RECORD IN THE WAR.

The most complete and comprehensive account of General Garfield's military career is found in Whitelaw Reid's "Ohio in the War," which was written many years before Garfield's nomination for the Presidency. When the time came, says this account, for appointing the officers for the Ohio troops, the Legislature was still in session. Garfield at once avowed his intention of entering the service. He was offered the lieutenant-colonelcy of the 42d Ohio Regiment, but it was not until the 14th of December that orders for the field were received. The regiment was then sent to Calettsburg, Ky., and Garfield, then made colonel, was directed to report in person to General Buell. On the 17th of December he assigned Colonel Garfield to the command of the 17th Brigade, and ordered him to drive the Rebel forces under Humphrey Marshall out of Sandy Valley, in Eastern Kentucky. Up to this date no active operations had been attempted in the great department that lay south of the Ohio River. The spell of Bull Run still hung over our armies. Save the campaigns in Western Virginia, and the unfortunate attack by General Grant at Belmont, not a single engagement had occurred over all the region between the Alleghanies and the

Mississippi. General Buell was preparing to advance upon the Rebel position at Bowling Green, when he suddenly found himself hampered by two co-operating forces skilfully planted within striking distance of his flank. General Zollicoffer was advancing from Cumberland Gap towards Mill Spring; and Humphrey Marshall, moving down the Sandy Valley, was threatening to overrun Eastern Kentucky. Till these could be driven back, an advance upon Bowling Green would be perilous, if not actually impossible. To General George H. Thomas, then just raised from his colonelcy of regulars to a brigadier-generalship of volunteers, was committed the task of repulsing Zollicoffer; to the untried colonel of the raw 42d Ohio, the task of repulsing Humphrey Marshall, and on their success the whole army of the department waited.

Colonel Garfield thus found himself, before he had ever seen a gun fired in action, in command of four regiments of infantry, and some eight companies of cavalry, charged with the work of driving out of his native State the officer reputed the ablest of those not educated to war whom Kentucky had given to the Rebellion. Marshall had under his command nearly 5000 men, stationed at the village of Paintville, sixty miles up the Sandy Valley. He was expected by the Rebel authorities to advance towards Lexington, unite with Zollicoffer, and establish the authority of the Provisional Government at the State capital. These hopes were fed by the recollection of his great intellectual abilities, and the soldierly reputation he had borne ever since he led the famous charge of the Kentucky Volunteers at Buena Vista. But Garfield won the day. Marshall hastily abandoned his position, fired his camp equipage and stores, and began a retreat which was not ended till he had reached Abingdon, Virginia. A fresh peril, however, now beset the little force. An unusually violent rain-storm broke out, the mountain gorges were all flooded, and the Sandy rose to such a height that steam boatmen pronounced it impossible to ascend the stream with supplies. The troops were almost out of rations, and the rough mountainous country was incapable of supporting them. Colonel Garfield had gone down the river to its mouth. He ordered a small steamer which had been in the Quartermaster's service to take on a load of supplies and start up. The captain declared it was impossible. Efforts were made to get other vessels, but without success.

Finally Colonel Garfield ordered the captain and crew on board, stationed a competent army officer on deck to see that the captain did his duty, and himself took the wheel. The captain still protested that no boat could possibly stem the raging current, but Garfield turned her head up the stream and began the perilous trip. The water in the usually shallow river was sixty feet deep, and the tree-tops along the bank were almost submerged. The little vessel trembled from stem to stern at every motion of the engines; the waters whirled her about as if she were a skiff; and the utmost speed that steam could give her was three miles an hour. When night fell the captain of the boat begged permission to tie up. To attempt ascending that flood in the dark, he declared was madness. But Colonel Garfield kept his place at the wheel. Finally, in one of the sudden bends of the river, they drove, with a full head of steam, into the quicksand of the bank. Every effort to back off was in vain. Garfield at last ordered a boat to be lowered to take a line across to the opposite bank. The crew protested against venturing out in the flood. The Colonel leaped into the boat himself and steered it over. The force of the current carried them far below the point they sought to reach; but they finally succeeded in making fast to a tree and rigging a windlass with rails sufficiently powerful to draw the vessel off and get her once more afloat.

It was on Saturday that the boat left the mouth of the Sandy. All night, all day Sunday, and all through Sunday night they kept up their struggle with the current, Garfield leaving the wheel only eight hours out of the whole time, and that during the day. By 9 o'clock Monday morning they reached the camp, and were received with tumultuous cheering. Garfield himself could scarcely escape being borne to headquarters on the shoulders of the delighted men.

These operations in the Sandy Valley had been conducted with such energy and skill as to receive the special commendation of the commanding general and of the government. General Buell had been moved to words of unwonted praise. The War Department had conferred the grade of brigadier-general, the commission bearing the date of the battle of Middle Creek. And the country, without understanding very well the details of the campaign—of which, indeed, no satisfactory account was published at the time—fully appreciated the satisfactory result. The discomfiture of Humphrey Marshall was a source of special chagrin to the Rebel sympathizers of Kentucky, and of amazement and admiration throughout the loyal West, and Garfield took rank in the public estimation among the most promising of the younger volunteer generals.

On his arrival at Louisville, from the Sandy Valley, General Garfield found that the Army of the Ohio was already beyond Nashville, on its march to Grant's aid at Pittsburg Landing. He hastened after it, reported to General Buell about thirty miles south of Columbia, and, under his order, at once assumed command of the 20th Brigade, then a part of the division under General Thomas J. Wood. He reached the field of Pittsburg Landing about 1 o'clock on the second day of the battle, and participated in its closing scenes.

The old tendency to fever and ague, contracted in the days of his tow-path service on the Ohio Canal, was now aggravated in the malarious climate of the South, and General Garfield was finally sent home on sick-leave about the 1st of August. Near the same time the Secretary of War, who seems at this early day to have formed the high estimate of Garfield which he continued to entertain throughout the war, sent orders to him to proceed to Cumberland Gap and relieve General George W. Morgan of his command. But when they were received he was too ill to leave his bed. A month later the Secretary ordered him to report in person at Washington as soon as his health would permit. On his arrival it was found that the estimate placed on his knowledge of law, his judgment and his loyalty, had led to his selection as one of the first members of the court-martial for the noted trial of Fitz John Porter. In the duties connected with this detail most of the autumn was consumed. Early in January he was ordered out to General Rosecrans. From the day of his appointment, General Garfield became the intimate associate and confidential adviser of his chief. But he did not occupy so commanding a station as to be able to put restraint upon him. From the 4th of January to the 24th of June, General Rosecrans lay at Murfreesboro. Through five months of this delay General Garfield was with him. The War Department demanded an advance, and when the spring opened urged it with unusual vehemence. Finally, General Rosecrans formally asked his corps, division and cavalry generals as to the propriety of a movement. With singular unanimity, though for diverse reasons, they opposed it. Out of seventeen generals not one was in favor of an immediate advance, and not one was even willing to put himself on record as in favor of an early advance. General Garfield collated the seventeen letters sent in from the generals in reply to the questions of their commander, and fairly reported their substance, coupled with a cogent argument against them and in favor of an immediate movement. This report we venture to pronounce the ablest military document known to have been submitted by a Chief of Staff to his superior during the war. General Garfield stood absolutely alone, every general commanding troops having, as we have seen, either openly opposed or failed to approve an advance. But his statements were so clear and his arguments so forcible that he carried conviction.

Twelve days after the reception of this report the army moved—to the great dissatisfaction of its leading generals. One of the three corps commanders, Major-General Thomas L. Crittenden, approached the Chief of Staff at the headquarters on the morning of the advance : " It is understood, sir," he said, " by the general officers of the army that this movement is your work. I wish you to understand that it is a rash and fatal move, for which you will be held responsible." This rash and fatal move was the Tullahoma campaign—a campaign perfect in its conception, excellent in its general execution, and only hindered from resulting in the complete destruction of the opposing army by the delay which had too long postponed its commencement. It might even yet have destroyed Bragg but for the terrible season of rains which set in on the morning of the advance and continued uninterruptedly for the greater part of a month. With a week's earlier start it would have ended the career of Bragg's army in the war.

At last came the battle of Chickamauga. Such by this time had come to be Garfield's influence that he was nearly always consulted and often followed. He wrote every order issued that day—one only excepted. This he did rarely as an amanuensis, but rather on the suggestions of his own judgment, afterward submitting what he had prepared to Rosecrans for approval or change. The one order which he did not write was the fatal order to Wood which lost the battle. The meaning was correct; the words, however, did not clearly represent what Rosecrans meant, and the division commander in question so interpreted them as to destroy the right wing. The General commanding and his Chief of Staff were caught in the tide of disaster and born back towards Chattanooga. The Chief of Staff was sent to communicate with Thomas, while the General proceeded to prepare for the reception of the routed army. Such at least were the statements of the reports, and, in a technical sense, they were true. It should never be forgotten, however, in Garfield's praise, that it was on his own earnest representations that he was sent—that, in fact, he rather procured permission to go to Thomas and so back into the battle, than received orders to do so. He refused to believe that Thomas was routed or the battle lost. He found the road environed with dangers; some of his escort were killed, and they all narrowly escaped death or capture. But he bore to Thomas the first news that officer had received of the disaster on the right, and gave the information on which he was able to extricate his command. At 7 o'clock that evening, under the personal supervison of General Gordon Granger and himself, a shotted salute from a battery of six Napoleon guns was fired into the woods after the last of the retreating assailants. They were the last shots of the battle of Chickamauga, and what was left of the Union Army was master of the field. For the time the enemy evidently regarded himself as repulsed; and Garfield said that night, and has always since maintained, that there was no necessity for the immediate retreat on Rossville.

SERVICE IN CONGRESS.

Practically this was the close of General Garfield's military career. A year before, while he was absent in the army, and without any solicitation on his part, he had been elected to Congress from the old Giddings district, in which he resided. He was now, after a few weeks' service with Rosecrans at Chattanooga, sent on to Washington as the bearer of dispatches. He there learned of his promotion to a major-generalship of volunteers, "for gallant and meritorious conduct at the battle of Chickamauga." He might have retained this position in the army; and the military capacity he had displayed, the high favor in which he was held by the government, and the certainty of his assignment to important commands, seemed to augur a brilliant future. He was a poor man, too, and the major-general's salary was more than double that of the Congressman. But on mature reflection he decided that the circumstances un

THE ASSASSINATION OF

der which the people had elected him to Congress bound him up to an effort to obey their wishes. He was furthermore urged to enter Congress by the officers of the army, who looked to him for aid in procuring such military legislation as the country and the army required. Under the belief that the path of usefulness to the country lay in the direction in which his constituents pointed, he sacrificed what seemed to be his personal interests, and on the 5th of December, 1863, resigned his commission, after nearly three years' service.

General Garfield continued his military service up to the day of the meeting of Congress. Even then he seriously thought of resigning his position as a Representative rather than his major-general's commission, and would have done so had not Lincoln urged him to enter Congress. He has often expressed regret that he did not fight the war through. Had he done so he would no doubt have ranked at its close among the foremost of the victorious generals of the Republic, for he displayed in his Sandy Valley campaign and at the battle of Chickamauga the highest qualities of generalship. A brilliant opening awaited him in the Army of the Cumberland. General Thomas wanted him to take command of a corps. President Lincoln told him he greatly needed the influence in the House of one who had had practical military experience to push through the needed war legislation. He yielded, and on the 5th of December, 1863, gave up his generalship and took his seat in the House.

He was appointed on the Military Committee, under the chairmanship of General Schenck, and was of great service in carrying through the measures which recruited the armies during the closing years of the war.

In the summer of 1864 a breach occurred between the President and some of the most radical of the Republican orders in Congress over the question of the reconstruction of the States of Arkansas and Louisiana. Congress passed a bill providing for the organization of loyal governments within the Union lines of these States, but Lincoln vetoed it and appointed military governors. Senator Ben Wade, of Ohio, and Representative Henry Winter Davis, of Maryland, united in a letter to the New York *Tribune*, sharply criticising the President for defeating the will of Congress. This letter became known as the Wade-Davis manifesto, and created a great sensation in political circles. The story got about in the XIXth District that General Garfield had expressed sympathy with the position of Wade and Davis. His constituents condemned the document, and were strongly disposed to set him aside and nominate another man for Congress. When the convention met the feeling against Garfield was so pronounced that he regarded his renomination as hopeless. He was called upon to explain his course. He went upon the platform, and everybody expected something in the nature of an apology, but he boldly defended his position, approved the manifesto, justified Wade, and said he had nothing to retract and could not change his honest convictions for the sake of a seat in Congress. He had great respect, he said, for the opinions of his constituents, but greater regard for his own. If he could serve them as an independent representative, acting on his own judgment and conscience, he would be glad to do so, but if not, he did not want their nomination ; he would prefer to be an independent private citizen. Probably no man ever talked in that way before or since to a body of men who held his political fate in their hands. Leaving the platform, he strode out of the hall and down the stairs, supposing that he had effectually cut his own throat. Scarcely had he disappeared when one of the youngest delegates sprang up and said : "The man who has the courage to face a convention like that deserves a nomination. I move that General Garfield be nominated by acclamation." The motion was carried with a shout that reached the ears of the Congressman and arrested him on the sidewalk as he was returning to the hotel. He was re-elected by a majority of over 12,000.

At the beginning of the XXXIXth Congress, in December, 1865, General Garfield asked Speaker Colfax to transfer him from the Committee on Military Affairs to that of Ways and Means, saying that in the near future financial questions would occupy the attention of the country, and he desired to be in a position to study them carefully in advance. The Military Committee, having on its hands the work of reorganizing the regular army on a peace basis, was the more important of the two at the time, but Garfield foresaw the storm of agitation and delusion concerning the debt and the currency which was soon to break upon the country, and wisely prepared to meet it. He began a long and severe course of study, ransacking the Congressional Library for works that threw light on the experience of other countries, and that gave the ideas of the thinkers and statesmen of all nations on these subjects. His membership of

18*

the Ways and Means also opened up a line of congenial work in connection with the tariff and the system of internal revenue taxation.   These two sources of income, gauged to the needs of the war, had to be changed to conform to the conditions of peace.   In the course of this work and of the investigations which accompanied it, he reached a conclusion upon the tariff question from which he never departed—namely, that whatever may be the truth or falsity of abstract theories about free trade, the interests of the United States require a moderate protective system.   In March, 1866, he made his first speech on the currency question, and took strong ground in favor of a speedy return to specie payments.

In the summer of 1867 General Garfield went to Europe, and made a rapid tour through Great Britain and the Continent. His health failed under the pressure of too much brain-work, and he took this means of recuperating.   This was the only year since he entered public life that he had been absent from a political campaign.   He returned late in the fall to find that Pendletonism—a demand for the payment of the bonded debt in irredeemable greenback notes—had run rampant in Ohio, and had taken possession of the Republican party as well as of the Democracy.   A reception was given him at Jefferson, in his district, which assumed the form of a public meeting.   He was told that he had better say nothing about his financial views, for his constituents had made up their minds that the bonds ought to be redeemed in greenbacks.   He made a speech in which he told his friends plainly that they were deluded, that there could be no honest money not redeemable in coin, and no honest payment of the debt could be made save in coin, and that as long as he was their representative he should stand on that ground, whatever might be their views.   The speech produced a deep impression throughout the district.   The next June the National Republican Convention took sound ground upon the debt and currency questions, and most Republicans who had been carried away by Pendletonism grew ashamed of their folly.

A LEADER IN FINANCE.

In the XLth Congress General Garfield was put back upon the Military Committee and made its chairman.   In 1868 he was renominated without opposition, and chosen a fourth time to represent his district.   On the organization of the XLIst

Congress, in December, 1869, General Garfield was made chairman of the Committee on Banking and Currency. The inflation movement was rapidly gathering force in the country, and men of both parties in Congress were swept into it by fear of their constituents. A cry was set up that times were getting hard because there was not money enough to do the business of the people. The West, particularly, clamored for more currency. General Garfield led the opposition to inflation. Finally, after a long fight in his committee with the men who wanted to throw out a flood of new greenbacks, he brought in and carried through Congress a bill allowing an addition of $54,000,000 to the national-bank circulation, and giving preference in the assignment of the new issue to the States which had less than their quota of the old circulation. This measure was a stunning blow to the inflation movement. The new issue was not all taken up for four years, and during all that time it was a sufficient answer to all demands for " more money " to call attention to the fact that there was currency waiting in the Treasury for any one who would organize a bank. Soon after the $54,000,000 was applied for national banking was made perfectly free. The New York gold panic came during General Garfield's chairmanship of the Banking Committee. Under orders of the House, he conducted with great sagacity and thoroughness an investigation which exposed all the secrets of the gold gamblers' plot which culminated in " Black Friday." He made a report which was a complete history of the affair, and the lesson he drew from it was that the only certain remedy against the recurrence of such transactions was to be found in the resumption of specie payments. He became the recognized leader of the honest-money party in the House and the most potent single factor in the opposition to inflation. He helped work up the bill to strengthen the public credit, which failed to get through during the closing days of Johnson's Administration, but was passed as soon as Grant came in, and was the first measure to which the new President put his signature. This bill committed Congress fully to the payment of the public debt in coin, and was the fortress around which the financial battle raged in subsequent years.

In December, 1871, General Garfield was placed at the head of the important Committee on Appropriations, a position which made him the leader of the majority side of the House. With his old habit of doing everything he undertook with the utmost thoroughness, he made a laborious study of the whole history of appropriation bills in this country and of the English budget system. He found a great deal of looseness and confusion in the practice concerning estimates and appropriations. Unexpended balances were lying in the Treasury, amounting to $130,000,000, beyond the supervision of Congress and subject to the drafts of government officers. There were besides what were called permanent appropriations, which ran on from year to year without any legislation. Garfield instituted a sweeping reform. He got laws passed covering all old balances back into the Treasury, making all appropriations expire at the end of the fiscal year for which made, unless needed to carry out contracts, and covering in all appropriations at the end of every second year. At the same time he required the Executive Departments to itemize their estimates of the money needed to run the Government much more fully than had been done before, so that Congress could know just how every dollar it voted was to be expended. The four years of his chairmanship of Appropriations were years of close and unremitting labor. He worked habitually fifteen hours a day. In addition to the demands of his own department of legislation, he took part in all the general work of the House, bore a leading part in all the debates involving the principles of the Republican party, fought without cessation a brave battle against inflation and repudiation, and omitted no opportunity to aid in educating the public mind to a comprehension of the importance of returning to specie payments.

Five times had General Garfield been chosen to represent the old Giddings district without serious opposition in his own party, and without a breath of suspicion being cast upon his personal integrity. With one exception, all his nominations had been made by acclamation. In his sixth canvass, however, a storm of calumny broke upon him. A concerted attack was made upon him for the purpose, if possible, of defeating him in the convention, and failing in that, to beat him at the polls. He was charged with bribery and corruption in connection with the Credit Mobilier affair and the De Golyer pavement contract, and with responsibility for the Salary Grab. His people, however, resented the slanders, and in the convention he was nominated by a majority of three to one. The opposition to him did not bring forward a candidate, but merely cast blank votes. His enemies then nominated a second Republican candidate. General Garfield met the charges against him before the jury of his constituents. He visited all parts of the district, speaking day and night at township meetings. The verdict of the election was a complete vindication of his character and actions, and in 1876 and 1878 his constituents nominated him by acclamation and elected him by increased majorities.

HEADING THE MINORITY.

The result of the elections of 1874 was to give the Democrats control of the House which met in December, 1875. Hitherto the legislative work of General Garfield had been constructive. Now he was called upon to defend this work against the assaults of the party which step by step had opposed its accomplishment, and which by the aid of the solid support of the late rebel element had gained power in Congress. One of the first movements of the Democrats was for universal amnesty. Mr. Blaine offered an amendment to their bill, excluding Jefferson Davis. Then followed the famous debate about the treatment of prisoners of war, opened by Blaine's dashing attack on Hill, continued by Hill's reply charging that Confederates had been starved in Northern prisons, and closing with Garfield's response to Hill. Garfield, by a brilliant stroke of parliamentary strategy, forced a Democrat to testify to the falsity of Hill's charge. He said that the Elmira, N. Y., district, where was located during the war the principal prison for captured rebels, was represented in the House by a Democrat. He did not know him, but he was willing to rest his case wholly on his testimony. He called upon the member from Elmira to inform the House whether the good people of his city had permitted the captured Confederate soldiers in their midst to suffer for want of food. The gentleman thus appealed to rose promptly and said that to his knowledge the prisoners had received exactly the same rations as the Union soldiers guarding them. While this statement was being made a telegraphic dispatch was handed to General Garfield. Holding it up, he said, "The lightnings of heaven are aiding me in this controversy." The dispatch was from General Elwell, of Cleveland, who had been the quartermaster at the Elmira Prison, and who telegraphed that the rations issued to the rebel prisoners were in quantity and quality exactly the same as those issued to their guards. Garfield's speech killed the Democrats' bill. They withdrew it rather than risk a vote. Mr. Blaine's transfer to the Senate soon after this debate left Garfield the recognized leader of the Republicans in the House. Mr. Kerr, the Democratic Speaker, died in the midst of his term, and in the election for his successor General Garfield received the unanimous Republican vote. Soon after, in August, 1876, came the dispute with Lamar. Lamar was the greatest orator the Democrats had, and was selected by them to make a key-note campaign speech. It was a sharp attack upon the Republican party, an appeal for sympathy for the " oppressed South," and an argument to show that peace and prosperity could come only through Democratic rule. General Garfield took notes of the speech. All his colleagues insisted that he alone was competent to break the force of Lamar's masterly effort. This speech is usually accounted the greatest of his life. It created a furor in the House. All business was suspended for ten minutes after he finished, so great was the excitement. One hundred thousand copies of the speech were subscribed for at once by members who wanted to circulate it in their districts, and during the campaign over a million copies were distributed. It contributed powerfully to the success of the Republican party in the Presidential campaign of that year.

After the election arose the dispute about the count of the votes of South Carolina, Florida, and Louisiana. President Grant telegraphed to General Garfield, under date of November 10, as follows : " I would be gratified if you would go to New Orleans and remain until the vote of Louisiana is counted. Governor Kellogg requests that reliable witnesses be sent to see that the canvass of the vote is a fair one.   U. S. GRANT."

Garfield went to Washington, consulted with the President, and then proceeded to New Orleans, in company with John Sherman, Stanley Matthews, and a number of other prominent Republicans. While on his way back to Washington, returning from New Orleans, he was again chosen by the unanimous vote of the Republicans of the House as their candidate for Speaker.

General Garfield opposed the Electoral Commission bill, but in spite of his opposition, when the bill passed he was selected as a member of the tribunal. The Republicans of the House were to have two members. They met in caucus, and were about to ballot, when Mr. McCreary, of Iowa, said that there was one name on which they were all agreed, and which need not be submitted to the formality of a vote—that of James A. Garfield. Garfield was chosen by acclamation. The second commissioner was George F. Hoar, of Massachusetts, who afterward presided over the Chicago Convention which nominated General Garfield for the Presidency. As a member of the Electoral Commission General Garfield delivered two opinions, in which he brought out with great clearness the point that the Constitution places in the hands of the legislatures of the States the power of determining how their electors shall be chosen, and that Congress had no right to go behind the final decision of a State. If there was nothing in the Constitution or laws of a State touching the matter, its legislature could appoint Electors, as Vermont had done after her admission to the Union.

Immediately after President Hayes's inauguration the Republicans in the Ohio Legislature desired to elect General Garfield to the United States Senate in place of John Sherman, who had resigned his seat to enter the Cabinet. Mr. Hayes made a personal appeal to him to decline to be a candidate and remain in the House to lead the Republicans in support of the Administration. General Garfield acceded, in the belief that his services would be of more value to the party in the House than in the Senate, and withdrew his name from the canvass, greatly to the disappointment of his friends in Ohio, who had already obtained pledges of the support of a large majority of the Republican members of the Legislature.

In the session of 1878 General Garfield led the long struggle in defence of the Resumption act, which was assailed by the Democrats with a vigor born of desperation. He also made a remarkable speech on the tariff question, in opposition to Wood's bill, which sought to break down the protective system. During the extra session of 1879, forced by the Democrats, for the purpose of bringing the issue of the repeal of the federal election laws prominently before the country, General Garfield led the Republican minority with consummate tact and judgment. The plan of the Democrats was to open the debate with a general attack on the Republican party in order to throw their adversaries upon the defensive as apologists for the course of their party. McMahon, of Ohio, was selected to make the opening speech. Garfield did not wait for him to make his

argument, but securing the floor ahead of him, delivered his famous " Revolution in Congress" speech, in which he attacked
the Democrats with such vigor and exposed with so much force
their scheme for withholding appropriations for the support of
the government, to compel the President to sign their political
measures, that they were thrown into confusion, and instead of
taking the offensive were obliged to resort to a weak defensive
campaign.   Driven from position to position by successive vetoes
and by the persistent assaults of the Republican minority, they
ended with a ridiculous fiasco.   Instead of refusing $45,000,000
of appropriations, as they threatened at the beginning, they
ended by appropriating $44,600,000 of the amount, leaving
only $400,000 unprovided for. The following winter the Demo-
crats recommenced the fight, but in a feeble, disheartened way.
They set out to refuse all pay to the United States marshals unless the President would let them wipe out the election laws.
General Garfield met them with a powerful speech on " Nullifi-
cation in Congress," in which he showed that while it was
clearly the foremost duty of the law-makers in Congress to
obey the Democrats had become leaders in an attempt to dis-
obey them and break them down.   General Garfield's last
work in Congress was a report on the Tucker Tariff bill.   In January, 1880, General Garfield was chosen to the Senate by the
Legislature of Ohio for the term of six years, beginning March
4, 1881.   He received the unanimous vote of the Republican
caucus, an honor never before conferred upon a citizen of Ohio
by any party.

HIS NOMINATION AS PRESIDENT.

Gen. Garfield appeared in the Republican National Convention at Chicago in June, 1880, at the head of the Ohio
delegation and as the leading supporter of Secretary Sherman
for the candidacy.   It was evident from the first that he was
one of the most popular men in the assemblage with the lookers-
on and visitors.   He was put upon the Committee on Rules and
Orders of Business and was made its Chairman.   This committee was important on account of the controversy regarding
what was known as the unit rule.   The report which was submitted and advocated by him abrogated that rule, but Gen.
Garfield appeared as a conciliator between the extremes of
opinion throughout.   He desired the withdrawal of Mr. Conk-

ling's resolution which proposed virtually to expel the West Virginia delegates who voted against his previous resolution that all members of the Convention would be in duty bound to support the nominee of the Convention, whoever he might be, and that no man should retain his seat in the Convention unless he was ready to do so. In his appeal in this case he said he regretted the action of the West Virginia delegates, but thought their explanation should be accepted. He would never himself vote in any convention against his judgment. In advocating the report of the Committee on Rules, he said that if the unit rule was adopted by the Convention he would stand by it, but he preferred a rule which would allow individual liberty, because it would be everlastingly right. When the time came in the protracted proceedings for naming candidates, Gen. Garfield urged the claims of Mr. Sherman in an eloquent speech, which drew the character of an ideal statesman, intended to apply to his candidate, but generally accepted as more nearly a portrait of himself or at least of what he thought a public man ought to be. In the voting a single Pennsylvania delegate began on the third ballot to cast his vote for Garfield. It was sometimes reinforced by one other, but only 2 votes were cast for him prior to the thirty-fourth ballot, when to the one from Pennsylvania were added 16 from Wisconsin. Gen. Garfield arose and questioned the correctness of the vote, declaring that his name was not before the Convention and no one had a right to vote for him without his consent. The Chairman ruled that this was not a point of order, and on the next ballot, Indiana added 27, Maryland, 4, and Mississippi and North Carolina, 1 each to the 17 previously given to him, making 50 in all. On the next and last ballot came the stampede which gave him the majority, and his unanimous nomination was then moved by Mr. Conkling, who expressed the hope that the same zeal, fervor, and unanimity that was shown in the Convention would be transplanted to the field, and that "all of us who have borne a part against each other here will find ourselves with equal zeal bearing the banner and carrying the lance of the Republican party into the ranks of the enemy." The motion was seconded by Messrs. Logan, Beaver. and Hale, on behalf of the supporters of those who had been the leading candidates before the Convention. Gen. Garfield was officially informed of his nomination in Chicago on the night of June 9, by Senator Hoar,

Chairman of the Convention, and accepted it in a brief speech, in which he laid special stress on his sense of the " very heavy responsibility" involved. Congratulations came in from all quarters, one of the first coming from President Hayes. While the nomination was disappointing to those who had with so much zeal urged the claims of others, it was generally accepted as that most likely to bring all elements of the party into harmony.

AS A CANDIDATE.

Gen. Garfield was greeted with enthusiasm on his return home from the Convention and during his subsequent visit to Washington, which occupied the latter part of June. The canvass opened with the meeting of the Republican National Committee on the 1st of July. On the 4th the candidate delivered a touching address at the dedication of a soldiers' monument at Painesville, Ohio. His letter of acceptance dated July 10, was made public on the 13th. In some respects it caused disappointment, and it was in this document that he gave expression to the opinion that the President should consult members of Congress regarding the qualifications of persons to be appointed to office. On the 6th of August a conference of Republican leaders was held, and Gen. Garfield was present. The candidate returned to his home shortly after the conference, in which he took no formal part, although he privately met the leading managers and workers of the party. On the 25th of August he attended a reunion of his old regiment at Cleveland, delivering one of those happy addresses which on such occasions came so easy to him. Aside from attending the Northern Ohio Fair at Cleveland, on the 9th of September, he spent most of the remaining interval before the election at his home in Mentor, receiving many visitors, singly or in delegations, and being overwhelmed with correspondence. A noteworthy incident was the visit of Gen. Grant and Mr. Conkling on the 29th of September, the former having presided and the latter spoken at a grand rally at Warren on the previous day. It has been said that Mr. Conkling's activity in the campaign began after that interview, but his speech at the Academy of Music, in New York, was delivered on the 17th, and in the interval he had been quite active in Indiana and Ohio. The candidate exhibited a constant desire to promote harmony and a cordial co-operation among all the leaders of the party. He appeared anxious that his nomination should heal all differences. Late in October he was annoyed by the forged " Chinese letter," which he promptly denounced in a letter to Chairman Jewell, of the National Committee, on the 23d of that month.

AFTER THE ELECTION.

After the election in November he continued to reside as before at Mentor, visited by politicians and others, though the last week of that month was occupied with a visit to Washington on private business. While at the capital he received many attentions, among them those of a delegation of civil service reformers, who delivered to him a paper setting forth their views of his coming duty in making appointments. In his reply he expressed the hope that he should have the co-operation of Congress in establishing all routine appointments on a secure basis, so that no removals could be made without cause. Before he left Washington there seemed to be an understanding that Mr. Blaine was to have the first place in his Cabinet, and that Secretary Sherman preferred not to continue in his position. From that time on to March there was constant speculation as to the formation of the Cabinet. Mentor was constantly visited by advising politicians, seekers for office, and seekers for information. Many of the leading men of the Republican party went there on invitation of the President-elect, who seemed to be anxious to obtain their counsel and to satisfy their views, so far as they could be reconciled with each other. His chief thought appeared to be for harmony in the party and a successful administration resting on its united support. Among those summoned to his home to consult with him were Mr. Sherman, Mr. Blaine, Mr. Conkling, Judge Folger, and others. Gen. Garfield took leave of his friends and neighbors on the last day of February and set out for the arduous position that awaited him with an evident feeling of solemnity and sadness. He arrived in Washington on the 1st of March, and speculation continued regarding his Cabinet, but he kept his own counsel, so far as the public was concerned, until after the inauguration.

AS PRESIDENT.

The President was inaugurated with an unwonted amount of display and amid general rejoicing and good wishes. His inaugural address was regarded as foreshadowing a firm and vigorous administration, a conscientious regard for the best interests of all sections, and a determination to promote harmony and good-will. On the day following the inauguration the Cabinet was announced and gave general satisfaction. There has been little to test the quality of the President except the incidents springing from the exercise of the appointing power. Since he took office there had been no session of Congress for legislation. The Senate was in session until the 20th of May, but its time was chiefly occupied in wrangling over the election of its officers. The question of calling an extra session was wisely decided in the negative, the plea for extending the maturing bonds of the government at a lower rate of interest having been hit upon. In exercising the appointing power the President did not uniformly satisfy his sincerest friends. The renewal of the nomination of Stanley Matthews for the Supreme Bench was deeply regretted by many of these, and attributed to some understanding with President Hayes. The chief incident of political interest had been the break with Mr. Conkling which had occupied much attention. On the 22d of March the President sent a number of nominations for office to the Senate, including those for District Attorneys and Marshals in this State and for the Collectorship at Buffalo. These were presumed to be in all respects acceptable to the Senators of New York. On the following day several other nominations were sent in, including those of William H. Robertson for Collector of New York, Edwin A. Merritt for Consul-General at London, and William E. Chandler for Solicitor-General. It was known that Mr. Robertson's appointment would be displeasing to Senator Conkling, but the President was quoted as declaring that he regarded the office as one of national and not local rank, and that he had no wish or intention to slight the New York Senators. Owing to the dead-lock in the Senate over the election of its officers, no executive sessions were held until May 4. It then appeared that Senator Conkling was determined to antagonize to the utmost the appointment of Mr. Robertson, on the ground that he had a right to be consulted and that no appointment displeasing to him should have been made. On the 5th of May the President withdrew all the other New York nominations with the evident purpose of compelling a separate consideration of that for the New York Collectorship. It soon became apparent that this could not be defeated by the New York Senators, and on the 16th of May they both resigned. Mr. Robertson was shortly after confirmed, the other nominations were renewed, except that changes were made in the Marshalship of this district and the Collectorship of Buffalo, and the political fight was transferred to Albany, where the President has had no part in it. Further than this the administration and the recent life of the President has been uneventful, though his sympathy with, and support for, those engaged in exposing and punishing the Star Route frauds should be recognized.

Upon those who ever saw him, President Garfield made a commanding impression, his height being six feet, his shoulders broad, and his frame strong. The head appeared unusually large and the forehead remarkably high. Blue was seen to be the color of the eyes and light brown that of the hair. In all things he has been temperate.

HIS HOME AND FAMILY LIFE.

The first years of General Garfield's married life were passed in Hiram, boarding with families of friends, and it was not until he went to the war that he saved money enough to buy a home. In 1862 he purchased a small frame cottage facing the college green, paying for it $800. About $1000 more was spent in enlarging it by a wing and fitting it up. The rooms were small and the ceilings low, as was the fashion in village houses of moderate pretensions, but the young housewife soon made the place cosy and homelike. This was the only home of the family for many years. While in Washington they lived in apartments. The lack of a settled home at the Capital, where the children could grow up amid wholesome influences, was seriously felt early in General Garfield's Congressional career, but it was not until he had been three times elected that he began to regard that career as likely to continue for an indefinite period, and sought the means of escaping from the disagreeable features of hotel and boarding-house life. He bought a lot on the corner of Thirteenth and I streets, facing Franklin Square, and with money loaned him by an old army friend put up a plain, square, substantial brick house, big enough to hold his family and two or three guests. As the boys grew older, however, and needed more range for their activities than a city house could afford, the desire to own a farm which he had always felt increased upon him. When he had paid off the mortgage on his house and had a little money ahead, he thought he could safely gratify his desire, and after a good deal of thought about localities, decided to settle in the vicinity of the Lake Shore Railroad on one of the handsome productive ridges that run parallel to Lake Erie. A farm of 160 acres was bought in the town of Mentor, Lake County, a mile from a railway and telegraph station, and half a mile from a post-office. The buildings consisted of a tumble-down barn and an ancient farm-house a story and a half high; but the land was fertile, the summer climate, tempered by breezes from the neighboring lake, was delightful, and the people in the vicinity were of the best class of farmers to be found in Ohio. Here the General revived all the farming skill of his boyhood days, holding the plough or loading the hay wagon or driving the ox team. Drainage, fencing, and other improvements absorbed all the money the place brought in, and the time spent upon it was highly enjoyed by all the members of the household, and every winter they looked forward to the adjournment of Congress and their release from Washington with pleasant anticipations.

General Garfield has had seven children, and five are living. The oldest, Mary, died when he was in the army, and the youngest, Edward, died in Washington about four years ago. Of the surviving children, the oldest, Harry, is fifteen; after him come James, Molly, Irwin (named after General McDowell) and Abram. Harry and James are preparing for college at St. Paul's school, in Concord, New Hampshire. Harry is the musician of the family and plays the piano well. James, who more resembles his father, is the mathematician. Molly, a handsome girl of thirteen, is ruddy, sweet-tempered, vivacious, and blessed with perfect health. The younger boys are still in the period of boisterous animal life. All the children have quick brains and are strongly individualized. All learned to read young except Abe, who, hearing that his father had years ago said, in a lecture on education, that no child of his should be forced to read until he was seven years old, took refuge behind the parental theory and declined to learn his letters until he had reached that age.

The manner of life in the Garfield household, whether in Washington or on the Mentor farm, was simple and quiet. The long table was bountifully supplied with plainly-cooked food,

THE HOME OF JAMES A. GARFIELD AT MENTOR, OHIO.

and there was always room for any guest who might drop in at meal-time. No alcoholic drinks were used. There was no effort at following fashions in furniture or table service. No carriage was kept in Washington, but on the farm there were vehicles of various sorts and two teams of stout horses. Comfort, neatness, and order prevailed, without the least attempt at keeping up with styles of dress and living, or any desire to sacrifice the healthful regularity of household customs, adopted before the General won fame and position, to the artificial usages of what is called good society.

Of study in the ancient languages and in history, in spite of a most active life, he has been extremely fond, and the house in Washington is stored with a handsome collection of books. In classical scholarship, it is doubtful if there have been many men in public life in his time who could have equalled him if put to the test.

THE NEW PRESIDENT.

SKETCH OF THE LIFE OF CHESTER ALAN ARTHUR.

CHESTER ALAN ARTHUR, the son of an Irishman named William Arthur, was born in Fairfield, Vt., on the 5th of October, 1830. After the customary New England schooling he entered Union College, in Schenectady, in 1845, and was graduated high up on the list four years later. Like his predecessor, Mr. Arthur supported himself while in college, and served his apprenticeship in the humble enclosure of a country school-house. After two years in a law school and a brief service as principal of the North Pownal Academy, in Vermont, Mr. Arthur came to New York and entered the law firm of Culver, Paisten & Arthur, after which, and until 1865, he was associated here with Mr. Henry D. Gardner. The law career of Mr. Arthur includes some notable cases. One of his first cases was the celebrated Lemmon suit. In 1852 Jonathan and Juliet Lemmon, Virginia slaveholders, intending to emigrate to Texas, came to New York to await the sailing of a steamer, bringing eight slaves with them. A writ of habeas corpus was obtained from Judge Paine to test the question whether the provisions of the Fugitive Slave Law were in force in that State. Judge Paine rendered a decision holding that they were not, and ordering the Lemmon slaves to be liberated. Henry L. Clinton was one of the counsel for the slaveholders. A howl of rage went up from the South, and the Virginia Legislature authorized the Attorney-General of that State to assist in taking an appeal. William M. Evarts and Chester A. Arthur were employed to represent the people, and they won their case, which then went to the Supreme Court of the United States. Charles O'Conor here espoused the cause of the slaveholders, but he, too, was beaten by Messrs. Evarts and Arthur, and a long step was taken towards the emancipation of the black race. Following this came the street car discourtesies, which Mr. Arthur put a stop to in a legal and definitive way. On the Sixth Avenue and one or two other lines,

CHESTER A. ARTHUR.

conveyances labelled " Colored persons allowed in this car" were run at long intervals, but on the Fourth Avenue and other east side lines not even this provision was made. Under these circumstances Lizzie Jennings, a respectable colored woman, neatly dressed, cleanly and of good appearance, the superintendent of a colored Sunday-school, hailed a Fourth Avenue car and succeeded in obtaining a seat in it. The conductor took her fare, thereby tacitly admitting her right to be a passenger, but hardly had he done so when a drunken white ruffian, who was seated in the car, demanded, " Are you going to let that —— —— nigger ride in this car ?"

" Oh, I guess it won't make any difference," said the conductor.

" Yes, but it will," replied the other; " I have paid my fare and I want a decent ride, and I tell you you've got to put her out."

Thus appealed to the conductor went to the colored woman and asked her to leave the car. She refused to do so. The car was stopped. The conductor attempted to eject her by force. She resisted bravely, crying all the time, " I have paid my fare and I am entitled to ride."

Her dress was almost torn from her back. Strong men stood by but gave her no assistance. Still she fought bravely for what she believed to be her right. The conductor could not eject her, and was compelled to call for the aid of the police. By their efforts the woman was dragged from the car.

The matter coming to the notice of a number of influential colored people they desired to make it a test case, and applied to Mr. Arthur for advice. He at once espoused their cause and took their case before Justice Rockwell, in Brooklyn. When the trial came on the court room was crowded almost to suffocation, and at one time serious trouble was threatened by those who believed that to seek justice for one of the black race was to do injustice to humanity.

Even the Judge seemed to share this opinion, for when the attorney handed him the papers in the case he threw them upon the desk, with the exclamation,

" Pshaw ! do you ask me to try a case against a corporation for the tort [the wrongful act] of its agent ?"

In reply to this Mr. Arthur plainly pointed out a portion of the Revised Statutes under which there was an undoubted right

19

of action. After examining it the Court concurred cordially
with the counsel, the case was tried, and, much to the delight
of the colored people, a verdict of $500 was rendered in favor
of the plaintiff.   The railroad company paid the judgment
without further contest, and at once issued orders that thereafter colored people be allowed to ride upon its cars.   Similar
action was soon after taken by all the city railroad companies.
At this there was great rejoicing among all the negroes in New
York, the Colored People's Legal Rights Association was established, and for many years afterward with much ceremony celebrated the anniversary of the trial which resulted as described.

ARTHUR IN THE WAR.

At the outbreak of the war Governor Morgan appointed Mr.
Arthur engineer-in-chief, then inspector-general, and in January,
1862, quartermaster-general.   No higher encomium can be
passed upon him than the mention of the fact that, although the
war account of the State of New York was at least ten times
larger than that of any other State, yet it was the first audited
and allowed in Washington, and without the deduction of a
single dollar, while the quartermasters' accounts from other
States were reduced from $1,000,000 to $10,000,000.   During
his incumbency every present sent to him was immediately returned.   Among others a prominent clothing house offered him
a magnificent uniform, and a printing house proffered a costly
saddle and trappings.   Both gifts were indignantly rejected.
When he became quartermaster he was poor.   When his term
expired he was poorer still.   He had opportunities to make millions unquestioned.   Contracts larger than the world had ever
seen were at his disposal.   He had to provide for the clothing,
arming and transportation of hundreds of thousands of men.
So jealous was he of his integrity that contracts where he could
have made thousands of dollars legitimately were refused, on the
ground that he was a public officer and meant to be, like Cæsar's
wife, above suspicion.   His own words in regard to this amply
illustrate his character: " If I misappropriated a cent and in
walking down town saw two men talking on the corner together
I would imagine that they were talking of my dishonesty, and
the very thought would drive me mad."   In July, 1862, he was
invited to be present at a secret meeting of the loyal governors,
held in New York, for discussing measures to provide troops to

carry on the war. He was the only person present who was not a governor, but his counsel and advice were none the less heeded on that account. Everything at that time was topsy-turvy and everybody upside down. One of the best illustrations of the lack of management, the haphazard fashion of transacting important State business, which prevailed during the early days of the war, is to be found in the manner in which the Ellsworth Zouaves were equipped and left New York. The regiment in question was made up of men who prided themselves upon their strength, drill and daring. It was, so to speak, an army unto itself, and under the independent system of organization already explained, comprised not only a full complement of infantry companies, but also a battery of light artillery and a troop of cavalry. All the infantry companies were not only armed differently, as they desired, but they contained, in some cases, 120 men, or fifty more than was, at the time, the regulation complement. So armed, about one thousand three hundred men in all, they were on their way down Broadway, after having received, amid great enthusiasm, a stand of colors, when orders were received through General Arthur from the War Department at Washington to the effect that the regiment could not be mustered into the service or leave the city until it had reduced and equalized its companies.

In pursuance of this command General Arthur, acting as quartermaster-general, issued instructions countermanding his original order for furnishing the troops with supplies while *en route* from New York to the South. The officers of the regiment, however, paid no attention to the order from Washington further than to beg General Wool, the United States commandant, to rescind it. To their petition was added that of many influential citizens and ladies. General Wool gave the necessary permission, the regiment marched on board the troop ship, and it steamed down the harbor.

Of this occurrence the Quartermaster-General was not informed for nearly an hour after the sailing of the ship; then an officer came into his headquarters and said casually,

" Well, the Firemen Zouaves have got off at last."

" Got off !" cried Arthur, in astonishment; " that's not possible. Orders have been received from Washington forbidding them to leave, and there is not a pound of provisions of any sort on the troop ship."

This was only too true. The regiment had actually put to sea without food sufficient for one man for a day. But the Quartermaster-General was equal to the emergency. In fifteen minutes he put himself in communication with an extensive contractor, made him an allowance of fifteen cents extra for each ration, and ordered him to hire every tug he could lay hands on, secure rations for 1300 men for five days, and hurry down the bay after the transport. This was done, and the troop ship, the officers of which had discovered the condition of their larder, having stopped on the way, was overtaken at the Narrows. The supplies were put on board and the same night the regiment was at last " off for the seat of war."

In the present days of peace and prosperity very few people realize that the city of New York in the spring of 1862 was threatened with total destruction. One Sunday morning during the period in question General Gustavus Loomis, who was then the oldest infantry officer in the United States regular service, flushed and out of breath, hurried into the Inspector-General's office, then occupied by Chester A. Arthur. For a moment he was unable to speak, and Arthur, offering him a chair, asked :

" What in the world has happened, General ?"

" The rebel ram Merrimac ! the rebel ram Merrimac !" incoherently gasped the other.

" Well, what about her ?"

" I have a dispatch from General McClellan that she has sunk two United States ships—that she is coming to New York to shell the city—may be expected at any moment—I am so out of breath running to tell you the news I can hardly speak."

" Running to tell me the news !" exclaimed Arthur. " Why in heaven didn't you hire a carriage ?"

" Hire a carriage !" replied the old army officer, lifting his hands in amazement; " hire a carriage ! why, that would cost me $2.50. I can't afford to spend so much out of my own pocket, and if I made such an expenditure on account of the government it would take all the rest of my official life to explain why I did so."

There was very much more truth than poetry in the latter part of General Loomis's remark. In those early days of the war it is a matter of record that an expenditure of $2.50 by an army officer for an irregular purpose, of no matter what character, and involving no matter what momentous results, would have furnished months of employment to half a dozen clerks in the War Department.

The State officers were not so bound by red tape, and when, in addition to his first communication, General Loomis informed General Arthur that McClellan had ordered him to place his shore batteries in position, and send vessels to the Lower Bay to watch for the appearance of the enemy, the latter lost no time in sending dozens of messengers in carriages in all directions to see that the order was carried out.

Unfortunately, however, prompt action on the part of the Inspector-General availed but little, for it was soon discovered that New York, for all practical purposes, was absolutely defenceless against such a naval monster as the Merrimac. The "shore batteries" spoken of by General McClellan in his dispatch did not exist. There were no heavy cannon in position on the so-called fortifications, and nearly all the cannon in the defences at the Narrows were marked " Shell guns," indicating that they could not be used to throw solid shot, and, as Loomis assured the Inspector-General, even for these guns there were not two rounds of powder in the harbor magazines. To remedy this alarming condition of things General Arthur set to work with every possible energy. All the available militia companies were put into the harbor forts, and a powder schooner arriving providentially from Connecticut, ample ammunition was soon served out. Luckily, as the event proved, all these precautions were unnecessary, for a few hours after the arrival of the first alarming news—news which never reached the general public, which on that bright spring Sunday was represented by crowds of well-dressed people on the principal avenues—General Arthur received a dispatch from General McClellan telling him that the Merrimac had been sunk by the Monitor, and that the danger to New York was passed.

At the end of Governor Morgan's term General Arthur returned to his law practice, and lucrative business soon poured in. Much of this work consisted in the collection of war claims and the drafting of important bills for speedy legislation. He was also counsel to the Tax Commission, with a salary of $10,000. In 1871 he formed the firm of Arthur, Phelps, Knevals & Ransom.

IN POLITICS.

It was in the year 1856 that Mr. Arthur began to be prominent in politics in New York City. He sympathized with the Whig party, and was an ardent admirer of Henry Clay. His first vote was cast in 1852 for Winfield Scott for President. In New York City Arthur identified himself with the " practical men" in politics by joining political associations of his party, and at the polls acting as inspector on election day. The inspectors were then elected each year, and prominent citizens were willing to serve.

General Arthur was a delegate to the convention at Saratoga that founded the Republican party. During these political labors he became acquainted with Edwin D. Morgan and gained his ardent friendship. Governor Morgan, when re-elected in 1860, testified to his high esteem of Arthur by making him Engineer-in-Chief on his staff. Mr. Arthur had for several years previously taken a great interest in the militia organization of the State, and had been appointed Judge-Advocate-General of the Second Brigade. In this position he was associated with many men who afterward took part in the war of the Rebellion and held high positions. Brigadier-General Yates, who commanded the Second Brigade, was a very thorough disciplinarian, and for several years required all the brigade and staff officers to meet every week for instruction. In this manner they became very proficient in military tactics on regulations, and the instruction proved to be of inestimable advantage to General Arthur in the responsible duties to which he was afterward called. In 1861 he was advanced to the position of Quartermaster-General, which he held until the expiration of Morgan's term of office.

INSPECTOR-GENERAL.

In February, 1862, Arthur was appointed Inspector-General, there being duty to perform with the armies in the field. In May, 1862, he went to Fredericksburg and inspected the New York troops under the command of General McDowell. He then went to the Army of the Potomac, lying near Chickahominy, and there carefully inspected the New York troops. In June of the same year the affairs of the country looked desperate. There had been defeats, regiments were getting thinned out, and it was evident a great levy would have to be made. Governor Morgan telegraphed General Arthur to return to New York. He did so, and was immediately requested to act as secretary at a secret meeting of the governors of loyal States, held at the Astor House on June 28, 1862. At this meeting President Lincoln was requested by the governors to call for more men. President Lincoln, on July 1, issued a proclamation thanking the governors for their patriotism and calling for 300,000 volunteers and 300,000 militia for nine months' service. Private knowledge that such a call was to be issued would have enabled contractors to have made millions. The secret was kept by all, however, till the proclamation was issued. The quota of New York under the call for 300,000 volunteers was 59,705. It was desired that these sixty regiments should be recruited and got to the seat of war at the earliest possible moment. In view of the fact that the greater part of the labor would fall upon the Quartermaster's Department, the request was made by Governor Morgan to Mr. Arthur that he should take his old post. He complied, and on July 7, 1862, again became Quartermaster-General and set energetically to work. He devised a new system for enlisting and caring for the troops, which was found to work very successfully. He established a camp in each one of the thirty-two senatorial districts of the State. The incoming of a Democratic State administration deprived him of his office in December, 1863.

COLLECTOR OF CUSTOMS.

Upon his retirement from office General Arthur resumed the active duties of his profession. His partnership with Mr. Gardner ceased only with that gentleman's death in 1866. Alone for over five years he carried on his law practice. It then became so large that he formed in 1871 the now well known firm of Arthur, Phelps, Knevals & Ransom. He became counsel to the Department of Taxes and Assessment, at a salary of $10,000 yearly, but abruptly resigned the position when the Tammany Hall officials at the head of the New York departments attempted to coerce the Republicans connected with those departments. Gradually he was drawn into political life again. He was very much interested in promoting the first election of President Grant, being chairman of the Central Grant Club of New York. He also served as chairman of the Executive Committee of the

Republican State Committee of New York. He re-entered official life on November 20, 1871, being appointed Collector of the Port of New York by President Grant. So satisfactory was his work that upon the close of his term of office in December, 1875, he was renominated by President Grant. The nomination was unanimously confirmed by the Senate without referring it to a committee—a compliment never given before except to ex-senators. He was removed by President Hayes on July 12, 1878, despite the fact that two special committees made searching investigation into his administration, and both reported themselves unable to find anything upon which to base a charge against him. In their pronunciamentos announcing the change, both President Hayes and Secretary Sherman bore official witness to the purity of his acts while in office. A petition for his retention was signed by every judge of every court in the city, by all the prominent members of the bar, and by nearly every importing merchant in the collection district, but this General Arthur himself suppressed.

VICE-PRESIDENT.

General Arthur then re-engaged in the practice of his profession as a partner in the law firm of Arthur, Phelps, Knevals & Ransom. In the fall of 1879 he was elected Chairman of the Republican State Committee, of which he had been a prominent member for many years before his appointment as Collector, and conducted the victorious campaign of that year, which ended in the election of all but one of the candidates of the Republican party for six State offices. In June, 1880, he was nominated for Vice-President by the National Republican Convention, held at Chicago; General Stewart L. Woodford proposed his name in the Convention, and the nomination was seconded by ex-Governor Dennison, of Ohio; General Kilpatrick, of New Jersey; Emery A. Storrs, of Illinois; John Cessna, of Pennsylvania; Chauncey L. Filley, of Missouri, and many others. He was elected in November and took the oath of office on the 4th of March last.

His bearing, as presiding officer of the Senate, produced a pronounced impression, and during the exciting scenes that followed the dignity of his manner and the fairness of his rulings won him the regard and admiration of the entire body. As a devoted friend of Senator Conkling General Arthur took great interest and an active part in the senatorial contest in Albany, and it was at the close of a peculiarly taxing week of work in his friend's interest that he was informed of the deplorable event that opened the door to his own promotion.

General Arthur was married in 1859 to Ellen Lewis Herndon, of Fredericksburg, Va. She was a daughter of Captain William Lewis Herndon, U. S. N., who in 1851–2 gained world-wide fame as commander of the naval expedition sent by the United States to explore the river Amazon. The heroic death of Captain Herndon, while in command of the United States mail steamship Central America, some twenty years ago, is still fresh in the memory of many, and was one of the noble deeds of which the American navy will always be proud. Mrs. Arthur died suddenly in the early part of January, 1880, leaving two children—Chester Alan Arthur, and Ellen Herndon Arthur.

On the death of the President the following telegram was sent to him, requesting him to take the oath of office as President:

"Long Branch, September 19, 12 a.m.

" *To Hon. Chester A. Arthur:*

"It becomes our painful duty to inform you of the death of President Garfield, and to advise you to take the oath of office as President of the United States without delay. If it concur with your judgment, we will be very glad if you will come here on the earliest train to-morrow morning.

"William Windom, Secretary of the Treasury,
"William H. Hunt, Secretary of the Navy,
"Thomas L. James, Postmaster-General,
"Wayne MacVeagh, Attorney-General,
"L. J. Kirkwood, Secretary of the Interior."

GENERAL ARTHUR'S REPLY.

The following response from General Arthur was received by Attorney-General MacVeagh in answer to the above dispatch announcing the death of the President:

"I have your telegram, and the intelligence fills me with profound sorrow. Express to Mrs. Garfield my deepest sympathy.
"C. A. Arthur."

In accordance with the desire of the Cabinet officers Vice-President Arthur took steps to be sworn in as President at once

19*

—and at 1 o'clock in the morning District-Attorney Rollins, Police Commissioner French and Mr. Elihu Root left President Arthur's residence in Lexington Avenue, New York, and proceeded up that street. At 2 o'clock Mr. Rollins and Mr. Root returned in a carriage in company with Judge John R. Brady. The gentlemen were at once admitted, and Colonel J. C. Reed, the private secretary of General Arthur, appeared shortly afterward.

About half an hour later Commissioner French arrived at the house with Judge Donohue.

THE OATH ADMINISTERED.

The entire party proceeded to General Arthur's front parlor, where the new President was found. Judge Brady greeted the General very warmly, and after a short conversation, the Judge took from a table near by a book containing the oath of fealty to the government, and administered it to the successor of General Garfield as follows :

"I do solemnly swear that I will faithfully execute the office of President of the United States; and will, to the best of my ability, preserve, protect and defend the Constitution of the United States."

OVERCOME BY EMOTION.

In the room at the time were Judge Donohue, Commissioner French, Elihu Root and Colonel Reed. The ceremony was simple, but not impressive. President Arthur's manly form towered above all, and he was evidently deeply affected. Several times he left the room, being unable to control his emotion. Judge Brady and Judge Donohue were also almost overcome by sympathy with both the deceased and living Presidents.

The room in which the new President took the oath of office is shelved with books. In the centre is a table, and the carpet is rich and dark. Paintings by old Italian masters, in Florentine frames, adorn the walls, and a bust of Henry Clay is in the corner, nearest one of the windows. The furniture is covered with white cretonne, and easy chairs and sofas abound.

Immediately after taking the oath President Arthur sank into one of the chairs in the room and buried his face in his hands. He was thoroughly overcome.

After a few minutes he arose and went up to the second floor, and the visitors departed at about 3 a.m.

THE INAUGURATION OF PRESIDENT ARTHUR AT WASHINGTON.

On the 22d day of September, at noon, there was a quiet and impressive scene in the Capitol, when President Arthur again took the oath of office and delivered a short inaugural address. The President had arisen at 7 o'clock in the morning, and after breakfast had received many callers. Among these were all the members of the Cabinet and several senators and representatives. The house in which the President is staying is near the Capitol and directly south of it. Only one street and the Capitol grounds lie between the dead Chief Magistrate and his living successor. The arrangements for the second taking of the oath had been very quietly made, and Sergeant-at-Arms Bright, of the Senate, had been directed to put in order the Vice-President's room, which is just in the rear of the Senate Chamber. Members of the Cabinet, senators, members of the House of Representatives, and a few other prominent persons had been invited to attend. A few minutes before 12 o'clock the President left Senator Jones's house, accompanied by ex-President Grant, Senator Jones, and several members of the Cabinet, and was taken in a carriage to the basement entrance of the Senate wing of the Capitol on the east side. The corridors leading to the foot of the private staircase reserved for the use of senators were deserted, having been cleared of all persons who had not been invited to witness the ceremony. The President and his companions proceeded to the Vice-President's room, and in a few minutes they were followed by others who had been invited. First came Secretary Windom and Secretary Lincoln and several members of the House. Secretary Blaine and Gen. Sherman in full uniform were then admitted. The next to come was ex-President Hayes, who was followed at 12.10 o'clock by Chief-Justice Waite, in his judicial robes, and Associate-Justices Harlan and Matthews. The Clerk of the Supreme Court brought in a small Bible, which he placed on a table in the centre of the room. Those who were present were standing in little groups silently awaiting the ceremony.

Very soon after his arrival, Chief-Justice Waite advanced to the side of the President, and the spectators formed in a circle around the table near which the President stood. The Chief-

Justice raised the Bible from the table, opened it, and passed it to the President, who placed his right hand upon the printed page. The Chief-Justice then slowly administered the oath, with his eyes upon the face of the President, who kissed the book and responded, "I will, so help me God." Near the President stood ex-President Grant, looking down, with his hands clasped behind him. At one side were Secretary Blaine and Justice Harlan, Attorney-General MacVeagh, and Secretary Lincoln. Facing the President, on his right was ex-President Hayes, and further away stood Senator John Sherman, with bowed head. On the other side were Senators Edmunds, Hale, Blair, Dawes, and Anthony, and Representatives Amos Townsend, McCook, Errett, Hiscock, and Thomas, ex-Senator Hamlin, Speaker Randall, and others. Speaker Sharpe and Col. George Bliss of New York, were also present.

As soon as the oath had been administered the Chief-Justice retired from the table and took a place in the circle of spectators. The President then drew from the inner pocket of his coat a roll of manuscript and read the following address:

For the fourth time in the history of the Republic its Chief Magistrate has been removed by death. All hearts are filled with grief and horror at the hideous crime which has darkened our land, and the memory of the murdered President, his protracted sufferings, his unyielding fortitude, the example and achievements of his life and the pathos of his death will forever illumine the pages of our history. For the fourth time the officer elected by the people and ordained by the Constitution to fill a vacancy so created is called to assume the Executive chair. The wisdom of our fathers, foreseeing even the most dire possibilities, made sure that the government should never be imperilled because of the uncertainty of human life. Men may die, but the fabric of our free institutions remains unshaken. No higher or more assuring proof could exist of the strength and permanence of popular government than the fact that, though the chosen of the people be struck down, his constitutional successor is peacefully installed without shock or strain, except the sorrow which mourns the bereavement. All the noble aspirations of my lamented predecessor which found expression in his life, the measure devised and suggested during his brief administration to correct abuses and enforce economy, to advance prosperity and promote the general welfare, to ensure domestic security and maintain friendly and honorable relations with the nations of the earth, will be garnered in the hearts of the people, and it will be my earnest endeavor to profit and to see that the nation shall profit by his example and experience. Prosperity blesses our country; our fiscal policy as fixed by law is well grounded and generally approved; no threatening issue mars our foreign intercourse, and the wisdom, integrity and thrift of our people may be trusted to continue undisturbed the present assured career of peace, tranquillity, and welfare. The gloom and anxiety which have enshrouded the country must make repose especially welcome now. No demand for speedy legislation has been heard; no adequate occasion is apparent for an unusual session of Congress. The Constitution defines the functions and powers of the Executive as clearly as those of either of the other two departments of the government, and he must answer for the just exercise of the discretion it permits and the performance of the duties it imposes. Summoned to these high duties and responsibilities, and profoundly conscious of their magnitude and gravity, I assume the trust imposed by the Constitution, relying for aid on Divine guidance and the virtue, patriotism, and intelligence of the American people.

At times his voice trembled, but his manner was dignified and impressive, and when he referred to the administration of his predecessor and his intention to profit by his example, he raised his eyes from the manuscript and spoke directly to his hearers. While he was reading many eyes were moistened with tears. The first to take the President by the hand after the ceremony and express sympathy and a wish that he might be successful was the Chief-Justice; the next was Secretary Blaine, and the third was ex-President Hayes. Ex-President Grant was one of the last. The remaining members of the Cabinet and the representatives came up in the order in which they had been standing. Then the two ex-Presidents quietly left the room and walked towards the rotunda. At first they had some difficulty in passing the guard, but as soon as they were recognized they were admitted. They then passed up to the catafalque, looked at the face of their unfortunate successor, and soon afterward departed from the Capitol.

A few minutes after the delivery of the President's address the room was closed to all except members of the Cabinet, who then held a conference with the President. At this conference a proclamation was prepared and signed by the President, designating a day of fasting, humiliation, and prayer throughout the country, in the following words:

By the President of the United States of America:

A PROCLAMATION.

Whereas, In his inscrutable wisdom it has pleased God to remove from us the illustrious head of the nation, James A. Garfield, late President of the United States, and,

Whereas, It is fitting that the deep grief which fills all hearts should manifest itself with one accord toward the throne of infinite grace, and that we should bow before the Almighty and seek from him that consolation in our affliction and that sanctification of our loss which he is able and willing to vouchsafe,

Now, therefore, in obedience to sacred duty, and in accordance with the desire of the people, I, Chester A. Arthur, President of the United States of America, do hereby appoint Monday next, the twenty-sixth day of September—on which day the remains of our honored and beloved dead will be consigned to their last resting-place on earth—to be observed throughout the United States as a day of humiliation and mourning; and I earnestly recommend all the people to assemble on that day in their respective places of divine worship, there to render alike their tribute of sorrowful submission to the will of Almighty God, and of reverence and love for the memory and character of our late Chief Magistrate. In witness whereof I have hereunto set my hand and caused the seal of the United States to be affixed.

Done at the city of Washington the 22d day of September, in the year of our Lord 1881, and of the independence of the United States the one hundred and sixth.

(Signed)   CHESTER A. ARTHUR.

[Seal.]   By the President.

JAMES G. BLAINE, *Secretary of State.*

ASSASSINATION OF LINCOLN.

THE shooting of President Garfield naturally recalls the assassination of President Abraham Lincoln. It will be interesting, therefore, to recite the scenes attending that event.

It was on the evening of Friday, April 14, 1865, that President and Mrs. Lincoln, with Miss Mary Harris and Major Rathbun, of Albany, son-in-law of Senator Harris, visited Ford's Theatre, at Washington, for the purpose of witnessing "The American Cousin," which was running at the theatre. The fact that this distinguished party was to be present at the performance had been duly announced in all the local papers, and the theatre was densely crowded. The Presidential party occupied a box on the second tier. The scene was a brilliant one, and all went merrily with the audience and actors alike until the close of the third act, when the sharp report of a pistol was heard, and an instant afterwards a man was seen to spring from the President's box to the stage, where, striking a tragic attitude and brandishing a long dagger in his right hand, he cried out, "*Sic semper tyrannis!*" and then, amid the bewilderment of the audience, rushed through the opposite side of the stage and made his escape from the rear of the theatre. The screams of Mrs. Lincoln told the audience but too plainly that the President had been shot. All present rose to their feet, and the excitement was of the wildest possible description. A rush was made to the President's box, where, on a hasty examination being made, it was found he was shot through the head. The President was quickly removed to a private house opposite the theatre, where, on further examination, his wound was pronounced to be mortal. This tragic occurrence of course immediately put a stop to the performance and the theatre was closed as quickly as possible. The assassin, in his hurried flight, dropped his hat and a spur on the stage. The hat was identified as belonging to J. Wilkes Booth, a prominent actor, and the spur was recognized as one obtained by him at a stable on that day. One or two of the actors and members of the orchestra declared that the assassin was no other than Wilkes Booth, and the evidence almost momentarily accumulating fixed him beyond a doubt as the author of the bloody tragedy. Almost before the audience had left the theatre it was known that the assassin, after he got out, made his escape on horseback.

SECRETARY SEWARD'S ESCAPE.

The news of this hideous tragedy spread like wildfire, and the greatest excitement prevailed throughout the city, dense throngs of persons congregating in the locality of the house where President Lincoln was lying. While the general excitement was at its wildest height, it became known that an attempt had been made to assassinate Mr. Seward, Secretary of State. At about ten o'clock a man called at the Secretary's house, stating that he had been sent by the family physician with a prescription for the Secretary, who was sick, at the same time stating that he must see him personally, as he was instructed to give particular directions concerning the medicine. He pushed his way past the servant, who had told him Secretary Seward could not be seen, and rushed up stairs to Mr. Seward's room, where he was met by the Secretary's son, Mr. Fred Seward, who said he would take charge of the medicine. The man dealt him a heavy blow, and, rushing past him into Secretary Seward's room, sprung upon the Secretary as he lay in bed and stabbed him several times in the neck and breast. Major Seward, another of the Secretary's sons, rushed to his father's assistance and got badly cut in a tussle with the ruffian, who after a hard struggle managed to escape from the house, and mounting his horse he had left at the door, galloped off, shouting out, " *Sic semper tyrannis.*" Surgeon-General Barnes was immediately sent for, and pronounced the Secretary's and Major Seward's wounds not fatal, but the injuries which the desperado had inflicted on Frederick Seward and the servant of the house were considered more serious. When it was known that Secretary Seward was not dangerously wounded the general anxiety was centred on President Lincoln, and while the scene in the streets was one of the wildest excitement and confusion, within the chamber where President Lincoln was lying all was sadness and stillness. Several members of the Cabinet had hastened to his side. Medical and surgical aid were obtained, and everything was done to relieve the suffering President. It was soon ascertained, however, that it was impossible for him to survive, the only question being how long he would linger. All through the weary hours of the night and early morning the President lay unconscious, as he had been ever since his assassination. He was watched by several faithful friends, in addition to near relatives. At his bedside were the Secretary of War, Secretary of the Navy, Secretary of the Interior, Postmaster-General, and the Attorney-General; Senator Sumner, General Farnsworth, General Todd, cousin to Mrs. Lincoln; Major Hay, M. B. Field, General Halleck, Major General Meigs, Rev. Dr. Gurley, George Oglesby, of Illinois, and Drs. E. N. Abbott, R. K. Stone, C. D. Hatch, Neal, Hall, and Lieberman.

MRS. LINCOLN'S GRIEF.

In the adjoining room were Mrs. Lincoln, her son, Captain Robert Lincoln, Miss Harris, Rufus S. Andrews, and two lady friends of Mrs. Lincoln. Mrs. Lincoln was under great excitement and agony, exclaiming again and again, " Why did he not shoot me instead of my husband ?" She was constantly going back and forth to the bedside of the President, crying out in greatest agony, "How can it be so !" The scene was heart-rending in the extreme, and all were greatly overcome. Mrs. Lincoln took her last leave of her husband about twenty minutes before his death. When she was told he had breathed his last she exclaimed, "Oh! why did you not tell me he was dying?" The surgeons and members of the cabinet, Senator Sumner, Captain Robert Lincoln, General Todd, Mr. Field, and Mr. Andrews were standing at his bedside when he died. The surgeons were sitting on the foot of the bed holding the President's hands and with watches observing the slow declension of the pulse, and such was the stillness for some few minutes that the ticking of the watches could be heard in the room. At twenty-two minutes past seven A.M. on April 15, the looked for but dreaded end came, and as he drew his last breath the Rev. Dr. Gurley offered up a fervent prayer for the deceased's heartbroken family and his mourning country. The President died without a struggle, passing calmly and silently away, having been in a state of utter unconsciousness from the time he was shot till his death. All present in the silent death chamber felt the awful solemnity of the occasion, and the scene was heartrending and touching. Mrs. Lincoln, shortly after her husband's death, was driven, with her son Robert, to the White House, where, but the evening before, she left for the last time with her honored husband, who was never again to enter that home alive.

Long before the President expired the authorities were perfectly satisfied as to who committed the terrible deeds, and the city and military authorities commenced investigation, and while the Cabinet and other Ministers were watching over the President every effort was made to capture the murderers. Couriers mounted on fleet horses rushed to and fro, and the sound of the hoofs of the horses was heard in all directions. The city and military authorities worked with energy and vigilance, and the tidings at last came that one of the horses had been captured, nearly exhausted, at the outskirts of the city, and that its bridle was covered with blood. The animal was identified as the horse ridden by the assassin from Seward's residence. This gave a good deal of hope that the author of the horrible crime might be captured.

THE EFFECT OF THE PRESIDENT'S DEATH.

The news of the President's death fell like a pall over the city, and before long every house was draped in mourning. It seemed that all were engaged in the sad tribute to the departed. The department buildings were tastefully draped, the War Department being literally covered. The pillars and the entire front were richly festooned with black. The hotels, private residences, and places of business were also appropriately dressed. In short, a mantle of gloom was thrown over the entire national capital. Flags from the departments and throughout the city floated at half-mast, and nearly all private and public business was suspended. The grief felt was wide-spread and the deepest gloom and sadness prevailed on all sides. The President's corpse was removed to the White House before noon, and a dense crowd accompanied the remains. After an autopsy had been made on the corpse it was embalmed and placed in a handsome mahogany coffin, on which was a silver plate bearing the inscription:

ABRAHAM LINCOLN,
Sixteenth President of the United States
Born February 12, 1809.
Died April 15, 1865

In the evening city councils, clergy, and others held meetings to officially express regret at the President's death. Although nothing was talked of during the day but the atrocious assassination and attempted assassination made by secession sympathizers and desperadoes, there was no disturbance of any kind, and by night time the streets were quiet and the excitement gradually subsiding. In the mean time every effort was being made to capture the assassins. Every road leading out of Washington was strongly picketed and every avenue of escape thoroughly guarded, and steamboats about to start down the Potomac were stopped. A rumor prevailed that Wilkes Booth had been captured, and this helped to keep the indignation of the people as fierce as ever and to keep up the excitement, though the rumor turned out to be without foundation.

THE NORTH IN MOURNING.

Sunday, the 16th, was a solemn and mournful day in Washington, as also in every city in the States. The churches were crowded, and not a sermon was preached but the tragic occurrence was touchingly alluded to. During this day it was learned that all members of the Seward family were recovering from their injuries, and general satisfaction was expressed that Secretary Seward had not fallen a victim to the assassin's blow. The interior of the White House all day presented a scene of overwhelming sadness. The body of the Chief Magistrate of the nation was temporarily laid out in one of the upper rooms of the house. The body was dressed in the suit of plain black worn by him on the occasion of his last inauguration, while on his pillow and over the breast were scattered affectionate offerings in the shape of white flowers and green leaves. During the evening it was made known that the funeral services would take place on Wednesday, the 19th, and that the President's body would be interred at Springfield, Ill. On Monday the person who assaulted Secretary Seward was arrested as he was about to enter the house of Mrs. Surratt in the little village of Uniontown. An intense excitement prevailed when it was learned that detectives were on Booth's track. Several person supposed to be concerned in these murderous outrages were placed under arrest. On Monday the body of the murdered President lay in state in the coffin, which was placed on a grand catafalque erected in the East Room of the White House. The room was

heavily draped in mourning, and a guard of honor surrounded
the coffin.   The populace by thousands gathered at the White
House and there viewed the body.   The trains during the night
and morning brought hundreds of distinguished visitors to the
city from all portions of the North.   All the streets leading to
the White House were thronged with people from early morn
till late at night, wending their way to the spot where rested the
sarcophagus in which was confined the cold and motionless form
of him who but a few days since had hold of the helm of the
ship of State.   The universality of the mourning was remarkable.   Old and young, rich and poor, all sexes, grades, and
colors, united in paying their homage to the great and illustrious
dead ; and one of the most touching sights was that of the
wounded soldiers from the hospitals, who came to have a long,
last look at the face of the late President and honored com-
mander-in-chief.

THE FUNERAL SERVICES.

On Wednesday morning a funeral service was held at the
White House, at which were present a large number of clergymen, representing various sections of the country.   The heads
of bureaus, the sanitary and Christian commissions, the Governors, assistant secretaries, Congressmen, officers of the Supreme
Court, the diplomatic corps, the judges of the local courts, the
pall bearers, ladies of the government officials, the chief mourners, President Johnson and Cabinet, the members of the family,
and the ushers.   The whole scene presented in the room was
one of solemnity, and a single feeling appeared manifest among
all, and that was grief.   The services were conducted by Rev.
Dr. Hall, of the Episcopal Church, in the city, and the funeral
oration was delivered by Rev. Dr. Gurley, pastor of the Presbyterian church in the city which Mr. Lincoln and his family were
in the habit of attending.   At the close of these services the
funeral cortege started for the Capitol.   Every window, house-
top, balcony, and every inch of sidewalk on either side was
densely crowded with a living throng to witness the procession.
The beat of the funeral drum sounded upon the street, and the
cortege marched with solemn tread and arms reversed.   The
procession consisted of a large military escort, including a body
of dismounted officers of the army and navy and marine corps.
Following these came the civic authorities, and after them the

funeral car, drawn by six gray horses. A long line of sad and weeping relatives of the deceased followed in carriages. Next came President Johnson, accompanied by Mr. Preston King, of New York, with a strong cavalry guard on either side. The rest of the procession consisted of the Cabinet and diplomatic corps, judges of the Supreme Court, and clerks of the departments, and was closed by 1,500 well dressed negroes of various organizations. The procession was one hour and a half passing a giving point; it contained 18,000 persons, and was witnessed by at least one hundred and fifty thousand people. After the body had been placed in the Capitol, Rev. Dr. Gurley read the burial service, at the close of which the outside procession gradually dispersed. The body of the late President lay in state in the Capitol all that day and through the night, attended by a guard of honor, and viewed by an immense number of citizens.

Early on Friday morning, 21st, the body was carried to the depot of the Baltimore and Ohio railway, and the distinguished party that was to accompany the remains to Springfield, Ill., left on their sad errand by the half-past seven A.M. train. The route was as follows, and the arrangements were all carried out to perfection, there being no delays on the journey: From Washington to Baltimore, Baltimore to Harrisburg, Harrisburg to Philadelphia, Philadelphia to New York, New York to Albany, Albany to Buffalo, Buffalo to Cleveland, Cleveland to Columbus, Columbus to Indianapolis, Indianapolis to Chicago, Chicago to Springfield. All the towns along the route were draped in mourning, and at the cities above mentioned, where the funeral train stopped, the coffin was removed from the funeral car and borne in solemn and majestic procession through the streets to the principal public building in each city, where suitable ceremonies were performed, and the sad procession in each city witnessed by thousands of citizens and visitors from neighboring towns. The funeral train reached Springfield, Ill., on the 4th of May, on which day the body of the deceased President was interred in the Oak Ridge Cemetery amid much funeral pomp and ceremony.

THE ASSASSINS ARRESTED.

It was some days after the assassination of President Lincoln before the indignation of the public was somewhat calmed at learning of the arrest of those implicated in the assassination of the President and in the assaults on the Seward family. A reward of $50,000 was offered for the arrest of Booth, $25,000 for the arrest of Atzerot, and a like sum for that of D. C. Harrold, the latter two being known to be specially implicated in the assassination and the attempted assassination. Lewis Payne was arrested, April 17th, at Washington at the house of Mrs. Surratt. On being taken before the servant of Mr. Seward's house he was immediately recognized as the person who attempted to assassinate Secretary Seward. With him were arrested Mrs. Surratt and others in the same house. Atzerot was arrested on April 20th, near Middlebury, Montgomery county, Md. On April 25th J. Wilkes Booth was overtaken by a party sent out by Col. L. C. Baker, special detective of the war department. Booth and Harrold had been traced together across the Rappahanock river at Mathias Point, Md., and were found on Tuesday evening, April 25th, in a barn about three miles from Port Royal. The barn was surrounded, and, although Harrold was willing to give himself up, Booth refused to surrender. Finally the barn was fired. Harrold then gave himself up, but Booth prepared to defend himself. Lieutenant Docherty, commanding the party, ordered Sergeant Corbett to fire, which he did through one of the crevices, and shot Booth through the head. Upon being shot Booth exclaimed, " It is all up now ; I'm gone !" He was found to be wounded in his head, and died about two hours after he was shot. The other important arrests made were Dr. Mudd, at whose house Booth was known to have stopped when in Maryland ; Edward Spangler, of Ford's Theatre ; Michael O'Laughlin, and Samuel Arnold. These, with Atzerot, Harrold, and Mrs. Surratt, were arraigned on Saturday, May 13th, and after a lengthy trial, Harrold, Payne, Atzerot, and Mrs. Surratt were sentenced to be executed, and were hanged on July 7th at Washington.

SHOOTING AT JACKSON.

The shooting of President Garfield by Guiteau on the 2d of July brought to mind at once, of course, the terrible details accompanying the assassination of President Lincoln by Wilkes Booth in 1865, and revived as well recollections of the attempted assassination of President Jackson in the Capitol at Washington on January 30, 1835. The extraordinary similarity which exists in the main circumstances attending the murderous attacks upon Presidents Jackson and Garfield is remarkable, although the former escaped by almost a miracle from the sad fate which has overtaken the latter.

General Jackson had entered in 1832, it will be remembered, on his second term as Chief Magistrate, and although his election decisively showed the popularity among the people of both Jackson and the political principles of his party, the opposition was sufficiently strong in numbers and sufficiently brilliant in the eloquence of its leaders to make the President's life anything but one of peaceful rest and enjoyment. Jackson's hot impetuosity, his strong personal and political prejudices, and the almost savage fury with which he was at all times ready to attack his enemies or defend his friends, served to fan to white heat any flame that was started in political matters of those days, and the Administration was almost continuously engaged in bitter political feuds with its opponents upon the questions of the hour. Calhoun, Webster, and Clay used their brilliant powers upon more than one occasion with great effect against Jackson, and the President's excitable, passionate nature and obstinate determination to carry his measures were only intensified by the withering attacks made upon him in Congress by these statesmen and their supporters. The times were troublesome ones at best, and party feeling was not quieted by any attempts on the part of the Administration to make rough ways smooth or by evincing a disposition to give way in its demands. The South Carolina nullifiers were a thorn in Jackson's side in their demands in regard to the abolition of import duties; the withdrawal of deposits from the United States Bank was another prolific source of anxiety; the French imbroglio added to the cares and political entanglements of the party, and the threatened impeachment of the President by the Senate served only to magnify the enmity between the administration and its opponents. Jackson's naturally stormy, vindictive disposition and proneness to abandon words for blows had often brought trouble upon him in the past, and great and well appreciated as were his public, military, and civic services, he had hosts of enemies, some of whom threatened him with personal violence. He was as much admired in certain quarters as he was thoroughly hated in others, and his ideas of the "code of honor" brought him into numerous personal encounters. Two serious public attacks were made upon him during the last four years of his Presidency—viz., those by Lieutenant Randolph and a man by the name of Lawrence. And it is this last to which reference is made as being in a remarkable degree similar to that made upon President Garfield yesterday, the similarity existing, not in the characters or disposition of the two Presidents, but in the character of the would-be assassins and their methods. The President and his Cabinet were present in the Capitol with official formality on January 30, 1835, to join both houses of Congress and a numerous body of citizens in ceremonies held in honor of a deceased member of the House from South Carolina. The usual ceremonies had been concluded, and the President, accompanied by Messrs. Woodbury and Dickson, had crossed the great rotunda and were about to step out on the portico when a man emerged from the crowd and advanced towards the President. When within eight feet of him he drew a pistol, and, aiming it at the President, pulled the trigger before he was aware of the man's intention. By a miracle, apparently, the cap missed fire, when the man drew another pistol and attempted to fire it. A second time the cap missed fire, and Jackson rushed at his assailant and disarmed him. Unfortunately for President Garfield, the pistol of Guiteau was sure and prompt, and did its work more effectively than did that of the assailant of President Jackson. The man was at once secured, and he gave his name as Lawrence. He conducted himself with the same cool indifference that has marked Guiteau's behavior since his arrest, and gave much the same excuses, saying he was deprived of his employment, and felt it incumbent on him to put the President out of the way by assassination, as he regarded the President as the cause of his own troubles and the country's political entanglements. The man was taken to jail, and his history and connections sought out, when it was determined that he was a lunatic on the subject and fixed in his determination to kill the supposed author of the difficulties mentioned. In his cell he remained tranquil and unconcerned as to the final result. After due legal and medical proceedings, Lawrence was finally committed to an asylum. Miss Martineau, who was an eye witness of the attempted assassination, gives a graphic description of the affair and its public effect in her "Retrospect of Western Travel."

THE END.

www.ingramcontent.com/pod-product-compliance
Lightning Source LLC
Chambersburg PA
CBHW020857130726
47900CB00014B/938